Enough Rope

PETER WINDRIDGE-SMITH

Published 2014 by pdsIdeas

Copyright © 2014 Peter Windridge-Smith

The moral right of the author has been asserted

All rights reserved

No part of this book may be used or reproduced in any manner whatsoever without written permission from the Publisher except in the case of brief quotations embodied in critical articles or reviews.

ISBN: 978-0-9928881-0-7

http://peterwindridgesmith.wix.com/p-w-s

This book is a work of fiction. Names, characters, businesses, organizations, places and events are either the product of the author's imagination or are used fictitiously. Any resemblance to actual persons, living or dead, events or locales is entirely coincidental.

For Hils…

The grateful thanks department –

To my readers: Margaret, Robi, John, Gill, Ali, A-K, Arthur, Sarah, Christine, Cathy, Peter, Paul & Michelle for your comments, suggestions and typo spotting skills.
To all at Monique's writing group for help & encouragement.
To Christian and Gunilla for assistance with Finnish language and realism.
To Immy and Sarah for your vocal talents.

A NOTE FROM THE AUTHOR

You can read this novel any way you like. You can skip to the last page first if you really want to. I wouldn't recommend it, but I can't stop you. No, all I've got is a suggestion. Take it or leave it…

Steven Carter is an amateur songwriter. Smattered through the text are the lyrics for twelve of his songs. If you visit http://peterwindridgesmith.wix.com/p-w-s you'll be able to listen to his demos online or download them for free. All I'm suggesting is that when you get to the appropriate places in the book, read the words and listen to the music at the same time.

If I was coming over all arty, I might say that the setting, lyric and music merge to provide an experience greater than the sum of its parts: the story interprets the song and the song evokes the story.

Otherwise, it's something a bit different. Why not give it a try?

Peter

CHAPTER 1

"It's my fortunate task to determine what's really going on in your head." The bald psychologist's southern states drawl seems completely out of place here. As if reaching into my mind, he adds, "My good old Mammy came from Alabama." That'll be why there's no translator. Our eyes make contact for a few uncomfortable seconds above the paper-stacked desk. Dr Hiltunen raises his eyebrows slightly inviting comment.

"It's not me; it's my world that's gone mad."

"Ah, projection. That's a mighty fine place to start. It ain't my fault, it's everyone else's."

"Well it feels like that sometimes." I can't keep the frustration out of my voice.

"Now, I've got to write this report. They may use it or they may toss it in the trash. So let's not get too concerned about it. There really ain't no point getting all hyped up." He spins his chair towards a small catering trolley and begins to make coffee. Without asking he pours two cups. He adds considerably more milk to one and passes it over. Just the way I take it... "I've done this for years and mostly I can tell if folks are just stressed about being here. That's quite a different thing than if you was hiding a deep dark secret."

There's nowhere to put the cup down amongst the clutter.

"Just set it on a stack. They're mostly not important."

Is this guy for real? He seems to be compensating for a lack of hair on top by the bushy profusion growing from his chin and jawline. What conclusions could I draw about that if the roles were reversed? He takes an audible slurp from his cup and places it on a seemingly precarious set of folders.

"So here's how it's gonna work. I ain't gonna ask too many questions. I want you to do the talking. I wanna know what you were thinking, what you were seeing, what you were smelling. Don't think no detail's too small. You tell it like it's happening all over again. Trust me, before long you'll be thinking of things you was sure you'd forgot. And they tell me you've got a good memory anyways."

Do they? What else do they say about me? I'm not sure I want this weird guy delving around inside my head. But I said I'd do this, so... "Where should I start?"

"Wherever you wanna. You gotta tell me your side of things. Start where you think it began."

Where I think it began... My mind flicks between channels on an internal TV. I've been immersed in the past these last weeks, trying to remember that incident, that glance, that word of revelation. It's difficult not to lose yourself: to drown in self-indulgent memory. Drown? Ah, that night, perhaps.

Hiltunen is waiting patiently, sipping at his coffee.

"It was..."

"Naw, no," he splutters. "I don't wanna hear no was. Live it."

"I couldn't help..."

"No couldn'ts neither. You got an education, yeah?" He grins like a kid proudly using grown up words, "No past tense, OK?"

I nod and shut my eyes for a moment, gathering the image.

+ + +

YOU CAN'T HELP WANTING to run your fingers through it. It's that kind of hair: long and slightly wavy, a deep luxuriant chestnut, falling almost untidily over her shoulders, some in front and some behind. She catches me staring and looks down to see if my drink is empty. I move my hand over the glass in the universal 'not quite finished yet' gesture.

"This is your first night, isn't it?"

"Mitä?" is all I receive in reply, so I roll out the standard phrase: *"Puhutteko englantia?"*

"What?" she repeats, this time in a pleasantly accented version of my mother tongue.

"I was trying to say, 'Do you speak English?' but I guess I got the words wrong."

The corners of her mouth rise slightly, revealing her opinion of my pronunciation. "Where you come from?"

"England."

"Really? My English is so bad."

"Don't worry; it's much better than my Finnish... This is your first night isn't it?"

"It show so much?" she says with an embarrassed grin.

"Well, you know, I had to be like Sherlock Holmes to work it out: you keep reading the price list and you haven't looked at your watch once. But the clinching thing is that I've been drinking in this bar for weeks and this is the first time I've seen you!"

She flashes an amused smile but I get the feeling she only understood half of what I was saying. "Why you..."

Loud music erupts from my shirt pocket. It'll be John texting why he's late. I pull out the phone, meaning only to press cancel, but when I lift my eyes she's already turning towards another customer. Nice timing, cheers mate. I jab the 'read' key, but it's not John:

'Dad has spare test match ticket. June 15. Do u want? U better be back by then. xx Abi'

Like she needed to ask... I thumb an affirmative before trying John again — still straight to voicemail. I suppose I'm going to have to hoick him out of his room. My eyes slip back towards the hair, but I turn, leaving behind an empty glass and a slightly guilty sigh.

- - -

"WAS THAT OK? Is that what you mean?" I ask.

"Hell, yeah," says Hiltunen, spinning a pencil round his thumb. "I can't say everything I'm remembering. There's too much."

"You're doing great. Don't over think it. Just carry right along."

+ + +

OUTSIDE, a tickling nose tells me it's at least -15: the moisture freezing on every in-breath. There hasn't been any new snow for the past week and the ploughs have done a thorough job clearing the roads and pavements to a bottom layer of compacted snow and grit: a carpet of coarse grade sandpaper which is much less slippery than it looks. Even with lying snow, the main street could hardly be called picturesque. The buildings are concrete boxes: shop fronts below, with two or three storeys of flats above. The overall impression is grey. Grey like black and white TV, with very little relief from illuminated signs above the plate glass frontages. The hotel wouldn't win any awards for architecture, either. Hardly distinguishable from a shoe shop on one side and jeweller's on the other, it presents a glazed facade, highlighted with polished steel. Grey again. It doesn't look much from the outside, but the food in the restaurant is excellent and the rooms are pleasant, even if the view from the window isn't.

'Home again.' The thought causes me to pause on the wide steps. Only two months and the Central Hotel is becoming home, and my house in Manchester is somewhere I once lived. Not good. I scrape my shoes across the slatted steel mat and the doors slide open. The tall frame of tonight's receptionist is half hidden behind the polished granite counter. I've a soft spot for Katri: very friendly, not intimidatingly pretty, just... nice really.

"Back so quickly?" she says.

"John seems to have forgotten we're going out tonight. Please can you give his room a quick call?"

Katri nods and reaches for the internal phone. She has to wait some time for an answer. "Mr McLeod? Your friend Steven waits in reception." Almost instantly she pulls the receiver from her ear and regards it quizzically.

"What did he say?"

"I not understand the word," she says grinning.

"Oh, yeah?" I'm not sure I believe her.

Katri sizes up my freshly ironed shirt and raises her eyebrows slightly, "You go to Copacabana?" I suspect she's winding me up.

"No, I'd be the youngest person there by ten years and anyway I can't do arm in arm dancing. It's not natural."

"It is good sometime." Katri's eyes twinkle.

"Hmm, I'm sure that when you're with your special man, pressing him close and moving to the music could be quite persuasive!"

"Oh, you are so.... what is word in English?"

"Cynical?" She nods. "Just you remember that my special woman is a thousand miles away and it's a tad inconvenient to go back to England just for a dance."

"I think she would not mind you practising."

"Now you're definitely teasing me."

"Me?"

A slightly dishevelled John appears from the lift. "Sorry, I just put the telly on for ten seconds an'..." Katri and I laugh as he holds his head back, eyes shut and mouth open.

"Näkemiin," I say over my shoulder as we leave at a trot.

"Not bad!" shouts Katri, in her best school mistress voice.

"Been burning the candle at both ends have we?" I say as we puff our way through the grid pattern streets towards the lake and the *LähelläMahi* Hotel.

"No more 'n you."

"I'm adding an extra day to my life every fortnight by missing those couple of hours sleep."

John regards me out of the corner of his eye with amusement, "Aye, but drinking in bars an' playing pool aren't exactly inspired ways to spend this time, now are they?"

"Well, that's why we're going tonight: we're fully immersing ourselves in the local culture."

"Fully immersing ourselves!" snorts John, patting the slight bulge on his left side. I realise that we have both, hopefully, brought our swimming trunks.

"Just in case", says John.

"But being Finland, I don't suppose we'll be expected to wear them", I add ruefully.

Our fears are realised as we are met by a betowelled Mikko in the hotel's plush changing rooms. "Welcome gentlemen. I thought you had, what is that phrase again: 'pigeon off'?"

"I think you mean 'chicken out', Mikko", says John.

"Ah yes, I thought you had chicken out."

"Are you calling us yellow?" I grin.

"Yes, as yellow as these tiles." He flourishes a hand but it comes to rest pointing to the swim shorts in John's left hand. "Ah you, Eng..." John's eyes narrow exaggeratedly. "You British: always trying to cover up. This is Finland!"

I glance towards John who shrugs. The phrase, 'This is Finland' usually means we are in trouble.

"Everyone else is here, hurry." Mikko hoists the towel from round his waist to over his shoulder and disappears through a panelled connecting door.

"Well at least we're not going to come last in the body of the year contest," says John. Mikko would run a walrus pretty close in a blubber competition.

We strip and shove our clothes into a couple of the gun-metal lockers. With my glasses safely tucked inside one of my shoes, I pull a warm towel over my right shoulder: Finland style. John, similarly attired, comments, "In for a penny, in for a pound," and reaches for the door handle. "Oh..." In our hotel, the sauna adjoins the changing rooms, but here we find ourselves by the side of a ten metre swimming pool.

"Cheers Mikko," I say, glancing around. Fortunately, there's no one swimming. John points towards an identical door in the centre of the opposite wall. He heads off over the tiles at a fast walk, the slaps of his bare feet echoing across the water. I follow, but can't help glancing towards another door to my right, on which, if I squint, I can just make out the brass symbol of a woman.

The Finnish guys keep winding us up about mixed saunas. "It happens all the time, no one bothers, no one stares. This is Finland." We're pretty sure this is bullshit, but only pretty sure... John heaves against the stiff spring and we walk into the heat trying to look confident. It's all boys. In fact, it's all *Suomen Kaapelitehdas* engineers: we could almost hold a project progress meeting in here. Mikko beckons us over; we lay our towels on one of the polished pine benches and sit on them.

"Found your way then?" says Mikko grinning. He receives a couple of sarcastic nods.

"Not first time in sauna?" says a guy I only know by sight, noting our seating etiquette.

"No. We sometimes use the one at our hotel. It's a good way to wind down after the factory," I say.

"Yes, very good if the customer is giving you a hard time!" says Mikko to general chuckles. They are good natured as the project is going quite well. He reaches forward and ladles two slugs of water from bucket to grid, through to the glowing coals below. Instantly, there is a huge gush of steam.

"Aye. It's so relaxing until someone does that." says John. The

Finns have a macho sauna thing going on where they only seem satisfied with the temperature if it's actually roasting them alive. John has a theory that none of them really like it that hot and any time someone blasts up the steam the sauna empties pretty fast. I catch his eye and notice that he is resting an open palm against his stomach. After a few seconds he folds his little finger, then his ring finger. Just after he counts off four, one of the guys stands and I catch the word *'beer'*. Five of them troop out. John casts me a knowing smile. The open door lets out the worst of the heat and I begin to enjoy the sweat.

"No alcohol before ice swimming." says Mikko in a tone that brooks no argument. I suppose that lager was quite a while ago...

"Are those guys not doing it, then?" asks John. "I thought it was a Finnish tradition."

"It is", says Mikko, but one of his colleagues adds, "But most Finns think it crazy." John and I exchange pensive glances. Mikko smiles: "Do not worry, gentlemen, you follow what I tell you and you will be OK. It is very refreshing."

"Where you from in England?" asks Kris, one of their draughtsmen.

John rolls his eyes ever so slightly. "Perth, in Scotland." There is plenty of emphasis on the final word.

"And me, Manchester."

"Ah, Manchester United. They have young player from Finland. Already he score one goal."

"Yes, Oksanen isn't he?" I'm not able to keep the sarcasm out of my voice and I notice Mikko chuckling.

"What is funny?" asks Kris, slightly put out.

"How many people already tell you about Oksanen, Steven?" says Mikko.

"Just about everyone else in Mahikkala..."

"And 'Where you from' is the number one question we get asked as well," adds John. "You only need, 'Why you come to Mahikkala?' for the full set."

"Oh," Kris's face morphs into an embarrassed grin as he realises his error, "and then when say working at *Kaapeli*..." He feigns a yawn.

"Yup, all those glazed over expressions when they find out we're engineers," I say. Everyone present nods or makes some grunt equivalent to 'been there'.

"Where are other two?" says Kris, trying a different subject.

"Mark and Keith?" He nods. "You'll ne'er get Keith to something like this. He willnae try anything; makes a little bit of England wherever he goes." John grins at the Finns and picks up some invisible cutlery. "Bacon, eggs and tea for breakfast, please." His attempt at a plummy accent is probably lost on them. For all his bluster, John is pretty anglicised these days.

"And the *LähelläMahi* restaurant is perhaps too expensive for Mr Hatfield?" says Mikko with raised brows.

"Very sharp, as ever, Mikko." I thumb towards him whilst addressing the other guys. "How do you ever get away with anything with him as your boss?"

"It take a lot of skill," comments one voice.

"And lot of food," adds another. Mikko's deep bass leads the laughter. The chuckles trail off, leaving only the low roar of the burner above the silence. The relaxing heat soaks through limb, torso, and brain...

I'm in Hanne's Bar. For some reason I'm still there after closing time. That barmaid with the red hair is facing away from me, clearing up. She glances over her shoulder, smiles coyly, and flicks her head forward sending a shimmer down those gorgeous locks...

A subtle change in my body's blood flow breaks my reverie. Not the thing to have happen in public. I've reached 'K' whilst mentally reciting the alphabet in reverse, when Mikko stands.

"OK. I think that is long enough. Follow me. Bring towels." The remaining seven of us file along to the end of the pool. Judging from the colour of Mikko's back, we'd better watch out that the hotel chef doesn't mistake us for a line of half boiled lobsters making a bid for freedom. He leads us through French windows on to a boardwalk which winds amongst towering trunks. Garden lamps line either side of the path, their warm light reflecting off the snow.

"Follow the yellow brick road," says John. It does look like that: not quite of this world.

"Mind your walking", says Mikko. There is frost on the boards and although our sauna heat gives immunity to the cold air, my feet feel like I'm stepping on nails. "When we reach the lake, one at a time, do not move away from the ladder, and no longer than five seconds in the water. I will count."

"Five seconds?" asks John.

"Yes. If you stay in longer than ten seconds you will not be able to climb out," says Mikko sternly. This seems pretty unlikely to me.

Just before we reach the lake shore, the boards end and we cross a snow covered path. Street lights trace its route through the pines in either direction.

"Is this a cross country skiing track?" I ask. I can see from John's nervous grin that he is equally concerned about the apparent lack of privacy.

"Yes", says Kris. "It is flat, good for beginner."

"But..." As if to answer my question a male skier appears to our left and passes by with a few pushes of his poles.

"Quickly!" shouts Mikko from the end of what must be a landing stage in the summer. Below him a wooden ladder disappears into dark ice.

"Starting to freeze already," says Mikko, mostly to himself, and reaches for a long pole clipped next to a lifebelt. The lake is white, snow upon ice, in every direction, except for two or three metres around the ladder where the surface is smooth and black. He expertly cracks the thin ice with the pole and flips sheets of it on to the thicker edges.

"Who is first? Come on Steven."

I stand with my back to the lake and put a foot down on to the first rung.

"Lower yourself in quickly and then let go."

I'm descending into a bath of numbness. My hands release the ladder and I slip into total submersion. My head pounds, the cold seemingly shrinking skull into brain. Something touches my feet and I have an irrational image of pale hands stretching to grip my ankles. I kick and more weed slithers across my toes. As I surface I hear Mikko counting. He has reached two. I start to tread water, but something is squeezing the life force out of me, strangling my breath. I realise that I've moved slightly away from the ladder and desperately reach towards it. Somewhere, in another world Mikko reaches five.

"Out now."

My right hand grips a rung. It seems like a superhuman effort to pull my body against the ladder, to reach up. Panic strength kicks in, I lift myself, and as my chest breaks the surface of the water, I'm present again. People are handing me my towel, patting me on the back. John is descending the ladder. A few seconds later he's standing next to me, large towel wrapped around his shoulders.

"Pretty intense, hey?" John says between shivers.

"Oh yeah," is all I can manage.

"Go on, back up to the hotel", shoos Mikko, "and make sure you get in the pool first. That will warm you up most quick."

As we turn to retrace out steps along the boardwalk, a mother, father and two pre-teen daughters ski into view.

"Imagine if we were in the UK!" says John. I glance down, our draped towels covering our upper torsos only and then to the landing stage where four naked men are shouting encouragement to the next masochist. The parents don't even look our way. One of the girls smiles in that slightly-amused-but-superior fashion that a Brit might reserve for a train spotter or bird watcher. And then they have slid past.

The hotel swimming pool feels like a hot bath. I've stopped shivering and I'm wondering if the others have left us any beer. Mikko pushes off from the side and glides towards the steps.

"There is no better way to get an appetite," he proclaims, climbing towards the changing rooms. As we follow, John winks at me and whispers, "Nae bad, but I can think of at least one more pleasurable alternative."

"I thought that just made old men like you go to sleep."

"Maybe for you English."

- - -

"NOTHING LIKE A BIT OF RIBBING." Hiltunen pushes his chair backwards and leans to search for the pencil which made a spin too far just as I was climbing into the water. "Be a lot less work for my kind if there was a bit more ribbing. Gotcha." He straightens up, the fallen retrieved. "You often away from home for long stretches?"

"No, it just worked out like that this year. I got on this big project and it was my turn to come to site. Most of the other designers had already done their stint. We try to pass the pain around."

"The pain?"

"Working away from home, it's disruptive; it isn't good for family life. You only need to look at some of the older itinerant guys who go from country to country, work site to work site. There's hardly one still with the mother of their kids."

"How've you been, working away from..." For the first time he opens the note book occupying a small area of stack free space directly in front of him. "... Abigail? Pretty name." I'm caught between acknowledging the comment and answering his question. I suppose he thinks I need a prompt. "You got two lives, huh? One out here with your work and your bars and one on the phone with your wife?"

"Yeah, it's weird how easily you swap from one to the other..."

CHAPTER 2

He badgered Terry for three weeks solid. Working conditions, health and safety, terms of employment, you name it, John quoted it."

"Just for some coats?"

"They are quite posh." I finger the navy blue 'Finnish Army' thermal jacket lying next to me on the paisley pattern bedspread. "I'd have given in to John after a week."

"I suppose that's why Terry does his job and you do yours." She's right; project management wouldn't be my thing. "You'll look funny, the four of you walking around in matching coats."

"Oh, I don't think I'll wear mine tonight. It's only a couple of hundred yards down the street to the pub." There's a snigger at the other end of the line. I just know Abi is rolling her eyes and shaking her head. "What?" I say, although I already have a suspicion.

"John just spent three weeks and you're not even… oh, never mind." She changes tack, "So you're out on the town again tonight?"

"Yeah, but nothing special, just a couple of beers; you never know, I might actually speak to someone who I don't work with."

"Er, Steve? Did you say you were going out for nine? Cos it's already five past…"

A BLAST OF GLASSES-STEAMING AIR welcomes me into the low lighting and dark wood ambience of Hanne's Bar.

"Over here you blind bat," shouts Keith above the hubbub of

chatter and mainstream pop. I squint over occupied tables towards the mirrored wall beyond whilst wiping my glasses on the front of my shirt. Mark is making exaggerated waving gestures in my direction. I put the specs back on and they promptly steam up again.

"You have a problem?" jokes a blurry Hanne.

"Who said that?" I drop the glasses into my top pocket and, holding my arms out in front of me in classic blindfold pose, I advance with my hands at chest height. I make a couple of sideways movements for effect but home in on Hanne across the copper topped bar. For a moment, I think she is going to call my bluff.

"I think you see well enough." I receive a slap on my left hand from a giggling Hanne as she turns away.

"It's not fair," moans Keith, shaking his greying head, "I've been wanting her to slap me for weeks."

"That wasnae on your hand though", says John.

"Mating polar bears off," says Keith casually.

"Do they get polar bears in Scandinavia?" I ask.

"Is Svalbard part of Norway or not?" says Keith.

"I guess so."

"And that's one of their main breeding sites, so it was a genuine Scandinavian themed oath and according to the rules, I don't owe you guys the next round."

"OK. Don't get your Discovery Channel knickers in a twist." Keith's pretend huff melts into a grin as he acknowledges that I have correctly revealed the source of his newly found wildlife expertise. "If you will play these ridiculous games..." I muse.

"Just adding a bit of spice to the humdrum."

"I can see that this is going to get bloody expensive." They're all laughing. "What?" My mind reverses back a few words. I raise my eyes heavenward and reach into my jeans pocket for some cash.

"Great steaming piles of reindeer poo," I mutter under my breath as I try to re-attract Hanne's attention.

My penalty round is half poured when Miguel walks in. He is also working at *Kaapeli*, but his company is installing some of the smaller equipment: toy stuff, we tease. His features are typically Spanish and even though he exudes an 'I know I'm good looking' manner, a sizeable proportion of the women in Mahikkala seem to find him irresistible. In the same way that people in the UK find blondes attractive because they're unusual (or at least they were before the advent of peroxide), Finnish women find dark haired guys fascinating. My light brown hair is probably a blessing.

Miguel swaggers up to the bar and pretend punches me in the stomach. "Hello Steven, how are you this good evening?"

"Fair to middling. Why is it such a good evening then?"

"I have come to see my future wife."

"Which one of your adoring crowd is it this time?" I ask, raising my eyebrows.

"Are you making a joke at me Steven?"

"Whatever gave you that idea, Miguel? Just tell me who she is and the date of the wedding. I can't bear the suspense."

"She work here. She has the long red hair and ..."

"Oh, I know the one you mean, she's new. Nice hair."

"Nice hair!" says Miguel, "You English have no passion; it is wonderful hair. You say she has just a nice body as well?"

"I can't say that I've really noticed," I reply with forced nonchalance.

Miguel raises his eyes in incredulity. "I cannot resist!" He draws a picture in the air with both hands drawing attention with a flourish to those parts which he admires the most. "I want to touch... I want to feel her hair on my chest. I..."

"Whoa there Silver," I gasp, in between guffaws. "Too much information!"

"Discussing the local wildlife again?" The other guys have wandered over to pick up their drinks.

"Is it that obvious?" I say, my shoulders still shaking with laughter.

"I think the whole pub could read Miguel's semaphore signals." says Mark.

"Speak of the devil..." I motion towards the woman in question who has just appeared half hidden behind a tower of clean glasses. On reaching the bar, she splits her load in half and puts both stacks down. As the second stack touches there is an ominous 'ping' and nimbly Hanne reaches out to catch the rest of the glasses as the bottom one shatters.

"Looks like you've got a smasher here, Hanne," shouts John over my head.

"It is third one tonight. It is good thing they come out of her pay." Hanne stares at our red head with a completely straight face.

The new barmaid seems embarrassed and taken aback at the same time. It is a cute expression in the nicest sense of the word. Then the corners of Hanne's mouth start to twitch and her eyes twinkle through her slope cut fringe. The surprised part of the red head's expression turns into even more embarrassment as she realises she is being teased. Sticking her tongue out at Hanne, she turns in search of more empties.

"She almost believed me," says Hanne, before taking Miguel's order.

We retreat to one of the tables and swap banter. All the time Miguel's head is following the progress of his 'future wife' around the room.

"You're right," I whisper to him. "She is trim."

"I am in love," he says with a self mocking expression. "Ah..." He downs the final third of his glass in one gulp and stands. We watch with amusement as he sidles round the bar to where the object of his affections has just started serving.

As he comes to a halt, Keith whispers in a perfect 'sheepdog trials' commentary voice, "Eight out of ten for the approach."

We explode with laughter and Miguel flicks us a scathing expression.

Keith continues, holding an invisible microphone to his sun lined face, "Has he been put off by the crowd? No, he's rallied and.... oh yes, a superb pick up."

Three tongues are simultaneously bitten.

Miguel's flirting seems to be going pretty well. She's laughing as she pulls his beer, but whilst receiving his change he asks something else and a look of uncertainty crosses her face, followed by a slight blush. She shakes her head, still smiling, and escapes to serve another customer.

"And it's always the one with the red collar that just won't go into the pen!"

I'm half way through swallowing a mouthful of beer and half of it comes back down my nose. "I wish you wouldn't do that when I'm drinking, Keith", I gasp.

And so the evening progresses through more tasteless banter, interspersed with glasses of tasteless beer, until John glances at his Beijing market 'Rolex' and stands. "So are we finally going to get either of you two into Copa tonight then?"

A scowl plays across Mark's baby smooth complexion and he replies, "No way, I'm expecting Jane to phone in a bit."

"You should have put a stop to that right away," says Keith. "My wife doesn't even know this mobile exists."

"I'm sure there's a happy medium somewhere." I cast a meaningful glance to John who returns it. His expression changes to reform the original question. "No, I'm far too young for that place," I answer.

"Your loss," says Keith, also rising.

Within minutes of them leaving Mark has also made his excuses and I'm alone at the table. I sup my beer slowly and glance ruefully towards the bar where Miguel is still trying his luck.

"Hey, where you from?" A woman slightly younger than me takes the seat opposite.

"England."

"Real English?" she repeats as if she doesn't quite believe it.

"Yes, Manchester."

"Oh, I not been there. I visit London. I love it!" Her lips part in a white teeth smile, contrasting with her dark lipstick. The whole black jeans, tie dyed top, heavy eyeliner look is bordering on Goth, but the platinum blonde hair makes it quirky. I kind of like it.

"There's a bit more to do there than in Mahikkala."

"Tell me about," she sighs.

"Hey, it's not all bad, you can go to Copacabana." She cuffs my hand with the back of hers and rolls her eyes.

Her face is suddenly serious, "Do I look so old?"

I hold up my hands, "No, no, I didn't mean that, you look…" A grin spreads and I realise she's teasing. "Got me," I say pulling an imaginary arrow from my chest.

She laughs and holds my eye, "I look?"

"You look… great." It comes out so naturally.

We continue to chat through a couple more drinks. It's an easy two way conversation, full of laughter and warmth. Heck, she hasn't even asked why I am in Mahikkala. 'This is a woman after my own heart,' I say to myself and in the echo of my words it hits me: where I am and what I'm doing. And in a double whammy, Ana – as I now know - raises an eyebrow and says, "Are real Englishmen as good at other things as they are at talking?" Careful, Steve, careful. I act dumb.

"What sort of things?"

She thinks I'm joking, trying to embarrass her, "Other things that men and women do together." A faux coy smile lingers on her lips. Damn, these Finns are so direct. There is a brief struggle for control of my mouth between my brain and my loins.

I smile weakly, "Of course we're excellent at that, but there's a little problem." I raise my left hand and spin the ring on the fourth finger with my thumb and pinky. She gazes quizzically, then light dawns. "Oh, in England this mean you have girlfriend, or are ma-"

"Yes, married," I interrupt.

She seems to consider for a moment. "You have children?"

"No."

"And your wife is in England?"

"Yes."

"Then no problem." She reaches out a hand. Oh, I am so, so tempted. My head swims; I feel the heat of a sudden sweat. I pull my hand from under hers and shake my head.

"There is a problem: in here", I point to my temple. She can see in my face that I mean it.

"But why?" She gestures towards herself.

"I enjoyed chatting with you, you're so... easy to like. I was flattered, I got carried away, I'm sorry." I leave the table, and head over to the outside door, trying not to look like I'm running. The bouncer receives his customary Euro and I step into the street.

I've now got majorly conflicting emotions going on in my head. These are not helped by the alcohol. My rational brain is thinking, 'Phew, that was too close'; my loins are chanting, 'What if? Why not? Who would know?' I try to block the animal thoughts with a firm, 'I would know and that would be the start of the problem.'

I'm greeted with an amused smile as the hotel door slides open, "What are you grinning about Katri?"

"The poor cold Englishman." She must think I'm shaking with cold. I'm not about to disabuse her of the idea.

"If I'd been out there any longer, I think I might have turned into a girl."

Katri looks puzzled, but low laughter rises from the short blonde curls poking above the computer monitor.

"Explain it to her, Erik," I say perhaps a little condescendingly. Erik is about three words through his explanation when Katri finishes translating. Her eyes narrow mischievously and she says straight to me, *"Ehkä you not much kutistu."*

I know she is taking the piss so I try to pretend I have understood every word. I'm not a good actor.

"Explain it to him, Erik," she parrots.

"She says, 'Maybe you not have much to shrink.'"

"Bah, humbug!" I retort, leaving two bemused Finns on the ground floor.

Soothed by the safety of a familiar room, my internal combat resolves itself into a self-righteous glow. I love Abi and her love has saved me. My head whirls with a familiar rush of lyric and melody: a song is forming. Lifting the dictaphone and small green note book from the bedside drawer, I start to hum and scribble simultaneously.

- - -

"WELL YOU ARE FULL OF SURPRISES. Engineer and artiste, huh?"

"I'm sorry, should I stay in your pigeon hole and collect train numbers?" I say, with a little pique. Hiltunen raises one hand in apology.

"So do I get to hear it?"

"You want me to sing?"

"No, just the lyrics will be fine." The corners of his mouth rise mischievously. "Don't want no one accusing me of torture."

Despite the teasing, I can't help but imagine piano, strings and melody as I recite:

Without You

When I wake up your elbow is the first thing that I feel;
the warmth of your breathing in my ear.
And I don't need to speak, because you know what I'm thinking:
one look will do.
And I don't need to tell you if I'm really hurting,
you just cry too.

You are soft sand on my feet;
a warm towel after the sea.
You are the mortar in my wall:
without you I can't stand at all.
You are a breeze at my back;
a beacon that shines in my black.
You are the butter on my toast:
without you, I'm average at most.

When we collapse on the sofa your legs curl around mine,
but somehow, still, your feet stay cold.
And if I should wonder, then you've thought it already,
whatever comes.
And I don't need to worry 'cause you'll be there beside me,
palace or slums.

You are red wine with my cheese;   (a full bodied Chianti)
the tissue in front of my sneeze.   (you catch all my mistakes)
You are the scent from my red rose:
without you it's all just a pose.
You are the rain on my seeds;   (gentle, life-giving water)
the storyteller of my deeds.   (but never telling tales)
You are the kiss that makes me well:
without you it all goes to hell.

Without you, without you, oh without you,   (Who would I be?
Without you, my castle will fall.   What would I do?
Without you, it's not right at all.   How can I even
Without you, I'm an empty shell.   think 'without you'?)
Without you, it all goes to hell.
I don't want to be without you.

Hiltunen's expression is neutral as I finish. "OK, so you probably think it's drivel. And hypocritical considering what nearly happened."

"I ain't no critic." His pencil begins to spin once more. "This Ana, Miss 'other things that men and women do together'..." As he quotes, his impressive eyebrows rise and fall. "...that kinda thing happen quite often?"

"A few times." I snort and shake my head. "Without me even trying."

"The lure of the unknown," says Dr Hiltunen, making it sound like a movie title.

"Being a foreigner kind of ups your rating, somehow."

He nods, "And that's kinda nice but kinda scary too?"

"Yeah, in fact, I had a similar conversation with Mark."

+ + +

CHAPTER 3

Mark sits opposite me in the site office. Office is a rather grand title for two off-white Portakabins knocked together, but you can't say you work in a shed can you? We're waiting whilst the new shop crane is load tested and both of us are putting off writing up Saturday's logbook.

"Do you think anyone has ever actually done it like that?" Mark lifts his head to see that I am pointing to a printout which Keith had tacked to the wall, underneath a part coloured progress chart. It claims to show Star reader's ten favourite sexual positions. My finger is next to number nine, 'the wheelbarrow'.

"Maybe, if you're a weightlifter and your girlfriend's a gymnast."

"You didn't say wife there, Mark!"

"Because..." Mark lifts one hand and gazes at the nails, considering, I suspect, if there is any possibility of growth since they were last bitten, "I reckon it's the sort of thing that you might try once, but you're quickly going to find that Mother Nature really does know best."

"So it's more likely with a girlfriend than a wife?"

"Yup", says Mark, pleased that his logic has stepped over my trip wire (or so he thinks).

"So, sex is more interesting before you're married, is it?"

"Ouch," says Mark, realising I've got him. "Has Abi ever asked you that?"

"Thankfully not. It's like being handed a shovel in a graveyard. Wherever you dig you'll find a skeleton."

"I suppose the right answer is that it's different."

"Yeah, but then what if you get asked, 'How's it different?'"

"Tricky."

The large fan heater drones above our heads, part of the 'cold weather' modifications that John ordered when he first arrived.

I start a new tack, "Mark?"

"Yes, Steven?"

"You know how you never stay out late?"

"Stop going on about that. The answer's no. You guys can relive your teenage fantasies if you want, but count me out."

I hold up my hands. "Hey, I know. I wasn't going to ask you. You've told me, it's a money thing, mainly, but is that all?"

"No. I just don't see the point."

Blood and stones come to mind. "OK, but is it your way of dealing with being away from Jane?"

Mark snorts, "What, you mean I stay in at night and get all homesick for my dearest darling?"

"I have met Jane, remember."

"Yeah, alright."

I try again. "No, what I mean is, do you stay in so you don't meet someone who might... you know, tempt you?"

Mark's brow furrows quizzically. "Yeah, I suppose there's a bit of that too. What happened on Saturday night then? You didn't?"

"No I didn't, but it was a close one. After you left, some girl, Ana..."

"A three letter name beginning with 'A'? I can see why you might have gone for her," interrupts Mark, unhelpfully. A deep revving sets everything in the cabin vibrating. I lift my mug from the table and take a sip whilst peering through the louvers. Just another rope truck.

"I don't know what I was thinking. She was friendly, so easy to talk to, I didn't see it coming."

Mark smiles at my unintentional innuendo and adds, "And then she just put her hand on your thigh."

"Well, metaphorically speaking, yes."

"And then what happened?"

"I legged it."

"Good, so, what seems to be the problem?" Mark transforms into a psychologist and I lie on his couch.

"Well, Dr Hatfield, I'm not sure if it happened again, that I'd do the same thing."

"So why did you leg it on Saturday night?"

"Because I love Abi."

Mark sees his opportunity to get me back for earlier: "So you think you might not love her as much in the future and give in to the next thigh touching Finnish sex kitten?"

"No, you git. Look, what I mean is, I do love Abi, a lot; masses; and that works fine for my brain. But my loins..."

"Steven Carter: never a simple word when a fancy one will do..."

"You know what I mean! The primal, animal part takes over and sometimes it seems like your brain switches off."

"The thrill of the chase."

"Yeah, hard wired into us for going after woolly mammoths or cave women."

"Whatever your preference!" laughs Mark.

"Hmm, that didn't come out quite right", I grin. "Don't tell Keith. I'll never hear the end of it." I pause, re-gathering the thought whilst wiping my glasses on an untucked fold of my polo shirt. "The thing is, the brain, it's a slow thing. Whatever anyone says, you don't fall in love in an instant. My love for Abi has been built up over years and so it would take ages for it to be worn down. But the loins lust and that can be instant and..."

"Involuntary?" inserts Mark.

"Oo. Now who's using big words? But, yeah, I mean, love can work, it should work. It worked on Saturday night, but will it work every time? I'm totally confident that my love for Abi will keep my brain under control, but what if the animal side is stronger?"

"Is it?"

"I don't know; that's what I'm afraid of."

"So don't test it out. Don't go out flirting when you're half pissed. Don't let the wild thing out."

"But I'll die of boredom, no offence."

"None taken." Mark taps his keyboard for a while with little enthusiasm. "Would it be different if Abi were here?"

"Of course", I say.

"Even if you still went out and she didn't?"

"Yes."

"Why?"

I ponder this whilst opening up the logbook file and scrolling down to the first blank page. "I think it has to do with immediacy. The loins need the immediacy of things like, 'will anyone see?'; 'will she find out?'; 'what if I bump into her when I'm out with Abi'. That's what keeps them under control."

"Stuff that'll really screw up your life," says Mark.

"Yeah. Of course, you know in your brain that it could happen anyway, but when your wife is a thousand miles away it just isn't so immediate."

"Maybe I should be Abi's spy and let her know everything you're doing?"

"Yeah right. And then she would think something was going on whether it was or not."

Mark rolls his eyes. "And I was so serious. No, what you need is a 'coping strategy'."

"You sound like the touch basers."

Just as he is formulating his riposte to this ultimate insult my mobile rings. The inspector has left and the crane is ready.

As Mark and I pick our way round sawn ends of reinforcing bar poking up through the roughly cast concrete, the seeds of a coping strategy (no, delete last), the seeds of a plan are forming in my mind. It's so simple. All I need to do is find a suitable victim.

- - -

"NOT EXACTLY THE BEST CHOICE OF WORDS under the circumstances, you think?" says Hiltunen widening his eyes. From the sudden heat in my cheeks, I'm sure I must be blushing. Bollocks.

"It's just a turn of phrase."

He makes a dismissive gesture with his left hand. "Sounds like you got a good pal in this Mark." The impish smile returns. "Even if he don't know the current lingo. Ain't no 'tell me about your problems' these days. Ain't no problems, only personal challenges. Speaking of which, I just got one little question: have you told your sweet Abigail about this Ana and the others?"

My eyes shift to the wood-block floor, "No, I didn't see the point in worrying her unnecessarily. I would tell her, but, it's been mad and, well, there's been way worse stuff being said."

"There sure has, there sure has... Pass your cup." I guess

compulsory caffeine is part of his technique. He waits until I'm once again enjoying the warmth in my throat before hitting me with it.

"And Arwen Saarinen, she was another in this long line of thigh-touchers?" I almost choke, a few drops of coffee escaping my mouth, spraying on to the nearest document. Bastard. He did that on purpose. Hiltunen pulls a cloth handkerchief from the inside pocket of his tweed jacket and begins to mop without comment. The ball is in my court.

"No, it was different, more like..."

"Don't tell it. Live it."

+ + +

CHAPTER 4

"Come on," I mutter. My stomach feels like it's beginning to eat itself. I'm loitering in the hotel's spotless reception area whilst the other guys finish getting changed, showered, etc. Erik is on duty but is deeply engrossed in the computer and doesn't seem to have noticed me. Katri appears out of the rear office and smiles a hello.

Finally lifting his eyes, Erik says, "You recover from the ice swimming yet?"

"How do you know about that? Is there no privacy in Mahikkala?" I say in mock offended tones.

"Small town..." he shrugs mysteriously, but Katri interrupts:

"Oh Erik, I know you from city think we all marry our brothers and ... what is English for talking like old woman?"

"Gossip?"

"Yes, we gossip all the time." She turns to me. "Do not believe him, he talk to John earlier in week."

Erik makes a 'what did I do?' face. There is a ping and the lift doors open to reveal Keith tapping a cigarette out of its box. I decide to answer the original question. "I can't say that I really enjoyed the cold water, but it was an experience."

"I think you mad to do it," says Katri. "Never!" She shivers at the thought.

"He's not still going on about his flirt with an icy grave, is he?" says Keith, crossing the granite tiled floor.

"I was just saying that it was an experience, but I don't think I want to repeat it."

"I cannot imagine..." starts Katri, but Keith interrupts, "No one wants to imagine Steve and John frolicking around in the snow naked, do they?"

All of us, including me, snigger.

"No," continues Keith, grinning at Katri, "The only way you'd get me on one of these sauna and ice swimming jaunts is if I got a personal invite from you and the rest of the reception girls."

"And how much chance do you think there is of that?" I say.

Erik makes the universal 'zero' gesture and Katri rolls her eyes as she retreats back into the office.

"Why do you do that?" I ask Keith.

"They like it really."

Another ping: finally, Mark and John.

"Something funny?" says John to Erik who is regarding us with a wide grin.

"Russian dolls." We are all in our navy thermal coats, all wearing black hats, and have all chosen blue jeans.

John raises his eyes heavenward. "Right then, purely for Erik's amusement let's form up in height order. By the left, quick, march." He pushes me ahead of him towards the double doors, adding to Keith on the way past, "That means you at the back, shorty."

There has been pre-agreement on pizza and when we arrive at the gaudy door, we find it is also Miguel's dinner of choice. He looks up apprehensively as we pass, no doubt wishing this town had a wider variety of eating out possibilities, but Keith and John head over to the furthest table and sit with their backs to the wall. Keith always says that he might as well have a view whilst he's eating. Mark and I can't be bothered to race for it most of the time. Tonight, Keith's 'view' appears to be the woman who Miguel is sitting with. Typically for him she's pretty close to stunning and wearing a tasteful, but unseasonably low-cut top.

The pizzeria is a Finnish chain similar to ones in the UK, but better, in our opinion. None of this deep crust rubbish where you pay for lots of dough and not much else. I order a four seasons and make my way through the plastic tables to the 'all you can eat' salad bar in lieu of a starter. As I squeeze coleslaw between my halved tomatoes and couscous, I find Miguel beside me, forking grated carrot and tiny radishes on to his plate.

"Things seem to be looking good for you," I say.

"Until you guys walk in. Please, do not spoil."

"Don't worry, Mark and I will keep hold of Keith."

Miguel gives me a grateful expression. I turn to check we are far enough away: "What happened to 'future wife' and 'I am in love'?"

"What you mean?" Miguel grins, wolfishly, "I am in love and there," he thumbs over his shoulder, "is my future wife." I shake my head, smiling.

"Miguel doesn't waste any time," says Mark as I retake my seat.

"No, he seems to work on the philosophy that a bird in the hand is worth two in the bush."

"Personally," says Keith between mouthfuls, "I always work on the opposite."

"Yeah, right. You'd shag anything in a skirt," says John.

"Like I said, the opposite, having a bird in the bush is worth having two in the hand." Groans all round.

Following our fill of pizza and Keith's jokes, we decide on pool for afters. A few streets away, slightly uphill from the lake, lurking between a furniture shop and a pharmacy is the entrance to the imaginatively named 'Snooker'. The club fills the first floor area above the pharmacy and has pretty much everything you need: half a dozen each snooker and pool tables and a bar. The decor is brick painted black with dark wood stained fittings to match the games tables, but in a snooker club who's looking?

We generally play pool as a four; two pairs alternating shots; Mark and I versus John and Keith. It's usually a fairly even match. I am the best, Mark is the worst, and the other two are somewhere in between. All of us are passable or better on the right day. The trouble is that tonight I am on fire. Every time I have a turn I'm potting four or five in a row. Even Mark is a little pissed off as he's not getting many shots.

"I'm sorry guys, you know how it is with me, I'll be missing them all again in ten minutes' time."

"That's what you said, half an hour ago," says Mark, watching me cut the final yellow into the middle pocket.

"All right, I'll sit out after this one for a bit. That one." I point to the bottom left pocket with my cue. The black rolls neatly along the cushion, wipes its feet and then falls into the pocket.

"I make that 5-0 to us." Mark doesn't sound too impressed with his victories.

John releases the balls with the next Euro and racks them up. "Steve, my glass's nearly empty." Cue virtuoso to servant in thirty seconds.

"Same again is it?" Three nods.

As I'm waiting at the bar a group of kids wander in. I say kids, they must be at least eighteen, ID cards being standard in Finland. Two guys and two girls, they park at the other end of the bar laughing at some story the tallest guy is telling. My Finnish can manage asking for four beers and giving over the right money, but I can't catch a word he's saying. I stand there smiling in the way that you do when everyone is laughing but you missed the start of the joke. One of the girls turns slightly and I realise that it's the barmaid from Hanne's: 'Reddy', as we've already christened her. I've never seen her out of the black-jeans-blue-shirt uniform before.

On the way back for the second two drinks, my movement causes her to glance in my direction. Our eyes meet briefly and I smile. There's a glint of recognition, but the taller guy is still talking and she turns back toward him.

A shelf along the wall acts as a table for drinks and I plonk myself down on a stool next to it and watch the pool. It's a much more even match: Keith and Mark have paired up and John is holding his own against them. Reddy and her friends have hired some snooker balls and the two girls are setting them up on a nearby table whilst one of the guys is feeding Euros into the light meter.

Keith notices Reddy and takes a few steps in their direction. "Hello. We've just seen your friend Miguel." She blushes deeply, cheeks clashing with her hair.

"Hey Keith, stop embarrassing her in front of her friends," I say, standing and moving in her direction.

The other girl is clearly asking Reddy who these blokes are and after hearing the gabbled answer, she says, "Where you from?"

"England," says Mark, getting it in first.

"'n' Scotland," growls John.

"You work here?"

"Yes," says Keith, "We spend all day tying each other up."

There is an awkward silence. You can almost see the translation cogs whirring in the woman's head. The taller guys who seems to have better English, says, "He is joking, Til. What do you really do?"

"Nothing so exciting, fortunately," I answer. "We work at the rope factory. Our company designs the machines they use to make the steel wire ropes."

The guy says, "Ah, 'tying each other up' with rope, I suppose that is the famous English humour." The Finns smirk superiorly.

The girl, who I'm guessing might be Tilia in full, says, "You move here?"

"Oche no, we're just here for a few months until the project is finished," says John. The chit chat continues for a bit until both parties gradually drift back to their games.

John has just missed an easy black when I find Reddy has walked back in our direction and is staring at me curiously. "Do you no play?"

"He's banned," says Mark answering for me.

"Apparently, I'm too good tonight and I'm spoiling their game," I say in a hurt tone. Reddy regards me with a hint of scepticism. I expect she's wondering if this is another wind up.

The good-at-English guy has obviously been listening and calls over. "Too good? Why don't you play him, Ar?" She throws him a look that I can't quite work out.

"Great." I take one of the Euros from the pile on our table and use it in the one next door. Reddy picks up the triangle and sets the balls. She has clearly done this many times before. I wave her to break off and she gives them quite a whack. However, luck is not with her and although the balls spread widely somehow none go in the pockets.

"Do you really just see Miguel?" she asks casually as I debate whether to choose reds or yellows. I stop myself from smiling. Now I understand why she came over. I roll the first red into the bottom corner pocket.

"Oh yes, he was having a pizza."

"He coming here?" Next one down.

"He might be," I pause as I walk round the table and sneak a quick glance. She seems slightly concerned as I hoped. "But, I doubt it." I grin as the third ball disappears into the middle pocket. "Has he been bothering you?"

"Not really, he is just…" She seems to be struggling to find the English word.

"Persistent?" I suggest sliding one into the top left corner. Blank look. "He keeps on trying?"

"Yes, very per-sistent." She tries the word out for size, smiling.

"Well, he did say he was in love." The smile disappears. I smack a straight red into the same pocket with a little bit of back spin on the white and walk to the head of the table, passing Reddy as I do so. She actually looks quite disconcerted and I lose my appetite for winding. I lower my head to see if I can reach my next ball through a gap between two of hers. "Don't worry. I think Miguel's love changes with his socks. He was with another girl in the pizza restaurant." Relief floods Reddy's face.

"She is his new 'true love', his new 'future wife'." I ape Miguel's accent very badly, but she still laughs. The gap is wide enough, my white finds it and another red falls. Suddenly, I realise that I have just potted six reds in a row and I'm on for an eight ball break. I can see Reddy counting round the table with her eyes. As I pass, I give her a conciliatory pat on the shoulder and say, "Easy come, easy go." I'm pleased with the ambiguity.

She shouts something to her friends and they come over. The final red sneaks into the middle pocket as planned, but even as I realise that we've gained a small crowd, the white travels way too far and I have an impossible shot on the black. The white and black are lined up quite nicely for the top right pocket, but one of Reddy's balls is sitting right in the jaws. The only thing I can think of is to bounce the black off two cushions back to the bottom left pocket, which I am leaning over. It's pretty much impossible.

"Oh, I don't know," I say, "this one," banging my hand on the rim of the nearest pocket. I bend and without pausing hit the shot as hard as I can. The white strikes the final ball at a completely unintended angle and speeds straight down the table. The black travels more slowly at right angles to it and hits the side cushion at ninety degrees. I almost look away from the table, but the two travellers which appear to have been going separate ways rebound off their respective cushions and home in on each other. The vigorous, youthful white strikes the circumspect black, transfers some of its energy and changes the black ball's path. I barely have time to lift my cueing hand out of the way as the final ball shoots towards me and thumps down into the nominated pocket.

I throw my head back in laughter at my outrageous luck, but everyone else is quiet. "Hey," I say, "that was a fluke. I'm not Paul Newman."

"Point to note in future," says Keith. "Gentlemen let the lady win."

I make an 'oops' face at Reddy. "Better make it best of three then."

In fact, she turns out to be just as skilful as I had suspected and although I do win the second game, we play the third and I'm losing heavily. We don't talk very much. Reddy keeps glancing back towards the good-at-English guy and talking to Til between shots. The third beer which has finally taken the edge off my pool prowess seems to have heightened my other senses. She must have used one of those berry shampoos earlier today and every time she passes, I receive an intoxicating waft of scented hair. Heavenly.

All too soon for me, the game is lost with an impressive long black.

"You not let me win?" she laughs, knowing that I didn't.

"Just ask these guys," I say. "Sometimes it all works and then a moment later it doesn't. Thanks for the game, anyway," I finish, rather limply, as she returns to her friends' table.

On the way back to the hotel we pop into Hanne's for our customary 'nightcap'. As the door man hangs our coats on one of the small glade of stands in the lobby, Hanne spots us and pulls up the left cuff of her royal blue shirt: no uniform privileges just because she's the owner. The time tells her everything she needs to know, "Four brandy cokes?"

"Aye, thank you," John answers for all of us.

- - -

"HAVE YOU EVER HAD BRANDY AND COKE?" Hiltunen's head snaps up in surprise. He shakes it. "Neither had I, but John is almost religious in advocating it as the last drink of the night to 'settle your stomach'. It seems to work pretty well too. I mean, I wouldn't have you wasting expensive brandy on it, but it's surprisingly not bad." Hiltunen nods slowly, waiting. "Look, I'm not sure if I'm going a bit off track here."

"There ain't nothing you can say that ain't important. We got all day."

+ + +

THE PLACE IS NEARLY DESERTED, but there's a bit of a scene going on in one of the dimly lit alcoves. An exceptionally drunk blonde woman is bawling her eyes out: hysterical sobbing, punctuated with garbled Finnish. One of the bar staff is sitting opposite her, talking slowly.

"What's going on there?" John asks Hanne.

"You not want to know."

We stand sipping our drinks, trying not to look towards the alcove. It's pretty awkward really. It's obvious that everyone else is doing the same. There's a strange fascination with someone who's clearly very upset and, well, if someone tells you, 'you don't want to know'...

Our curiosity is sated by the woman herself. She lurches up from the table, leans precariously against a pillar and walks unsteadily towards the bar. Her white jacket, wet down one sleeve, flaps open as she sways. There is an exchange between her and Hanne. Now I can't understand the Finnish, but it went something like:

"A double vodka."

"I think you've had enough."

"I've got money."

"I'm not going to serve you anything except water."

"Bitch."

"Drink this, while I decide whether to throw you out or not."

Whatever, the upshot is: Hanne glaring at woman; woman glaring at Hanne, but grudgingly taking a sip of water from the glass which has been placed in front of her. To the side, the door man has moved several steps closer.

The woman glances sideways along the counter without taking the glass from her mouth. Close up, I can see she was probably beautifully made up at the start of the evening, but all the mascara has run and now she wouldn't look out of place at a Kiss concert. "Are you married?" she says to Mark who is nearest.

"Yes," says Mark simply, pulling at one of his neatly trimmed sideboards, unsure of what is coming next.

"You do not hit her, no?"

"Of course not."

"Even if you have lot of beer?"

"I never have a lot of beer."

"Ah, good boy. Why I not marry good boy?"

"Is she problem for you?" says Hanne who is following the conversation whilst wiping glasses.

"No."

"Are you from England?" The woman surveys the rest of us.

"Well, Britain, yes," I say. This is no time for one of John's whinges.

"Do men hit wife in England?" Her eyes fall back on Mark.

"Maybe a few do. But they can go to prison for it."

There is a pause. I think she wants to say something but doesn't dare say it and none of us really want to be the first to ask. It's pathetic really. We're pathetic. Society's silly inhibitions are pathetic. Abi once volunteered doing the admin at an abused women's refuge, so I guess I feel the most guilty first:

"I'm Steve. This is Mark, John, Keith. What's your name?"

"Daina."

I just come straight out with it, "Does someone hit you then, Daina?"

Daina slips the jacket off her shoulder and lifts the side of her pale pink top to just under the bra strap. There are multiple yellow black bruises from her hip all the way up. "The last time he drink too much beer..." She doesn't need to elaborate. "Tonight he is out. I brave, I stupid. I think, I go out get drunk too. Not hurt so much. But now so late. He at house. He think I with other man..." she starts to cry again. "Scared..." sob "...go home"

"You need to tell the police," says Mark and puts a comforting hand on her shoulder. She steps back like his touch is electric. "Shit. Sorry. I wasn't thinking."

Daina continues to take backwards steps, "Who believe drunk woman?" she says, turning to head unsteadily towards the women's toilets.

"Do you know her?" Mark asks Hanne.

"Never see her before. Her Finnish is terrible. We have tried to call her a taxi home since one hour."

"It doesn't sound like a clever idea for her to go home," says Mark.

"Not my business," says Hanne. My head flicks up in surprise: it's not the attitude I'd expect from such an 'in-charge' sort of woman.

"What about taking her to the police?" says Mark.

"The police will say it is private thing between man and woman." It's like being transported back to the UK in the 1960s.

"So how badly does he have to hit her before the police will listen?" I add vehemently.

"What if he kills her?" says John.

Hanne seems as surprised by our concern as we are by her lack of it. "I do not know. This is not England. In Mahikkala the police are all men. They probably think drunk wife should be hit."

"And you think that as well, Hanne?" says Mark.

Daina re-appears from the toilets. She has cleaned herself up and now looks a bit less like a panda. Using every table and chair back for support, she wobbles towards us.

"Have you got any family or friends round here where you could stay?" I ask.

"No. Just his parents."

"Couldn't you tell them?"

"Ha," she gives a brief humourless laugh. "They hate me. Never believe me. I hear his father call me 'Russian whore' once. See me like this, he probably hit me also."

We are silent. She really is in a bad position.

"You're from Russia, then?" says Mark.

"No," spits Daina. "Latvia. 'Russian' worse insult than 'whore'!" There is another long pause. The nationalistic fire that briefly lit Daina sputters out and she whimpers softly, "I think I go home now and have my hitting."

"You've got to leave him," I say. "Go back to Latvia."

"He come looking, find me, hurt me really bad." She scrabbles in her bag for her mobile phone and turns it on. Immediately, it pings for three missed calls. Someone is searching for her. Although they are happy little notes, the rings sound like a funeral bell to me.

Hanne reaches over the bar, takes the phone out of Daina's hand and presses the off button. Anger plays on Daina's face, but Hanne says, "I will take you home. Maybe if I say you with me, he not hit you." Daina's expression melts to gratitude.

A few minutes later, Hanne and Daina leave through the back door and we are politely ushered out of the front by the other staff who have been left to close up. We feel like we should do something, but there's nothing we can do and, anyway, we are abroad and the language would defeat us.

Back in my hotel room, I'm telling Abi all about it. I think she's going to lay into me for not doing more, but as ever she surprises: "Poor woman, that's awful. You can't go to the police if she doesn't want to. Imagine if they turn up when her husband is at home. He'll be all polite and charming and then the minute they leave she'll be beaten to a pulp."

"What can we do then?"

"I don't know. I don't think you guys can do anything. Maybe Hanne could try to persuade her to phone a relative in Latvia. If she has any, that is."

"I'll ask Hanne tomorrow."

"Even in the UK with refuges and more sympathetic police it still takes years sometimes before women try to leave. Some never even try."

"I can't imagine ever hitting you…" my voice trails off.

"Gosh, this has really affected you, hasn't it?" she says. "You don't often go soppy on me." I hear a slight snort which means she's grinning, "No, I suppose I can't list wife beating amongst your many faults."

"Thanks very much." I roll my eyes. Why do I do that when she can't see? "I can feel a song coming on, by the way."

"About this?"

"Yes."

"Got a title?"

"I was thinking *Enemy within*."

"Good one. You can't sing it though."

"Why not?"

"It's got to be a woman's voice for a song like that."

"You're probably right. I'll ring up Madonna tomorrow, shall I?"

"Oh yeah, now where did I put her number?"

Enemy within

He was so very charming; totally into romance.
He swept me off my two left feet,
taught me the way to slow dance.
(what happened to that gentle dancer?)

He called me beautiful princess,
said he would never let me go.
I called him my gallant prince:
how in the world was I to know?
(what happened to that knight in armour?)

Did I do something wrong or was our love lies?
Every time you hit me, part of my heart dies.
When you held me up close, I'd like it so much.
Now I start to shiver at your slightest touch.

He said he'd love to protect me,
hold me tightly, keep me well,
He said marry me quickly,
I was completely in his spell.
(why couldn't I see what was coming?)

Then the jealously started:
Who was that man you're talking to.
You're disrespecting me princess,
and you know that will never do.
(I tried to say, he wouldn't listen)

Did I do something wrong...

But now the enemy is within my bed,
and the enemy is within my head,
and the enemy is within my car,
but the enemy won't let me go far.

Did I do something wrong...

Sorry Madonna, this seems to have turned out a bit R&Bish. I wonder if Beyoncé is available?

CHAPTER 5

There's a lull at the bar and Hanne moves towards us. "Well Steven, I did my good deed." She is obviously pleased with her correct use of the idiom.

"With Daina? What happened?"

"I took her home in my car. She lives *Laakso* Road. Big house. The husband wait at the window."

"What was he like?" asks Mark.

"Like a normal man, quite good looking. I got Daina out of car. She can hardly stand up. She shakes so much. I lift her down the path." Hanne makes a gesture showing Daina had put one arm round her neck. "We walk halfway and then the man comes out. He puts her other arm over his shoulder and we carry her in."

"That was brave of you - to go in," I say.

"Maybe stupid," says Hanne, "but I just want to see. Lovely inside, nice furniture, tidy, like when sell a new house."

"Like a show home?" says Mark.

"Yes, like that. We put her down on sofa. I say I am Daina's friend Hanne. He says to Daina, 'So you been out drinking with your friend Hanne?' and Daina only says 'yes' in small voice."

"Did he seem scary?" I ask.

"No, he was normal. He thanked me nicely and show me out."

"So you think she was making it up?" says Mark.

"No," says Hanne in a hushed tone, "I think she is in big trouble. When I drive, the man is watching me again from the window. Why is he doing that and not looking after his wife?"

"Maybe he was just waiting for the kettle to boil?" says Mark.

"Maybe," says Hanne, "But what do you call your wife?"

"Err... her name, Jane?" says Mark, furrowing his brow.

"When you not use her name, what then: darling?"

"Oh, okay, we don't really use pet names. Maybe sometimes 'sweetie' when I'm joking around, but..."

"Not 'little mouse'?"

"No, it sounds a bit..." Whilst Mark struggles for the right word, I interrupt.

"He calls Daina little mouse? What is he, then, the big fat cat?"

"It sounds more like a name for a little girl than for your wife," says Mark, finishing his thought.

"Just a small thing," says Hanne, "but it give me shivers up my back when he said it."

Keith, who has been half listening, turns, "Oh Hanne, I've been trying to give you shivers up your spine for weeks now."

Hanne smiles through pursed lips and rolls her eyes. "Keith, can you ever do serious talk?"

"Why would I want to do that?"

"Maybe I go visit Daina in a few days," she says and turns towards a proffered ten Euro note.

Keith and John are talking work, but my mind keeps turning around Hanne's words. That pet name is too creepy not to make it into the song. What rhymes with 'mouse'?

and the enemy is within my house,
and the enemy softly calls me 'little mouse'.

"Oi, dreamer, it's your round." Keith bangs his empty glass on the table and my head jerks up towards grinning faces.

"Sorry. Your conversation was so riveting..." I retaliate, heading towards the bar.

The staff are sporting new black badges with *Hanne's Bar* in large gold lettering. 'How tacky', I ponder, but then smaller type beneath the logo catches my interest. Unfortunately, Reddy has seen fit to pin her badge half way down the slope of her left breast and therefore propriety dictates that I don't stare too hard in the aforementioned direction.

It takes a little more time to order than expected as I discover that 'whisky and dry' does not translate too well and in the end Reddy has to show several mixer cans and I point to the correct one. Rather ironically, she then tells me that the 'Finnish' name for this mix is 'whisky ginger ale'. Sometimes the language barrier just makes you feel stupid.

Whilst she is adding ice to my hard won drink, I am able to see the text, and it is a name: Arwen. That rings a bell somewhere, but I can't quite place it. She turns and throws the ice scoop across the bar, landing in the sink with a satisfying 'plop'.

"I don't know, a couple of weeks on the job and she's an expert already," I joke. It's now my turn to be on the receiving end of the tongue.

"Any of you guys recognise the name Arwen?" I ask, putting the first two drinks into waiting hands.

"Why?"

"Because it's Reddy's name. They've all got new badges."

When I return, John says, "It doesnae sound Finnish. Is it Welsh?"

"No, I think it's from a film or a book," I reply, racking my brains.

"Why are you so bothered anyway?" asks Keith, stirring as always.

"I'm not really, I just know I've heard it before."

MY QUERY IS ANSWERED by my literary encyclopaedia of a wife: "Lord of the Rings. You know, she was the princess who got married to Aragorn at the end. She was supposed to be the most beautiful woman in the world. Why do you ask?"

"One of the barmaids here is called that."

"Does she measure up?"

"How do you mean?"

"Is she the most beautiful woman in the world?"

"Well, she's not bad. Not nearly as good looking as you though, dear!"

We make gagging noises at each other.

"Just don't get any heroic ideas about whisking her back to your castle."

"Chance would be a fine thing."

"Thank you very much," says Abi in a mock hurt tone.

"I meant of having a castle, not doing any whisking."

"Hmmm..."

CHAPTER 6

"I know we're currently on programme, but I really think we have an opportunity to get our ducks in a row and with a bit of out of the box thinking, we could pick the low hanging fruit now and accelerate this project." Terry is in full flow, his voice booming almost painfully across the cramped meeting room. He's in his element and has a suitable bit of TBS for every situation. TBS: that's 'Touch Baser Speak' in its more polite acronym. The other one starts Total... He's trying to persuade the bemused row of *Kaapeli* engineers to reorganise some work so that the new wire rope line will start up early. He's making it sound like he is suggesting this because he loves to make his customers happy and save them money. The thing is that everyone round the document strewn table knows full well that finishing early will save us money too and that is really what Terry has on his mind.

We engineers think that this kind of posturing is pointless and fools no one. It's obvious that what he's suggesting is, in TBS, a win-win, so let's just get on with talking about how we might do it.

John glances at his watch and catches my eye. It's coming up to my chosen time in the sweepstake. Surely any moment Terry's going to do it: "...so I'll get Steven to touch base with the designers back in the office and..."

I don't hear what Terry has just volunteered me for as I'm too busy subtly clenching my fist in a smug victory salute. Mark starts to cough, presumably to cover up a snigger. Terry stops mid sentence, vaguely aware that something else is going on, regards Mark quizzically, but then forges on. Bless him, he's in his own little management world. Anyway, his timely use of the fabled phrase has bought me all my drinks for this evening, so he's alright by me.

IT'S AMAZING how much better Scandinavian gassy lager tastes when someone else is paying. On a light summer evening it would be pleasant to perch on a stool next to the wide plate glass frontage of *Laiska Lohi*, but tonight sofas seem more snug.

Keith is studying two women sitting close to the large island bar. The low glass topped table in front of them is empty. "I see some APs are in tonight," he says, grinning at John.

"What are APs, then?" says Terry.

"Oh, they're one o' the more unusual bits of Finnish culture that we thought you ought to experience," says John.

Keith chips in, "A little bit expensive, but well worth it."

Terry has his back to the bar, so he hasn't seen anything. "It's not one of these rocket fuel vodkas is it, because I really can't afford to get too pissed?"

"Nothing like that," says John, "but you will, most likely, meet them at the bar."

Terry turns, but gets no clues. He knows we're winding him up, but he's worked with engineers long enough to know not to bite too hard. "'Meet them'? So we're talking about people?"

"Could be," I say.

"When you get the next round in, just let it happen, go with the flow," John says, "It's worth it just for the entertainment."

"Look, lads, you're not setting me up for anything too..."

"No Terry, you'll still respect yourself in the morning," says Keith.

"We're just giving you a head's up," says Mark. We all stare at him. It's an intervention with glorious comic possibilities. As ever, Keith is first off the mark:

"We're signposting what might happen."

"Making sure you've got them on your radar."

"We wouldn't want you to firm up too soon." All of us except Terry dissolve into giggles, sorry, make that hearty masculine laughter.

"Well I can see the joke's on me tonight. You'd best drink up then, hadn't you?"

The next minute or so is filled with the silence of four men who seriously want to get to the bottom of their glasses. "Once more unto the breach," mutters Terry rising from the table. He leans against the granite topped counter, waiting.

Right on cue, the two women join him. They tilt their styled heads slightly and smile lipstick. Obviously having clocked our English, one says, "You like to buy us drink?"

Terry glances suspiciously from the women, who are young, blonde and not at all unattractive, to us and back again. "Why not, what would you two ladies like?" He adds a couple of white wine spritzers to the beer order.

"We sit with your friends?" asks the other AP.

"Of course," says Terry as he carries over the first load of drinks. Rather than sitting next to each other, they each take one half of the two empty sofas.

"I'm Steve, this is Mark, Keith, John, and the very important looking guy carrying the drinks is Terry."

"Yeah, he's our boss" says John.

"The one with all the money," adds Keith.

Terry rolls his eyes and retakes his place next to the taller of the two women.

"My name is Fiia and she is Kristiina. Where you are from, why you here?" Four of us groan inwardly at the inevitable question. Terry, always ready to fill a pause, helps us out, "We're all from the UK. These guys are engineers, we're working on the project at the rope factory. It's going to be the biggest in Europe." I can see eyes starting to glaze over. "I'm the project manager."

"Are you from Mahikkala?" asks John, changing the subject.

"No. Here for university."

"Ahh, students," says Keith, "Never any money."

"Everything expensive," Fiia shrugs.

"Especially clothes, make up, and alcohol," says Mark. The APs seem a little disconcerted and Keith signals Mark a 'not yet'.

"Yeah, it's amazing how much Mark spends on lipstick," I say. Smiles return.

Fiia leans towards John, "Do you like here in Mahikkala?"

"It's better than China. At least there are a few decent pubs. The food's OK, and most people speak English."

"But very cold?"

"Well, we can always warm up in a sauna."

"You like sauna?"

"Steve and I do, but the others... Come on guys, why won't you have a sauna?"

There is a bit of pause, broken by Kristiina grinning, "Perhaps shy about taking clothes off?"

Keith peers down his nose, "That, my dear, has never been a problem. I just don't like being roasted alive."

The flirty type chit chat continues through several more rounds. The APs are gradually becoming louder and drunker. Just a little bit longer...

"Isn't it your round now?" says Terry.

I throw a what-do-I-say-now expression towards John.

"Steve doesnae have to pay this evening," he answers. "He won a little wager. We do that sometimes."

"Makes life a bit more interesting," I say. 'Please don't ask what I was betting on,' I add silently.

"Oh, yeah, what were you betting on?"

Just as I'm debating whether to lie or not, my saviour puts her hand on my shoulder. Reddy is standing beside me, leaning so that our heads are at the same height

"Hi."

"Hi."

"Not working tonight?" says Mark.

"No working day. So we come to other place." I turn to see the other three from the snooker club sitting at a table nearer the window. The 'good at English' guy raises a hand in greeting.

Reddy whispers in my ear, "We want to tell you, these women, they..."

I move my mouth next to her ear, "Don't worry," I breathe, "we know all about the alcohol prostitutes. Just watch."

When I turn back, Fiia and Kristiina are fidgeting with their straws. I may as well start it now.

"So if it's not me, then who should buy the next drinks?" John nudges Terry and subtly shakes his head. There is silence.

Mark joins in, "Well I just got the last round, so it can't be me."

"Or me," says Keith.

"So who's been knocking back expensive mixers and hasnae paid for a round yet?" says John, turning towards Kristiina. We all follow suit. Kristiina looks down. Fiia says a little defiantly, "We ask if you like to buy us drink."

"Well, aye, the first one, maybe. Terry here is very generous. But after that, you joined the round," says John.

"What this mean, 'joined the round'?" says Kristiina.

"In the UK, if you have more than one drink with some people then you have to buy them all a drink when it's your turn. It's only fair."

"Sorry, we not know about that," says Fiia.

"Well now you do, so mine's a lager please." Neither Fiia or Kristiina move.

John waits a few seconds. "Is there a problem?"

Kristiina says quietly, "We have no money. We thought you buy all drinks."

"Why would we do that?" Keith asks.

There is a pause, Kristiina stares at Fiia, clearly willing her friend to say something. I wonder if they're going to run right now. It would be a shame.

"Because you like us," says Fiia.

"Oh that's alright then, because I really like you," says Keith and puts a hand on her closest knee.

"And I do to," says Mark.

"I prefer Kristiina," says John and nudges Terry who is beginning to catch on.

"Oh me too," says Terry, stretching his arm along the sofa behind her.

"And I thought I was the lucky one tonight," I say. "So how's it going to work then guys? Are you going to flip a coin for who goes first?"

Fiia and Kristiina exchange confused glances.

"Save the best for last maybe? Which one do you like best Fiia?"

"What you mean?" says Fiia.

"Well in England if a man likes a woman, he talks to her, he tells her how lovely she is, but most of all he tries to buy her a drink. Because when she finishes that drink she hasn't paid for, she's agreeing to go to bed with him."

I hear a little gasp from Reddy beside me.

"Usually it's one man and one woman, but here, well, we're two against four, so to speak and, as broadminded as these guys are, I'm sure they'll not want to be at the same time, so you'll have to pick who goes first."

"I hate going second," says Keith to Fiia in a breathless whisper.

Fiia and Kristiina share a horrified expression and both jump up from the table. "No, we, sorry…" They virtually sprint to the door as we collapse in laughter.

"You guys are naughty," says Reddy shaking her head and chuckling. She notices that her hand is still on my shoulder and removes it with a slight squeeze. "All what you say about UK is not true, no?" As soon as the words are out she realises her mistake.

Keith pounces, "Why, would you like me to buy you a drink?" She sticks out her tongue and retreats back to her friends with a roll of her eyes.

"I thought they were real pros to begin with," says Terry.

"So did we first time," says John. "There's lots of them do it, mostly students."

"They come out with no money and then latch on to some gullible looking older bloke. Keith really thought his luck was in the first time," says Mark.

"But they're not interested in anything except your wallet," says Keith, "Which is why they never come near you, Mark."

Terry ignores the banter, "What was it you called them, again?"

"APs – alcohol prostitutes," I answer, "They swap flirting for drinks. It's strange, a lot of them seem quite nice girls really. They just don't realise how bad it makes them look."

- - -

"HAW, HAW, HAAW." Hiltunen's laugh could have been lifted straight from a Disney cartoon. "I sure wish you'd bumped into some of my sassy little undergrads. They'd 've called your Keith's bluff till his pants were down and then high tailed it off with them."

"You have students?" This seems highly unlikely.

"You're looking at the favourite guest lecturer at Helsinki, Turku… hell, I get all over." Maybe they find this 70s throwback amusing? He continues to chuckle as he reaches for his coffee.

+ + +

CHAPTER 7

The large digital thermometer on the right of the square glows a sweaty +1°C as we pass. The thaw has made the pavements particularly treacherous, with a lubricating film of water covering the compacted snow. Even the extra gravel chips are making little difference. We totter along awaiting that inevitable slip which will lead to derision and a wet backside.

"Someone was asking about you today." John has his full 'I know something you don't' voice on. I grow fins and jump into his net.

"Who?"

"Yeah, you should have been in Hanne's earlier," Keith butts in.

"Why?"

"She was asking questions about you." John grins, pleased with the progress of his drip feeding.

"So are you actually going to tell me what happened or do I have to spend the whole evening squeezing blood out of your stones?"

"Now who's going into a huff?" says Mark.

"Look guys, if I buy the first round can we cut the bull?"

"Spoiling our fun," mock whines John.

With a half drunk lager and some garlic bread in front of him, John is a bit more forthcoming. Unfortunately, we seem to have to go back to the start. "Guess who was working at Hanne's."

"Err... Hanne!"

"Come on."

"I don't know, Reddy?"

"Now why do you suppose he came up with that name so

quickly," says Keith putting a hand on my shoulder with exaggerated tenderness. I shake it off.

"I had to pick someone. What did she say then?"

"We were joking with her a bit. Somehow we got on to English introductions: how are you, my name is… that sort of thing. Then she says something like, 'There are four of you, yes?'"

"And then she said, 'What is the big one called?'" interrupts Keith.

"Which, of course Keith couldnae resist," continues John.

"I just wanted to know what she meant."

"Yeah, right. Anyway, Keith now gets the poor lass completely confused by asking her to define exactly which dimension was 'big' and how she knew about it."

"You git," I admonish Keith, "Her English isn't really that good."

"But she looks so lovely when she blushes," says Keith. "I did tell her that she meant 'tall'."

"In the end," says Mark, "and only because Hanne told you off."

"I take it that she was asking my name then?" I say and instantly regret it.

"You can see how he got his degree, can't you?" smirks John.

"Yeah, yeah, but it's funny how people always describe me as tall. I would've expected her to ask about the good looking one."

"Then we really wouldn't have known who she was talking about," says Mark.

I suck on my beer and wait for more. I'm still waiting when I take in only bubbles having unknowingly reached the bottom of the glass.

"Is that it then? She asks my name and immediately it's front page news for 'Gossip Monthly'. How sad are we?"

"This is Mahikkala…"

- - -

"BUT WHY'S SHE ASKING? That's what I'd be thinking. She must be interested if she's asking." Hiltunen's eyebrows rise to form a question.

"I suppose I was thinking something like that."

"And you felt a little guilty about it?"

"Maybe, but I needn't have worried."

+ + +

"... CHINESE, darts at O'Grady's and then a club, maybe."

"Have fun." There's nothing in Abi's tone, but I still feel like I need to justify myself.

"You know the dancing here's different, it's more of an activity, less of a meat market."

"I know you like to strut your stuff... twinkle toes," she says, teasing.

"Quit it. At least I don't 'daddy dance'."

"You just continue in your own little deluded world."

"Bum head!"

"Poo breath!" We both giggle at the ultimate insults borrowed from our four year old niece.

O'GRADY'S is the inevitable Irish Pub that has a prominent position on one side of Mahikkala's market square. They're the same the world over. I don't know whether someone sells a franchise. Maybe there's a 'start your own Irish pub' book. If there is, the decoration section would read something like:

a) The pub should have dark wooden beams across the ceiling.

b) There should be a long central bar with a brass lined upper surface.

c) The walls need to be festooned with various Irish memorabilia and several tricolour flags.

d) Ensure that the layout is unusual with several alcoves and sub-rooms. Customers will think that this adds 'atmosphere' but in fact it should be designed so that it is impossible to move from one part of the space to another without passing close to the bar.

Miguel has joined us in the darts alcove and he's dividing his time between 'Killer' and girlfriend. She's still the same one as at the pizzeria. This must be some sort of longevity record. I can see why.

"Come on Miguel, get him," cries Elina. He has just become a 'killer' again after Keith had hit his treble. He takes aim at the 16s with his final dart and hits the double.

"*Yes, vedä turpaan!*" says Elina, her mane of blonde hair flicking across my shoulder as she throws her head back.

"What did that mean?" I ask.

"You say in fight when you hit."

"OK, maybe we would say 'take that'."

She considers for a moment. "Is that why the pop group call itself that?"

"Who knows what goes on in the mind of Gary Barlow." I fail to hit my segment at all.

Miguel and Elina are discussing where they are going next. It's weird to hear two non-native speakers discussing in English.

"Aren't you learning Finnish?" I say to Miguel.

"Yes, I know all important words: *beer, food, sänky*."

"What was that last one?"

"Bed," says Elina widening her eyes. "Miguel says you like to dance."

"I have been known to."

"We go to Clarity soon, want to come?" I have a flashback to a teenage self being asked a similar question by someone else's gorgeous girlfriend. Why was it always someone else's girlfriend?

"Maybe, but on a Friday? I'll feel old." I glance down at my casual shirt and jeans: not really very 'street'. "My jeans aren't half falling off, for a start," I shrug.

"Come on," says Miguel, "Think of all the young women."

"I am married, you know," I say. Miguel gives me a 'and what has that got to do with it?' shrug in full view of Elina who narrows her eyes at him. He grins and plants a kiss firmly on her pursed lips.

"Come on Steven, you not go to Copacabana!" He pulls Elina from her chair and they rock towards me, arms in ballroom pose, giggling. It's true, I've no wish to join in with Keith and John's granny grabbing exploits and Mark will soon disappear back to bed.

"Oh, alright," I say. I'm not really sure this is a good idea.

"I dance with you," says Elina, receiving a faux jealous expression in return from Miguel. "Well, one time." I feel so much better. Not.

I don't get another turn at darts. Mark, showing an uncharacteristically brutal streak, finishes me off before turning his attentions to Keith. Miguel is soon knocked out too and the three of us make our excuses.

THE BEST THING about Clarity is its name. I just love the irony of calling a place where drunk people peer through theatre smoke and strobe lights, Clarity. Genius! Elina drags Miguel straight on to the dance floor so I take the route to the bar. It's not a night to be in any way agoraphobic and one of Finland's idiosyncrasies is much in evidence. There is a word in Finnish for 'excuse me', but they consider it perfectly normal to guide someone gently out of the way without asking them first. Trouble is, once everyone has had a few beers, the guiding often feels like shoving. John nearly threw punches until he realised they didn't mean anything by it. Strangely, Keith often finds himself blocking the path to the women's toilet.

I feel a minor sense of achievement having reached a spot on the lecher's balcony without spilling my or anyone else's drink. The balcony stretches along three sides of the dance floor. Fixed stools line the glass and chrome handrail come shelf. I suppose I'm a bit different from most of the observers up here. I'm not scanning for a target or staring enviously at the more expert strutters of their stuff. I'm not sulking because no one has picked me out. I'm just spectating wistfully, wondering what it would have been like to be here ten years ago.

I'm nearly down to the bottom of my vodka Red Bull (when in Rome...) which I have drunk far too fast. Come on then Steve, there's no point being here unless you dance. I'm a bit gangly, not all that muscular, but whatever Abi may say, I can move. And I love it. So I step out on to one of the less crowded corners and lose myself in the rhythm.

It's pure visual dating tonight: all about fleeting eye contact, which way you're facing, how close you're dancing to whom. I know the rules, but I'm trying to play it neutrally: smiling, but then drifting away; moving close but not staring. I just want to dance. The music morphs up a gear to a more hardcore trance beat number and I find myself being sucked nearer the centre of the floor by the whirlpool of bodies. I catch sight of the back of some red hair. No, can't be. It disappears. I reach that point where I'm dancing at full pelt. I should be tired, but I'm not. I should be sweating, but I'm not. I'm floating. Maybe this really is a trance. Wouldn't it be great to close my eyes? And then there she is, an angel of laughter, in front of me, bouncing and twirling to the beat.

You know that feeling when you're suddenly roused from a deep sleep and your head aches with all the wake up juices throbbing inside? It's like that now. My head temporarily forgets to control my legs and I almost fall. I try to make it look like a move, but judging from Reddy's face, I'm not successful. I shrug and then repeat it to the rhythm, reach out for her hands and halve the distance between us. We dance, fingers locked, guiding each other's arms in patterns as the music seems to lead. Her blue-grey eyes are burning into me, but I'm not looking anywhere else. The music is winding to a climax and we both stop dead as does everyone else familiar with the ending. There is a second of silence followed by a long slow chord. I let go with my right hand and flourish it whilst bowing low in costume drama style. Perhaps a bit over the top, but as I glance up, it has made her laugh. Another track starts, but Arwen grabs the hand of her friend, (Til was it?) who I notice for the first time, and beckons me to follow.

We pass under one corner of the balcony, through some heavy swing doors, into a side room. It's surprising how much volume the doors block out, but every time they open a deafening blast follows.

"Wow, that was intense," I say as we perch on three stools surrounding a high level circular table.

"You really," she pauses to remember the phrase, "in-the-zone."

"Good dancer!" adds Til.

"Thanks." Then to Arwen, "You surprised me back there!" I place my hand over my heart and gasp.

"I know it. I mean it!"

"You nearly fall over," says Til. Both women are laughing. I stick my tongue out, but hold Arwen's gaze. A gust of noise from the opening doors renders conversation impossible for a few seconds.

"Would you two like a drink?" They laugh louder.

I'm slightly confused, but then Til says, "I will buy. Just in case!" and I remember back to the night with the APs.

"Well, OK, I'll have a vodka Red Bull, thanks." Til slips off her stool and my eyes meet Arwen's once more. It doesn't feel uncomfortable.

"So Arwen, I hear you know my name."

"Yes, Steven."

"Steve for short."

A small smile plays on her lips. "And the Scotland man he also call you *'steevi'*. She pronounces the word in a Finnish accent.

"Yeah, I don't know why John does that." I stop while the doors open again. "Stevie doesn't mean something awful in Finnish does it? You know, like smelly feet or something?"

"Not awful, just funny."

"Go on then, tell me."

"I not know the English word, but when we go in Harri's boat on lake, it what he call the part that goes up at the front." She traces the curve of a keel across the table top and taps her finger at the end of the line.

"Hmm, I suppose we call that the prow." She shrugs. I stare at her with exaggeratedly narrowed eyes. Under my gaze her expression dissolves from feigned innocence into a smirk. "Are you being rude, young lady?" The smirk turns into a grin and I roll my eyes. "Anyway, talking about names, Miss Fairy Princess."

Arwen's grin turns sheepish. "My dad like to read." She lifts her hair at one side. "Look, no sharp ears."

"I..." Another blast of music. The bleached streaks in Til's hair glow slightly blue under the UV light that bathes the small bar in the corner where she is still waiting. "Is it just you and Til here?"

"Yes, Kari and Harri not like to dance."

"Harri is Til's boyfriend?" I saw them holding hands in the snooker club.

"Yes, and Kari is my boyfriend."

"Oh..." I don't know why this hits me out of the blue, it's fairly obvious really, but I clearly hide my disappointment very badly. Why am I disappointed?

Reddy's cheeks colour slightly. Then she smiles, head shaking slightly and puts a warm hand on top of mine. "No." She glances towards her friend. "Til always say I too friendly with all the boys."

I let her hand rest there a few seconds and then smile back, "Well, this boy is married anyway." Her hand shoots back as if I have nipped it.

"Oh, I... sorry, I..." Reddy seems far more surprised than I expected. I decide to be adult about it and interrupt:

"Don't be. I suppose I am kind of a little jealous. I know I shouldn't be..."

"No," she says, her expression unreadable.

Someone opens the door again and I experience my loudest ever slightly awkward silence. It's a welcome distraction when Til places three vodka Red Bulls on the table. The thumping beat subsides, I glance back at Reddy and halt the glass part way to my mouth. "Perhaps too many of these."

Til looks from me to Reddy and then asks her something in Finnish. I can't follow the short conversation, but I know it's about me. It seems like Til is telling her off, but I can't be sure.

"Your wife is in England?" asks Til.

"Yes."

"Do you have children?"

"No. Maybe sometime." I'm worrying about the direction this is headed, but the tack changes.

"What is name of your wife?"

"Abi."

"She like to dance?" Reddy joins in with the interrogation.

"Yes, a lot, but she wouldn't like it tonight. Saturday would be better."

"Til prefer older music too."

A little retaliation is called for, I feel, but I have to wait for another gush of music. "Kari is very good at English."

"Yes, he spend last year in UK. University exchange."

"Which one?"

"Oxford."

"Oh, clever guy." As I say this, I realise someone is standing next to me.

"I looking for you everywhere," says a glowing Elina, completely ignoring the others. "I want my dance." Her demeanour brooks no argument. She is already facing back towards the door as she takes my hand and starts to pull me up from the stool. I follow Reddy and Til's glances towards the laces and flesh of Elina's backless top and make a 'what can you do?' expression.

"Miguel's girlfriend," I say as I straighten up. Reddy's expression changes from surprise, to something, to amusement. Was that relief? Relief that I'm going, or relief about what? I'm being tugged away from the table and I start to say, "Always, someone else's girlfriend!" but end up shouting it as the volume rockets. I'm not sure whether they hear, and I have to turn and concentrate on the woman in hand.

I'm dancing again, but my mind is back with Reddy. What did that look mean? Why should I be bothered? Isn't this perfect for my plan? What about Abi? Clarity. *See you in clarity.* Good line.

Later I search the side rooms and the dance floor but I can't find her. I leave, ears ringing, and trudge back home. My head is full of dance beats, melodies, and lyrics as the hotel door slides open.

"Had fun, Steven?" says Erik whose snoozing I have disturbed. I can barely hear him and point to my ears.

"Ah, you must have been to Clarity."

I nod. "I also found out that John's been calling me part of a boat." Erik's brow furrows. "He calls me Stevie – *steevi*."

Light dawns across his face. "It is not a usual word. Who told you about this?"

"I bumped into Arwen, she works at Hanne's Bar."

"Ah yes, red hair?"

"That's the one. Still it could be worse, my name could mean stupid or something."

"No the word for stupid is *keith*." he says, pronouncing in a Finnish accent.

"No, really?" Erik grins and I realise he's winding me up. "Don't you wish it was, though? *Hyvää yötä*," I say on my way to the lift.

"Good night."

As soon as I reach my room I recall that moment on the dance floor and start to write:

Clarity

Suddenly, I see you in clarity.
My mind wakes up, the blurriness has gone.
Just look, don't think,
standing on the brink.
I never thought that you could be the one.

Drifting away, across a crowded dance floor;
drawn by the tide, towards your distant seashore.
Floating away... or am I sinking?
Caught in a swirl... what am I thinking?
Floating away... dry land is shrinking...
The answer always out of reach,
then suddenly... clarity.

OK, so they're not the most inspired lyrics ever, but, hey, this is a dance song: it's about the beat!

CHAPTER 8

"The floor level is OK as well," Mark says, his eye still peering through the theodolite. He pulls at the short hairs of his left sideboard: something is wrong somewhere. One of the swaging machine gearboxes doesn't line up with its motor. It's only a tiny part of the wire rope factory, but Mikko found the problem before we did and it's always a bit embarrassing when your customer says 'and how is this meant to fit together?' So here we are on a Saturday afternoon, trying to measure which part has been made wrong, or is out of place or whatever.

"That's good. You know John was telling me about a Taiwanese project where they cast one whole section of the concrete floor at the wrong height."

"Nightmare," says Mark moving the theodolite nearer to the corrugated wall so he can see the shaft ends protruding from the motor and gearbox. "How was Clarity last night?"

"Loud. I've still got hissy ears."

"And dancing with Elina?" Mark raises his eyebrows.

I blow air out of my mouth to indicate her 'hotness'. "I don't know where Miguel finds them."

"That's the annoying thing about it: they seem to find him."

"Imagine all the tricky decisions, though, with that many beautiful women throwing themselves at you."

"It's a nice problem to have," says Mark aping Terry's boom. "Hey, you're wobbling the ruler."

"Don't make me laugh then." Mark has taken a line of sight over the motor shaft and I am holding a steel ruler vertically up from the end of the gearbox shaft. It's not the most accurate method, but it'll do for now.

"You're drooping a bit."

I straighten up the ruler but can't resist the innuendo which I'm sure Mark has set up for me: "That's not what Elina said."

"Yeah, right," says Mark, "I bet Miguel was standing there sharpening his axe, the whole time you were dancing with her. There's seven millimetres between them."

"When I saw them dancing, I can assure you that most of the time there was zero millimetres between them."

"Shaft heights, you dope."

"I know. Seven exactly?"

"If you're holding that ruler right then pretty close."

"Hmm. Where did I put that gearbox drawing?" I find it sitting on top of a power supply cabinet behind me. "Anyway, dancing with Elina wasn't the highlight of the evening. I bumped into Reddy. She can really move."

"Oh."

"Hey, don't go all puritanical on me. We danced and laughed and got on really well," I pause for effect. "Right up to the point where she told me she had a boyfriend and I told her I was married."

"Huh?"

"Yeah, it's perfect. You know how I was talking the other week about the temptations of the women out here and you said I needed..."

"A coping strategy," interrupts Mark in Terry's voice again.

"Yup, well, I've worked it out: a sure fire, one hundred percent guaranteed, way of ensuring that I stay a good boy, but can still go out on the town." I pause as something catches my eye on the drawing.

"Go on then," says Mark in the long suffering tone of one who has heard my wacky ideas before.

I make Mark wait while I subtract a couple of numbers using the calculator on my mobile. "It's simple, I'm going to fall madly in love with Reddy."

"And that helps because?"

"Because when you're first in love with someone, you can't think of anyone else, you're totally obsessed and, well, just remember when you were a teenager, if that girl wasn't interested, it just makes it worse."

"So let me get this straight, your grand plan to stay faithful to Abi is to fall in love with another woman?"

"Yeah, but it's never going to go anywhere."

"But don't you think it's a bit..."

"Ha haa," I interrupt and start to laugh. "It's upside down."

"What, your brain?"

"No, this." I rotate the gearbox drawing by 180 degrees. "The 'box can be installed either way up and for some reason the shaft sits seven millimetres higher if it's upside down."

"It looks symmetrical to me."

"I know, I bet that's what the fitters thought and of course if they've got a 50/50 chance, Sod's law always applies."

Mark breaks into a broad grin. "Monday's meeting is going to be a classic." It was Mikko's fitters who installed the gearbox the wrong way up.

I check my watch. "Come on, I can think of better things to do on a Saturday afternoon."

"What time is Katri's birthday thing?"

"She said meet up with them in Clarity at eleven. You are going to come, aren't you?"

"Yesss."

- - -

"HEY, NOW THAT IS SOMETHING, Mr Carter. That is something..." Hiltunen's shoulders are shaking. "I ain't never heard that one before. 'Falling in love to stay faithful'... Sure as hell sounds like you should've been listening to your pal."

"I know." My head moves from side to side in disbelief. "If only I'd taken any notice... But I was so unsettled by the 'thigh-touchers'." We share a smile about this phrase which is clearly going to pass into both our vocabularies.

"So you decided to pour something over the fire to put it out. Trouble is, you chose gasoline, right?"

"Hindsight's a wonderful thing, hey?"

"If folks had one percent foresight instead of one hundred percent hindsight, I'd be straight out of a job."

+ + +

KATRI is having a birthday meal out with some of the hotel staff, and, presumably because we're slightly amusing company, we've been invited along to join in with the clubbing afterwards. Whilst Fridays at Clarity are firmly aimed at the more hardened punter, Saturdays have broader appeal and the volume is considerably reduced.

"You always buy each other drinks. Why?" asks Erik, as John's back recedes into the crowd. Katri, Erik, Raakel, and Dea have already each bought their own drink.

"I don't know. It saves us all from fighting our way to the bar, I suppose."

"But what if there were ten of you?"

"Then we'd probably split into two or three rounds," says Keith. The other three Finns move closer. This is obviously a strange bit of 'English' culture that they have been dying to ask about.

"What it mean 'round'?" says Raakel.

"The shape of Steve's belly after too much pizza", says Mark and makes a half circle motion in front of me.

"You can't beat a four seasons," I comment. I see the confusion in Raakel's eyes and help her out, "Sorry, 'round': it means we each buy the drinks in turn; going round in a circle." I point out each of us in turn as I say the last.

Erik is not done yet, "But what if you only buy three drinks or five?"

"Then someone pays less, or more than the rest," I say.

"Not everyone likes buying rounds," says Mark. "It's not like everyone in the UK..."

Keith interrupts, he is very old school about buying drinks, "If someone buys more or less drinks one day, we remember it for next time. It evens up after a while." He glances disparagingly in Mark's direction. "We soon notice if someone isn't paying their way."

I've witnessed this argument before and try to head it off at the glare stage.

"Basically," I say, shrugging to the Finns, "we do it because it's polite."

They love this image of Britishness and all grin.

"The polite Englishmen buy each other drinks and say please and thank you." Erik manages a pretty passable posh English accent on 'thank you' which causes hysterics among his female colleagues.

"At least we don't push people out of the way without asking," says Keith finding an alternative injustice.

John returns with the full round clamped precariously between his stretched hands. "So when are you going to show us all up with your fancy dancing then Steve?" he says, as we unburden him.

"Not just yet, more lubrication required."

Katri is being pushed forward laughing. Dea and Raakel are ignoring her protestations. "It Katri's birthday so she dance with everyone," says Dea.

Raakel spots Mark trying to hide behind John and grabs his hand. "You first, Mark," she says.

"But, I can't..."

"Come on, you can't refuse a woman on her birthday," says Keith.

"Go," says Raakel. Mark looks hesitantly from us to Katri, to the dance floor, and then to Raakel who smiles encouragingly.

"Oh, all right then," and he takes Katri's hand. Probably the less that is said about Mark's dancing the better. On a TV show the host would kindly call it a 'game attempt'. John makes no complaint, but only fares a little better. He Dad dances, but with confidence.

"How do you charm all these middle aged divorcees in Copacabana then John?" I ask, as Katri gives up and drags him back to us giggling. "It can't be with your dancing skills."

"He doesn't know how to dance unless he's wearing a kilt," says Keith.

"Aye, an' a pair o' claymores on the earth to step o'er," says John, broadening his accent.

I've never seen Keith dance before. I suppose it shouldn't be a surprise. He likes to think he has all the verbal moves too. Completely ignoring the fact that there's a fast pop song playing, he takes Katri in a ballroom hold. Somehow making an asset of his height inferiority, he glides and twirls her through the gyrating crowd. Katri has clearly done this sort of thing before and seems to be enjoying herself in spite of it being Keith. I only see her wince twice when he pulls her particularly close.

And then it's my turn. "Aren't you worn out yet?" I ask, as we walk out in the lull of an intro. She shakes her head and smiles. As the beat begins I grin impishly and begin to point to ceiling and floor,

Travolta style. Katri pulls my arm down, mock frowns and wags a finger at me. She continues to wag it whilst starting to dance. I twist my hips to the beat, turn sideways, and point at my bum. I'm daring her to spank. She makes as if she is going to, but instead of her hand, I receive a gentle kick instead. I laugh, grab her still wagging finger and try to twirl her like Keith did. She goes round, but it doesn't seem quite right, not graceful.

"Not really my thing," I shout in her ear.

"What your thing, then?" she shouts back.

I take one hand and pull her closer, I can feel her pulling back slightly, so I take the other, but let her recede. I sway her arms to the beat and then move one out sideways. She's not used to this: her arms are resisting, so I release one hand and smile into her eyes. I can't read her expression and I wonder if I've overdone it, but she retakes my free hand and meshes fingers. Now she's making the shapes.

"Careful, you'll be pointing in a minute," I shout. She grins, but the music starts to fade and we make our way back towards the bar with the fingers of one hand still interlocked.

Mark widens his eyes at me as we approach. Dea says something which makes Katri's cheeks colour and Raakel giggles.

"What?" I say to Mark. I find I am no longer holding Katri's hand. Did I let go?

He leans towards me. "That was pretty intimate, wasn't it?"

"Was it?" I'm actually surprised. "It wasn't meant to be. We were just having fun." 'like brother and sister' I add to myself. Mark shakes his head and turns towards Erik, who has reappeared with a tray. On it are eight drinks held in strange metal cups that look like stretched shot glasses. The liquid they contain appears to be black and slightly oily.

"I buy a round, Finland style," says Erik grandly.

"Are we meant to drink that?" asks Keith.

"Finnish speciality: Salmiakki."

"Are you afraid?" says Dea, reaches for a cup and downs its contents in one. With our male pride challenged, we all follow suit. It tastes like a cross between aniseed and cough medicine. Strangely, at this time of night that doesn't seem so bad.

"Yuck," says Mark. From Katri's face, she's hasn't enjoyed it any better.

"Ah, a falling down drink," says John.

"A what?" I ask.

"Like Tequila with salt and lime: keeps you wanting more..."

"...until you fall down," I finish for him.

"It also one of the cheapest drink here," adds Erik.

"There you see, they can't even give the horrible stuff away," says Mark.

"Who wants another?" says Keith.

MY FIRST THOUGHT in the morning is, 'when did I hit my head on the wall?' Then I remember the liquid reason for my distress. "Bloody black stuff," I announce to the wardrobe. I run through the latter parts of the evening in my head. Good, there are no gaps.

Breakfast is a slow and careful affair, but I do feel a great deal better for it. Nothing like scrambled eggs and meat balls after a heavy night! As I sip on my fifth glass of orange juice, I ponder Katri. Was I really flirting as much as Mark reckoned? It didn't feel like flirting. I don't fancy her. But what's not to fancy? Dancing with her just wasn't... it just wasn't... the same as dancing with Reddy. Cool. It actually is working.

I'M STILL CONGRATULATING MYSELF when I phone home later in the day.

"Mark actually went to a nightclub? You're not finally corrupting him are you?"

"No. It was Katri's birthday and she asked him directly, so he couldn't really get out of it. Anyway, what do you mean corrupting?"

"I thought Mark was the good husband who stayed in and didn't spend all night dancing with blonde beauties!"

"They're not all blonde you know."

"Oh well that's OK then," Abi replies ironically.

"Anyway, how was your work night out?"

"We ate in Ricardo's. Olivier ordered two bottles of Chianti, so you can imagine how loud it got."

I grin at the mental picture of inebriated librarians arguing over some great literary controversy: like whether Darcy or Knightley was more fanciable.

"And then, don't faint, we went out dancing too."

"Jenny still trying to find a man?"

"Oh yes, but when she suggested 80-90s night at the Cottonmill, we didn't really need much persuading."

"Did they play 'Fool's Gold'?"

"Yup, and it was one of the few times that I was glad you weren't there. Why must you wave your head about like that?"

"Mostly because I know it winds you up. That's genuine indie dancing I'll have you know."

"Looks genuinely stupid to me."

"Cheers... so did Jenny find anyone?"

"Maybe." Abi pauses.

"What?"

"Well it was a bit embarrassing really. Jenny had been smiling at this guy for ages and finally he comes over to where we're standing, and we all thought he was going to ask Jenny, but then he asks me to dance."

"Ha, haa, so you're the good little wife who gets asked to dance by hunky English blokes whilst her husband's away on business."

"Touché. No, I did my matchmaking duty and said I was taken, but Jenny liked to dance."

"Not really a good start is it?"

"No, but you never know, they did swap phone numbers." She changes tack, "Is work going well, you sound pleased with yourself?"

How does she do that? I answer quickly, "*Kaapeli* have blamed us for something and Mark and I have just found out that it was actually their fault. So it's going to be an interesting meeting tomorrow."

"Oh well, have fun playing with your big boy's toys. I need to do some exciting ironing for tomorrow. Love you. Miss you. Wednesday, yeah?"

"Yeah, I'll ring about eight your time. Love you too. Bye."

I push the disconnect button feeling slightly underhand. Somehow I don't think explaining that I'm actually pleased because my plan is working would go down too well. Not when that plan involves falling in love with a rather attractive redhead. And she provided me with such a good get out. Still, I am doing it for Abi...

- - -

"I REALLY DID CONVINCE MYSELF that it was OK, that my plan was an 'innovative solution', just like I'm supposed to come up with at work." I shrug. "There is a sort of logic behind it."

Hiltunen shakes his head. "Don't go putting your trust in logic. Most of the nastiest decisions in history been justified using logic. Strange new religion preaching freedom? There'll be slave riots. Rome could fall! Logic says throw them Christians to the lions. Shut 'em up, make an example. That one didn't work neither!"

"Bit late for advice now," I mutter.

"Maybes you thought it was for the best of reasons, but it seems to me you was actually justifying letting your eyes wander. And two doses of love ain't never a happy mix. Same as drinking your beer... and your vodka too."

I throw back my head and let out an ironic chuckle. "Drinking my vodka too, hey?" He couldn't have chosen a more appropriate phrase.

If I have confused Hiltunen he doesn't show it, but merely raises those eyebrows as an invitation to continue.

+ + +

CHAPTER 9

I'm gazing at Reddy's back as she returns some glasses to the narrow shelf above the optics. Her hair is up in a full pony tail, revealing a milky neck, appearing all the paler due to its close proximity to those deep chestnut locks. There's something about the back of a woman's neck: kissability. She turns and catches me staring. Our eyes hold: I'm feeling brave and I don't look away. After a second or two, Reddy looks down and smiles. She glances sideways at Hanne who raises her eyebrows. Hanne says something in Finnish and Reddy disappears into the kitchen. I glance towards Hanne who regards me for a moment and then makes a slight chuckle.

"What?" I ask.

"Nothing."

I finish the last sip of my brandy and coke and decide that it is an opportune moment for a pee. Opening the door to the gents, I glance back to see her smiling and shaking her head. When I face forward, I decide I must be drunker than I thought. Rather than the dull green walls and acrid smell of the gents I am confronted by pure white walls and stainless steel worktops. There is a noise of rummaging behind the furthest worktop. A hand reaches up and places an unusually shaped glass on the metal surface. I know that hand. Reddy straightens up and lets out a tiny gasp as she sees me.

"Hey, you not allowed in here."

"I didn't mean to, I must've got the wrong door."

She glances down at the glass and then back at me.

"I've never seen a glass like that. What drink is it for?" I ask taking a couple of steps closer.

Blushing slightly, Reddy lifts the glass and absentmindedly rubs a mark off the outside with her finger nail. "It a lover's cup." Her eyes meet mine, "In old times, Finland woman fills cup with berries and vodka."

"Ah, berries and vodka, what else?" I grin holding her gaze. There's something in her eyes.

"She find her man, they drink from the cup, and then…"

"And then?" I find I have walked to the opposite side of the work surface. We are only a metre apart.

"They make love." Our eyes are still locked. I reach out my right hand to touch a lonely strand of chestnut which has become detached from the hair band. From there it is a small distance to move my fingers to the hairline behind her ear. We are both leaning. Our lips meet lightly and we linger in that first intimate touch. I start to pull closer, meaning to kiss deeper, but she makes a little cry in her throat. We are both at full stretch and I realise that a steel edge is digging hard into my groin. Reluctantly, I let go and Reddy tips back. There is a line across her shirt just above the belt.

"There's something between us," I say.

"And it is long and hard," she replies, eyes sparkling. Who knew that she likes a dumb innuendo as much as I do?

"Who told you about that?" I move round the end of the surface and reach out again but she holds me away with the flat of her empty hand against my chest.

"Not here."

I am led by the hand out of the kitchen. I'm expecting Reddy to let go as we cross to the bar, but she holds on. Hanne doesn't seem at all surprised.

"It look like you have everything you need, Arwen," she laughs. "You go, I finish."

We cross the deserted bar to the outside door. The teeth of the night air reminds me that I have left my coat behind, but there's a different heat keeping me warm now.

"Where…?" I start to ask.

"Just follow."

We walk half a block in the opposite direction to the hotel, turn the corner and I'm led up a stairway to a first floor balcony passage.

Someone told me that Reddy still lived with her parents just out of town. I guess they were wrong. After a few metres, she stops, pulls at a light chain round her neck and inserts the key hanging from it into the lock of the second doorway.

"Never lose it," she says and pushes the door.

I do a double take - it's my hotel room, but, no, there's a kitchen area off to the right. Still, the same parquet floor, the same pine cupboards, the same blue curtains?

"It..." I start.

"...looks like hotel room," she finishes. "My uncle does furniture, painting for hotels and shops. He has some extra." She shrugs, as if to say, 'it's better than nothing' and heads over to the kitchen units. I sit on the bed and pick up the cup which she has left on a low table between it and the TV. The curves of the glass are clearly intended to mimic those of a woman. As Reddy approaches, I hold it out at eye level. She raises her eyebrows questioningly.

"Just comparing shapes," I say.

"Design by a man," she laughs, taking it from me and adding a generous quaff of vodka. She puts the cup back on the table and tops it up with a carton of cranberry juice. "This near enough," she says, and smiles archly.

My head is a whirlwind of emotions. I've never been here before. This doesn't happen to me. What... But before I even think it, she is sitting next to me, offering me the glass. I take a sip of the bittersweet liquid.

"English..." she sighs, rolling her eyes and drinks a huge gulp herself. I take the cup back and as I tip it she jogs my arm. Cold streams out of the corners of my mouth. I put the glass down and start to reach for a tissue in my pocket, but firm hands hold my arms above the elbow and I feel the touch of that tongue, so often shown in jest, on my neck. She traces the purple trail up past my chin to the corner of my mouth and our lips touch again. My arms are released and as I nibble at her top lip, I reach behind her head and gently pull off the hair band. I explore her mouth, eyes, neck, whilst all the time running my fingers through her hair. Oh that hair! I plant kisses on the side of her neck and it tumbles over my face. I breathe in deeply: recently washed hair, mixed with the heady scent of warm woman — the best smell in the world.

"More," she breathes, untwining her head from mine and reaching for the cup. She intentionally allows it to run out of her mouth, down her neck, and on... I take the glass and push her gently backwards. Starting at her mouth I go with the flow: chin, neck, breast bone, cleavage, each a new domain to be explored and savoured. I pause to undo a couple of buttons and realise that my crotch is pressed hard against the edge of the bed and the bulge is straining hard against my weight. I'm so turned on, it feels like I'm about to... no... I've never had that problem, unless...

I'm suddenly in two places at once: conflicting hormones throb through my head as I mentally flap: trying to grab hold of the image of open shirt, pale skin, and deep chestnut hair that is fluttering out of my mind on a gust of consciousness.

"Oh, crap," I groan. I'm lying on my front in my hotel bed drenched in sweat, breathing heavily. Beneath me I recognise that feeling of teetering on the edge. I tense, but it's too late. I flip over to save the sheets and sigh in the face of reality. As my heart rate slows, I find myself in what it amuses Abi to call a 'sticky situation'.

The fluorescent red digits show that it is five minutes before the alarm is due to go off.

- - -

HILTUNEN is guffawing again.

"Did I get you?" I say, grinning through the low autumn sun which has just begun to play on the side of my face.

"Course not. I'm a pro-fessional." His eyebrows twitch in contradiction to his words. "You really dream any of that?"

"Oh yeah, every last drop." We share another moment's mirth until I remember how inappropriate it might appear. I straighten my face, "It would be funny if it weren't so serious." The heat returns to my cheeks.

"Something's still funny, whatever happens after," he shrugs, rising and shuffling over to the window.

"It was so vivid though. Amazing how your brain can weave its own story out of random nerve pulses."

"If they are random," inserts Hiltunen, struggling to close the louvers.

"I think you pull the one on the other side."

"Never can remember which is which. There we go."

"Thanks." I reopen my right eye fully. "I have a little pet theory - I probably nicked it from somewhere - that when you dream, your brain is doing its filing: sorting everything you learned the day before into virtual drawers."

"You watch a horror movie and then dream about zombies..."

"Yeah, that kind of thing, but not always – no, I reckon every time your brain opens a drawer to put something in, some of the contents leak out. Sometimes the leak mixes with what is going in, sometimes it doesn't. Then your brain tries to make sense of all those leaks. So I feel a bit guilty about Reddy when I'm talking to Abi and lo and behold I dream about shagging her."

"No giant leaps there."

"OK, how about, I don't know what Reddy's flat might look like, but there's a whole load of 'leakage' about my hotel flowing about, so her bedsit looks like my room?"

"You ain't been reading one of those 'Phsycobabble for Beginners' books have you? Pain of my life they are."

"No. I just like thinking about it; trying to spot the links; where the weirdnesses might come from."

"Aw, a natural. Go on then Mr Thinker, impress me."

"Well, I bet you're interested in us drinking from the same glass and as for the barrier between our first kiss, there'll be a whole chapter in your report on that."

"All I needed was for you to say Hanne was wearing one of your mammy's tops, and padded cell here you come." My head rises sharply, but it's clear from the psychologist's face that he's not serious. He pushes his chair back slightly and stretches his legs. "No, I already got the feeling that anything to do with you is gonna be way more convoluted."

I nod, pulling one corner of my mouth sideways in regret. "If only I was sitting here worried about an accidental drunken shag."

+ + +

DURING BREAKFAST, the simultaneous feelings of frustration and relief which follow a dream with such a dénouement fade, but I'm amazed at how guilty I still feel. I can hardly look at anybody. Ridiculous. You can't help your subconscious, can you? And yet, as

I hand a linen bag over the reception desk, it feels like Dea's eyes are accusing me.

"Recovered from Saturday night?" says Erik, appearing from the office.

"Never touching that black stuff again," I say. Dea laughs, but my mood isn't lightened. This misplaced emotion even takes the edge off my enjoyment of Mikko's squirming when the subject of the swager gearbox is raised at the morning meeting.

Imagine if it had been real. What would I be feeling then? Let that be a lesson to you, comes the paternal toning of my conscience. I must make sure I don't get carried away. Good job Reddy has a boyfriend. What happened to the boyfriend in the dream?

I should be writing up the minutes, but I can't get my mind off vodka and cranberry juice. The other guys are off on the site somewhere. I pull a sheet of paper out of the printer and try to exorcise my demon:

Dream Lover

I must be fast asleep and dreaming,
something's not exactly what it's seeming,
but the way you're looking at me:
I've never seen you seem so hungry.

And when I close my eyes, your stare,
the light reflecting in your hair:
the after-image burns so clear,
I blink again and you're still here.
You're my dream lover: do I dare,
reach out and test my savoir-faire?

You must be a hallucination.
It's the only rational explanation
for the sparkle in your wide eyes;
and your impish grinning at my surprise.

And when I reach out for your hand
your touch is more than I can stand.
You put my hand on your waist's curve
and so dissolve my last reserve.
You're my dream lover: now is when.
Take a deep breath, count to ten.

You must have had a knock on your head.
It's the only likely reason instead
for the moisture on your full lips,
and the sureness in the sway of your hips.

And now I'm holding you so close:
a passion potion overdose;
inebriated by your love,
a bumblebee in a foxglove.
You're my dream lover: come to bed,
or is this all just in my head?

    I'm not sure whether that's made it better or worse? I fold the paper and slide it into the inside pocket of my thermal jacket. Probably best not to show Abi this one, just yet...

CHAPTER 10

I'm gazing at Reddy's back as she returns some glasses to the narrow shelf above the optics. She turns and catches me staring. Our eyes hold, and I smile. She smiles back, politely, but glances towards Hanne. It's a look that says, 'You see, what I mean.'

Hanne says something in Finnish and Reddy disappears into the kitchen. Hanne regards me for a moment and then says, "What is problem this evening, Steven?"

"Nothing," I lie. My left hand is trembling slightly, this is too similar. I steady it against the bar.

"You stare at Arwen since you sit down. Now you look like you see a ghost. You make her uncomfortable. She has a bad day anyway."

"Sorry, I..."

"Where are the others?"

"O'Gradys. I just had to check something..."

"Well, you check it for the last hour," says Hanne with a tone of exasperation.

"No, it isn't like that, it's silly, you'll laugh." Hanne's expression convinces me that being laughed at is probably the best option. "I had a dream. It started with Arwen putting some glasses up on that shelf and then you sending her into the kitchen. I've been waiting to see if that happened and it just did."

Arwen walks out of the kitchen carrying a stack of perfectly normal half litre glasses.

"Hey, Steven was dreaming about us last night," says Hanne. Putting an arm round Hanne and mischievously resting her head on the older woman's shoulder, Arwen says, "and what we do in your dream?"

I must be blushing, because they start to giggle, "Nothing like that..." I say. "I know this sounds a bit weird, but what's on that chain you wear, Arwen?" I indicate part of a pale silver chain just showing above the back of her shirt collar. She appears a bit disconcerted.

"Sorry, it's none of my business. Only, in my dream it was a key."

Arwen shakes her head slowly, and pulls out a heart shaped locket.

"Oh well, there goes my prescient dream."

"Prescient?" Hanne is interested: there aren't too many English words she doesn't know.

"Tells what happens in the future."

"Like.." she pauses, trying to recall, "like crystal ball?" I nod.

"Do you believe in this?" asks Arwen with sudden interest.

"In here," I point to my head, "I think it's stupid. In here," I point to my heart, "well, I'm sitting here aren't I?"

"What this key open?" asks Arwen.

Hanne says something, in Finnish, that is clearly rude. Arwen gives her a look as if to say, 'who are you talking to?' Chastity belt, would be my best guess.

"A door, just a silly dream," I shake my head and try to change the subject. "So does that locket have a picture of lover boy in it?" Immediately, I see that I have said the wrong thing. The smile crumbles from Arwen's face and moisture starts to appear in the corners of her eyes. She dashes into the kitchen.

Hanne turns to follow but answers my apologetic, questioning look with a terse whisper, "Lover boy is not lover boy anymore." Then she glares at me and thumbs towards the door.

I clench my teeth and breathe in. *"Sorry..."*

I leave, making very sure I know which door I'm passing through. Bollocks, this isn't meant to happen. Great big stag moose's testicles. The delights of Guinness and darts have lost their shine, so I trudge to the hotel, a tight brow forewarning of an impending headache.

"Are you OK?" says Katri, as I pass through reception.

I glance towards her concerned smile. "I think I'm feeling worried and excited about the same thing at the same time and it's doing my head in." I leave the comment hanging and walk straight into the lift.

"WHAT HAPPENED TO YOU last night?" says John, in between bites of a banana which I'm guessing he picked up from the hotel breakfast bar on his way out.

"Yes, we missed your feeble attempts to throw some arrows," says Keith.

"I haven't got the belly for it."

"Now, now," says Keith whose figure is a closer approximation to the dart player ideal.

"I wonder what it could be at Hanne's Bar that you found so much more interesting?" says John.

"Or who?" says Mark.

I'm not in the mood to be wound up: "Yes, I went to Hanne's. Yes, Reddy was there. No, I got a headache and went to bed early. No, there was no mad passionate anything going on. Does that cover it?"

"Keep your thermal long johns on," says John, tossing the banana skin across the office. It misses the bin.

"Judging from that throw maybe I should've played last night."

John does not comment, but picks up his hard hat and says, "Keith and I will be at the second stranding line." A blast of cold air plays across our knees.

Mark picks up the banana skin from where it is still lying. "Gorillas," he comments as he takes a couple of steps back and underarms it straight in. "What really happened last night, then?"

"What I said." I twist the dial and the fan heaters' drone rises.

"How long have we been living in each other's pockets?"

"Too long."

"Then what's up?"

"Nothing."

"Be like that then."

"Yes, dear." We both chuckle as the domesticity of this argument becomes apparent. Mark stays silent, engrossed in whatever he's typing as I follow the usual arrival routine: turn kettle on, shoes off, overalls on, site boots on, tea bag in cup, wait for useless 10 Euro kettle to boil, press power button on PC.

"Come on you useless piece of..." I glare at the blank blue screen. Somewhere across the site the metallic screech of an angle grinder sums up my mood.

"Reindeer poo?"

"Yeah. One day I'm going to race the PC and the kettle."

"Mm," says Mark continuing to tap his keyboard.

"Maybe they should change the saying to 'a watched PC never boots up.'"

"Maybe." Tap, tap, tap.

"Alright," I take a preparatory sip of hot tea. "Reddy split up with her boyfriend."

"Talking about reindeer poo."

"Yeah, that's not how the plan is supposed to work."

"I suppose not," says Mark, "and so..."

"And so... what?"

"What happens now? Did she split because of you?"

"I don't know the details. I don't think so... but she was upset."

"So she was dumped?"

"Maybe, I don't know."

"So you've got a possible rebound situation going on?"

"Don't say that."

"So you don't want to – what's that thing Keith says - get inside her ermine bloomers?"

"No. I mean, well, who wouldn't, but Abi..."

Mark cocks his head to one side, "You know what I would do."

"I'm not going to hide in my hotel room for a month until it all goes away."

"You'd probably fall in love with the cleaner." Mark ignores the gesture I'm making above the monitor, "So you've either got to be really nasty to her."

"No. That's not my thing."

"I didn't think so. Or you could act so stupid that there's no chance that she'll fancy you."

"Easier, maybe I'm already doing that?"

"Trouble is some women kind of like that. You'll just have to be careful."

"Oh, great advice there, Sigmund."

"You can pay me in free shots next time we play pool," Mark pauses and regards me with concern across the top of the screens. "You do want Abi, don't you, not this Arwen?"

"Yes... of course"

"Don't let Abi hear you sound that convinced."

CHAPTER 11

"Two Caffrey's and two Guinness," says Keith, returning from O'Grady's ubiquitous bar with a tray full.

'Beer, darts, and banter again', I sigh inwardly: the best of a bad job. Wouldn't it be so good to eat baked beans on toast, drink hot chocolate, curl up on my own sofa and laugh at rubbish telly with Abi? Is this what they mean by home sickness? We're playing standard 501 down and for some reason, the distraction of imagined homely delights has improved my aim. For once I'm actually winning. I retrieve an 81 from the board and start to make the mental subtraction.

"Look who just walked in," says Keith. I turn to see Arwen and Til threading their way towards the bar. I lose count.

"And now who's distracted," says John as I stand over-long with chalk poised, trying to refocus on the matter in hand.

"You've got 52 left," says Mark.

"Thanks." I write it down without checking.

The women order their drinks separately and disappear into one of the alcoves round the corner. Either they've not seen us, or they're pretending they haven't seen us. I really want to talk to her, but I know Keith and John will pounce. I play my turns, but keep on glancing towards the tricolour hanging from the far end of the bar. Mark catches my eye one time, but he makes no comment. All throwing prowess deserts me and I limp towards the humiliation of double one with the others catching up fast. I bust myself first dart with an 18: "Right, that's it, I give up," I strop, "I need to pee."

Having relieved the easiest of my tensions, I find myself walking past the flag rather than back towards the dartboard.

"Hi, I've never seen you two in here before." The words are out of my mouth before brain is engaged. Fortunately, the cliché doesn't seem to translate. Til looks up and smiles. Arwen looks... well, I'm not sure how she looks. She seems engrossed in the destruction of a Caffrey's beer mat.

"We no been here for ages," says Til.

"You're not big fans of Guinness then?" I point to their drinks which appear to be vodka Red Bulls.

"No, it taste like earth," says Til making a face.

"And what's wrong with that? Nothing like a lovely bit of earth. Even better when they leave the worms in." They smile weakly. Arwen finally joins in, glancing up from her project, "What it means, worms?"

"Small, long, pink animals that live in soil." I wiggle my finger in the time honoured kids' song way.

Til catches on first: *"Kastemato."* They both pull disgusted faces.

"May I..." I gesture to one of the two vacant chairs on the opposite side of the table.

"Yes," says Til. She glances at Arwen and raises one eyebrow archly, "Ar tell me that you dream about her and Hanne." Arwen frowns slightly at Til.

"Does everyone in Mahikkala know about that now?" Arwen's expression hasn't changed and I decide it's not the moment for another crass joke. I continue quickly, "It was just a silly dream." Then to Arwen, "I'm sorry. I think I upset you the other day."

"It OK, how could you know?" says Arwen simply.

"Hanne explained a little: it's always difficult when someone breaks up with you."

"He not break up with me, I break up with him." There is defiance in her voice.

"Then why so sad?"

She turns the mat, selects a different corner and begins to separate the green print from the cardboard below with a neatly shaped nail. Without raising her eyes, she says, "Because I love him."

"Then why..."

"You ask like Til," she says, her reproachful tone as much for her friend as for me.

"*Sorry.*" I say and receive a weak smile for my attempt.

"He is very difficult, but sometimes very amazing also."

There is an uncomfortable pause. The mat is now completely stripped on its top side. I can see a bit of wetness in the corners of Arwen's eyes. Done it again, dope. Somehow it just seems right to put my hand on top of hers and say, "Smile, it really does suit you." A smile comes, but so too do two tears which roll down the outside of her cheeks and hang on the curve of her jaw. She wipes them off with the back of her hand and stands.

"*Excuse me,*" she says. Til starts to rise but Arwen puts a hand on her shoulder to hold her down and walks off in the direction of the toilets. My eyes follow her back until it disappears.

I shake my head. "She seems very sad. I always say the wrong thing. That's the second time I've made her cry this week."

Til gives a despairing shrug, concern showing in her dark shadowed eyes. "She cry to me twenty times. I know nothing in her head. I think she and Kari are OK, but what I know?"

"He hasn't done something bad to her has he?"

"No, he not like that." She lifts the part skinned mat and brushes the paper fragments off the table with the side of her hand. "Kari is clever, he know how to make people do what he want, but he is... he, what you say? He not hurt fly."

"But..."

"I see Ar in sauna, she not hurt," Til interrupts with a finality about the subject. "She say she not know why she break up. It just not feel good. Kari keep try to phone her, see her. That why we here, Kari never come here."

I indicate with my eyes that Arwen has just reappeared from the toilet. Her hair had been gathered at the back, but she's taken the clip out and it falls across her shoulders as she sits down. That, together with Til's sauna comment, makes a heady combination in my mind. I erase an image which starts to form.

"Steven, tell me about this dream." She seems to be forcing herself to cheer up. I wonder what I should leave out.

"Hanne asked you to go to the kitchen to get something. Then I needed to go to the toilet, but when I opened the door, I was in the kitchen."

"But toilets are other side of bar from kitchen."

"I know, but you know what dreams are like."

"Did you pee in sink?" smirks Til.

"No, I only do that at your house," I say, making a face which says, 'yes, I can give as good as I get.'

"*Yuck.*" This seems to be one of the few words which sounds nearly the same in English and Finnish.

"I am in the kitchen?" says Arwen, bringing me back on track.

"Yes, you were looking for some special glass."

"Special glass?"

"Yes, you called it a lover's cup. Some old Finnish tradition about men and women drinking out of the cup together. There's not anything like that really, I suppose?"

Arwen and Til exchange a few words. I can't catch any of them.

"What?"

"You dream about the lover cup?"

"Yes."

"We both drink out of cup?" asks Arwen.

"I didn't say that."

"We both drink out of cup or no?" I'm surprised by her serious tone.

This is awkward. "Well, yes, eventually..." I mumble to the table. A gulp from Til raises my eyes: her face is stony.

"You and Arwen both drink from the cup?"

"Yes, but..."

"In Finland we have..."

"Poem," inserts Arwen.

"Poem that say, 'If drink from cup in evening, marry in morning.'"

"But..." I try to start.

"But you already married," says Til. Her eyes are accusing. "You hurt Ar even before start."

"But it was just a silly dream," I say. I can feel my heart rate rising. What major cultural faux pas have I made?

"I have to tell your father, Ar."

I look to Arwen for some kind of sanity. She stares back with a flat expression. "Steven, this really bad." There is a pause. She turns the beer mat, peeled side down and staring intently at the remaining logo, says, "It like in UK, when a woman let a man buy her drink and then no want sex." Her shoulders are shaking. Til lets out a snort of laughter.

"Gits," I shudder with a mixture of relief and embarrassment.

"Absolute gits." Arwen and Til are rocking with delighted hysterics at the success of their wind up. Til gasps for breath, "What it mean, git?"

"It means you two. The exact definition of a 'git' is you two, right now." I shake my head, "I can't believe I fell for that."

"Your face," says Til.

"Poor scared Englishman," says Arwen cupping her hand over the back of mine in mock concern. We sit for a moment whilst the laughter subsides.

"So what we do after we drink from magic cup?" says Arwen.

"I'm not saying any more about it," I say, folding my arms.

"We Finnish women, we not be embarrassed," says Til.

"It's not YOUR embarrassment that I'm worried about."

Til and Arwen look at each other and chorus, "Please."

"Well I'm glad to see someone in Finland has finally got some manners, but I'm still not telling you."

"Not telling them what?" says Keith who has appeared next to the table with John and Mark just behind.

"None of your business," I say, perhaps a little too vehemently.

"No need to get shirty, we just thought we'd see where you'd got to."

"Aye," says John to the girls, "We were in the middle of a game of darts and Stevie here wanders off to take a leak and ne'er comes back." Arwen catches my eye, grinning slightly as John takes nautical liberties with my name. There's no way I'm letting on about that.

"We had no idea where you'd gone," adds Mark.

"It's so nice of you guys to show all this concern," I say, the irony heavy in my voice.

"I'm so sorry about my rude friend," says Keith spotting two now empty glasses. "Would you ladies like another drink?"

I can't resist a brief raise of my eyebrows. Arwen and Til both snort. Keith's eyes pass from me to them and back again.

"Oh yes," he says, "I'd forgotten you were there that night."

"Watch out," I say, "Once Keith starts talking, there's no stopping him. In the end you'll do just about anything to shut him up."

"Now, now, Steven, jealousy doesn't suit you. Just because your girlfriend finds me strangely attractive."

"Strange, yes, attractive, well, what do you think?" I ask Til.

"Maybe for my mother," she grins.

"Can you get me a date with her?" says Keith seemingly unperturbed. Til looks slightly taken aback and then giggles. You have to admire his cheek sometimes.

I notice that Arwen is silent and regarding me with annoyed eyes. I think I know why. "In case you, or your mother, were wondering," I say to Til, "Keith is just as married as I am." I shift my eyes to Arwen's, "which also means he knows full well, that no one is anyone's girlfriend." Her expression softens as I hoped it would.

Sometimes I think Keith is as insensitive as a charging rhino but he does have his own warped sense of honour. He puts a hand on my shoulder and says, "Being married's not a problem, Steve, it's a benefit. It shows how much experience I've got in keeping a woman satisfied."

"Sometimes you really do sound like a Viagra advert, Keith," says Mark. We all laugh, but the unsaid corollary doesn't escape my notice, that if a thing applies to one married man it most likely applies to another: Keith's way of an apology.

"We go now." Arwen stands, pulling at Til's arm above the elbow as she does so. Til seems momentarily surprised, but allows herself to be lifted upright.

"Moi moi," I say, having learnt the slang goodbye from Hanne the other day.

"Moi moi."

"Oh woops, did we scare her off? I'm so sorry," says Keith as I stare at their retreating backs. John waves his hand in front of my eyes, "Another Caffrey's, please, when you've finished." John and Keith walk back towards the dartboard, leaving Mark standing next to the table.

"You've got it bad, haven't you." It's a statement not a question.

I stand up. "It doesn't work unless I've got it bad." Mark rolls his eyes.

9:55AM ON SUNDAY MORNING: Just time to fall out of bed, throw on some clothes and roll down to breakfast before they stop serving. Meatballs, scrambled eggs and baked beans, washed down with several glasses of orange juice do wonders for the potential hangover, but they don't stop my mind from racing. A long snowy walk is required, I think.

I drive for ten minutes to a local beauty spot and park up. It's very cold again, but the pale sun has me sweating inside the thermal coat before I've gone half a mile along the lake shore.

So the question for today is: what would I do if? What would I do if Arwen said something like that girl in Hanne's? What would I do if she fell in love with me? Can you find yourself tempted to the point where no one could resist? Stand back, think analytically; problem solving, that's what you're meant to be good at.

Suppose I did sleep with Arwen. Would I feel guilty? Of course, madly guilty. So guilty that I'd end up telling Abi? Maybe. Would she ever forgive me? Pass. If I didn't tell her, would it always gnaw away at me inside? Would it change the way Abi and I are together? How can you know?

But suppose Arwen did throw herself at me and I walked away. Would I always regret it? Definitely. Would I think about what might have been, wistfully, when I'm 80? Probably. Would that regret gnaw away at me, poisoning my life: spoiling it with Abi? Who knows?

- - -

"WHICH IS BETTER, then, guilt or regret?"

"Aw, that's an easy one: definite versus indefinite. Definite's always worse. You know you done something bad, you'll never know how things might've turned out. Course different folks react in different ways... but don't stop, I enjoy it when you philosophise."

+ + +

SOMEONE HAS CLEARED SOME SNOW from the lakeshore, revealing a bed of pebbles. I bend to pick one up and, like others before me, toss it across the snow free ice to the other side. My gloved fingers affect the aim and the stone strikes a log frozen fast about a third of the way across. It bounces off, but the new angle takes it nearly parallel to the shore and it comes to rest, stranded in the middle.

If I did have an affair... affair: what a euphemism, 'an affair of the heart', how romantic, how lovely, how un-life-wrecking-sounding. 'Cheat', say it like it is. If I did cheat on Abi would I fall in love, well, more than I am at the moment: properly in love? Would Arwen be better for me than Abi? Would my life be more interesting? It'd definitely be different. Different can be good... at least to start with. But could I stand breaking Abi's heart? Could I stand the thought of leaving behind someone who knows my most intimate thoughts?

And what if I leave Abi, go with Arwen and then that all goes reindeer udders to the sky? Then I'm left with nothing and it would be my own fault. Better to stick with what you know. But if it seemed really, really good with Arwen, would I take the risk? What you know versus the greener grass in the other field. Which to choose?

I reach the foot of the lake where a pine pole walkway crosses the frozen outlet.

'Ha, ha, very funny', I accuse life in general. Talk about crossing bridges before I come to them. This is probably all in my head. She probably has no interest in me at all. This splitting up thing is just a coincidence. But we do get on, and she does keep touching me. So what? She's probably just one of those tactile people. But what if? Round and round and round.

Frustrated, I slog up the path to the trig point. I have the view all to myself, and for the first time I feel a slight breeze on my left cheek. The panorama down to the lake and its surrounding pines is usually pleasant rather than stunning, but today something strange is happening. The whole atmosphere seems to twinkle. I'm inside one of those paperweights full of liquid and glitter and someone has just shaken it. The breeze is blowing tiny ice crystals off the tree branches. They're so small they hang in the air like dust, sparkling in the sun. It's one of the most beautiful things I've ever seen. Moisture appears in the corners of my eyes.

"Who are you feeling sorry for, you steaming wolf turd," I shout out loud. There's a noise of moving branches down the slope to the left. Probably a startled moose, but thoughts of hungry bears chase me down the last half mile to the car park in double quick time.

- - -

"BEAUTIFUL, AIN'T IT, when that happens with the ice? I only seen it a couple of times... walking's not really my thing." The belly protruding between the open lapels of his jacket had already given that away. He must've followed my eyes. "Maybe's it should be," he adds.

"Was all that stuff just bollocks?" Hiltunen frowns slightly. I clarify: "I can't remember exactly what I was thinking, but that was the kind of thing. Does she, doesn't she, what if this, what if that? And I didn't even know if she liked me."

"And anyway you weren't even interested because you're married."

"Yes, exactly."

"Seems to me, Mr Thinker, that you don't have no trouble asking the right questions, you just don't always listen to the answer."

+ + +

CHAPTER 12

Last time we were in *Laiska Lohi*, I picked up a flyer which was obviously advertising karaoke. A couple of minutes' work on the internet and the rest of the words translated as 'every other Wednesday'. I am alone in this masochistic pleasure. At least, I was alone, but it seems that I have accidentally crashed part of a Central Hotel work night out. At any rate, I'm sitting with Raakel, Katri and Erik.

"So none of you are going to sing?" I say.

"No, we just like to listen," says Katri.

"And laugh," adds Erik.

"No Mark?" asks Raakel, "or the other?"

"No. Keith and John have gone to play darts and Mark said he didn't want to listen to me make a fool of myself: he gets that at work all day."

As they laugh at my self-deprecation, the guy who is currently singing has just realised how high the chorus of 'Lady in Red' goes. It's not pretty. "Rule number one of karaoke," I say, "Never, ever do a song that you haven't tried out at home first."

I had real trouble finding any on the list that I fancied. Too many 60s numbers that I don't know, or female ballads which are obviously out and there's no way I'm touching the likes of Chris de Burgh.

"When your song?" asks Raakel.

"After the next one. Excuse me a minute."

I'm settled in front of the central urinal when someone leaves the gents, shoulder barging the heavy door wide open. It's on a very slow return spring and I notice to my amusement that I am in full view of the sofas I have just left. I've clearly been in Finland too long: it was 'to my horror' the first time I experienced the lack of those funny little double door arrangements that we reserved Brits take for granted.

I resist a childish temptation to wave; my hand, obviously, thank you. Of course, no one looks anyway. What's interesting? Zipped and washed, I return to the strains of 'My heart will go on.' It's a valiant attempt, the woman is no Celine, but her prow is still above the water.

"That toilet door is distinctly un-English," I say, pretty much rhetorically. Erik, who has heard us complain about this type of thing before, answers, "We do not waste money on two doors here," without turning his head from the singer.

"Steven," starts Katri, somewhat apprehensively, "Is really that people have carpet in the bathroom in England?"

"Yes?" I'm not sure where this is leading.

"Yuck," say Raakel and Katri together.

"Inhottava," adds Raakel making a face.

I look to Katri for help, "Disgusting."

"It is warm under foot."

"But what happen when man... misses."

"Misses what?" I play dumb.

"When he pee over the side," says Katri, starting to colour up.

"Oh, that never happens to English men," I say, trying to keep a straight face.

"Why not?"

"Well, we're not boasting, but..." I leave the implication hanging. Dangling, perhaps I should say.

Erik, who I didn't think was listening, laughs loudly and turns back towards us. The two women are rolling their eyes, and I receive a playful slap across my nearest shoulder from the back of Katri's hand. I spread my hands wide, "Well, if you are going to ask things like that!"

"We go to the bar," says Erik, he and Raakel rising from their settee. Katri and I are left behind with our half finished drinks.

"Are Erik and Raakel..." I ask.

"No," says Katri. There is something strange in her voice. I misinterpret it.

"Not you and Erik?"

"No," she laughs. "I not sure Erik interested in women."

"Plays for the other team?" She frowns. Maybe that doesn't translate well. "Gay?"

"Maybe. Maybe, just not interested."

"So, if it isn't Erik, who is your boyfriend?"

"No boyfriend." There's a touch of melancholy which I haven't seen in our usual chit chat. I've always just assumed that someone like Katri would be in a steady relationship.

"Are these Finnish guys mad?" I say with mock indignation.

Her lips rise, but her sky blue eyes don't smile. "The one I like is already taken," she says.

"Oh, that's the worst," I say, "When I was a teenager, I had this friend, Pete. He was much better looking than me; had all the lines. We always fancied the same girls. He always got them. I never did. It used to drive me crazy seeing him with them."

"But you married now."

"Yeah, what was that woman thinking?" Another mirthless smile.

"I think it your turn now," says Raakel, returning drink in hand. The karaoke man is beckoning.

A simple rhythmic guitar leads and I follow. 'Chasing cars': Snow Patrol. Perfect for my voice: not too high, not too fancy, just a great melody. I haven't really got a lead singer type voice, no edge, no gravel, but at least I can stay in tune. The song reaches its denouement and I'm surprised to hear a smattering of applause, not just from my table, where Raakel's whooping is, frankly, a bit over the top.

"That really good", says Raakel as I retake my seat, back towards the mic.

"It's just about picking the right song."

"I think it very brave to sing on own," says Katri, "I could not."

"Or very stupid," adds Erik grinning at my new found fan club.

"Cheers," I say, raising my glass slightly off the table. Erik pulls up a cuff to reveal his watch. He mutters something to Raakel, who glances toward Katri and then shakes her head.

"You sing again?" asks Katri.

"I don't know, maybe." The intro to the next song has started. "Now this is brave," I say, "or stupid," directing the last towards Erik.

"She good. Always sing here," says Raakel.

I take a sceptical mouthful of beer and almost choke on it in my haste to turn round as the singing starts. I recognise that...

Arwen is inflating the room with a power that belies her slight frame. 'Oh bollocks, she sings too,' I think. It really is the best karaoke version of this song that I've ever heard. Not that you hear it very often; women don't dare; like trying to do Freddie Mercury if you're a bloke. It's one of those songs that just doesn't work unless you blast it out. Most people are too nervous. Of course, I'm enthralled. There is no one else in the room; just auburn hair and a surprising voice, singing the perfect song for someone who's hurting. Have 'You got the love', Arwen?

She knows the lyrics off by heart and hardly looks at the screen. Her eyes seem to be searching through the tables for someone. She's staring straight at me, declaring her love... or is it someone in front or behind? I remember that the two small spotlights make it difficult to see much at all.

Arwen's ovation puts mine firmly in its place. Everyone is clapping. I join in with the whoopers and whistlers. She raises an open hand in front of her half turned face and smiles a mixture of pleasure and embarrassment as she heads back to her seat on the other side of the island bar.

"Wow, I had no idea she could sing like that," I say.

"Queen of Mahikkala karaoke," says Raakel.

"Big deal!" says Erik.

"Good one," I say to Erik complementing his sarcastic idiom.

"Er-iii-k," says Katri.

"You know her?" asks Raakel.

"Well, just a bit. She works in Hanne's Bar. I've spoken to her a few times." I try to be nonchalant. "In fact, I think I'll just go and say hello, you know, one great artiste to another." I suppose only Erik gets the joke. He's the only one who smiles anyway.

Arwen is sitting at a table across from an older woman. A bloke who might be the woman's partner is sitting beside her. I recognise both of them as previous singers. "Where does her massive voice come from?" I say to the woman, indicating Arwen with my right hand. The woman gives me a pained smile and shakes her greying head.

"No English," says Arwen.

"Ah, *sorry, no Finnish*," I say, receiving a proper smile this time.

"Where does that voice come from?" I repeat to the woman in question this time.

Arwen shrugs her shoulders, "I heard you not so bad yourself."

"Nothing like you. Wow... No Til this evening?"

"No, she say she not sing if I do. She say I too good. Like your guys say when you play pool."

"Ah, the curse of the virtuoso," I say, rhetorically from the blank look. "Is this the lonely singers' table, then?"

"Yes, you want to sit?" says Arwen indicating the sofa beside her.

"Well, yes, but I'm sort of with some other people. Just a minute." I move a couple of yards to where I can see my table around a raised section of the bar which houses the cash tills. It's empty. Strange. I glance towards the toilets, then the main door. The back of a pink coat is just disappearing past the left hand window. Raakel? Shrugging, I rejoin Arwen.

"They seem to have gone," I say sitting down.

"Another one?" she asks, holding out the song menu.

"Maybe, there aren't many I know."

Before I can take it, she pulls the booklet back and starts to leaf through it. Her eyes narrow: considering, "Beatles?"

"No, too high. Most of them anyway."

"Tom Jones?" she says grinning.

"Yeah, right," I say in a disgusted voice.

She continues her perusal until her face lights up. "Perfect song for funny Englishman." Her finger is pointing at 'I'm too sexy' by those Adonises known as Right Said Fred.

"Too much hair," I say pulling a bit of my tousled fringe down towards my eye.

"Please," she says, throwing me a look that even an Archbishop would have difficulty resisting.

Unfortunately, I do know this one, having done an ill advised, partly inebriated performance at one of Abi's work Christmas parties. "OK, but only if I get to choose one for you too."

"OK, *good*, you want me to give your number?"

"I haven't given you my number... yet," I say tapping the mobile shaped bulge in my trouser pocket. Arwen rolls her eyes, notes the number on the karaoke menu and then bats me playfully across the top of the head with it.

"Are you singing another one already?"

Shrugging, she rises from the table. A drum intro begins and her simple, figure hugging top blazes white in the spotlights. As her voice rises towards the chorus, I shake my head ever so slightly and exhale, nostrils flaring. She's really on a downer this evening and that makes me want to hold her even more. 'It must have been love': she sings it beautifully, hauntingly, you can hear the rawness. They are her own words, not written by Per Gessle in the 80s, but the outpourings of her own wounded heart, surely?

"You're going to make me cry, if you sing any more like that," I say as she retakes her seat amid more enthusiastic applause. Arwen looks deflated, she's just pinned her heart on her sleeve and now reality has returned.

"You should do this for real," I say, "You're good enough."

"What you mean?"

"You should sing in a band. Your voice is amazing and..." I pause, considering how to say this without sounding creepy, "you've got the look, too."

"I love to sing in musical."

"Mamma Mia, Cats..." I ponder; now what would suit her voice; "Evita, that sort of thing?"

"*Joo, joo,*" she says, forgetting about English. "Sing on stage, London West End, Broadway," her eyes sparkle at the holy words.

"You'd be great." Then I fling wide my arms and do my best opera impression, "Don't cry for me Mahikkala!" I expect to get a smile for my trouble, but instead I seem to have pulled the magnetic slider across Arwen's face and her joy disappears like the kid's sketch.

"Who come to Mahikkala? Who hear me..." she glances round, "here?"

"You could make a CD, send it off? What about musical school?"

She sighs, "Music academy at Kuopio. I have place last year, but..."

"But what?"

"Kari, he..." she hesitates, "No. I not... I..." She checks her watch.

"Big step to leave everyone behind?"

She nods.

"Are you still avoiding him?"

Another nod.

"You're not worried that he'll find you here?"

"Hockey train on Wednesday, not finish until 10 o'clock."

I decide it's probably best to change the subject. "You know, I try to write songs. They're probably no good, but I like doing it." I do seem to have distracted her.

"What you write about?"

"What I'm feeling, things that I see, stuff like that. I've written a few since I've been here. All about you, obviously," I joke and receive a moist pink rebuff.

"You have to show me."

"Yes." But not *Dream Lover*, or *Clarity*, what about... I am tapped on the shoulder by the other woman at the table. I'd forgotten they were even there. She points towards the compere, who is waving the mic at me. Oh, heck, I put on my best growl and step forward.

Now the thing about comedy songs is that you can't just stand still and sing them. You've got to act the part. Fortunately, I have had enough beers so that charading the over-the-top 'I'm too sexy' lyrics comes naturally.

It begins with the suggestive undoing of my top two shirt buttons and continues with some lyric modification to include 'Finland' (never hurts to play to the home crowd!). By the time I'm wagging my finger at the outrageous thought of moving to the music, people are beginning to laugh. I walk forward swinging my hips 'fashion-model' style and try to complete the effect with a spin. The microphone cable catches round one of my legs and I miss the next line whilst laughing in disentanglement. The patrons are in stitches. And we haven't got to the pièce de resistance yet. At the appropriate line, I wiggle my backside in the most ridiculous way I can think of. Abi would recognise it as an impression of her Mum's cat when annoyed. I hear a loud whistle from a direction that I suspect could be Arwen. Shame on her!

And so on until the abrupt end when I slam the mic back on its stand and march off in a mock huff. My ovation is the loudest and most raucous of the night so far.

Arwen is shaking her head, her shoulders still bouncing. "I not laugh so much, since..." I spin on the spot and crash down on the sofa. It sets all three round the table off again. Arwen leans forward and rests her head on the crook of my elbow for a moment. She turns her head sideways, beams up at me and says, "Just what I need." As she sits up, one side of her hair flows across the backs of my fingers.

"Together," says the man on the other side of the table, waving his finger at Arwen and I.

"N..." I start to say.

"Sing together," he says firmly. "Duet."

"What do you think?" I say.

In answer she reaches for the song menu. After five minutes we're not having much luck. There aren't many duets and most of them need a much stronger male voice than mine. Our matchmaker has also been studying his menu. He passes the booklet across to Arwen with his finger indicating a particular song.

"'Nothing's gonna stop us now'?" she asks. The verbal contraction sounds strange on her lips.

"Starship?"

She nods.

"I'd forgotten that was a duet. *Miksei?*"

A flicker of disconcertment plays across Arwen's face. "Hey, you know some Finnish."

"Only a few things. I learnt *'why not?'* from John. He picked it up, straight after *'Two beers, thank you'* and *'my friend will pay'*."

"Oh yes, most important things," says Arwen sarcastically.

I shrug. "So we're gonna do this one then?"

"Nothing's gonna stop us..."

I walk to the table where the compere has his laptop and point to the song. "Steven and Arwen. Duet."

"Very good. After next," he says over a somewhat screechy and rather too drunk Rhianna impression.

"Steven," starts Arwen. She has a weedling manner about her.

"Yes, Arwen?"

"You still not told me what happen at end of your dream."

'Rhianna' has finished and the man from our table is starting a Finnish ballad.

"We're on next."

"Stop..." she pauses to remember the phrase, "changing subject."

"You can keep on asking, but I'm not going to say," I grin, shaking my head. There is a pause whilst she considers her next form of attack.

"Did we kiss?"

"I'm not saying." I try to keep my expression from giving anything away. She holds my gaze. She is going to stare me into submission. We both start to laugh but don't look away. I'm weakening. I'm going to have to break away before I fall into those eyes.

"I'm still not going to tell you," I say, avoiding looking directly at her, "and you know why?" I pause for effect. "Because it's far too steamy for your young ears."

Her expression seems to encompass disconcerted, pleased, annoyed and amused all at the same time and she colours very slightly.

"Come on, we've got a song to sing," I say and take her hand.

The ballad is obviously coming to its climax and we stand behind the lights waiting for its end. His voice is much better than mine.

"You should duet with him," I say into Arwen's ear.

"We done it, before. Our voices, they not fit together."

"Strange," I muse whilst applauding loudly.

We take the 'stage' and the karaoke man brings out the spare microphone. Before he hands it over he announces 'Nothing's gonna stop us' followed by some comment from which I can pick out only 'Steven *and* Arwen'. I furrow my brow in query, but Arwen just rolls her eyes and shakes her head. The intro begins; it's me first. In true duet style I hold eye contact and sing to her. I'd forgotten how intimate the words are. I feel a bit light headed. Maybe this song wasn't such a good idea. She sings back to me, reaching out her free hand to take mine. She's acting the lyric so well…

And then a weird thing happens as we start the chorus. Her voice is so much stronger than mine, so much more its own instrument, but together they meld into something greater. It's like my voice is designed to be her accompaniment. She can hear it too and widens her eyes. We slip back into the separate verses, but all the time I'm longing to return to that chorus. This time she doesn't sing in unison, like on the original, but takes up a harmony line above mine. Her voice is static electricity. Not only are the hairs on my arms responding, but it seems like my voice is being pulled, stretching out the tone into something richer… The attraction is primal, unavoidable, inevitable.

I catch my breath in the guitar solo. We are grinning at each other, a pair of teenagers after their first deep kiss: wondering if it gets even better. We turn to face the room…

Arwen stops singing for three words. I glance quizzically towards her. She grimaces an apology, but her voice, so liquid a moment ago is now freezing fast. I follow the wild look in her eye to Kari, standing between the nearest two sofas, arms folded, face unreadable. We don't even bother to sing the fade out.

"That was quite a performance," says Kari, as we return to the table.

"She's an amazing singer." He nods.

The applause is somewhat muted. Arwen, looking extremely uncomfortable, sits. Kari takes my seat.

"Maybe I'd better leave you two to it," I say.

"No, stay," says Arwen. The sofa opposite is now empty, so I perch on the edge of it. I try to catch Arwen's eyes, but there are tears in them and I can't read her expression. I'm not sure I should stay, but…

Kari stares at Arwen for several minutes. He seems sad and bitter, but resolute. *"Why…"* Arwen finally explodes. I can't follow it after the first word.

"Because I love to just sit and look at you and I haven't been able to for some time." He answers in English.

"Why English?" Arwen asks as if out of my own head.

"Because if you want your married English friend to stay, it is not polite to talk in Finnish." Did he accentuate married?

"OK, talk," says Arwen in a resigned tone.

"Why are you avoiding me? Don't you know I have been looking for you all week? Your mother says, sorry, but she doesn't want to talk. Til says talk to Harri. Harri says talk to Til. I'm going crazy!"

"I sorry," says Arwen in the tone of an obstinate child. "I just want alone."

"Do you still love me?" Kari cuts to the heart of the matter. Arwen is silent. "Because I still love you, *muru.*" Some pet name? He gives her (and I hate to admit it) a very genuine weak smile. I feel sorry for this guy. Been there, sort of. There is silence for some time. I mean not actual silence, we're in a karaoke bar, but between them it's outer space.

Arwen finally breathes into the vacuum. "I still love you, but… you make me crazy."

"I know, I try to be too clever," he stops talking in English and carries on in his native tongue. My green and hairy feeling grows as I see Arwen begin to relax, so I reach for the song list and start flicking through. Every so often I sneak a glance. It's quite plain she still loves him, but she's fighting hard. What's she fighting? Is he too small town? That doesn't fit with his time at Oxford. Maybe it was getting too serious and this is just jitters? Arwen glances my way and our eyes meet. Hers are wells of sadness and confusion. I feel paternal.

Kari turns, "Sorry, we are ignoring you."

"No, no, you carry on."

"Are you going to sing again?" he asks.

"You should see him do 'I'm too sexy', it was so funny," says Reddy. The first smile in a long while.

"No, I don't think so... but," my eyes alight on a particular song. Oh, it's perfect, I can fix this. I can do the decent British thing and fix this. "Arwen chose one song for me. I still have to choose a song for her."

"Steven, I know I say, but..."

"Come on..." I look at her, then slide my eyes to him. "Please. This one."

The compère is starting to tidy up. "Just one more?" I ask. "For them..." pointing back to Reddy and Kari who are once more deep in conversation.

"OK," he shrugs. I point to Pat Benetar's 'We belong'.

"Right now," I say back at the table. Reddy seems reluctant. "Trust me." I pull her out of her seat. "You too," I say to Kari.

"I don't sing."

"You won't have to." Then for his ears only I whisper, "Put my cheque in the post." He regards me curiously.

"You stand here – sing." I more or less have to put the mic in Reddy's hand.

"You stand here – stare adoringly." I make a thumbs up behind my back for the music to start and quickly sit in the nearest seat. Reddy stands awkwardly waiting for the words to scroll, but she's a singer, she won't be able to resist. I hope... She starts ever so softly, eyes widening as the appropriateness of the lyric dawns on her. Kari stands paralysed in her unwavering stare.

By the end of the second verse, the colour is returning to her voice and the hairs on the back of my neck are anticipating the chorus. It's even better than I imagined. Reddy reaches out a hand towards Kari leaving him in no doubt where he 'belong's. He throws me a quick, grateful look over his shoulder. I flick my head to the side in acknowledgement: 'You see!'

By the last chorus, her free arm is round his waist and she points the mic for him to make a game attempt at the last line. Their lips meet in a long deep kiss amid loud cheers and whistles. I stand with everyone else.

Reddy detaches herself from Kari and bounces over. She nearly knocks me down with the force of her hug. It's not a lover's hug, but it is intimate. "Thank you, thank you," she whispers in my ear. Then she pulls back to look me in the eyes and kisses my closed mouth. "How you know?"

I shrug. "Well, it would have worked for me."

She regards me with a quizzical eye and leaves me with, "Your wife lucky," as she bounds away.

'Maybe she is, or maybe I don't deserve her,' I ponder as the taste of lip balm reaches my tongue.

I KEEP THINKING about 'Nothing's gonna stop us now'. Such a cheesy lyric and yet for a moment it felt like nothing would. The way our voices joined: magical, intimate, too intimate. Mustn't follow that line of thought too far. But, if I could just crystalise that feeling: what a song it would make. There's only one possible title, and of course, it has to be a duet:

Harmony

MAN - I used to sing in solo: the music sounded alright to me.
But play a note on its own and you'll never hear if it's off key.
So when I heard your voice sparking off my own: electricity,
and, when I heard your tone melting into mine: concentricity.

TOGETHER - Ahh, ahh, aah...

TOGETHER - Our hearts beat the same time.
Our words fall into rhyme.
Our voices rise in sweet harmony.
Sing with me tonight.
Our feet walk the same path.
Our smiles find the same laugh.
Our music picks out a melody.
Help me play it right.

WOMAN - I used to sing in solo: who would I need to accompany?
I never thought I'd need you, but the song it played out differently.
So when I heard your voice interlocking mine: curiosity,
and, when I heard your tone complementing mine: luminosity.

TOGETHER - Ahh, ahh, aah...

TOGETHER - Our hearts...

- - -

"IT'S STRANGE, you start writing about one thing and it changes into something else. When Abi and I first met, loads of things that we said, thought, did, seemed to fit together so neatly. Like music in harmony... She wasn't as keen as I was to start with: still in solo career mode. Her head stayed there for a while, but in the meantime her heart had slipped off its shoes and curled up with mine on the sofa. Her song played out a bit differently to how she'd planned. And we do complement each other so well." Hiltunen is resting his chin on his fingers, one eyebrow raised sceptically. "So that's what it's about... You do believe me, don't you?" The corners of my mouth turn up as I say the last.

"Uh, huh..." says Hiltunen, not one hint of affirmative in his voice.

+ + +

CHAPTER 13

"Bring Mum's vol-au-vents through will you Steve?"

Abi's sister, Claire, is in organising mode and just because I arrived home at 11pm last night doesn't mean I'm exempt from little jobs. I work my way round the edges of the throng towards one end of the long buffet table. Reg swipes a cheeky one off the tray as I pass.

"I see my girls have got you working hard, Steve. Family trait I'm afraid." He receives a dig in the ribs from my mother-in-law for his trouble. "Oi, I'll spill my drink."

"Those look nice," says Sue, an old uni friend of Abi's.

"Something I whipped up this afternoon," I say, "Try one," I offer the plate to her and her husband. What's his name? Sue gives me a quizzical look as she bites into the perfect pastry.

"Thor no, I'm joking, Brenda's been cooking for months."

"Thor?" says... Charles, that's him.

"Sorry, forgot where I was, it's a long story. I just need..." I say and make another move for the table. This time I make it unmolested. Now, what would be a suitable reward?

"I saw that." The birthday girl herself pinches my side.

"Still no flab, though."

"I don't know how you manage it with all that restaurant food."

"We do a lot of walking." I smile at Abi; she is glowing. "I can't believe Claire invited everyone off my list of possibles. It's heaving!"

"It's great. Thank you." She pulls me forward by my tie and kisses me gently.

"Get a room." We turn to see the library girls laughing at us.

"We're not the ones who were just seen inspecting their new boyfriend's tonsils in the car park," says Abi. Jenny blushes sweetly.

"Where is the man of the moment?" I say.

"At the bar." This is rather an overstated description for a bare topped table with a number of tapped kegs overhanging one side.

"What's it like in Finland then?" asks Olivier.

"Cold."

"No, you know, what's the place like? What are the people like?"

"It's a bit weird, it ought to be really pretty: lots of snow, pines and lakes, but round Mahikkala it's mostly flat, so you can't really see much of a view. It's kind of the epitome of the phrase 'you can't see the wood for the trees'."

"So are all the women statuesque blondes?" asks Jenny, who is petite and mousy.

"There are quite a few of those..." I pretend to be daydreaming and receive a playful cuff from Abi. "But, of course, they're all incredibly ugly compared to English women. And you know I prefer brunettes anyway," I add, moving my hand through the back of my wife's shoulder length hair. An image of a red mane flowing down the back of a royal blue shirt slips into my mind. I banish it.

"There're a lot of things that are just the same as here," I continue, "but there are some strange differences. I mean, take the Finnish attitude to nudity... I launch into my funniest stories: the ice swimming, revealing toilet doors, etc. Part way through Abi drifts away: she's already heard these more than once.

"OK, I'LL STOP embarrassing my increasingly ancient wife." Abi is standing next to me, smiling in a slightly resigned, but not annoyed way. I can just about make eye contact behind the large bouquet she is clutching.

"I'm hoping that you'll end this speech before I retire," she twinkles.

"Ouch! Well, all that remains is the thank yous. Firstly, thank you to everyone who has been giving Abi help whilst I've been away. It's really appreciated... although the offer of dancing tuition was probably beyond the call of duty." I stare towards Jenny and Olivier who are snorting with laughter. Jenny's boyfriend is shifting from one foot to the other looking sheepish. "Also a big thanks to Brenda and Claire for their amazing cooking and organising. (Reg carries on more flowers.) Thanks to Andy for letting us borrow his Scout hut (bottle of Talisker) and thanks to Salford Super Sounds for my forthcoming embarrassment on the dance floor. Reg will be giving you your cheque later." (The spot lights flash.)

My father-in-law looks up sharply, but his surprised expression melts into a grin, and joins in: "Worth every penny to see Steven move. I'm not going to call it dancing…"

"So have I forgotten anything?" I smile towards my four year old niece. It's well past her bedtime, but, hey, this is special.

"Present!" Leia shouts, pleased to play her part.

"Oh, was I meant to buy someone a present? Well, I did get one little thing. Now where did I put it?" I rummage through my jacket pockets, then wink at Leia. She walks towards Abi who bends and puts her bouquet to one side. Leia hands her a long slim black box wrapped with an emerald ribbon. The ribbon has number 30s embossed along its length.

She recites with a child's practised exactness, "From Steven to my wife Abi, who I like rather a lot, really."

Abi takes the box, glances up at me quizzically, and pulls the ribbon. Even in profile I can see from her expression that I've chosen well. The moment I walked into that jeweller's, I knew it was the right place. Abi pulls the necklace from the box and joins the clasp behind her. She straightens up and above her low cut black dress six polished ovals sit in an inverted triangle, each inset into a silver mount and joined to the others in a lacework of flat silver chains. A further two stones, one each side of the central delta, are mounted upon the slightly thicker neck chain; all are exactly the same shade of green as Abi's eyes.

We stare, in our own cocoon, the outside world irrelevant.

"Beautiful… and the necklace."

Abi moves closer and asks in a low, wondering voice:

"How did you find it?"

"There's a shop in Helsinki. All sorts of silver, ethnic type stuff, just your sort of thing. I wanted something really 'wow', so I sat down with their designer. We got the colour match from one of the photos on my phone, she sketched a few things and, well, you haven't got a posh necklace."

"I have now. It's amazing. Thank you." She reaches forward and kisses me tenderly. Somewhere else people are cheering and whistling. "Now I know why Claire said I had to wear this dress."

"Yeah, she had to know roughly what it was because of Leia, but no one saw it before you."

A thought passes across her face, "It wasn't too expensive was it?"

"No, serpentine's not like diamonds or anything."

Abi leans back down to our niece who is sitting on the floor watching us with an intensity that only small kids can. She whispers in her ear and then signals for everyone to quieten down.

Leia jumps up, walks towards me and shouts loudly, "Auntie Abi says thank you and she likes you quite a bit too." The whoops and whistles resolve themselves into a chant of 'dance, dance, dance!' Who started that? I have my suspicions.

Inevitably the DJ starts with 'Happy Birthday', you know, the old one by Altered Images. I hold Abi's hands and we start to move. Fairly soon our relaxed start is overtaken by some fairly vigorous bopping from one or two people who remember the track the first time round and are therefore a tad old for such antics. After a couple of songs, one of our amusing friends tips the DJ off about 'Fools Gold'. As the intro starts Abi holds her hands over her eyes. She parts her fingers peering through to see me waving my arms madly and moving my head side to side in that curious circular motion performed by the Stone Roses and their ilk.

"Come on, just imagine you've taken far too much of numerous illegal substances and let your head go," I shout over the music. "It's your birthday, you've got a duty to embarrass yourself!"

I don't believe it. She's actually doing it. I've known her for seven years and this is the first time she's tried it. I pause as I watch the rolling head and flailing arms.

"Oi, don't stop, I don't want to be the only idiot."

I turn to the others on the dance floor, "Come on, compulsory indie dancing." By the end of the song there is a sizeable contingent of head-wavers.

"I need to sit down, my brain feels like it's been rolled around inside my skull," complains Abi.

"That's cos it has," I say helpfully. We take two plastic chairs, close to the buffet. The swarming hordes haven't quite got the better of it yet.

"Daddy, can I have another cake?" Daddy is ignoring his four year old. "Can I have another cake?" Now I see that Daddy has heard, he's just chosen not to reply. "Daddy!" again followed by an indignant grab at Chris's elbow.

"I can't hear you," says Chris.

"You know Leia, you'd fit in very well in Finland." She turns towards me looking puzzled, "They don't have a word for 'please' there either."

"Uncle Steven, please can I have another cake?"

"Well, that's up to your Dad, but I think now you've said the magic word..." Chris nods. I turn to see Abi watching me talking to the little girl. A strange expression passes across her face.

"They don't have a word for 'please' in Finnish?" says Chris.

"Well, the books say you can add 'you're welcome' or 'thank you' to questions, but I never hear the Finns doing it; just asking the question seems to be polite enough. They think all our 'please's are ever so quaint."

Abi tucks her feet up and leans so she is lying half on her chair and half over my legs. She turns her head to regard me.

"What are you grinning about?" I say.

"I'm just happy..."

We sit, watching the dancers in our own blissful silence. A flash of red hair on the dance floor flickers in the corner of my eye. Surely not? No, it's just Ellie, next door's daughter been at the wash in / rinse out again. Get out of my mind, please.

WE'RE LYING IN BED. It's Sunday afternoon and my airport taxi arrives in two hours' time. Tiny specs of fluff swirl in a needle of light, the low winter sun finding a gap in the curtains.

"Steven."

"Abigail, darling."

"When you go dancing, who do you dance with?"

"Errm, three or four half naked eighteen year olds. Why is there a problem?"

"Oh, that's alright then..." Abi's old style alarm clock ticks through the pregnant silence.

"Usually by myself. You know me, I like to get lost in the rhythm."

"Yeah, my neck's still sore from yesterday." I caress it with exaggerated concern. After a minute or so she says, "Usually?"

"Well, for instance, I danced with Katri because it was her birthday and so did everyone else."

"Even Mark?"

"Even Mark." My lips begin to explore her hairline. She doesn't move: something's still bothering her. "And I've danced with Miguel's girlfriend and one of the barmaids from Hanne's Bar. It's a bit like it used to be here years ago. You dance with everyone because it's something to do: it's fun. It doesn't mean anything."

"Tell me about Katri."

"She's nice, really friendly. All the hotel staff are: they've made us long term guests feel like part of the family. But Katri, well, she's the... nicest."

"What does she look like?"

I lift myself on my arms so we're face to face. "I don't fancy her, OK?" Abi raises an eyebrow. "Maybe, if I'd met her ten years ago, but, anyway, she's interested in someone else. She was complaining that she likes a guy who is attached and so I told her about Pete and how I always used to be in love with his girlfriends."

"I just don't get what they all see in Pete."

"Well you do have very strange tastes, my love."

"Very strange," she agrees and reaches up to nibble my bottom lip. She pulls back, "Who is Katri's taken man then?"

"I don't know, she didn't say."

Abi pushes me on to my side and sits up. I'm studied by deep glittering eyes in the semi-darkness. "What exactly did she say then? Give it to me word for word." She knows I'm pretty good at this, having lost a few who-said-what arguments in the past.

"I asked her if she was going out with one of the other receptionists, Erik, and she said, 'no, she didn't have a boyfriend.' She looked quite sad, so I said, 'Are these Finnish guys stupid?' to cheer her up.'"

Abi rolls her eyes.

"What?"

"Go on."

"Then she said something like, 'The one I like is already attached,' and I went on about Pete for a bit."

"Poor girl. Is that it?"

"No, she said, well, I was married now and I made some joke about..." I grin as I remember, "what could that woman have been thinking?"

Abi ignores the jibe, "Did she laugh?"

"No. Like I said, she seemed quite morose about the whole subject. I was trying to make her feel better. It didn't work."

"But normally she does laugh at your jokes?"

"Yes?"

Abi is shaking her head, smiling in despair, "She was talking about you, dope."

"What do you mean?"

"You're the guy that she fancies, the one that's taken."

"I am not."

Abi ignores my protestations, "I suppose I should be grateful that you have no idea about what women are thinking." She ruffles the hair on the top of my head and the corners of her mouth rise mischievously. "She fancies you," she says in her best playground voice.

"She does not."

"Does too."

"Does not."

"Double does with cherries on..." I stifle her with a kiss that becomes deeper.

Drawing back for a second, I whisper, "I know what you're thinking now."

She pulls me downward, grinning. "Lucky guess."

- - -

CHAPTER 14

"I'm sorry, but I'm bursting for the toilet."

Dr Hiltunen glances towards the clock hanging above the window. Judging from the gloom barely seeping round the blinds it must have clouded over. "We might as well break for lunch, anyways." He motions towards the door with an exaggerated sweep of the hand and says in an ironic tone, "I'm sure the guy out there will show you the way."

By the time I return, sandwiches, fruit and cake have appeared on the trolley. I eye the slice of chocolate sponge lustfully.

"One of the catering firms does an 'English afternoon tea' so I thought you might like it – for a change."

I restrain myself from saying, 'Hell, yeah' in Hiltunen's accent. "Thanks."

"You dig right in first. I'm trying to go easy."

I'm halfway through my second sandwich when I realise that this is going to be a working lunch. "So, you went on back home, but I'm guessing that didn't fix it."

"I'm here aren't I?" I shrug.

"You and Miss Arwen seem to be playing a fine little dance, up till now."

"I think that was the problem. It was all so slow... Nothing seemed too wrong."

"Them's often the worst. Folks put up this big umbrella to catch the rain storm, but they don't realise the mist seeping in from the sides will get 'em just as wet in the end."

"And there was me, telling myself I was making a bigger umbrella... using mist!"

"Don't sound such a clever plan now does it?" I comfort myself with the chocolate sponge. "Any good?" asks Hiltunen, reaching for what, despite his earlier comment, must be his third sandwich.

"Not bad. It's not up to my mother-in-law's standard, but that's a pretty high marker."

Hiltunen fixes me with a considered stare. "Not once today have you said anything about your own folks." His expression morphs into a broad grin as he exaggerates the clichéd phrase. "So tell me, Mr Thinker, a little about your family."

"There's not much to say. Only child; Mum died nearly ten years ago; Dad's in a dementia home."

"Uh huh." He grunts, seemingly without embarrassment and picks up his pencil. "Your folks older when they had you?"

"Late thirties. I think they'd given up."

"And when the pressure's off, it all starts working again."

"Something like that."

Hiltunen scribbles a couple of notes and then raises his eyes to mine. "My mom died before her time too. Tricky ain't it?"

"You don't know till it happens. There's no word for it. Loss, sad, grief, they're just words, they don't describe it."

"I was so angry, I used to have to go out and shoot something to calm down. How about you?"

Is this some kind of trick question? I wouldn't put it past this guy. I choose my words carefully. "I've never been into the hunting thing, but yeah, I was angry; angry at the world, at the injustice of it, not at anyone in particular. Strokes, they're just so random."

"Your Pop's illness had begun by then?"

"Perhaps he was a bit forgetful, but nothing major. I always think it was Mum's death that pushed him over. Now he doesn't even realise she's gone."

"Shoot. That's like being hit by a Chevy and then run over by a truck... You were pretty much on your own, then?"

"Yes, well, no, not for long, I met Abi soon after."

He nods, notes that I seem to have finished eating and reaches out a hand for my plate. "You about ready to re-start?"

"I didn't realise we'd stopped," I say, passing it over.

"Occ-u-pational hazard," he says whilst re-stacking the trolley.

"Ain't no such thing as meaningless chit-chat... We must be getting close to the crime now?"

It's the first time he's mentioned it. I kept expecting him to say something right at the start. I nod. Hiltunen is watching closely. I'm going to have to relive it all. A sigh escapes as I ponder what came next. Just back from Abi's party, that means...

"You want to hear some more about Daina? That wasn't going too far off track?"

"It's your show, just live it like you done before."

+ + +

CHAPTER 15

The horn marking the end of the first period is above ear-splitting, more like skull-reverberating. Players swoop off the ice and cheerleaders bounce down the aisles to take their places at the rink side. The excited chatter of hopeful home-side fans almost drowns the canned music.

"Your team are winning for once," I comment to Mikko as Mark and I squeeze past.

"Much time for that to change," says Mikko, his tone that of the long suffering fan, whose bottom of the table team is well used to receiving a stuffing from the big boys like TPS.

I spot a small stick man symbol and follow the arrow through a tunnel beneath the concrete stands. A queue of fidgeting women snakes away from their relief, barring the entrance to the gents.

"Steven!" My arm is grabbed as I make my way through.

"I didn't take you for a hockey fan, Til."

"Everyone here is hockey fan," she shrugs. The blonde streaks in her hair seem to have turned purple since we last met. "We have not seen you since a few days."

"I went back to England."

"Ah, nice time with wife?" Til grins.

"Yes, actually, really good." I pause. "Is Arwen OK now?"

"Yes, she really happy. She tell everyone how you make her sing to Kari, how you get them back together."

"I think it would have happened anyway." Til holds my eye.

"She also tell me about you singing, about singing with you. She talk about you more than Kari!"

I shrug. "Well, we both like to sing."

Til screws her eyes up slightly as if staring straight through into that part of my brain which I am trying to suppress. "Hmm, you very strange man Steven," she says and shakes her head.

"Confused might be a better word," I say, indicating with a flick of my head and a grimace that my bladder is straining.

"Lucky," she says, shifting from one leg to the other as I pass through the empty doorway.

MARK shuffles back along the row carrying four paper wrapped burgers. He looks slightly shaken.

"Mark's just discovered the arena prices, I see," says Keith, but it's more than that.

"Do you remember Daina?" he asks, ignoring Keith.

"Woman being beaten up by her fella?" says John.

"Yes. Over there." We follow his finger to where the seats start to curve round the end of the rink. Slightly higher than us, a blonde woman is sitting beside a man in a padded jacket.

"That's Daina?" I ask. Mark nods. "Bastard." No one points out that I forfeit the next round of drinks. Even from here, the plaster cast up her right leg is obvious.

"She might have just fallen over," says John.

"Oink, oink, oink..." says Keith pointing up at an imaginary pig flying past.

"Is that the bloke?" asks John.

"I think so, from what Hanne said." As we are watching, Daina reaches between her feet and pulls up two crutches. She pendulums down the steps with the confidence of someone who has been using them for a while.

"'scuse me again, Mikko," I say. He looks up in surprise at my haste. I trot down the steps and along the tunnel. Daina rounds the corner into the toilet area moments after I do and lets out a gasp. I wondered if she wouldn't recognise me, but she clearly does.

"Are you alright?" Is all that comes into my head.

She stands open mouthed for a couple of seconds and then quickly glances behind her. "I fine. No problems. Anything I say, last time in bar. I very drunk, I not make much sense. Forget it."

"What happened to your leg?" I ask.

"Slip on ice, hit post," she says, but colours slightly.

"Unlucky." I pause. "Are you sure there's nothing we can do? My three friends are here too." I not sure what I mean by this. Have I been watching too many films?

Another nervous glance back towards the rink, a shake of the head that seems to accelerate into a shudder and then she thrusts the crutches forward. "Leave alone, thank you." Her eyes are fixed to the floor as she reverses awkwardly against the toilet door spring. The hooter sounds for the third period. I don't really have any option but to wend my way back to my seat.

Mark is incensed; I don't think I've ever seen him so angry. He even agrees when John suggests we wait for them outside and break the husband's legs. Keith is silent. I find myself, unwillingly, being the voice of reason: "But we can't just do vigilante stuff. He might deserve it, but we'd probably end up in jail too."

"We'll tell the police then," says Mark.

"We've been through this last time. Even if this was the UK, if she won't say anything, there's not much can be done."

"And we'd be risking her being beaten up for our trouble," says Keith, finally joining in.

"So we just watch the game and do nothing?" flares Mark.

I shrug.

AS WE JOSTLE our way through triumphant crowds, John and I become separated from the others. It doesn't really matter, we're all going in the same direction. A young redhead crosses the stream just ahead of us. It's not her, but I begin to day dream of duets and the touch of chestnut hair. Always back to the hair. Get out of my mind, woman. I should be imagining birthday parties and Sunday afternoons. What is wrong with me?

John glances towards me, "Dreamin' 'bout red hair and tight jeans again, hey?" he says with surprising insight.

"Got me." I pull the imaginary arrow out of my heart.

"That's what I'd be thinking if I was a bit younger." He considers for a moment. "Is it serious with her?"

"There is no it. I'm married, she's got a boyfriend."

"There will be. I've seen how you look at her `n` how she looks back."

"No. It's just like a stupid teenage crush."

"'cept you're not a teenager, are you?"

"I do love Abi."

"I didnae say you didn't... I love Janice."

"Anyway, it's useful. If I'm mooning over Reddy I'm not running off with any other girls, am I?"

John laughs, "Brilliant," he tries to copy my accent, "I'm sorry darling, I only made love to her, so I wouldn't shag anyone else."

"Nothing's going to happen."

"You keep telling yourself that," says John in strangely wistful tone.

The crowds thin by the time we reach the market square and take our homebound exit. "Maybe there is one thing I could do about Daina," I say, as we pause in front of familiar doors, still two blocks from the hotel.

"I'll leave you to your good deed then," John smiles, adding a conspiratorial wink.

But inside, the reason for John's amusement appears to be absent. I wait for the flow of punters to ease. "Hanne, did you ever go back to visit Daina?"

"Yes, two times, but never reply. I think perhaps she was there, but she not open the door."

I shake my head, "We went to the hockey tonight."

"You are become a real Finn," she laughs.

"We saw Daina there, she had a broken leg."

The smile evaporates from Hanne's face. "You think he did it?"

"If it looks like a rat, and smells like a rat."

"He is a rat," finishes Hanne. "Did you speak to her?"

"Yes, she said she slipped over."

Hanne shakes her head. "She very scared. I go again, but not tomorrow. Soon." She looks me up and down. "Brandy coke? On the house?"

DESPITE John's supposed sleeping draft, a whirling mind and churning stomach are keeping me awake. So John thinks she looks back, does he? No, don't think about that, think about Abi. The digits of the bedside clock glow 12:20. Twenty past ten: she's probably watching telly, half sitting, half lying on the sofa, legs curled up under. She does look back doesn't she? Remember dancing in Clarity. Her eyes. Doing it again. Get out of my mind. Out of my mind. *I must be out of my mind, can't get you out of my mind.* Hmm. I give in to the inevitable and turn the light back on. Now, how to write this song without it sounding like that one by Kylie?

Out of my mind

Why do I think the things I do?
My mind keeps slipping back to you.
Where will my subconscious take me?
Bury my head, try not to see.
Has my sanity all gone?
I'm becoming an automaton.

I must be out of my mind, can't get you out of my mind.
I must be out of my mind, can't get you off my mind.

Can't keep my mind off your flaming red hair.
I know it will burn me, I think I don't care.
I've got a fever, you are the cause.
Obsession is dripping from each of my pores.
I've got a fever: a raging hot fever;
I've got it bad now, I'm caught in your claws.

Can't get you out of my mind...

Maybe I need a reboot up the backside?
Maybe a stirring pep talk at the track side?
All I know is: you are in my mind
I can't let this life of mine unwind

Can't get you out of my mind...

- - -

"INTERESTING..." comments Hiltunen as I finish reciting.

"Obviously it's all exaggerated to make the lyric sound better," I say, shrugging.

Hiltunen nods. "Sounds kinda like you were beginning to see the problem, though." His pencil starts to spin once more. "You write the music for these songs too?"

"Sort of. In my mind I can hear the melody or sometimes even the full band playing, but I can't write it straight down on to a stave, so I hum or sing bits into a Dictaphone."

"What kinda thing are you hearing for this one?"

"It's a weird folky type melody; starts with one of those big drums. I don't even know if it'll work. These songs, they're not totally finished. They might change if I ever get to record them properly. You can't really separate the words and the music. They affect each other. If you have a bit of a tune and then you try to put some words to it, they often alter the timing or even the notes. And the same the other way round."

"You dream of being a pop star like, err... Reddy?"

"No," I say, although I find myself smiling ruefully. "Professional songwriter would be my perfect job: all the royalty cheques with none of the hassle."

"So she was gonna be the star and you was gonna write her hits?"

"No. We never talked about that."

"But I bet you thought about it?"

"Maybe..." I can distinctly remember daydreaming along those lines at least once.

Hiltunen sighs whilst shaking his head. "And all this pent up stuff came a bubbling out one day I suppose?"

"I wasn't going to say anything. I just got forced into it."

+ + +

CHAPTER 16

Maybe it's because the work level is ramping up, maybe I'm just being careful, but I've only been to Hanne's Bar a few times since arriving back from the UK and each time it doesn't seem to have been one of Reddy's shifts. The coin can only fall on tails so many times though...

"Ah, we'll let you get the first round then," says John as he spots a familiar figure reaching up to the optics.

"So generous." I am left standing, twenty Euro note in hand, whilst the others move off towards Keith's favourite perch.

"Steven, I not seen you for ages," says Reddy. "Four beers?"

"As usual," I nod.

"Til tell me you go back to England," says Reddy as she lets the first two pour from the taps.

"Yes, just for a few days. It's a lot warmer there."

"You have good time?"

"Yes, great; big family party. Lots of food, drink, dancing."

"Nice. How is..." A short guy with close cropped blonde hair interrupts her with his drinks order. She fobs him off with *"Hetkinen,"* takes my proffered note and goes over to the till. Several other people are now queuing up.

"Very busy!" she shrugs as she hands me the change. "Are you singing Wednesday again?"

"I guess so," I say automatically. I take the first two glasses and deposit them in waiting hands. As I pick up my second load, she is handing the blonde guy his change.

"You still to show me one of your songs."

I smile and nod as she turns to the next punter.

"I HOPE you're going to issue everyone with a set of earplugs," says Abi.

"Like I need for your snoring," I retort.

"I do not snore!"

"Yeah you do, occasionally. Cute little snuffles really: like a hedgehog poking around in leaves."

"Thanks a lot. I'm feeling a bit prickly after that analogy." I can tell Abi is grinning at the phone, pleased with her wit.

"Sorry. I did say cute."

"And that makes it better?"

"Maybe not." There is a short pause.

"So, what are you going to sing then?" says Abi.

"I don't know, I'll see how the mood takes me. Anyway, I'd better be going. Can't keep the adoring fans waiting for too long."

"Speaking of which, how is Katri?"

"She's OK. She hasn't expressed her undying love for me yet, if that's what you mean."

"She's not coming to watch you sing, then?"

"No, she'll be keeping the bed warm for when I get back."

"Oh, very funny. Just be careful, OK?" I think I detect a slight sigh.

"I will... It's only a couple more months. Love you."

"Love you too."

I press the disconnect button. Abi's almost barking up the right tree. Once again I feel slightly duplicitous, but what am I meant to say? Maybe I shouldn't go, I consider, as I slip the battered green notebook into the inside pocket of my thermal coat. No, that's daft. She's back with her boyfriend. We just share a common musical interest. But which of the songs do I dare show her?

"Have a good evening," calls Erik from behind the reception desk as I pass.

"Will do."

By the time I reach the plate glass doors of *Laiska Lohi*, I have decided to play it completely safe and just show her the words for *Without you*. It's probably the best one anyway.

The first thing I hear as I enter are familiar lungs belting out 'I will always love you': the Whitney Houston version from that film with the guy from Robin Hood in it. What was his name? Leaving my coat on one of the multi-armed stands next to the door, I transfer the notebook to the back pocket of my jeans and make my way round the island bar until I can see Reddy in full flow. She's wearing her hair in a French plait thing today. It adds an air of sophistication that I've not seen before. What did she have to go and do that for?

The song finishes and as she steps away from the lights I am spotted. She waves and points towards one of the low tables - where Til is sitting - before backing away in the direction of the toilets.

"*Hei*. I didn't think you came to these things," I say to Til as I plonk myself on the sofa opposite.

"I not singing."

"Fair enough." A thought occurs and I ask the question without thinking. "Kari didn't ask you to come did he?"

"No, why you think? Oh…" Til regards me for a moment. "No, I come myself," she pauses, deciding whether to say something or not, "… for same reason."

I don't ask what the reason is. I know a good friend when I see one. "Fair enough," I repeat and pick up the song menu. Yes, they have got it.

Arwen appears at Til's shoulder, "Steven," she says and leans to half hug, cheek to cheek. I receive a wonderful waft of berry scented shampoo as she pulls back.

"Thank you again for other day," she gushes.

"Can't have you looking sad all the time, can we?" I say shrugging.

"Have you choose a song?"

"Yes." I stand with the song list in my left hand, "Would either of you like a drink while I'm up?" They both grin, but I roll my eyes – that joke is past its sell by date.

"*Why not?*" says Arwen. "Two vodka lemonade," she smiles glancing towards Til who nods her acceptance. "Please."

When I return from my little circular tour, tray in hand, I find the two women eyeing each other with a mixture of sisterly love and exasperation. "What have you two been arguing about?" I ask.

"It not matter," says Til.

I place the tray on the table and sit. The small book digs into my backside. I take it out and place it beside my drink.

"Did you take a song?" asks Arwen.

"Yes, I did bring one," I say, gently correcting this most common of mistakes. "I write everything down in here to start with: lyrics, notes, all sorts of stuff. It's a bit of a mess." I hold the book open at some pages containing lots of crossings out and additions between lines.

"Do all English write like this?" asks Til.

"No, my hand writing's terrible... so I usually print it neatly when I've worked most of it out. I turn over a couple of pages and pass the book over. It's like waiting for a teacher to mark your book. I sit, scrutinising their faces for traces of approval.

"What is beacon?"

"A fire people lit on a hill as a signal, long ago."

They continue to read. Arwen finishes first and catches Til's eye. Til shrugs in a 'maybe I'm wrong' sort of way.

"Well?" I ask.

"I like. I like a lot. Is there a tune?" says Arwen. I try to start the chorus, but I am competing with someone singing slightly off key in Finnish. It's impossible and I shake my head, laughing.

"You miss your wife. Is about her?" says Til.

"Maybe, maybe it's just a song," I say, playing the artiste.

"There are more?" says Til starting to thumb through the rest of the pages.

" Yes, but.." I snatch the book out of her hands, which stay in reading position as she looks up in surprise. "They're... not finished." I see she got as far as *Enemy Within*. "Oh, maybe this one is OK." Can't do any harm. I put the green notebook back into her bemused hands.

After a few seconds, Arwen says, "This about that woman who Hanne try to see. Yes?"

"Well, she gave me the idea, yes, but the rest's made up." The out of tune singer has reached a welcome finale and I hear my name called out over the mic. "Didn't realise I'd be on so soon," I say, jumping out of my seat.

The compere spots me squeezing between sofa backs and the iconic sound of a Brian May guitar intro hastens my steps. I know what you're thinking: Rule #2 of karaoke – never do Freddie. And I'd agree with you... except for 'Crazy Little Thing.' It only works because Freddie's not doing Freddie, he's doing Elvis, so the vocal stays in a range that mere mortals can attempt. Needs a bit of practise though. I take a breath and push my voice down my throat. It's going pretty well, until I have a horrible thought: I've left my notebook in Til's hands. My mind is momentarily distracted and I stumble over the lyrics. I recover for the chorus, but can't muster any great enthusiasm and finish the song by numbers. Did they keep turning pages? What have they read? I leave the mic to muted applause and squint towards our table. My song book is sitting closed on the table between them. They're both staring at it.

Something always happens to spoil things doesn't it? I try to make light, "Did I forget to tell you that it bites?" Both women give weak smiles. Neither of them speaks. "What?" I ask. I know what, at least I think I do, but I'm not going to make it too easy for them.

Til, sharp as ever, cuts to the heart of it, "The other songs, they look finish to me."

"They're not... totally... I didn't say you could read them," my indignation melts into resignation, "but you have... so..."

Arwen takes a deep breath, "I not understand all the words, but... you meet someone in Clarity, you sing with someone, you dream someone."

"And I can't keep my mind off her flaming red hair," I add.

"Clever words," says Til.

"Thanks," I acknowledge the complement with zero pleasure.

Arwen ignores this little interruption. "Steven, you married."

"I could say they're just songs. They don't mean anything."

"But it would be lie, like songs not finished," says Til. I let that one pass, more intent on blue-grey eyes.

"You write beautiful song about miss your wife," says Arwen.

"I know."

"And you get me back with Kari..."

"I know."

"Why you do that? If..."

I shrug. "It seemed the right thing to do."

"English gentleman!" says Til whose expression is smug but concerned. Arwen throws her a scathing look. I think I know who the argument was about. I glance awkwardly towards Til, gathering my thoughts.

As if reading my mind Arwen says, "Til can you buy me another vodka? Pleeease." There is plenty of sarcasm on the final word.

Til rises somewhat reluctantly and when she's out of earshot, I begin: "I'm sorry," I say, fixing Arwen with my gaze, "but I've liked you since the first time we spoke." I pause to let that sink in. "Obviously, I'm married, so I've tried to keep it just an idle fancy." Arwen frowns slightly with incomprehension. "I tried to think of you like I might think about a film star," she nods, "but things keep happening to make it too real: we dance together and it feels good?" She doesn't deny my question but her eyes are not giving anything away. "We have a laugh together; we both like singing and when we sing together it's like... well, it's like electricity. Wasn't it?" There's still no response from the other side of the table. "I thought I had it under control. I went home, I had a good time with my wife and family, but every time I saw someone with long red hair..." I fade off. Arwen's eyes shift down to her lap where she is flicking her left thumb nail with her right index finger. I continue, "Tonight I thought, I'll just come as a friend, I'll show you my song, I'll make sure we don't sing any duets, no problem. And then there you are when I walk in, singing 'I will always love you' with your hair done up in that beautiful way and I'm melting before I even sit down." I shrug, "I'm sorry, I can't help it."

When Arwen raises her head I can see there are tears in her eyes.

"I'm sorry, I didn't mean to upset you. It's my problem, not yours."

"Stop say sorry," says Arwen forcing a smile. Her milky brow furrows, "You just not think me like that. You must not," she adds with surprising vehemence.

I hold up my hands in surrender. "I'll try," I say weakly.

There is an awkward pause and I become aware again of the surrounding tables and the old Finnish guy from the other week crooning out a dance hall number.

"I think I'd better go," I say and reach across the table for my notebook.

Arwen catches my hand and squeezes it, apologetically. "*Dream lover!*" she says with a slightly amused snort as if she can't comprehend how the male brain works.

I redden and retrieve the song book. "Better take this with me. Anyone might read it."

CHAPTER 17

I'm a bit reticent about this. It just feels like a bad idea somehow. Like standing at the bottom of a sandstone cliff in a rain storm... something might slip.

"What are you looking so glum about, Stevie?" says John. "Reddy'll be there, I bet."

"Yeah, yeah..." That's what I'm afraid of.

Hanne's bouncer peers at us above a temporary sign which has been taped to the tinted glass. He opens the door and then closes it quickly behind us. Unlike a usual Thursday at 7pm, it's not deserted. An eager crowd is milling in front of the bar. The two staff, neither of whom I recognise, are standing around, shifting from one leg to the other in anticipation of the rush. Something seems out of place, not quite complete, and I realise it is the lack of Hanne. An elegant woman with hair extravagantly curled around the top of her head and a low cut tawny dress detaches herself from the crowd and meets us half way across the room.

"Good, you got my message, we just about to begin," says the woman in Hanne's voice. We all do a double take.

"Hey, you scrub up well, Hanne," says Keith, kissing her on the cheek.

"Specially for you Keith..." Hanne lets that settle on his surprised expression and then snorts with laughter. "Come, I do this in Finnish and English." She ushers us towards the throng. A path opens up for her towards the other doorman who is waiting arms outstretched. As she reaches him, he lifts her in one smooth movement so that she is sitting on the bar facing us. She smiles with almost motherly pride and starts her speech saying each line in Finnish and then English. "Five years ago I buy this place. I use some money I inherit from my parents." She looks at us enquiringly and we nod the correct usage of the word. "But I also have loan from bank... At the end of last month, I pay off the loan... So now I own all of Hanne's Bar." There is a loud cheer.

"I can only do this with my wonderful staff..." Several people in the crowd whoop and, like Hanne, I now recognise them in their civvies. And there is Ar... Reddy at the back with Kari. Her eyes slip sideways in my direction, but mine move away like opposite poles: back to Hanne.

"...and my best customers." We join in the general shouting and clapping.

"So as a big thank you, for the next hour, all drinks are free!" She pauses and people edge forward slightly. *"Viisi, neljä, kolme, kaksi, yksi, mene!* Go!"

Imagine a rugby scrum but with drinks and slightly more shoving. The two bar staff aren't taking orders, they're just leaving all the taps running and putting glasses on to the counter the second they're filled. After a mad first fifteen minutes, everyone has slowed down slightly and started to get more adventurous. True to her nationality, Hanne has been handed a huge bottle of Koskenkorva and is pouring out triples from the wrong side of the bar to all takers. A hefty proportion of the bottle is finding its way into her own glass.

"Hey, this is your party," says John. "I'll do that."

Hanne smiles and hands the bottle over.

"You need to watch him," I say, and gesture, "one for you, one for me, one for you, two for me."

"Shut up and drink," says John forcing a glass into my left hand. I still have half a Lapin Kulta in my right. I'm momentarily at a loss as to which glass I should drink from.

Mark spots my dilemma and apes Terry, "Nice problem to have."

"Don't use your TBS on me," I say and hold my arms in a cross: warding off his evil. I only spill a small amount of lager. I'm taking alternate swigs when Dea, Erik, and Raakel swirl past. Erik nods at us. "You've got people from the Central hotel here?" I say to Hanne.

"Yes, they..." she grins sheepishly and then laughs, "they send people here."

"Oh," I say, realising the implication, "and I thought they were giving me an honest recommendation!"

"They were, I think."

"But a few free drinks don't hurt, hey?"

"Only the head in the morning," says Hanne and sweeps away to speak to someone else.

By 7:45 I have drunk several lagers, at least two large vodkas, a bottle of some Belgian dark ale and a gin 'n' tonic: all on an empty stomach. At the far end of the now slow motion and wobbly bar, someone starts chanting, "salmiakki... salmiakki..." It starts to appear on trays.

"There is no way any of that chemical waste is entering my body," I announce to no one in particular.

Mark, who seems in a slightly better state, says, "How about whiskies?"

"Bloody too right," I say, loud enough for Keith to hear. He's just about to pounce, but I spike his gun with, "and I'm quite happy to get in the next sodding round for any of you twats."

"Doesn't that count as three rounds?" says Keith limply, wishing he had thought of this first.

"Coming up," I say, heading towards the free bar.

I'm half way through my third double Bell's when what sounds like an alarm clock goes off behind the bar. Hanne, who has now forgotten or is incapable of English, shouts something out, bows to the crowd and wobbles on the way back up again. There is a mixture of cheers, clapping, whistles and what I assume is drunken Finnish banter. As a last hurrah, the bar staff pass over a couple of large boxes filled with crisps, peanuts and the like. We grab handfuls and retreat to one of the alcoves.

"Now that, my fwiends," says Keith with a mouthful of peanuts, "is what I call a happy hour."

"You're nae wrong," says John. He spots Hanne standing with her back to us a few metres away. "Hey, gorgeous!" I notice a muscle twitch in Hanne's neck, but she doesn't turn round. "Aye, I mean you, darlin'."

This time Hanne turns, eyebrows raised. "Great start," says John, ignoring her expression, "What's the score for the rest of the evening?"

"Oh, I forget Engliss," says Hanne slurring slightly. "Shoon, hot food will come. Buffet." She pronounces it like what the wind might do to a flag. The alcohol has relaxed our manners and all four of us unthinkingly grin.

"What ish sho funny?" says Hanne.

No one wants to be the one to say. I give up first.

"You say it boo-fay. It's actually a French word. Bound to be really, being about food..." Hanne looks slightly put out, so I continue quickly, "But don't worry about it, your English is just about the best of anyone I know here. It's certainly better than John's." I ignore the muttering under his breath which I suspect is comparing me to some Scandinavian animal's nether regions. "Are we going to have dancing?" I point towards the rear area of the room, where the usual tables have been cleared. A guy whom I presume must be the DJ is fiddling with dials behind a substantial portable desk. Either side are dark metal racks containing speakers and disco lights.

Some of the lights begin to spin as Hanne answers, "Tonight we have third night club in Mahikkala." The DJ raises a hand towards Hanne, who nods. She turns back towards me with a mischievous expression. "Sho, Shteven, becaushe you are sho rude to me, you have to make up." For a second I have visions of lipstick and eyeliner, but that's not what she means. "You do first danshe with me."

I regard the glammed up Hanne, who is supposedly almost 10 years my senior, but you'd never know it from appearances. "Well, it's a dirty job, but I suppose someone's got to do it." (the old ones are still the oldest...) I attempt to stand, but the crisps have done little to dull the alcohol and I wobble part way up. I bang a hand down on to the table, narrowly missing a couple of empties to steady myself.

"Looks like you may have to hold him up," says Keith as I take Hanne's warm hand, which is still shaking from her giggles.

"Jealous!" I mouth over my shoulder, as I am led through the LED patterns now tracing themselves across the floor.

"Arwen tell me you are good dansher," says Hanne flashing a wide smile.

"Did she," I mutter. I can't help but glance to my left where Reddy is resting her head on Kari's shoulder. I don't think Hanne notices; she's already raising a thumb in the direction of the DJ.

The squeaky keyboard intro of 'Money, money, money' rips out of the speakers. If this guy has eleven on his dials, he just used it. Hanne grimaces and makes a 'turn it down a bit' gesture. With her other hand she beckons people: despite supposed international rivalries, there's nothing like an ABBA song to get the Finnish on to a dance floor. Before we even reach the first chorus Dea and Raakel are with us and several more are up.

It normally takes me a while to get going, before I start the 'silly stuff' as Abi would say, but tonight, well, how shall I put it? The joints are already fully lubricated. So it's straight in with a pretend tango, which almost causes us to go sprawling, followed by handing out invisible bank notes in the chorus. Hanne shakes her head, amused eyes raised. The 'dancing' continues in the same vein through the next few songs, until a breather is called for. We park at an empty table close to the bar. She smiles, moving her head closer.

"Steven, you dance so funny tonight."

I shrug and gesture a swig of an imaginary drink. Out of the corner of my eye I see Reddy leading Kari towards the gyrating bodies. I glance sideways. She's wearing the inevitable little black dress, but that's not what has caught my eye. Against the black, her chestnut mane is shimmering. It's an unusual style: mostly down, but with two thin braids appearing from above her left ear, curving back over her shoulder. They're held tight by post box red bands.

I flick back to Hanne, whose eyes are also returning from the same direction. Was she following my gaze? Our eyes meet and Hanne says, "Was there something you were wanting to ask me?"

Of course there is, I want to know what Reddy really thinks about me. I want to know if there's turmoil in her head like there is in mine. Has she confided in you Hanne? But I don't say that. I don't know what Hanne is on about. The only reply I can think of is an uninspiring, "What sort of thing?"

She holds my eye and I think she's about to speak when Keith's jovial tones interrupt, "We can't have you monopolising the party girl all night, can we Steve." He takes Hanne's right hand, and asks very formally, "May I have the pleasure of this dance Madame?" I can see that Keith has also found how well the polite Englishman act goes down. In spite of the despairing look she gives me, she allows herself to be pulled vertical. As she passes close behind my stool I say, at a volume for her ears only, "Watch out for his left hand."

I spin on the stool slightly to watch Keith put his left arm round Hanne's waist and quickstep her away. He really does do that well, to any sort of music. My eyes follow their progress for a few seconds but inevitably my gaze strays elsewhere. Kari can dance, but it's a bit mechanical, not natural, but learned, like a Tony Blair hand gesture. Reddy, on the other hand, is swirling her hair and moving her body in fluid motions that echo the music. I can't think of a reason why anyone would want to look anywhere else in the room. What did Hanne mean? Has Reddy told her something? Why am I bothered? Stop thinking about her. Get out of my mind!

I don't notice her head start to turn until it's too late. Our eyes meet and we both look away rapidly. She must have seen that I was staring. But she looked too. Why did she do that? 'Oh Arwen...' I sigh under my breath.

A pair of fingers click in front of my face. "Food," says Mark, pointing to the three trestle tables in the corner where a man in white is pulling foil off the tops of various dishes. Steam is rising appetisingly.

"Good spot." I stand and follow him. I'm most of the way through various delights which wouldn't normally share a plate when Hanne breezes past.

"What is that?" she asks, indicating the reddish mush.

"Curry with lingon berry sauce. Who knew they'd go so well together? Try it!"

"How much he had to drink?" laughs Hanne.

"Loads," says Mark after swallowing.

"Bar still open," twinkles Hanne. What a trooper. She turns as if to move on, but pauses half way. "Steven, good tip... about left hand."

I grin and raise my eyebrows, "You're welcome, Madame." I say, imitating Keith's tone.

"I need something to wash this down with. Want one?" I ask Mark out of politeness.

"Why not?"

"Sorry, have you been replaced by alien party Mark?"

He shrugs, "It's going to be a bad morning whatever now."

"You're not wrong there."

We're about a third of the way down our lagers when I notice Arwen back at her table, without Kari. Automatically, I stand.

"Where are you going?" says Mark. "Oh, I see," he adds, following my gaze.

"Kari left you on your own?" I ask.

She raises her chin and smiles, but I can see apprehension in her eyes. "Toilet."

"Interesting hair," I indicate the braids. "Nice." She's wearing a lot of makeup, but I think I spot a small blush. "Would you like to dance?" It just comes straight out from that supposedly suppressed place in my brain, surprising me almost as much as her.

"Steven," she studies me for a moment. I suppose she sees a drunk, confused bloke. "Not good idea."

"It's just dancing..."

"Is it?"

What was I expecting? But the alcohol drowns any sense. "You think you're looking at a drunk, confused man, don't you?" She shifts on her stool uncomfortably. "Except right at this moment I'm totally clear on one thing. If you come and dance with me now, you won't want to stop."

"Steven," she says in a pained voice. Then more urgently, "Kari comes."

"Hello Steven," says Kari in a friendly tone. "Chatting up my girlfriend again?" I stiffen, but try to hide it with a shrug as I realise he is joking.

"Well, if you will leave her alone in a room full of drunks... what do you expect?"

He smiles, "I could hardly take her into the toilets with me."

"Can't see that that would be a problem in Finland." In spite of herself, Arwen grins and screws up her nose at the thought. There is a pause and I'm wondering how to excuse myself, when Hanne's amplified voice emanates from behind me. "Everyone dancing!" She beckons exaggeratedly from beside the DJ and the beat of the trusty 'Macarena' begins.

As I move forward, I spot Mark and the three from the Central Hotel hanging back near to the buffet table. "Come on, the birthday girl has spoken," I shout above the music. Raakel and Dea glance at each other and then turn to grab Mark and Erik's hands. The guys look for a moment like they are going to stand fast, but then shrug at each other and give in to the tugging. Out of the corner of my eye, I see Arwen is also dragging a protesting Kari forward. Gradually, almost everyone presses in, and the ninety degree turns are becoming quite hazardous.

You know how this beat is quite hypnotic? Well, guess what has caught my eye? I drift forward until I am dancing directly behind her and have a perfect view. It seems so natural to reach out and place my hands on Arwen's waist as we both lower into the wiggle. I feel her twitch, under my touch and her head turns. Her face ignites in pure fury and I stumble backwards holding my hands up by my sides in apology. A shove in the small of the back, which turns out to be courtesy of Erik, keeps me on my feet. Arwen's expression softens and she turns back. What was I thinking?

I CAN'T GET THE HEAT of her anger out of my mind. She's never looked at me like that before. My heart feels branded, left charred by the molten stare. Oh, hark at me. This is just some girl from a bar who you hardly know. 'Sober up,' I think, sipping another whisky.

"Why does he sing that high?" says Mark, amazingly still present at twenty to two.

"Trousers too tight," grunts John, who I'd thought was beginning to doze.

"What?" I try to engage my brain.

"He's supposed to be this mega chick magnet? Yeah? So why does he sing like his balls haven't dropped?" Mark is in alcohol philosophy mode. He isn't making much sense.

"Who?"

"Justin Timberlake. This song." Mark gestures in the direction of the few people who are struggling to keep up with 'Rock your body.'

I catch on to where he's going with this, "You mean these pop guys who pose around in their videos with tens of scantily clad dancers but sing like girls?"

Mark nods. "Imagine going up to a woman in a bar and saying in a squeaky voice higher than hers, 'Fancy going somewhere quieter?'"

"Always use that line do you?" says John, amused.

"Worked on Jane," says Mark, presumably just bantering, "But women wouldn't find it attractive would they?"

I smile across the table at John. It's strange seeing Mark with his hair down. "No I can't imagine they would."

"I mean, there's Barry White and Chris Rea, but tell me one other male pop star who sings in a deep voice?" John and I fail to think of a name. "There, you see?" says Mark.

"It's one of the great mysteries of popular music," I shrug.

John smiles at my sarcasm and then indicates over my shoulder with his eyes. "Reddy's boyfriend's making things easy for you."

"Shut up."

Arwen is facing away from Kari, towards the dancers, with her arms folded. Kari is slumped back in his chair wearing an exasperated expression. I'm not sure what the prelude to this was. After a few seconds she turns, flashes a forced smile and tries to pull him forward. Kari is clearly going nowhere. Arwen turns back, refolds her arms and crosses her legs tightly.

The music morphs from Mr Timberlake to another upbeat dance track: one of those American women.

"I'm just going to dance the last couple before the slow ones start," I say and stand. I pass close in front of Arwen, but purposefully don't look. When I start to dance I face the other way, imagining her gaze drilling into my back. As the track progresses, the flow of dancers gradually rotates me and I risk a quick glance out of the corner of my eye. She's facing Kari, who is still scowling. Safe, I turn fully. There are a couple of sharp words in both directions and catching me unprepared, Arwen snaps her head away from him and finds herself facing straight at me. It's too late to look away, so I stare. Her eyes lower, but not instantly.

The foolish, pickled part of my brain takes this as an invitation and in a moment I'm standing in front of her saying, "You look like you want to dance." She doesn't say anything but glances towards Kari. I interpret this as asking for consent, so I say, "Kari, you don't mind her dancing with me for a few minutes, do you? No slow dances!"

"She can do as she likes," says Kari, slowly and deliberately.

I turn back to Arwen and part of my brain thinks: back off, sit down, go home; the other part reaches for her arm and says, "Come on, this is a good one."

"No," she says simply, but I still have her wrist, cool under my grip.

"Please... You know I don't bite." And as I say this I try to lift her out of her seat. In my inebriated state, I pull a little too hard and against her will she begins to rise. Seeing her grimace, I immediately let go, causing her to jerk back down the couple of centimetres to her stool.

"Ow," she says, rubbing her wrist.

I'm mortified. "*Anteeksi,* sorry. I thought you were messing around."

She regards me carefully and slowly shakes her head, "Steven... Stop being arsehole."

I give her a watery smile of extinguished hope and blurt out, "I'm sorry, I can't help it," before my voice cracks too badly. In the background, the corners of Kari's mouth rise at what he thinks is my self-deprecating humour, but the reference to a previous conversation is not lost on Arwen.

The two braids hang in front of her bare left shoulder and I stare into her questioning eyes, taking one last deep breath of Arwen, before I turn away from Reddy. I've almost made the relative privacy of the toilets when I hear a Scottish voice call from my left, "Nice technique, Stevie boy." I push against the door without turning.

I suppose the toilets in a bar are a pretty common place to have a wake-up call. To think, 'What the hell am I doing? Why am I even thinking about this woman when I have Abi? Stop creating problems that needn't exist.' I close the lid and sit in one of the narrow traps. The sliding home of the bolt shuts out Finland. I'm in the scout hut at Abi's party, she's just thrown me an expression of such love that it makes me choke up. That must be why I'm crying. I'm sitting in Gary's front room when a friend of his walks in. "This is Abi," he says. Was I alive before then? I'm lying on my back with Abi's head resting on my shoulder, her breath tickling my chest hairs. Now this is what feels right.

Silence breaks me from my reverie. I squeeze myself out of the cubicle and regard my reflection. The eyes are red under my specs. I take them off and splash water in my face. Out in the bar, Hanne is talking into the mic. I glance at my watch, having to hold it up close to my face to focus: 2am, she must be chucking out. Putting my glasses back on, I step, blinking, into the bar where the house lights reveal the detritus of the evening. Mopping of the sticky floor has already begun in the far corner.

"Thought we were going to have to come in and get you," says Mark.

"Something in my eye."

"Oh aye?" says John, conveying disbelief but respect for my privacy in two words.

"What happened to Keith," I ask, realising he is missing.

"Went off with someone's mother about an hour ago," says Mark.

"That's a thought I don't need," I say, waving goodbye to Hanne, who is bending to pick up a fallen wrapper. We join the queue to retrieve our coats and swap them for a few Euros; after all it's been a cheap night.

As we step out into the bite of the street, I notice Reddy and Kari up ahead, standing on the edge of the pavement where a road crosses the pedestrian area. I can hear raised voices from here. Reddy is shouting through tears at Kari who is replying in short sharp bursts like you might to a slow-to-catch-on child. As we pass, Mark stands on a particularly crunchy spot of snow; her head flicks round at the noise, followed by her eyes rising toward me appealingly.

I hold my arms apart, palms forwards. "Hey, I'm not doing it twice," I say, and start to cross the road towards the hotel. Part way, a thought occurs to me.

"Guys, I'm not that tired. I'm going for a tramp next to the lake. I need to clear my head. See you in the morning." Neither Mark nor John seem surprised and raise their hands in farewell before falling into step with Dea and Raakel who must have left just behind us. Before the polished stone of the central bank obscures my view, I glance back to see Reddy standing with her hands on her hips and Kari apparently talking fast.

It's only five minutes' walk down *Pankkikatu* before you reach the lakeside park. I wait for a couple of late taxis to pass and then traverse the dual carriageway without waiting for the crossing lights to change. This is technically illegal in Finland. "Go on, arrest me!" I dare an outraged lamp post. On the other side I'm straight into forest.

Taking a walk in a forest by a lake in the middle of the night would sound nuts to someone from the UK, but this is Finland! It's what - quarter past twoish - and in a couple of hours the first hardy cross-country skiers will be preparing to get their ten laps in before breakfast. The track I'm walking along is used by these muesli addicted Adonises, so it's wide and has regular lamp posts - you can't ski in the dark, can you? There are several routes of varying difficulty, and many intersections enable a myriad of alternatives. I'm making for the path closest to the lake shore. If I walk right round, I'll eventually pass the wooden pier where Mikko took us ice swimming.

Mind you, even if it was a run down estate in Manchester, I don't think I'd feel unsafe. The mixture of alcohol, food, and dancing has left me in that state of mind where I might wobble, the world might spin slightly, but I'm totally absorbed in myself and nothing is more important than the point I'm trying to make. It's surprising how eloquent frost sprinkled pine trees can be in such a debate.

"It was a pretty good plan, I mean, I haven't looked at another woman since I got hooked on Reddy. What? Oh yeah, sharp as your needles aren't you? Straight to the heart of the issue. Well, it was her fault for being so damn fanciable. I mean, what were the chances of us having so much in common? And if she'd only been completely uninterested, then..."

"Mmm, yeah, you could be right, she probably is completely uninterested. It's all been in my head, hasn't it?"

The next lamp post is rigid in its silent assent.

"How old are you Steven? Thirty-one, and you're acting like a fifteen year old."

A branch points accusingly.

"Yes, and a drunk misogynist fool, too."

A picture of Abi with a hurt and angry expression pops into my mind.

"You'd look like that, if you knew. Not you," I say to a six foot pine which has somehow missed the Christmas cut, "Abi." The two syllables of her name bounce off each other inside my head until they find a way out through salty water. I'm not sure how long I continue to sob, but the backs of my gloves are white with a mixture of freezing tears and snot by the time I am finally aware of my surroundings again. A quick glance towards the next distance marker shows me that I'm about a quarter of the way round the lake. The alcohol anaesthetic must be wearing off, because I discover the weak point in my apparel. With hat, gloves, scarf and thermal coat, my body is toastie, almost sweating, but my feet are... Well, where are they? I stamp and can just about feel something. A warm hotel room suddenly feels very appealing and I turn.

"What I need to do is lay low for a while," I blow in between sharp breaths. I'm walking at top speed. "Keep my nose clean." I wipe it again on the back of my right glove for good measure. "Be a Mark."

An image of Mark holding forth about squeaky pop singers springs from nowhere. He has got a point. What about a song with a low vocal. Why shouldn't it work? In fact, what about a song ABOUT singing in a low voice? The seeds of a comedy song start to split and green shoots emerge. A title, I need a title. 'Low'? No. 'Deep'? Yes: full of possible double meanings. How to start?

Deep

Would you fancy a man who talked like a girl?
Would you, would you really?
Squeaky voice and your heart's all in a whirl?
I don't think so, not even nearly.

So will they answer me this question?
'cause it's been buggin' me so long.

Why do you sing like your pants are broken, not your voice?
Attract some bats if you really have to, guys that is your choice.
But if you want to snare a real beauty, don't twitter and cheep,
'cause everyone knows girls like it deep,
oh yeah, everyone knows girls like it deep.

Did someone buy them their first razor today?
'Cos that is what it sounds like.
Maybe it's not just the penny that hasn't dropped
when they step up to the mic.

So will they solve this strange conundrum,
'cause it just seems so wrong?

Why do you sing like your first chest hair grew yesterday?
Guys, let me tell you there's a far more sexy way:
If you want to catch a real stunner,
don't bleat like a sheep,
'cos everyone knows girls like it deep,
oh yeah, everyone knows girls like it deep.

They like it deep...

    The plate glass doors of the Central Hotel coalesce in front of me. My mind wrenches with that 'how did I get here?' feeling. You know the one: you're driving home, thinking about that tricky problem at work; suddenly, you're outside your house switching off the engine and you've no recollection of turning off the by-pass or crossing the high street. You did stop and look, didn't you?

    I wave at Katri whilst scraping the snow off my shoes. She buzzes me in, "You look happy, Steven." I must be smiling about the song. I shrug with a grin.

    "You not as drunk as others?" she continues.

    "Oh, I probably am." I can feel lyrics fading. "I'm sorry Katri," I say pacing past the desk, "I'd love to stop and chat, but I've got to write something down before I forget it."

    Katri's slightly put out face slides out of view behind the closing lift door and I begin to hum again.

CHAPTER 18

We're as talkative as coffin bearers. The gentle purr of the site office fan heaters might as well be a jet engine straining before takeoff. Every rustle of paper makes me wince. Tapping on keyboards has been totally banned for at least the morning.

John gives in to the inevitable first. "It's gonnae have to be a full site inspection then," he whispers. We all nod.

As we cross the rutted snowscape the final exterior building panels are being lowered into place: royal blue corrugated sheeting, its gloss already somewhat dulled by a mixture of dust and frost. Mikko is supervising. He regards our pale faces, water bottles, and notes, with an amused expression, our winces as the crane engine revs. "Aha, site inspection morning, I see," he says rather louder than necessary. "I speak to you in afternoon."

Mikko has been around the block long enough to know that when you're too hung over to do any real work, a site inspection is a good excuse for a head clearing stroll, with plenty of deep breaths and a minimum amount of concentration required. Occasionally, we even find something that needs noting down. After an hour or so, Mark and I have got as far as the dies, whilst John and Keith have descended into the hydraulic cellar to check the recently cast standby pump foundations. We are just about up to quiet conversation.

"What was going on with you and Reddy last night?" says Mark out of nowhere.

"That noticeable was it?"

"You looked like you were hell bent on showing her what a bear's backside you can be."

"Maybe, I was... subconsciously," I muse.

"It didn't look like there was much thought going on."

"We were all pretty drunk. What would Jane say?" Mark turns away. He can be so touchy about that. I sit down on a convenient electric motor and continue, "I guess I've been a bit stupid, a bit infatuated, and it all came out in one go. I mean, all this falling in love with Reddy to stop me being interested in other women. It's just swapping one problem for another."

"Swapping a small problem for a big problem," says Mark with feeling. "Trust you to choose just about the most attractive girl in town."

"That was supposed to be the point: that she was unobtainable... I didn't think it through very well, did I?"

Mark shrugs. "And it's not like Abi isn't really nice." He almost sounds jealous.

I smile ruefully. "I know... the phrase that springs to mind is 'hoist by my own petard'".

Mark shakes his head, "More like, give a man enough rope and he'll find a way to hang himself."

"Perhaps they should change that proverb to 'send a man to Finland and he'll find the most elaborate way possible of screwing up his relationships'," I suggest.

"Doesn't really trip off the tongue, does it?"

We both laugh and the hammering inside my skull seems to have shrunk from pile driver proportions to something more domestic in size.

- - -

"I THOUGHT I'D FIXED IT. That was the end of it." Hiltunen blinks and leans forwards as he realises I'm addressing him directly. "She was out of my head. For the first time in months, I wrote a song that had nothing to do with her at all."

"You think?" The psychologist's eyebrows are raised.

"Oh, come on. It's a comedy song. It's innuendo. You're not going to start asking me who I was thinking *'likes it deep'* are you?"

"No, Mr Thinker, I ain't." He stops the pencil mid twirl and jots a couple more notes. The slight smile on his lips fades as he writes. "This little head clearing stroll of yours – that was in the same forest as..."

"Yup. Yet another way in which I'm totally screwed. I was congratulating myself that I'd pulled back from the edge, that I'd rescued myself from any life-cocking up possibilities, and all the time I was totally screwed." Hiltunen keeps his head lowered but furrows his forehead just enough so he can scrutinise me through his eyebrows. "Mind you, even later that day, I was getting the feeling that something had gone to shit."

+ + +

"IT CAN'T STILL BE YOUR SHIFT," I say to Katri as I enter reception using the back door from the car park. It's 6:30pm and she was on the desk last night, and this morning.

"I work late shift, then evening shift."

"Ah, so you've been sleeping while I've been at work?"

"I not sleep well in day." I peer a bit closer and see the tiredness under her makeup.

"And you drew the short straw last night," I say with a sympathetic smile.

"Short what?" Her expression is quizzical.

"Drawing the short straw. It means being unlucky. You missed Hanne's party."

She shrugs, "Somebody have to work... But what is short straw?"

I smile inwardly at the Finns and their love of idioms! "It's a game you play to decide who does the bad job. Someone gets some straws or sticks and cuts them so they're all the same length except one short one. Then you hide them in your hand with only the ends sticking up. Whoever picks the short one has to do the bad job."

"Ah." Comprehension dawns across Katri's face. "I think in Finland we say nearly same thing: *'veti lyhyen korren'*.

I dutifully repeat the phrase.

"It means 'pull short end of the stick', but we say it if someone do the unlucky job, just the same." Katri raises her eyebrows. "Short one is always bad!"

I roll my eyes and tut, "So they say... Of course, I wouldn't know about that, obviously." And in the cold light of day this morning, I was worrying about the Deep lyrics being too rude! It's all in the head of the beholder.

The phone rings and I lean against the counter whilst Katri takes a booking. She taps away on the keyboard, gripping the receiver between ear and shoulder. I listen to see if I can catch the 'goodbye'; there seem to be so many different words for it.

"...*kuulemiin*" says Katri and replaces the handset. I've not heard that one, but before I form a linguistic question, she lifts one corner of her mouth and says, "So you not too busy to talk to me today?"

"Sorry about last night. Was I a bit rude?"

Katri shrugs, non-committally. I guess I was then.

"I was a bit drunk and I had the words of a song in my head and I needed to write them down before I forgot."

"You write songs?"

"Yes, well, a bit. They never really get played anywhere. They're probably rubbish, but I enjoy doing it," I shrug my slight embarrassment at the subject. But this is something Katri didn't know about me and it has obviously piqued her curiosity.

"What the song about?"

"Oh it's just a joke really. It's about why male singers, pop stars, rappers, even metal bands sing in really high voices. They spend the whole time trying to look sexy, but..." I raise my voice to falsetto, "this is not very macho is it?"

She laughs, "I never think it, but it is strange." Then her expression alters. "I wonder if you write love song about beautiful karaoke singer?"

"No, that was the previous one," I banter back in automatic self defence. But it's not Keith winding me up, it's Katri, and from the start of a frown I see she's taken me literally. "Hey, I'm joking," I say and then think, 'am I?' Well, technically, *Harmony* wasn't the previous song I wrote. OK, I'm splitting hairs.

Katri stays silent.

"Whatever anyone has told you, it isn't true. I'm a one woman guy." She raises her eyebrows questioningly. I can imagine Abi doing exactly the same thing. "Look, I'm not going to deny that I find..." Should I name the name? "...Arwen attractive. We get on really well, but I'm married: I might think about it, but I'm not going to do anything."

"Ah, good boy," says Katri, but she doesn't seem convinced. Why do I feel the need to justify myself? It occurs to me that if Abi is right about Katri's feelings, then I do have a killer argument.

"You don't believe me do you?"

She shrugs. "Many men say this at home, but in hotel you see different."

"I'm sure you're right, but not everyone. Not Mark for instance."

"Maybe you ask Raakel where she go after party?"

"No, surely not?" My mouth is open. Cracks begin to appear in one of the cornerstones of my Mahikkala life.

Katri shrugs again.

"No, I can't believe it. I'd know."

"Believe it," she says simply. My head is in a whirl, but I'm not going to let this revelation beat me.

"Well, maybe everyone else is doing it, but not me."

Katri is amused by my earnest defence. "It something men do," she says in a resigned tone. "I say too much; save argument for your wife."

I slap both hands down flat on to the counter, "No, I'm not having you believe that. You see, Arwen isn't the only woman in Mahikkala that I find attractive." I hold eye contact. "There's also this hotel receptionist..."

"You need watch out for them," she interrupts, her smile having turned rueful.

"So it would seem, but this receptionist has such warm eyes and we talk together so easily. She finds silly innuendos as funny as I do and even though I recently found out that she has a very poor view of most men..." Katri's eyes soften and begin to glisten with moisture. "... when she smiles with tears in her eyes, it would be very easy to fall for her." One lonely tear runs down a pale cheek. I feel mean as I finish, "But I'm not going to, because I married someone else first and she's great too."

"This receptionist is sorry," says Katri. She takes a deep breath and reaches past the printer for a tissue. As she dabs at her eyes and cheek, she adds, "Sorry, I not believe you."

The lift pings and a tall blonde man appears. He glances from Katri to me curiously, but apparently makes no comment. He asks a short question, Katri motions to the left and I catch the name 'Hanne'. After the doors have closed behind him, I say, "Another free drink earned."

"Yes, I have many next time." She regards me, purses her lips to one side and makes a decision. "Someone called Tilia visit this afternoon."

"Ah..."

"She ask if Arwen spend the night with you. No one see her since party. I know you come in late, I think maybe you..."

"I see. No, I wasn't doing anything like that. I was walking round the lake feeling guilty for ever fancying her in the first place. I was a bit drunk at the party. I asked her to dance and didn't take 'no' very well. I think a lot of people saw."

Katri nods as if she already knew this, "Tilia was quite scared for her. She not answer her phone."

"Well the last time I saw her she was having a blazing row with her boyfriend. They probably kissed and made up and have been at it like rabbits all day. You know how it can be after an argument."

"Yes..." says Katri with an expression that seems to mix wistfulness with pain. I wonder what that's from? "Steven," Katri says in a suddenly more businesslike voice, "you help me with something?"

"Just so long as it doesn't involve any unbuttoning." She rolls her eyes. "Sorry, I spend so much time around Keith, sometimes one just pops out... What is it you want?"

Katri passes me a colourful laminated card with her neatly manicured fingers. It appears to be a cocktail menu for the restaurant. "We make up some new drinks for special meals. Can you read English names. Are OK?"

I scan down the list and stop at the third one, "You'd probably say 'head banger' not 'head hitter'". Katri makes a note. "Oh," I dissolve into a fit of giggles.

"Which?" says Katri, as I steady myself against the counter.

"You can't," I gasp for a breath, "call it that!" Katri follows my finger to the second last entry. Someone has clearly tried for the same effect as a Bacardi 'breezer' but the name they've plumped for is 'Fresh Wind'! Katri looks puzzled. "It would be fine," I laugh, "if it wasn't that in England we use 'wind' as a polite word for 'fart'."

'Perkele,' swears Katri. (I don't know exactly what it means, but you hear it a lot.) "I glad I not copy all of them yet," she snorts with one hand over her eyes.

"Oh, that has cheered me up. I am so going to dine out on that one for months," I say, still grinning, as I make my way to the lift.

CHAPTER 19

Mark has joined me for a pre-dinner beer at Hanne's. It is Saturday, but it's still unusual. I think I know why. I'm wondering whether and how to broach the subject when Hanne asks, "Recover from the party now?"

"Just about," I reply, "Great bash."

"You not seen Arwen today, Steven?"

"You're the second person to ask me that. I don't know why anyone thinks I should know where she is," I reply tetchily. "I suppose she's with Kari."

"She not with Kari. She should be here now," says Hanne, slight concern in her voice.

"Maybe she's finally decided to leave it all behind and follow her dream. She had a place at Kuopio music academy, you know?" From her expression, this seems to be news to Hanne. Perhaps it's not the sort of thing you discuss with your boss. Hope I haven't said more than I should. "She did seem in a bit of a strange mood on Thursday night," I continue.

"I thought that was because you kept pawing at her," says Mark. Hanne turns away to serve another patron.

"Talking about pawing on Thursday night, I heard something very interesting about you and a certain receptionist."

Mark's face pales and contorts. There's something slightly scary about him that I've never seen before. Should've stayed quiet. When he speaks it's in a slow, carefully controlled tone, "I didn't hear what you just said... and if you're my friend... you'll never talk about it again."

"Rutting elks," I exclaim, not having believed the truth of it until now, "Sorry man."

"It only takes one slip..."

"To screw up your life," I finish for him, nodding in agreement.

We're sitting facing each other, staring down at our beers in the silent understanding known as brotherhood, when my head jerks sideways. The force of the blow knocks me off the stool and my ear pounds against the bar before I slip downwards. Before I hit the ground a heavy boot catches me in the ribs, and again in the right kidney. I try to curl up, protecting my head with my arms. I can hear Mark and others shouting. My attacker swings again, but the foot strikes the wood above me and then stops.

I uncurl slightly, the metallic taste of blood in my mouth and peer up between my forearms. Through the blur I can see Mark and the bouncer holding Kari's arms behind his back in a tight lock. Kari is gibbering in Finnish. I can't see the detail of his face but I suppose he sees my eyes.

"I know it was you, you bastard," he shouts with a mixture of venom and agony. "What did..." He falters under a verbal onslaught from Hanne who has stepped between us. Even Mark and the bouncer seem to be backing away from her tirade, dragging a struggling Kari with them.

Hanne waves dismissively towards the door, takes a quick glance towards me and concludes in English, "I not want to hear it. There is no reason for fight in my bar – period." She turns, reaches to the floor and bends to slide my surprisingly intact specs over my ears. "Careful, you lie on all broken glass."

With her assistance, I slowly rise up to a sitting position. My head is pounding and I feel slightly sick. My tongue feels round my teeth for the source of the blood. All seem present and correct; I think it must be a split lip.

"Are you OK?" asks Hanne, as I prod tentatively against my side where the kicks landed. It doesn't feel like anything is broken but I bet the bruises will go all the colours of the rainbow.

"I think so. Oh." The wetness I had assumed to be sweat on my left arm appears to be a small patch of blood surrounding a shard of glass which has pierced my shirt in about the place you have injections. My immediate, unthinking reaction is to tug at it. The sliver does come out, but its departure is followed by a stinging pain which causes me to breathe in sharply between my teeth. The flow of blood quickens. It's not spurting out like I've severed an artery or anything, but it is dribbling fast.

"Have you got a towel or something?" I ask, but Hanne is already on to it. A wet flannel followed by a clean tea towel is thrown across the bar. I unbutton my shirt and slide the left arm out of the dripping sleeve. Hanne sets to work mopping my arm so we can see the source of the damage. She has a firm businesslike touch.

"You weren't a nurse in a previous life, were you Hanne?" I ask.

"No, but my sister has two boys. When I stay I spend lot of time cleaning blood from knees."

"I remember that phase."

"Oh..." Hanne chuckles with relief. I follow her eyes up my stained arm and join in.

"A lot of blood from a very small cut."

"Hold." I take over pressing the towel against my shoulder and Hanne straightens up, arching her back to stretch out of the hunched position she had taken over me. The ringing in my head is subsiding and I'm able to think about what happened.

"What was that all about?" I say to Hanne.

"Kari make no sense."

"But it's something to do with Arwen, isn't it?"

Hanne shrugs and turns. "I told them to throw him out," she says indignantly, leaving me, back propped up against the bar, sitting next to a puddle of beer, blood and glass.

Kari has been released and is now standing half bent over, gripping one of the coat stands for support. The bouncer is poised inches from him, clearly ready to pounce on any unexpected movement, but his face seems strangely unsure. Not that Kari looks like he is up for a continuation. Sobs are pulsing through his body; tears and snot are pouring off the end of his chiselled nose. I don't feel any anger; it was all too sudden, unexpected. There wasn't any goading, any posturing, just wham. Does he think I spent the night with Arwen too?

Hanne stops to exchange a few words with Mark who is glancing uncertainly from Kari to me and back again. I wish I could hear what he said because Hanne rushes to Kari, lifts his chin and stares into his tearful eyes. Kari nods to Hanne's question. Her shoulders start to droop, but she turns towards the doorman who lifts a mobile from the case clipped to his belt and makes a call. His face is being scrutinised by Hanne and Mark. Kari just stares at the floor. After about twenty seconds, the doorman closes his eyes and flails the side of a fist against the wall. Hanne gasps and pales. Mark grabs the nearest empty chair and slides it behind Hanne who sits down heavily. Pressing the disconnect button, the bouncer mumbles a couple of sentences through a shocked and contorted face. Hanne shakes her head, tears flooding down her face.

I don't care if I still feel groggy, I need to know what's going on. Releasing pressure from my arm I use the bar to pull myself up. A small amount of blood oozes out of the wound. I wipe it and reapply pressure as I pass tables, now empty, their few patrons having moved round to the other side of the bar, out of harm's way. It feels like I've just stepped off a ship after choppy seas: the perfectly still floor is rolling slightly. I steady myself on the back of a convenient chair.

"What's happened?"

Hanne raises her blotchy face but doesn't answer.

"Arwen's dead." I twist my head sharply towards Mark. The sudden movement is not a good idea, but physical pain is irrelevant. My brain is far too intent on searching Mark's face for traces of this being some elaborate wind up. I find none.

"No..." There doesn't seem to be anything else to say. There is silence between the five of us. A numbness settles. I stare vacantly until I realise that I'm staring straight at Kari's boots which ten minutes previously had been intent on kicking the crap out of me. My eyes trace his legs and torso upwards to find him staring back.

"I'm so sorry, man," I say quietly, "but why?" I gesture back towards myself with my left hand. Kari glares for a few seconds and then makes a dive towards me. The bouncer springs forward, Mark makes a grab for an arm, and the punch falls short and wide.

"I think..." gasps Mark, still struggling for a better grip, "Kari thinks... you had something to do with it." The arm lock is reinstated and they force Kari upright.

"You can't be serious," I say holding Kari's eye. I can see that he is.

"After the party here, you didn't go to your hotel, you turned down the road to the left. Where you go?" he spits.

I furrow my brow quizzically and shrug. "I went for a walk by the lake. I needed to sober up and think about a few things."

A flash of triumph plays across Kari's broken face, "And what happened when you met Arwen?"

"I didn't meet Arwen, I didn't see anyone."

"They found her by the lake," says Kari with the finality of ultimate proof.

I seek confirmation from Hanne who nods. She inclines her head towards the doorman. "Matti work as a policeman once. He ring a friend. They not say much, but they find body of young woman in forest by the lake this morning. Police think it is murder."

"What sort of sick bastard..." I start, shock turning to anger.

"You should know," says Kari tauntingly, then his voice turns bleak, "They say she was naked when they found her. What did you do?" He struggles for a moment but the grip is too tight. The doorman grunts a couple of words and Kari reluctantly relaxes.

I've had just about enough of this. "Look, Kari, I seem to remember that the last time I saw Arwen, you were having a big row with her: shouting, crying, the full works. Wasn't he?" Mark nods in agreement. "What were you arguing about? Maybe she said no to you and you couldn't take it? You've clearly got a temper." I indicate my various scars. "You seem the most likely suspect to me," I finish, taking a step forwards.

Hanne puts a firm hand on my knee and uses it to pull herself up to stand between us, "Boys, it not either of you. It some sick pervert. The police will find him." She looks from me to Kari, "You think Arwen want to see you two fight? She is dead. Stop think with your balls, think with your heart." She turns having seen the effect of her words on our faces and claps her hands together twice, "Everybody drink quickly and leave, we closing." She repeats it in Finnish.

A few minutes later, I'm walking back to the hotel with Mark, thick heavy snowflakes sticking to my thermal coat. Kari is being escorted by Matti in the other direction. I have no appetite for dinner. As the plate glass doors slide open, I see Raakel behind the counter, twirling a lock of hair round her pen. Mark's step falters slightly but he carries on staring intently towards the lift button until his finger touches it.

"What happen to you?" Raakel calls, but chit chat seems meaningless.

"Don't ask," I say, part turning, but not breaking my stride in Mark's wake.

I'VE NEVER WATCHED the local TV channel before. I don't know why I am. I'm not going to understand anything even if there is some news. The contestants on some mindless game show are answering questions. Each time they get one right (I suppose) a stepping stone appears in front of their partners who are trying to cross a fluorescent blue pool. If they get it wrong then a stone lowers. The audience is enjoying the frequent splashes. How can they carry on as if nothing has happened? Don't they know?

The credits can't roll soon enough, but I don't want to look away in case I miss it. Eventually, the one dry contestant collects the keys to their new car and the adverts begin. Please let it be the news next. It's not; it's the Finland lottery draw. Who will be lucky tonight? The draw is only a short program and soon hopefully-boring-looking titles begin to play. A smart man sitting behind a desk confirms that this is, finally, the news.

Almost immediately they cut to a snow speckled reporter standing on a ski track in a night-time forest. Behind him, temporary arc lights reveal a hive of activity behind luminous yellow tape. There is a large orange tent off to the right. Attached to the side of it, a curved plastic tunnel stretches back towards the track. Crime scene investigators, officers with dogs, contractors attaching extra guy ropes: all are decked out in serious cold weather gear against the rising blizzard. I wish I could understand more Finnish. Still, I don't suppose the reporter's really saying much. The police won't have given anything out yet. The picture flicks back to the studio and a photo is superimposed to the side of the presenter. I squint at it. It is Arwen, but it must be 2 or 3 years ago: she's still a girl. She's got a perm and her hair's not red, it's plain mousy brown. The newsreader says the name: Arwen Saarinen but that's all I can catch.

They cut again, this time to an official looking man with a shrewd face and slightly greying temples. He is flanked by uniformed officers on the front steps of what I recognise to be Mahikkala police station. He is obviously reading a carefully phrased statement and answers no questions. The camera pans sideways to another man, wearing an immaculate dark suit. Can't be a family member, he seems far too together. He makes compelling hand gestures as he talks. His face shows apparent pain but no tears. Local politician saying that he and the rest of the community are shocked and saddened, I bet: just another photo opportunity.

The main presenter reappears, this time with a photo of a saw mill to his right. I hit the red button and let myself fall back, tears running down the sides of my face and on to the bedspread.

- - -

"I NEVER EVEN KNEW HER SURNAME until I heard it on TV," I say, blinking away the wetness forming in the corners of my eyes. "Arwen Saarinen - she wouldn't have needed a stage name."

"And that beautiful red hair..."

"Was from a bottle... Yeah, I mean, obvious really. Who actually has chestnut hair?" Hiltunen nods, but does not comment. His face remains neutral, like an undertaker's, whilst he waits for me to continue. "It sort of completely knocked me out. I knew her so superficially and yet it felt like the world had ended."

+++

I'M AWOKEN BY MUSIC and an insistent tickling from my jeans pocket. It's 12:25am. Bollocks, forgot to phone Abi. Still prone on my back, I flip open the mobile. Before I even speak:

"Were you ever going to get round to phoning me then?"

"Sorry, I... I just forgot. It's been a bit mad here today."

"Are you alright?" says Abi with her usual sixth sense.

"Fine," pops out automatically, but then my brain catches up with my mouth. "No, actually I'm not alright, I'm pretty crap really."

"What is it?"

"You know how I've told you about Hanne's Bar? Well, one of the women who works there has been killed."

"What, in a car crash?"

"No, it seems like it's murder."

"Gosh." There's a pause. "And you knew her quite well?"

"She's always been friendly to us. She's the red haired one with the strange name: Arwen, you remember?"

"Oh yeah. Did you say you'd danced with her?"

"Yeah, we bumped into her and her boyfriend quite often when we were out."

"He must be going out of his mind."

"Believe me, he is." I pull my knees towards me and roll sideways so that I'm in a sitting position facing the mirror. The right side of my lip is purple with scab and a reddening bruise is forming across my jaw. "I think I was one of the last people to see her. There was a party at Hanne's on Thursday."

"You never told me you were going to that."

"No, we didn't even know about it until an hour beforehand. She was celebrating paying off her mortgage. We had a free bar for an hour. It was absolutely mental. Everyone was wrecked."

"Even Mark?"

"Well, he's never as bad as the rest of us," I say, loyally.

"You're drinking too much, you know? I'm worried."

"I'm OK. It was a one off. Anyway, Reddy was there."

"Reddy?"

"Arwen. Keith's nickname. He was going to call her 'Duracell', you know, the one with the copper coloured top."

"Not very original."

"No, that's what John said, so he changed brand to 'Ever Ready' and the Reddy bit stuck." I pause, "Now I've lost my track."

"You were saying Arwen was at this party."

"Yeah, and when we left, she was having a massive argument with her boyfriend on the street outside. No one's seen her since then."

"Do they think it was the boyfriend then?"

"I don't know. I don't think so."

"Wow, so you might be interviewed as a witness then?"

"Maybe," I shrug to the walls.

"How exciting!"

"Hey, this isn't one of your whodunnit novels," I snap, "this is real life. It isn't exciting, it's... complete shit."

I think Abi is surprised by the force in my voice, "Sorry, I... It's just so far away. It doesn't seem real," she mutters.

"It does to me."

Now that Abi's on the back foot, I'm hating this conversation even more. I'm tiptoeing round the truth. I haven't lied, I'm just not saying everything. But I still feel devious. She should be yelling at me. But there's no point upsetting Abi over nothing, is there? I mean, nothing happened and nothing can ever happen, can it? The thought causes me to well up again.

My voice cracks slightly as I continue, "She was just so friendly and funny, and young... It seems so unfair."

"Bless you, you're crying aren't you?" Abi has always loved that I cry. No macho posing for her.

"Maybe... Anyway," I sigh, "Did your Mum choose a sofa then?" I say, grasping at a straw of normality. The lack of enthusiasm must be very apparent in my voice.

"You don't really want to chit chat do you?" says Abi.

"Not really. I'm sorry, it's just..."

"It's OK. I've not been doing much anyway. Steve?"

"Yes?"

"Close your eyes."

"They're closed."

"I'm giving you a big hug."

"Thanks," I say, in a whisper. "Love you."

"Love you too. Bye."

"Bye."

The wave of grief laden sleep that took me earlier has now completely passed and I pace the room. I know what I want to do, but somehow it seems... unfaithful. I clean my teeth, put my stained clothes in a linen bag, turn the TV on and then off again.

"I'm sorry Abi, but I have to do this," I say out loud. It takes no effort to write; no inspiration is needed, no pondering on lyric or melody. All I have to do is grip the pen and my heart pumps the ink on to the page. All I have to do is listen and the silence of your extraordinary voice weaves a melancholy tune: a requiem for you.

Requiem for you

You lit up the room without trying.
Seemed your life was defying
anyone not to like you.
When you smiled it made my heart warm:
thermal spring in a snowstorm.
Now it's all frozen over.

I want to scream against the world,
my banner of rage is unfurled,
but I don't know where I should wave it.
I want to make somebody pay
and let the lynch mob have its day,
but that won't bring you back now, will it?

Stolen, out of time;
Clocks will never chime;
All that I have is an imprint on my mind.
So much left to do;
Missed your grand debut;
My star, this is a requiem for you.

You loved living life in a whirlwind.
Seemed like you must be destined
for the extraordinary.
The future was yours for the taking.
So much more than heartbreaking
that you never will see it.

I want to scream...

Stolen...

    Dictaphone to ear and book in hand, the trembles and sniffs of a cracked voice transform into a full orchestration as I listen to the night's pain. It's probably the best thing I've ever written. I hate it. Outside, a plough is beginning to scrape the freshly fallen snow from the street. The grating of bucket against tarmac is the sound of the futile cleansing of a dirty world. I decide it's time for a shower.

CHAPTER 20

Erik stares, mouth open in feigned shock as I walk past him for breakfast at 7:01am. He doesn't receive the pithy response that his cheek expects. OK, so usually I'd be down almost 3 hours later on a Sunday, but I'm not normally up all night and humour seems... pointless. I shrug and pass by into the dining area. A generous helping of meat balls and baked beans, a couple of pieces of toast and I'm still unsatisfied. Would fruit or cereal be any better? Erik interrupts my coffee sipping reverie:

"Steven, there are some men in reception who want talk to you."

"OK, I'll just be a minute." I gulp the last few mouthfuls, choose a particularly shiny apple and walk through to the front of the building. Have I forgotten about some supplier arriving for a meeting tomorrow? The older of the two men does seem familiar. He raises a leather wallet towards me which displays a metal crest with the same Finnish word across the centre as I've seen on black and white cars. I place him as the man reading the statement on the news last night. Police, then, already.

"Steven Carter?"

"Yes."

"Detective Chief Inspector Aaltonen." He indicates the other, stockier, man: "Detective Sergeant Kotka. We ask you some questions." He turns towards Erik. "Can we use back office?"

"Of course," says Erik and ushers us past the end of the counter. I've never been into the hotel office. I haven't missed anything. The Inspector heads round the small pine meeting table to take the high backed 'power chair' at the end. He indicates that I should take the seat to his left. Detective Kotka closes the door behind him and sits opposite me. There's a slightly intimidating pause whilst he unzips his overcoat and reaches deep into layers for his phone.

I pass the apple from hand to hand. "I suppose this is about Arwen then?" Inspector Aaltonen raises his eyebrows questioningly. "I saw you on TV last night. It's a terrible thing."

He nods. "We try to talk to everyone who was at the Hanne Bar last Thursday evening. You were there with three other English? Mark Hatfield, Keith Smith, John McLeod?"

"Yes, but John won't thank you for calling him English."

"Ah, proud Scottish?" says the Inspector, a brief humourless smile playing on his lips.

"Yes."

"You were at the bar all evening?"

"Yes, we were invited to Hanne's party. She'd paid off the mortgage on the bar."

"We already speak to Ms Ryti," interrupts Kotka. He receives a quick glance from Aaltonen.

"Is that Hanne?" I ask. "I'm sorry, I don't know anyone's surname."

"Hanne Ryti, yes," says the Inspector, pulling his fingers along his stubbly jaw. I suspect he has been up all night as well. "You were asked to the party, but you do not know her well?"

"I suppose we're some of her best customers. We talk to her quite a bit. I think she considers us friends... I hope she does."

"This is how you know Ms Saar.., Ms Arwen Saarinen also."

"Yes, she works... worked at Hanne's Bar. She was friendly."

"And pretty," adds the detective.

"Yeah..." I say, casting Kotka a quizzical glance. Without thinking I take a bite from the apple. There's an embarrassing silence in which all I can hear is my own chewing. I feel my cheeks colouring as the two policemen wait for me to finish.

"I'm sorry, I was in the middle of breakfast when you..." I place the apple on the table and my hands in my lap.

"You see Ms Saarinen at the party?" The Inspector leans forward ever so slightly.

"Yes, I spoke to her a couple of times. She was with her boyfriend."

Kotka taps the smart phone on the desk in front of him, scrolling back through some text. I guess notepads have had their day. "Mr Varis?"

I look blank.

"Mr Kari Varis?"

"Kari, yes."

"She is normal. She say nothing strange?" asks Aaltonen.

I pause, trying to recall how she seemed. "I don't know. Did Hanne tell you there was a free bar?" Aaltonen nods. "So almost everyone was drunk. I suppose she was too. I think her and Kari were arguing about something. They certainly were afterwards." Out of the corner of my eye, I see the detective tap some notes.

"You see Arwen after the party?"

"Yes. As we left..."

"We?" interrupts Kotka.

"Myself, Mark and John."

"Mr Keith Smith?"

"I don't know, he left earlier."

"Continue," says the Inspector.

"As we left Hanne's we saw Arwen and Kari standing on the street corner, opposite the bank. She was shouting at him when we passed."

"You hear what they say?"

"It was in Finnish," I shrug. "Ask Kari."

"We will," says Aaltonen.

"Dea and Raakel, receptionists from this hotel, were just behind us. They might have heard something."

"Ah, thank you." The inspector says a few words to Kotka in Finnish.

"What time?" asks Kotka.

"Just after 2am. Hanne threw us all out at two, so I suppose it must have been about ten past."

"Then you go back to hotel?"

Again I feel heat flowing into my cheeks: I know how this is going to sound. "Err, no. I think Mark and John went straight back to the hotel, but I went for a walk to clear my head."

"And where you walk?" asks Aaltonen.

"I went down the street with the bank on it, across the main road and through the wood to the lake. I was going to walk all the way round, but my feet got cold so I turned round and..." I trail off. Both men are sitting bolt upright. I glance from one to the other. "I know... I went for a walk through the wood where her body's been found. But I didn't see anyone at all. Do they know what time she died?"

Aaltonen recovers his neutral pose and says, "We wait for test results. What time did you come back from this walk?"

"I'm not sure. About three maybe? Katri may know, she was on reception and saw me get in."

The Inspector holds eye contact with me for a moment as if trying to read my mind. Then his gaze drops slightly. "Mr Carter, how you get that cut?"

Shit, I'd forgotten about what I must look like. I become conscious of the ache too, now it's been mentioned. There isn't any way round this. "Kari punched me last night in Hanne's Bar."

"Kari Varis?" says the detective.

"Yes."

"He was in the Hanne Bar last evening?"

"Yes."

"Why did Mr Varis hit you?" asks Aaltonen.

I stare at the apple for a moment. The gleaming white bite mark is beginning to turn brown at the edges. They'll find out from someone else anyway... "He seemed to think that I had something to do with Arwen's death."

"And why he think that?"

"I don't really know. He was putting two and two together and making five." I lift my shirt to show the red bruises on my side. "He's got a temper."

Inspector Aaltonen purses his lips, "You want to make charge?"

"No," I shrug, "I think he's got enough problems at the moment."

He nods and stands. "Thank you Mr Carter, that is all questions for now. You not go back to England soon?"

"Not for another month at least."

"Good, we may need to see you again."

"Whatever I can do to help," I say passing back round the reception desk. Kotka says something to Erik and I catch the name Hatfield. Mark's turn next then.

I DIDN'T FEEL like going out tonight so I've had a meal in the hotel restaurant accompanied by that most distracting of companions: a good book. I'm just finishing off my glass of house red when Mark parks himself in the empty seat opposite. The waiter looks questioningly in his direction, but Mark shakes his head.

"I've been out for a burger," he says by way of unnecessary explanation.

"Healthy." I comment, placing the open novel face down on the cloth. "How was your interview this morning?" Mark seems surprised. "I was first. I heard them calling you down," I say in explanation.

"It was OK I suppose. I've never been interviewed by the police before. It's a bit scary."

"I know what you mean... Did they ask about me?"

Mark shifts uncomfortably, "Um, yes, they asked if I knew where you walked to and if I saw Arwen follow."

"Did you?"

"No, she was still shouting at Kari when I last looked. Anyway, I just stopped off at Hanne's to see if there was any news. Apparently, Kari's done a runner. The police are looking for him everywhere."

"So, he did it then?"

"Looks like it. But why did he hit you?"

"Maybe he just doesn't like my face," I shrug.

"It is an improvement."

"Thanks a bunch, mate." I grimace at him and then regret it. The soreness is always worse the day after. A thought occurs to me, "Did they ask you what you did when you got back to the hotel?"

"No, thank Woden."

- - -

"YOU'RE NOT going to write up word for word what I've said are you?"

A slightly frustrated expression plays on Hiltunen's face for a moment. "Why do you say that?"

"I've been blabbing about Mark's, err... indiscretion and I said to him I wouldn't tell anyone. It isn't relevant. There's no point mangling his life too." This wretched psychologist with his stupid accent and his 'just live it' has had me saying all sorts of stuff I didn't mean to.

"What makes you think his life ain't already up the creek?"

"Maybe it is, but I don't want to be the one to add to it." I glance round the office, determined not to be the next one to speak. It's full of clutter, but I'm struggling to spot anything really personal. There are box files, stacks of paper, the odd magnetic desk toy thing, but where are the photos, the awards, the 'world of tractors' calendar? It's almost as if it has been staged. My eyes slip towards the other side of the desk where a bemused smile is playing on Hiltunen's lips. Maybe he's just paranoid about being analysed by his patients. I suppose that would be prudent.

"Ain't gonna say no more until I agree? Is that it?" He raises one eyebrow. "Remind me how old you are?"

"Thirty-one going on three and a half," I say in the voice of a petulant child.

Hiltunen snorts and shakes his head. "I ain't gonna tell on your pal Mark. But not 'cause I think hiding it's the right thing. It'd just be a whole lot better coming from him."

"You think he should confess and take what comes?"

"Hell, yeah."

"But doesn't that go against what you were saying earlier about the definite thing always being worse?"

"Haw, haw..." I've set off Hiltunen's cartoon laugh again. "You got me there, Mr Thinker." He pushes his chair backwards, waiting until the chuckles subside. "Folk's heads aren't like your engineering. There ain't no hard rules. You gotta take it case by case. Case by case..."

+ + +

CHAPTER 21

"Come on, Stevie, it'll take your mind off it. Too much thinking is ne'er any good," says John through my half open door.

"Alright then, but I'm not going to Hanne's. Not yet."

"We donae have to." I pick up my wallet and key card and swing the thermal coat over my shoulders.

"We were thinking pizza," says John as the lift door slides back revealing Mark and Keith loitering in the lobby. Most of Saturday night's snow has been trucked away to wherever they dump it, but there are still a few mounds awaiting collection. As we pass one, a couple of kids, too old for the game really, are sliding down from its 1.5m summit. John pulls up short as one of them overshoots on to the pavement in front of him, laughs and picks himself up.

Eating is a quiet affair. Despite John's best intentions, our minds are still only on one subject. Even Keith is subdued. However, we are unanimous on darts and decent beer for afters. What else is there to do?

"Terrible thing this Arwen," says the barman as he lets the Guinness fill the first glass.

"You knew her?" I ask.

"A little. Small town, I see most people. She work at Hanne's Bar, people say."

"Yes, we often saw her in there."

"I see you talking to her in here few week ago? And her dark hair friend?"

"Yes, she was always very friendly." I don't really want this conversation and leave Mark to bring over the rest of the drinks.

I am as useless as ever at 501 down, but I try to give the darts my full concentration. After a few legs, John and Mark have two each, Keith one, and only I have none. Just hit the twenty this time, I think, but the first dart hits the five and overcompensating, the second hits the one.

"Er, Steve," says Mark hesitantly. I turn to see Til standing just inside the main door, but it's a Til I've never seen before: no makeup, puffy eyes, un-washed hair. She beckons. I can see a wild look in her eye, like you see in photos of kids in a war zone. As I come to a halt a metre away, she moves one foot slightly backwards.

"Oh Til, you must feel like you've lost a sister," I say. She nods, blinks and says, "Steven, look me in the eyes and say you not do it."

"Not you too." I almost stamp one foot like a petulant child. "Have you been talking to Kari?"

"Say it."

"You, of all people, Til, should know I would never have done anything to hurt Arwen. You know I thought she was amazing." She continues to hold my gaze. It's disconcerting the way she does this. I feel naked, but I'm not going to look away. Eventually her expression softens.

"She did like you. She never say, but I know." There are tears in her eyes.

"Arwen, Arwen..." I say shaking my head and reaching forwards. We hug, a desolate wet hug with no warmth, just a brief sharing of pain. I can feel her tears soaking through to my shoulder.

Til pulls back, "They arrest Kari. But I know he not do it."

"The last time I saw them, Arwen and Kari were arguing really badly."

"I know it," she says. "Kari wake Harri out of bed at two thirty Friday morning. He think she leave him. He think she go to you."

"I never saw her again. You sure about Kari?"

"I know him, Harri know him all our lives. He cannot do this."

"He can try to kick me to a pulp," I say pointing at my blackening jaw.

"Kari do this?" Til appears less sure of herself.

"And this," I say, raising the right side of my shirt. "Saturday night, just before he disappeared."

She puts her hand to her mouth, then shakes her head. "No, he do this because he think you hurt Arwen. Can be only reason."

"Maybe he couldn't stand her leaving him again?"

Til shakes her head. "No," she says with the finality of faith. "I go meet Harri at police station." She squeezes my right arm, turns and is gone. Her cloud of sorrow remains in the room. As I turn back towards the darts, several people look quickly away and I realise how quiet it is. Like the barman, I suppose everyone knows who she is.

The guys are standing wordlessly watching my approach. Mark hands me the final un-thrown dart. I sling it with venom. It misses; strikes the chalk board to the left; falls. No one bothers to pick it up.

"IT'S ALWAYS THE BOYFRIEND," says Abi with the certainty of a hundred crime thrillers to back her up.

"I hope they've got it wrong. He seemed quite a nice guy... really," I add, my jaw aching slightly from talking. It's a good job we've never got into skyping. Sitting open between TV and minibar, my laptop displays a news photo of a young man, towel over his head, being bundled into a police car. The man's build, the same as Kari's, seems to belie my hope.

"I suppose there'll be a trial," says Abi.

"I guess so, I don't know how it works here."

"You might be a witness." I can hear worry in her voice.

"What?"

"They won't make you stay out there until it's finished will they?"

"No," I say automatically, "No, I'm sure not. I suppose if I was needed, work would have to pay for me to come back here for the days I give evidence. It must be in their insurance somewhere. But it wouldn't be for a long time."

"Good," says Abi sounding unconvinced. She's been with me long enough to tell unsubstantiated waffle when she hears it. "Cos I'm missing you today."

"I'm missing you too." More than ever. "I think I'm ready to hear your Mum's sofa saga now..."

CHAPTER 22

We're not meant to be testing any of the stranding lines for another three weeks, but Terry is keen that we press on with the job as quickly as possible. Frankly, it's nice to be busy. Less time to think...

You always hope everything will work first time. It rarely does. Reels of pre-drawn wire have been shipped in from a rod mill; all the motors have been spun up and tested; Mikko is standing close to the big red E-stop button just in case there is a major problem. There's a certain sense of anticipation amongst all of us, contractor and client. It's one of the best bits of engineering: actually seeing your baby start to work. Someone somewhere in both companies will be moving a small green diamond on an electronic progress chart to indicate that on this Tuesday, 'commissioning' began. It doesn't even matter if nothing works to start with, the 'milestone' has been reached. And early too. Terry will probably be sending a self-congratulatory email round to all the directors before the day is out. If he's feeling benevolent he might even mention that the engineering team have done well. I'm not getting my hopes up.

We do get a strand out of the end, but it's a bit ropey, if you'll pardon the pun. It's deformed: too tight, but it's a start. We let it run for a couple of metres, Keith slowing down the rotation in manual mode, but it doesn't make any significant difference and we stop to consider options. Seemingly the die is not right for this size wire, or the wire is not the size we've been told. We power down the machine and send Mark back to the office for some measuring equipment.

"Always something when start up," says Mikko, but he doesn't seem that bothered.

"Not to worry, I've seen this many a time," says John. We turn as the hiss of a warm air curtain heralds the opening of the side door. We are expecting to see Mark return, micrometers in hand, but instead one of the labourers appears. He approaches and whispers something in Mikko's left ear.

"Steven, it seem there are two policemen at the main gate who want to talk to you."

"Oh... thanks." I glance towards John who waves me away with a no-problem-we-can-handle-it-without-you expression. Did they forget to ask something last time? I take the tunnel across to the main gate / canteen building, its newly glossed walls unconsciously aping the winter above.

"Cold today," says Inspector Aaltonen staring out of the plate glass windows of the waiting area beside the visitor's entrance. Every car has engine heater cables trailing from grey posts dotted along the ends of the parking bays. Beyond, deep, pristine snow has turned ornamental bushes into jelly-mould humps.

"Yes, even for here," I reply. The car thermometer read -32 as we drove in this morning. Detective Kotka has already taken one of the armless easy chairs. I am ushered on to a capacious settee where Aaltonen joins me. He crosses his right leg over his left, rests his left arm along the rounded back, and half turns towards me, uncomfortably close.

"Mr Carter, I have spoke to Kari Varis..."

"I heard you arrested him," I interrupt.

"Hmm. He is... how you say? I see it on your 'Bill' program."

"Helping with inquiries," inserts Kotka.

"Yes, that it." The inspector nods to his partner. "Kari Varis say that Ms Saarinen break up with him on street corner by the bank. Then she walk off quickly to follow you. Why would he say that?"

"Maybe he wants to blame me for something he did?"

"Maybe," says the Inspector. "I ask him why she would follow you and he say that she liked you. How well you know Ms Saarinen?"

"A bit, I've spoken to her quite a few times, but I don't know her anything like as well as Kari or Til do." I pause suddenly realising that I've been using the present tense. "I suppose you would have called us new friends."

"You are married and she was pretty girl," says Kotka, suggesting the question with his raised eyebrows.

"No, nothing like that, we just liked the same things."

"Things?" asks Aaltonen.

"Dancing, karaoke, having a laugh."

The inspector puts an index finger to his mouth in thought. "Is possible that Ms Saarinen like you more than you think?"

Whatever Til says, Arwen didn't seem interested on Thursday night. The inspector waits patiently as I consider my answer. "No, I don't think so. I think she loved Kari. A few weeks ago they split up and I actually got them back together again. She seemed pretty pleased about that."

"You got them back together?" repeats Aaltonen.

I shrug. "Yes, I persuaded Arwen to sing Kari a karaoke song, a love song, and by the end they were all smiles and kisses."

"Man of many talent," says Kotka wryly, practising his idioms. "You dance with her on Thursday?"

At the edge of my vision I think I see Aaltonen's right hand make a small gesture. My eyes flick that way but it's still again. If it did move...

"No. She didn't dance much that night."

"Did you ask her to dance?" The questions swap back to Aaltonen.

"Yes, a couple of times, but she said no. Doesn't sound like she was secretly in love with me, does it?"

"No," says Aaltonen. "You may think this strange question, but did you touch her at all at party? Hug? Shake hands?"

"No," I start, "Hang on, yes, I held her wrist one time I asked her to dance and..." I blush slightly at the recall, "I grabbed her waist during the 'Macarena'." Aaltonen raises his eyebrows questioningly, but Kotka says a few words in Finnish and puts his hands out in front of him, palm first, one at a time, smirking slightly. Aaltonen nods once.

"We like to take DNA sample, so if we find any on wrist or clothes we can know if you," he says.

"Of course," I say. Seems like a good idea. The detective reaches into a pocket and produces a sealed packet of swabs and a plastic bag.

"Just rub in mouth and then put in bag." I do as bidden and hand it back.

"Thank you Mr Carter, we not keep you from work any longer," says the Inspector, standing.

I watch them leave through the sliding doors, somewhat bemused. It was hardly worth them coming, I didn't seem to tell them anything worthwhile. Still, I suppose police work is full of fruitless interviews.

CHAPTER 23

A smiling Mikko slides the water jug across the canteen table and forks another chunk of liver. I'm not a great fan of offal in general, but the berry sauce makes it bearable, and besides there isn't any other option left, we're so late for lunch.

"*Kiitos.*" I pour myself a glass and comment to John, "So we'll do the 31 machine on Friday then?"

"You've got enough reels for that, haven't you Mikko?" says John.

"Yes and we cut them this time!" A few chuckles rise against the background of clangs and rattles emanating from behind the serving hatch: the sounds of loading industrial dishwashers, I suppose. Everyone is in a jovial mood. Across in the new building a perfect hundred metre length of 19 wire rope is coiled up on a pallet. A laminated piece of A4 card with the words "First strand" in English and Finnish is taped to it. In Mikko's pocket is a digital camera with soon-to-be-emailed photos of the team standing behind the fruits of our labours, proudly grinning under logoed helmets.

Yesterday, things hadn't seemed so positive. When Mark measured the wire we found it was oversize. Mikko was embarrassed. It would be days before he could get replacements. We searched to see if we had supplied any larger dies for different strand configurations that might work, but nothing doing. This morning Mikko turned up at our site office complaining that the wire mill sales director was not answering his phone. 'Surely they'd have checked the size,' we all said. That was when I had a thought. 'I don't suppose they've left an over gauge length on the front of the reels?' We virtually sprinted out of the office.

It was so daft, you had to laugh. For the first 30 metres or so, the wire on each reel was too thick, then it quickly decreased to the expected diameter. Normally they cut that bit off at the mill before sending out the reels. Mikko quickly assembled his team of labourers and after some cutting and rethreading, here we are: all satisfied smiles.

It's almost 3pm before we finish lunch. Mark stands first and carries his tray over to one of the empty racks.

"Back to the grindstone, I suppose," I say and follow. Before Mark has finished sliding his tray home, the heavy double doors to his left are swung open by one of the security guards from the gate house. She is followed by Inspector Aaltonen and two uniformed officers.

"More questions?" asks Mark, but Aaltonen ignores him and continues towards me. His expression is very serious, grim in fact.

"Put down your tray," he says. I'm only five yards from one of the racks, but he is standing resolutely in my path and I suppose he means right here. I place the tray on a table to my left, a look of puzzlement playing on my face.

"Steven Carter, I arrest you for murder of Arwen Saarinen."

"Wha..?" My head snaps up towards the Inspector and I take a step backwards. Two pairs of strong hands grab my arms and push me sprawling on to the table. The glass on my tray is upset, spills its inch of remaining water, and starts to roll towards the edge. Involuntarily, I try to reach forward to catch it, but I'm in a vice, cheek pressed against the hard surface. As my wrists feel the cold touch of metal, I can only watch the glass roll agonisingly on, reach the edge, fall with a surprising pop.

I'm yanked back upright, handcuffs secure. "You have right to a lawyer before you answer questions or you may stay quiet." The two uniforms start to march me towards the door. "Which is his coat?" says Aaltonen to Mark, who can only gawp and point. Before I reach the door I see him take a blue plastic bag from his jacket pocket and start to unfold it.

John's shout follows me down the corridor: "Hang in there, Stevie, I'll make some calls..." People press themselves against the wall or peer out of offices as we pass. The remaining guard opens the gate beside the usual rotary barrier and we are into the lobby. A ridiculous thought occurs: I haven't signed out. I suppose John will sort that out.

There are four police cars parked across the main gate. Four cars! Any minute someone is going to jump out of one of them and shout 'you've been framed'. They are all empty. I start to shiver without my coat as we head for the leftmost car. One of my guards opens the rear door and slides across to the passenger side. The other pushes me on to the seat by my shoulder and indicates that I should shuffle across to the middle. He follows, slamming the door behind him, completing the unpalatable Steven sandwich. Silence.

"What now?" I say.

"Wait," says the man on my right. Somebody does speak English then.

"But I haven't done anything... I thought you already had Kari?"

"Wait, Aaltonen." I've had better responses from pine trees. Still I don't think these two have been chosen for their conversational abilities. After ten simultaneously boring and panicky minutes, I see Aaltonen, Kotka and another man illuminated behind the glass doors of the security office. The Inspector and Kotka descend the steps towards us, whilst the other man turns back and heads towards the plant.

"Why have I been arrested?" I repeat as the Inspector slides into the passenger seat. "What has Kari been saying now?"

Aaltonen turns his head slowly. There is no compassion in his eyes. He says slowly and deliberately, as if it is a painful duty: "Mr Carter, I must advise you not to talk until you have lawyer."

Abi always says I never listen. "Why are there so many police cars? What is everyone else doing?"

"We search."

"For what?"

I get no answer, but Kotka pushes the gear lever to reverse and we ease into the road.

THE TRANSLATOR has taken an age to arrive and now she is eyeing me warily. Aaltonen notices and sits her in a chair on the opposite side of the appointed lawyer. People already think I'm a monster... Let's just sort out this misunderstanding and I can get back to the hotel before someone rings Abi and everything goes pear shaped. The inspector nods to the lawyer, who speaks in Finnish. The translator, compelled by her task, finally meets my eye and I move the corners of my mouth into an acknowledging half smile.

"You understand that you are here because the police have reason to suspect you in the murder of Ms Saarinen?" Her speech is precise but with a heavy Scandinavian accent.

"Yes, but I'd love to know why they think that." Although I'm sure everyone in the room already knows what I have said, the lawyer, Aaltonen and the other detective wait for the translator to finish. This is going to be a slow process.

"I would advise you only to answer the question that is asked," says the lawyer through the translator.

"OK."

There is a small hiatus whilst Kotka connects a flash drive to a small contraption on the centre of the institutional desk and presses the red button. He speaks a few careful sentences towards the recorder. I catch my own and a few other names, but it is not translated. Aaltonen clears his throat and begins, one sentence at a time.

"Give your full name."

"Steven Leslie Carter." Even in such a situation, I wince at my middle name.

"You are being questioned in connection with the murder of Arwen Saarinen... I must remind you of your rights... You do not have to say anything, but it may be better for you if you do..."

"I am happy to help catch her killer," I say. The inspector raises his eyebrows even before the translation is complete.

"Tell us about your relationship with Arwen Saarinen?"

"You already asked me about this."

"I am asking again."

"She worked in a bar where I go for a drink. Hanne's Bar..." I stop for the translator, "We talked and joked like people do with bar staff," I shrug.

"And you met Ms Saarinen outside of her work as well?"

"Yes. But not on purpose... It's not like we arranged to meet..."

"And where did these accidental meetings happen?" I can't tell from the translation, but I think Aaltonen is being sarcastic. I pause to remember.

"In the snooker club, in Clarity night club, in *Laiska Lohi*. If you like to go out, Mahikkala is quite small," the translator raises her hand and I pause, "so you keep bumping into the same people."

"Did the relationship become physical?"

"There wasn't a relationship. We became friends."

"But you wanted it to be physical?" Why is he believing Kari's rantings?

"I'm married," I hedge.

Aaltonen leans forward, "Answer the question."

"You do not have to answer," inserts the lawyer.

I pause, glancing at the youngish Kotka, "No, it's OK, I will answer... Detective Kotka, do you want to have a physical relationship with Hanna Pakarinen?" The three Finnish men in the room grin despite the circumstances. I've just named last year's Eurovision singer, whose dark haired smouldering seems to have caused quite a stir amongst all these blonde Finns.

"Mr Carter, just answer the question."

"I'm going to, but only if Detective Kotka gives me an answer first."

Kotka glances towards Aaltonen, who shakes his head. When I hear the inspector's next comment I realise there is a keen brain behind the greying exterior.

"I will answer your question... If I was young, free, and single of course I would fancy Ms Pakarinen... but I am married."

"But you still find her attractive?"

Aaltonen shrugs as if it's unimportant, "Yes, of course."

"So it's the same with Arwen... She was very attractive, but I'm married... So if you ask did I want something physical, the true answer is: part of me did... But it was a small part... Just like a small part of you wants Hanna Pakarinen... That doesn't make me a murderer, does it?"

Aaltonen shakes his head. Not one of his wire brush hairs moves out of place. "No, that alone does not make you a murderer."

"What does then?"

He ignores the question, "So, for the record, Ms Saarinen and you were not having a sexual relationship?"

"No."

Kotka's eyes flick towards his superior and back to me. I still don't see why this is so important.

"So how do you account for us finding some of your," the woman pauses, trying to recall the word, "semen on Ms Saarinen's body?"

My mouth drops open and I sit gawping at the inspector. I heard the words, but my brain refuses to believe it. A cobweb fluttering between the pale green walls and matte white ceiling to the left of Aaltonen's head suddenly becomes intensely interesting: anything to avoid thinking about the implications of those words. Kotka clears his throat. My mind wrenches back into gear. I've sat next to Abi through enough crime dramas to know I'm in serious trouble.

"It can't be," I say. "There must be some mistake."

"There is no mistake," comes back the reply from Aaltonen. "DNA matches well above the legal requirement."

"A mix up between different samples, then?"

"No mix up, but your lawyer can do independent tests if you would like." Kotka seems slightly annoyed. I guess he handles the samples and I just questioned his competence.

I want to raise my hands in a conciliatory gesture but they are still cuffed behind my back. "Look, I don't mean to question how you do your job, but I know I've done nothing, so there must be a mistake somewhere... Either that or someone is trying to make it look like I did it..."

Aaltonen purses his lips as if I have said something slightly distasteful, but not wholly unexpected. I recognise his first word, but have to wait for the rest, "Who would want to make it look like you did this?"

"The real killer."

"The real killer," says Aaltonen under his breath, in English, then through the translator, "Who is this?" He is staring intently at me.

I shrug, "I suppose you don't think it's Kari any more. If it's not him, then I've no idea. Some sick maniac." Aaltonen sneers with disgust.

"And how would this 'sick maniac' have some of your semen?" How would he? How the hell would he? I can't think of anything. I can't think... It's not cold in the interview room, but I start to shiver.

"Any answer?"

"I don't know." I sound like an obstinate school boy, caught out by a teacher's cold logic. There is a pause. Aaltonen is watching me shake. I try to stop. Come on, relax. Relax? I'm handcuffed in a room where everyone believes I'm a killer. How can I relax? My chest tightens and it hurts slightly as I breathe in. Is my heart going to burst out between my ribs? Kotka seems to be enjoying my discomfort. Aaltonen just stares impassively.

He formulates his next question: "You stated previously that after you left Hanne's Bar... you went for a walk in the woods by Lake Mahi? Is that correct?"

"Yes. I wish I hadn't, but I did."

"You wish you had not?"

"Of course, if I'd not gone into the wood then Arwen might not have followed and she might be alive now."

The lawyer says something quickly and the inspector purses his lips again. "You do not have to say any more, Mr Carter," the translation comes through. I look quizzically at him and shrug.

"Arwen might be alive now, if she had not followed you?" asks Altonen.

"Maybe." Why is he tormenting me? I feel guilty enough about that anyway. His eyes slide sideways and the younger officer takes his cue.

"I can understand," Kotka says, through the translator. "She was beautiful. Anyone would want her... I am sure you did not mean to... It was a game that went wrong, yes?"

"What are you talking about?" I say in bewilderment.

"She met you in the wood. It was your dream come true... But then something happened, yes?"

"Wha? No. Oh." My mind clicks back over the last few sentences. "You think I'm about to... Look, I never saw Arwen in the wood. I never saw her after I passed her and Kari on the street corner. I just went..." The translator raises her hand. The time waiting for her to finish only increases my frustration. "I just walked in the woods and then went back to the hotel. I didn't kill her. Honestly, I didn't." Any composure that remains bursts and tears flood down my face. My nose starts to run. I can't even reach my shoulders to wipe it there. The officers just sit and watch me drip. Perhaps embarrassed by the indignity, the translator pulls a tissue from her left sleeve. Aaltonen waves it away.

"You said Ms Saarinen would be alive if she had not followed you?"

I close my eyes. Please, make it go away.

"Mr Carter?"

I take a deep breath and open them. "You told me that Arwen followed me. I don't know why she did that... But if she hadn't, then she wouldn't have been walking round a wood in the middle of the night and might not have got herself killed by some maniac."

Aaltonen sighs, "For the record, you say it was not you. You did not kill Arwen Saarinen?"

"Of course not, I wouldn't kill anyone." I stare appealingly through droplet speckled glasses at each of the officers in turn.

"Mr Carter, save your pleading for the courthouse," says Aaltonen. "You say you were in the wood where Ms Saarinen was killed.... You don't deny that a part of you wanted her... We find your semen in her body, but you deny you are having a sexual relationship... I believe for some reason, that I will find out, you raped and killed her."

As I listen to the translator numbness descends. Kotka leaves the room and the lawyer tells me that he has gone to fill in the charging document. I am made to stand and turn for photos. They take another DNA swab. Two burley officers enter and one undoes the handcuffs. The DNA man digs about under my fingernails with what look like small plastic cocktail sticks. He bags the dirt he extracts. Then the fingerprint pad. As my fingers are rolled across the ink and on to the paper, I remember having done this before. A vision of paint filled sponges, ink pads, cut potato shapes and small messy aprons fills my mind. How did I grow up to this? When it is finished, without thinking, I move to stretch my aching arms above me at 10 and 2 o'clock. One of the officers takes a step forward. What does he think I'm going to do? Abi would be able to tell him I couldn't fight my way out of a paper bag. Abi... oh, Abi. My mind suddenly returns to focus.

"I've got rights, haven't I? Innocent until proven guilty is the same here, right?"

"Yes," says the lawyer, "You have the right to legal help and you have the right to keep in contact with your family, work and whatever else is reasonable until the trial."

"What about bail, or is that just in the films?"

"No. Rules are different here, but even in your own country, bail is not allowed for serious crimes like murder."

I didn't know that. "But I can make a phone call?"

"Yes."

"Can I do one now? I need to talk to my wife before anyone else does." Aaltonen, who has been watching the forensics, raises his eyes quizzically.

"They will record the call," says the lawyer through the translator.

"It doesn't matter. She just needs to hear this from me first." I look questioningly toward the inspector.

"After this," he says in English.

PICK UP, SOMEONE, PLEASE... Come on, it's the main library number, somebody must be there. It continues to ring. I press the disconnect button and try Abi's mobile again; still straight to voicemail. Back to the other number; wait. After nine rings, I hear a familiar voice and talk over her greeting.

"Jenny, hi, it's Steve, I've got to talk to Abi right now." Maybe the line's bad. She doesn't seem to catch the urgency in my tone.

"Oh, hi Steve, how's it going in the grim north?"

"I need to talk to Abi, is she there?" I say, ignoring the small talk.

"I'm afraid she's with an author at the moment. We're in the middle of a signing." Jenny sounds a little put out and falls back on professionalism, "Shall I leave her a message?"

"No. I'm sorry Jenny, but this is really important. You're going to have to drag her away. I don't care if it's J. K. bloody Rowling."

"Steven, you're scaring me."

"I'm scared. Just get her now. Please..." I press my back teeth together repeatedly, urging the passage of time. My jaw is beginning to ache before I hear scrabbling at the end of the line.

"Steve, are you there?"

"Abi." I find myself temporarily unable to say anything else.

"I don't know what you said to Jenny, but she's standing here white as a sheet, I hope..."

"Abi..." My voice cracks as the contrast between her sweetly familiar tone and the institutional colour scheme in front of me short circuits my senses.

"Steve, you're crying, what is it?"

I close my eyes and draw a shuddering breath. "Abi, you need to sit down. I'm not joking; this is not one of my wind ups; I've never been more serious. You remember how I told you that the woman I knew, Arwen, has been murdered?"

"Yes, it was the boyfriend, wasn't it? You're not going to have to stay for the whole trial are you?"

Shit, in any other circumstances that might be funny, thinks the small part of my brain clinging to reality. It all flows out in a rush. "Probably, yes, because they arrested me this afternoon and now I've been charged with murder and they say they've got proof that I did it, but I didn't, and no one will believe me..." Silence. "Abi, say something."

There's a sniff from the other end of the line, then a gulp and a small voice says, "Where are you?"

"I'm in a police station in Mahikkala. I'm in a room with nothing but a table and a phone and half the police in Finland are outside listening to what we're saying."

"No," she whispers. It's a statement, a question and a plea all at the same time.

"Abi. I need you to be rational. I need you to think. I don't know what's going on out here, but I'm going to need help. Is your friend Charles still a barrister?"

"Yes, but he specialises in environmental law. Pollution cases and stuff."

"But he knows the system. They've given me a Finnish lawyer; I don't know if he's any good and I have to speak to him through a translator and I don't really understand what's going on."

"This is real, isn't it." It's not a question this time. Come on Abi, if I was ever glad you were so obsessed with crime novels, it's now. Tell me what I should do. "I'll ring Charles, he'll know what to do. Has anyone contacted the British Consul over there?" This is more like it.

"I doubt it," I say, "Unless John has been doing something. They took me out of work: in the dinner hall, in front of most of the project team."

"They'll understand. Mistakes happen."

"I hope so," I can't help but sigh.

"Steven?" There's a pause. "They haven't beaten you up or anything, have they?"

"They were a bit rough when they arrested me, but I'm OK. I'm not in central America or anything." The shakes have returned and they must be audible.

"I've never heard you sound this scared."

I struggle to hold the receiver still. "Abi, please get me out of here..." My voice cracks on the last word.

"Steve, listen." She waits until I answer.

"I'm listening."

"I love you."

"I love you too."

"We'll work this out."

"OK." We spend a few moments listening to each other's breathing. My trembles fade.

"You've got some kind of legal protection with your work insurance, haven't you?" says Abi.

"I think so, but I've never really read the small print." The door opens and the inspector enters. He taps his watch. It is clear my time is up. "Abi, they've just told me I've got to stop."

"No, already?"

"I don't know what the rules are."

"OK, I'll ring Charles, I'll ring your work. I'll get the government involved. Hang on in there, OK?"

"OK."

"Oh, and I'm coming on the first flight I can get." Aaltonen takes a step towards me and makes a sign for putting the phone down.

"Love you."

"Love..." I miss the last as the inspector presses the disconnect button.

"Come, you have to sign charge sheet." Maybe it's my imagination, but Aaltonen seems slightly uneasy.

- - -

"IS THERE ANY POINT me going on? You must have heard everything you need by now?"

"Hell, no. I wanna hear everything right up till you walk through my door."

"But how can anything else be relevant?"

"Ain't nothing happens that ain't relevant."

This constant refrain is beginning to piss me off. "Look, if you want to know about the rest of the case why don't you just read the file. If you can find it." I wave my hand dismissively towards the piles on his desk.

"Hey now Mr Carter, we've been all amicable up till now. Let's not fall out when the going gets tough." Hiltunen stares until I hold his eye. "Can't have been easy, going through that all over again. Scary being arrested, 'specially in a foreign country."

"'specially when you didn't do it," I say, voice full of dejection.

"As you say..."

"I'm sorry, I'm just a bit disappointed. Raking over it all again; I was hoping I'd remember something."

"No flash of in-spi-ration?"

"No."

"It might still come. Look at this way, is it better talking to me or going back to your cell?"

+ + +

CHAPTER 24

I expect the door to clang shut with a resounding echo, a mournful tolling to proclaim my incarceration. It clicks shut, just like anyone's front door. No echoing door and no chipper Fletch lying on the top bunk making some amusing observation about life behind bars. Instead, I have a bench bed with mattress, small sink and stainless steel toilet for company. In the corner above the door, the lidless eye of a CCTV camera stares from inside a reinforced cage. Will someone be watching my every move? Even when I wipe my backside?

I've never seen a cell in real life before. Everything I know is from the telly and I expect, just like 'Porridge', it's all wrong. This isn't even proper prison, just a secure police cell, but it's the first time I've ever been locked inside anything.

Tomorrow I go to court. It all seems so fast. My appointed lawyer, Mr Rintala, says this is just procedure. After charging, I go straight to the district court. The judge checks that all the documents are in place for me to be held on remand and then they defer doing anything for two weeks whilst the prosecutor organises a summons. It's a ten minute job: 'Nothing to worry about.' But... I'm going to court and no word from Abi or anyone else yet. I'm going to court and I haven't done anything. I'm going to court...

I sit on the bed with my eyes closed. I'm in a small basic hotel room close to one of the big rope factories up near the Mongolian border. There's no TV, no one that speaks English, nothing to do except wait for the meeting in the morning. I could go out any time I want to, but what's the point, I'll just lie here and relax...

"STEVEN LESLIE CARTER you are a citizen of the United Kingdom?"

"Yes."

"And this is your passport?"

The small maroon booklet is handed across. They've obviously been through my suitcases.

"Yes."

"You have been charged with the murder of Ms Arwen Saarinen. Do you understand?" This court translator is so skilled he even speaks with the same gravitas I can hear in the Judge's Finnish.

"I hear the words, but I don't understand." Mr Rintala glances in my direction with an expression of slight annoyance.

"What don't you understand, Mr Carter?" says the Judge.

"I don't understand why I have been charged with this crime."

"From the preliminary papers I have seen, the police believe they have overwhelming evidence of your guilt."

"I know. I just don't understand how they have that evidence when I haven't done anything."

A brief look of exasperation flits across the Judge's face as the translator finishes my words.

"Mr Carter, this is not the time to hear evidence. We are just here to ensure that there is sufficient cause to detain you on remand pending the start of a trial. There will be ample time for you to prepare your defence." He picks up a wad of papers and taps them level on the desk. "This case will be quite unusual... You are a British citizen and given the seriousness of the alleged offence... I expect your Attorney General might be involved... There is also the matter of translation which always complicates..." The Judge turns towards my lawyer. "Mr Rintala, the clerk will inform you of the exact date and time when the official summons will be issued." He addresses me again, removing his half moon reading glasses.

"Mr Carter, you have, I suppose, family and friends?"

"Yes."

"Such a case as this will inevitably cause a big sensation in the press... Already, in this morning's papers... Whatever you may or may not have done... you should warn them to expect bad things from the newspapers... Be careful who they speak to."

I hadn't thought about the press. The tabloids will have my name in about two seconds. I hold the Magistrate's eye. *"Kiitoksia paljon,"* I say in my most polite Finnish.

He looks away and mutters just audibly in English, "No need more victim."

ABI'S PHONE IS OFF. Two hours waiting to be taken to the 'comms' room and I can only leave a message. I should use the time to ring someone else, but there isn't anyone else I want to talk to. I hope it means she's in the air.

Shaking my head, I pull my credit card out of the reader next to the phone and pass it back to the burly officer hovering near the door. I've been told that I'm allowed to keep some stuff in the cell, but it's at their discretion to refuse things they consider dangerous or inappropriate. What do they think I'm going to do with a bank card?

I hold my hands behind my back for the cuffs to be reapplied. My guard won't open the door unless he's done this first. I wince as he tightens them one notch further than I think is strictly necessary.

"Go," he barks as the door opens. This guy seems like he really wants to pummel me. There is a cold hatred in his eyes. I bet his little sister was at school with Arwen or something like that. I see it in all their eyes: the officers, the translators. I might have killed their little sister, or their daughter, or their girlfriend. Murderer. Monster. And they've all got guns... An image of hundreds of Mahikkalans carefully polishing their hunting rifles in front of the TV rears into my mind. They shake their heads as the newsreader reveals more lurid details about the death of their beloved daughter. My arms start to tremble again. A small snort causes me to turn my head slightly. He does not try to hide his derision.

We reach the cell; I enter first, stop and tense, expecting the rough removal of my binds. A coarse skinned hand firmly grips my right forearm, but before the key is inserted there's a shout down the corridor. My captor turns and swears under his breath.

"You have visitor," he mutters. Abi. It must be Abi. Oh, it will be so good to see her. I have to swallow my disappointment when ten minutes later John, Mark, and a man I don't recognise troop into the interview room under escort. One officer remains, immovable in front of the closed door. John glances sideways towards the muscle bound guard and then questioningly at me.

"He'll stay. I think it's for your protection. After all, everyone thinks I'm a dangerous criminal."

John shakes his head. Mark stays strangely still as if waiting for me to prove something.

"Am I glad to see familiar faces," I say. "Are you guys OK?"

"Managing," says John, "but..."

Mark interrupts him, "Steve, you look like a ghost."

I shrug. "I'm bloody wetting myself, aren't I?"

There's an awkward silence. Then John remembers himself. He tilts his head slightly to the left where the immaculately suited stranger is sitting. "This is Mr Wilson from the embassy. He's got some news for you."

"Mr Carter," says the short man. "Henry Wilson. Pleased to meet you." I'm sure he isn't. "I wish it were in better circumstances."

"I'd shake your hand, but..." I shrug again. It's just about the only gesture I can manage.

He ignores the irony and continues, "Both Mr McLeod here, and your wife have been in contact with the embassy." I mouth, 'Thanks,' towards John. "We often find we can be of some assistance, particularly when British nationals find themselves in serious situations such as yours. Your wife wishes to tell you that she has tried to get messages to you, but she's had some difficulty with..." He glances towards the door. "...red tape." I nod.

"She's arriving in Finland this evening. We'll send one of our cars for her."

"Thanks," I say. At least this bureaucrat appears to actually do things. It's a start.

"At Mr McLeod's suggestion we've booked her a hotel in Lahti."

"Not here?" I'm surprised.

John screws up his face slightly before answering, "Steve, I thought it was best. It's... it's a bit hot in Mahikkala at the moment."

"Wha..?" My brain is struggling to imagine a searing sun turning all the streets into rivers. Then I remember all those polished guns.

"Oh Thor, is it really bad? I'm sorry."

"You've nothing to be sorry about Stevie. They'll all have to apologise when they realise what a stupid mistake they've made."

"Thanks," I say quietly.

"And you don't need to carry on with the Thor rubbish."

"I know. It's just habit. What are people doing?"

"It's not really what they're doing, it's what they're not doing," says John. "Most people have stopped talking to us... They willnae serve us in *Laiska Lohi*."

"Hanne's been great, telling everyone that she knows you didn't do it, but..." Mark trails off.

"...but she's in the minority?" I finish.

"Yeah. Keith's even stopped going to Kopa for a while." Somehow this seems more scary than anything else.

"I didn't do anything. You know that, don't you? Anything at all..." I hold Mark's eyes as I say the last.

"We know," says Mark quietly.

"Anyway, it's probably best if Abi doesn't stay here for a while. At least until it's cooled off a bit. It's only half an hour down the motorway." John always knows what he's doing.

The embassy guy has been quiet, but, sensing a pause, he clears his throat, "Your wife also said that they are trying to find a British barrister who also has some experience of Finnish law. They've got someone in mind but he's on another case. I think there may be some arm twisting going on. Our Ambassador got a phone call from the Attorney General's office this morning asking for details about your situation. It seems someone is shaking trees for you."

"That'll be Abi," I say, "She's done quite a bit of charity campaigning in the past. I've seen MPs wilt in front of her onslaught." Even I can hear the pride in my voice. Mr Wilson nods.

"They're saying there's forensic evidence," says Mark. He can't help himself. John glares at him.

"I know," I shake my head. "Someone's got it in for me, that's all I can think, because I know it wasn't me."

"Helluva situation," says John shaking his head. "I brought you this." He hands over a new copy of *War and Peace*. "I know it's a bit heavy, but there wasn't much choice in English. It was the longest thing I could find." The edges of his mouth raise slightly, "I figure you might have a bit of time for reading."

"Yeah, I figure I might," I say forcing my mouth into a smile.

"It was either this one or *Crime and Punishment*..." The three of us all laugh a bit too loud. Mr Wilson sits bemused by John's gallows humour, but it's the first time I've laughed for days and I'm grateful to him for both gifts.

CHAPTER 25

Almost twenty-four hours later finds me sitting in the same plastic chair. I'm confused. I was expecting Abi, but I've been told that my British lawyer has arrived. I've been staring at these pale green walls for half an hour. Still at least they're different walls and the cuffs are off this time. My head is beginning to nod with the hypnotic plainness when the door opens. Abi's friend Charles takes one step into the room and politely indicates that my guard should leave. Some sort of question is just beginning to form, when from behind the fawn rain coated figure Abi herself appears. I start to stand, but Charles gestures with one palm downwards and I stay seated. Abi pauses, Charles's hand on her shoulder until the door is closed.

"Right then, boys and girls, I'm just going to stand over there facing the corner and whistle to myself for a bit, OK?" My eyes flick from Abi to Charles in bemusement, but before I look back she has landed in my lap and I'm enveloped. It can't be real, but the bruise on my ribs is aching with the tightness of her hug, our tears are mingling where our lips meet in salty union, and the smell of her skin fills my nose. My Abi. I don't know how long passes, but a small clearing of the throat from the corner causes her to pull away. I can see in her eyes that she doesn't want to have to think about realities.

"Charles, what the hell?"

"Couldn't let Abi come out here all on her own, could I? After all, I wouldn't have got very far with Sue if Abi hadn't put me straight on a few things back then; big favour to repay, really. Besides, Sue didn't give me much choice – already had my bag packed before I was home from the office."

"Thanks," I say. Charles's chipper manner is feeding my strength as much as the warmth on my lap.

"I was also able to use my small knowledge of Finnish law..."

"He had his nose in a huge tome all through the flight," inserts Abi.

"... to play a few tricks. It seems that anyone can be nominated as your legal counsel, or Advocate as they call it here." A conspiratorial grin spreads across Charles's face. "I believe you've been introduced to Mrs Carter, your new Advocate." Charles points towards Abi and my mouth falls open.

"The police hated it. But Charles just spent half an hour pointing out the rules and their lawyer said they had to accept it. It means I can visit for much longer and they can't listen to what we say," gushes Abi.

"I think it would be best not to rub it in too much though," says Charles, running a hand through his slightly surprised hair. "Hence the waiting to shut the door."

"Yeah, I guess so. The officers all stare daggers at me as it is."

"Have they hit you?" asks Abi, running a finger along my jaw where the bruise has begun to fade towards yellow.

I purse my lips. Here it is, the start, the point of no return: "Err, no, that was from when Kari, Arwen's boyfriend, punched me."

Abi sits up straight, a slight frown playing on her brow.

Charles makes wide eyes at me over Abi's shoulder and says, "I think now would be a good time to go through the facts as you see them. Of course, we've had nothing from the police yet."

"But how's this going to work?" I glance from Charles to Abi and back again. "I mean, no disrespect, but Abi knows about as much about Finnish criminal law as I do. And I could write that on the back of a stamp."

"Ah, you see that's the beauty of our little game. Finnish law states that if you appoint an Advocate who cannot appropriately defend you – and sorry, Abi darling, but you can't – then the state is obliged to appoint a competent counsel to help."

"Is that going to be you, then?"

"No. Initially it'll probably be this Rintala, but we're organising a chap called James Hainsworth to come out next week. Absolutely the right person. On his way to becoming the youngest QC since... what's his name and, crucially, he did an exchange with chambers in Helsinki – so he's qualified for the Finnish Bar."

"And he's available?"

"Well, things are being arranged..."

"How did you swing that?"

"It's amazing what can happen when your wife plays tennis with the wife of the Attorney General," says Abi turning to smirk at Charles.

Charles shrugs and says, "Sometimes, I wonder whose career it actually is."

"Behind every great man, there's a scheming woman, hey Charles? When are you going to sit in the high court then?"

Charles smiles modestly, but doesn't deny it. "One step at a time. I'm not a judge yet."

"Soon though." says Abi. It's a statement rather than a question.

"Ask Sue!" says Charles ironically, "Anyway, enough about me. How did you get yourself into this mess then?"

Abi slips off my lap and takes a chair on the opposite side of the table next to Charles. Her face is a study in apprehension overlaying hope. I watch as she repeatedly sucks her bottom lip inwards and runs her teeth over the top of it. Charles: he's seen it all before. Despite his matey demeanour up till now, I see a flicker of seriousness cross his face as he produces a leather bound writing pad from his briefcase, places a dictaphone in the middle of the table, pulls a surprisingly cheap plastic biro from his jacket pocket. He follows my eyes, "Just keep losing all the posh pens Sue buys me. Costing me a fortune to replace them. Now..." He presses the record button.

"There's not that much detail of your case in the papers: lots of headlines, lots of outrage, but not many facts. As far as I've been able to find out," he flicks a couple of pages of the pad, "we know this: One, a nineteen year old woman called Arwen Saarinen has been found dead in the woods by Lake Mahi. Two, a Mr Kari Varis, was initially arrested, but later released without charge. Three, you have now been arrested and charged with murder..." he glances sideways at Abi, "and I believe rape as well."

I can see in her face that none of this is news to her. I expect Charles has been steeling her up gradually, making comments like 'always a few secrets', 'no one's a saint', 'need to expect some surprises'.

"Other than that, everything else is rumour, or at least unconfirmed. We can't just sit with our hands under our arses until we see the prosecution's papers in full, so we'll need to know everything that you know. Got to start somewhere, so... How did you know Ms Saarinen?"

I start to clean the wetness from my glasses on the corner of my shirt. "She was one of the staff at Hanne's Bar which is the nearest pub to the hotel, so we often drink there."

"'We' being?"

"My work colleagues Mark, John, Keith, and myself."

"And so you got talking?"

"Well, not much, actually in Hanne's Bar, but Mahikkala's quite small so we often bumped into her and her friends."

"What are the names of these friends? Sorry to interrupt the flow, but it all might be important," says Charles. 'Thorough', I think. I hope the other guy is as good.

"I don't know all the surnames, but they mostly went round as a foursome: her boyfriend is called Kari Varis, then her best friend is Til, Tilia, and her boyfriend is Harri."

"And where did you meet?"

"In the snooker hall: she was pretty good at pool; and in the Irish bar." He looks up questioningly, "O'Grady's in the town square." I can't help glancing at Abi. "And one time she almost knocked me over on the dance floor at the 'Clarity' nightclub."

"Was she a good dancer?" The question, inevitably, from Abi. There's no point lying.

"Yes, but that was the only time I danced with her, and you know what it's like here..." Again the questioning look from the barrister. "Everyone just does it for fun. Asking someone to dance here is no more suggestive than asking them if they want to play pool or something."

"OK, anywhere else?" says Charles, running a hand through his hair again.

"Err, yeah," I can feel a guilty flush coming on. "It turned out that we both loved karaoke, so a couple of times I sat on the same table as her and we talked about songs and stuff. She had an amazing voice."

"Sounds like you had lots in common..." I'm not liking Abi's expression.

"Yes, but it was only friendship. In fact, I don't even know if she actually thought of me as a friend. She had a boyfriend, she knew I was married. It wasn't like we ever arranged to meet on our own or anything like that. I even got her back together with Kari after they split up."

"Her relationship with Kari Varis was stormy?" Charles sits forward slightly.

"I think they argued a bit. Reading between the lines, I think she wanted to try for professional singing and he wanted a nice little stay-at-home wife."

"And they split up?" asks Charles.

"Yes. She didn't say why, that's only my guess, but you could see that they both still loved each other. They were like two kids who blamed each other for breaking their favourite toy: each too proud to get the glue out and mend it."

"But you got them back together?" Abi's expression has softened.

"Yes. One time at the karaoke I persuaded Arwen to sing to Kari and it did the trick. Pat Benetar's *We belong*, the words were so perfect."

"Steven Carter's musical relationship counselling," says Charles ironically. "So how did this Kari end up punching you then?"

"Well, that brings us to the night she was killed, sort of," I say, glancing apprehensively toward Abi. "Here's where it gets a bit embarrassing. I was a bit of a jerk. Everyone was so drunk." Her face is hardening. I raise a conciliatory hand, "Nothing really bad, just stupid." I take a deep breath and continue. Best to get it over with fast. "Hanne, who owns Hanne's Bar..."

"Original name," says Charles under his breath.

"...had a party on that Thursday night to celebrate paying off her mortgage. It was a free bar for the first hour. Everyone got absolutely wrecked. You can imagine. Anyway, at some point I decided to ask Arwen to dance, but she turned me down. I think that was a red rag to a very drunk bull. A bit later, everyone was dancing the Macarena and it seemed like a good idea to put my hands on her waist as we did the wiggly bit. Sorry, Abi, I wasn't thinking straight." Abi seems caught between feeling annoyed or relieved. Before she can decide my fate, I continue, "and there's more. She started having an argument with Kari and I went to ask her to dance again... I know!" I say shaking my head, "I tried to pull her out of her chair. I thought she was messing about, but I nearly pulled her arm out of its socket."

"Not your finest hour," says Charles. Abi is silent.

"But that did sober me up a bit. I did apologise... profusely. Then I went and hid in the toilets out of shame."

"Sounds like a typical drunk night out," says Charles and I flick him a grateful glance. "So Arwen and Kari argued again at this party?"

"Yes, and when we all left they were really going at each other on the street corner. That was the last time I saw her."

"On the street outside Hanne's Bar? At what time?"

"Must have been about ten past two, I know Hanne chucked everyone out at 2am sharp."

"And then you went back to the hotel?"

"No, that's the really bad thing. I was going to go straight back, but I was still a bit drunk and feeling a bit stupid, so I thought it would be a good idea to go for walk to clear my head."

"And where did you walk?" I have a feeling Charles has already guessed the answer.

"Through the woods along the shore of Lake Mahi."

"Oh, Steve..." says Abi, in a half whisper of realisation.

"Not good," comments Charles, "and the police know this?" I nod.

"But I didn't do anything, I didn't see anyone, I just walked around for a bit until my feet got cold and then I went back to the hotel."

"And at the same time, someone else was killing Arwen, or at least dumping the body, in the same wood?"

"That's what the police say."

"So how does Kari Varis punching you come into this?"

"That was later, on the Saturday night. Mark and I were sat in Hanne's just chatting and suddenly, wham, Kari knocks me off the chair and starting kicking seven bells out of me. I didn't even see him coming." I lift my shirt front and Abi's hand goes to her mouth as her eyes take in the multiple black bruises. Charles lets me continue in my own time. "After Mark and Hanne's bouncer had pulled him off, he started babbling about me having killed Arwen.

He said they found her body, naked, in the woods by the lake. I don't know how he knew that, but it's a small town; whoever found her probably told him before the police. He was mad and dead sure it was me. I think the police have been listening to him too much."

"But they did arrest him?"

"Yes, to start with. But then everything changed because of the forensics."

"Um, I've seen a rumour online about that," says Charles, for the first time diffident.

I stare into Abi's grey-green eyes, "You've got to believe me when I say this isn't true, but the police say they've found my semen on her body." Charles's face reveals that it's worse than he's read.

"But how..." says Abi.

"I wish I knew. Either there's some weird mistake or someone's out to get me big time."

Charles clears his throat, "It's difficult to see how anyone could have planted such evidence. The police took a DNA swab I suppose?"

"Yes, from my mouth. They said it was to eliminate me. But then next day they're putting on the handcuffs."

"Do you suspect someone in the police?" says Charles.

"Maybe, but the inspector, Aaltonen, doesn't seem that type of guy. He seems honest, and really sharp."

"Then it must be a mistake," says Abi, giving me a wan smile. She trusts me, I think. I really wasn't sure how she'd react.

"Whichever way, I'm up the proverbial creek and as for the paddle, well, someone threw it out to make room for forensic evidence," I say with a mirthless grin.

CHAPTER 26

The first fortnightly reassessment of my remand has already passed. It was pretty much another formality. I didn't even speak except to give my name. There was a debate about James taking over the appointed Advocate role from Rintala. In just about his last act before leaving, Charles suggested that, being a foreign national, my case was bound to become complicated and perhaps it was in everyone's best interests to have them both on the defence team. That seemed to satisfy the judge.

The thing that gets me is the time everything takes. It's going to be summer before the hearing even begins and then they will adjourn it for months to allow for case preparation time. I mean, of course I want my defence to be well prepared, but I'm the one who has to sit in a cell waiting.

At least James now has some paperwork. Just enough to make sure the judge agreed there was still a case to answer. It's a game. James hasn't actually said that, he's far too professional to call all this crap a game, but I can read between the lines. The police have to finish their investigation. Then they release the documents to the prosecutor and the court issues a summons. But of course everyone is doing their own investigating, trying to get a head start. Otherwise we'll all be sitting around with our thumbs up our backsides for the next eight weeks. Eight weeks! I'm already sick of reading. Abi keeps bringing new books, which is great, but I just want to go for a stroll, stop off at a pub, eat some cheese and onion crisps. And they estimate eight more weeks until the police hand over the files.

"I'm still here then," I say as an officer closes the interview room door behind Abi and James.

"Yes," says James, pulling a laptop out of his bag, ignoring our kissed hellos, "They ought to have transferred you to somewhere with more facilities by now. You can't stay in a police cell. Do they even let you exercise?"

"They take me down to the canteen late in the evening and we walk laps." I pause, "But I really meant, I'm still HERE."

James gives a rueful smile, "I'm afraid we're in for the long haul on this one." He regards me appraisingly, "The hearing was reasonably successful though."

"Was it?"

"I know it doesn't seem like it when you read this," he pulls a clear plastic wallet from one of the side pockets of his bag, "but really, their case is all based around this semen evidence, and we already knew about that. Any time there are no surprises in court, you're halfway there."

Abi reaches out to hold my left hand and squeezes it reassuringly.

"I've already got Rintala chasing the police for some of the sample. We'll get it tested here and in the UK just to be sure," says my barrister. "We knock that down and their case crumbles."

I've not had any reason to disagree with Charles's assessment of this guy so far. Likeable, youthful – barely older than me, but still with a certain authority that makes you listen.

"You really ought to be transferred to a proper facility," says James, returning to our previous thought. Both Abi and I look doubtful. "Don't worry, I'll check everything out first, but really, a proper facility..."

"Do you mean prison?" I interrupt.

"Remand centre," James clarifies. "Specifically for people awaiting trial." He makes a slight frown. "Sometimes they might be attached to correctional facilities but certainly here in Finland there is no mixing of ..." he pauses, struggling for the politically correct term.

"Inmates?" say Abi. He nods.

"But what's the point? I'll still be in a cell?" I say.

"Yes, but you would have proper exercise and communication facilities, perhaps the chance to carry out some activities. From what other clients have told me, boredom is your main worry. This temporary arrangement the police have here is not very satisfactory."

I shrug, "OK, but don't you need to stay around here?"

"It would be convenient if you were still close to Mahikkala. I seem to remember visiting a place north of Helsinki in the past. That can't be too far, maybe no further from Lahti." He glances at Abi.

"Away from here, the officers might not be quite so vociferous. I worry about you." Abi forces a smile.

"There is that," I say, rubbing the sore skin around my wrists.

"OK." James taps the interface pad on his laptop. "Oh yes, er, Steven, your request to have a guitar has been denied. Apparently the strings are too dangerous." I can almost hear the Q.E.D. in his tone.

"What am I going to do, garrotte somebody with them?" I snap. Not that I'd really expected them to say yes.

The barrister ignores my rant and types a couple of sentences. "Is there anything else we need to talk about before we begin?" he says, without looking up.

"Steven..." Abi shifts in her chair, "I was wondering, what about your Dad?" Dad, gosh yes. I haven't even given him a thought. For the first time ever it crosses my mind that it might be a blessing. What would he have thought?"

"Should someone try to tell him?" Abi continues when I don't answer.

"What would be the point?" I sigh.

"Alzheimer's," says Abi in answer to James's raised eyebrow.

"It's more than two years since I had any sort of recognition from him. He just sits there."

"And asks where your Mum is all the time," adds Abi and then makes a pained face. I give her hand a squeeze of reassurance. It wasn't the wrong thing to say. My Mum. You know, after my Mum, Arwen is probably the closest person I know who's died? Mind you, is Dad really still alive? A slight wetness forms in the corners of my eyes. I raise my head with a sigh. James is staring intently at me.

"So... take me back to the party at Hanne's Bar. Is there anything more you can remember?"

CHAPTER 27

If you thought the architecture of Mahikkala was uninspiringly grey and blocky, wait till you see Korikylä Prison. Let's just say that they didn't waste any Finnish taxpayer's money on making it look pretty. A central courtyard is surrounded on three sides by buildings and on the fourth by a high concrete wall. The remand centre takes up the whole east side. From my window - yes! my very own half metre square sheet of bullet proof glass - I can see real prisoners in their blue shirts exercising behind high and sharp looking fences which divide the yard. James was right, it is better here: no handcuffs for a start and I'm allowed to walk outside every day. OK, it's only on the east side of the yard, the only green I can see is some pine trees on a rise in the far distance, but it is outside. The snow has been gone for weeks. Yesterday, eight huge long necked birds flew over in a shallow V formation. Everyone looked up to see freedom flying north for spring. I squint out of the window, but there's nothing in the sky today. The buzzer alerts me that my door is about to open. I turn and stand with my arms by my sides.

"Lawyer time," says the tall, thin guard. Whilst not exactly friendly, these guys are at least civil. I'm just another murderer to them.

Abi, James and Lars Rintala are already seated on the moulded plastic chairs in visiting room three when I enter. Abi puts her arms round my neck, kisses me and pulls away. It's too brief. I regard her carefully. She's cleaned herself up, but she should know better. "You've been crying," I say.

"I'm afraid it's not good news from the re-tests," says James in a matter of fact voice. "Unfortunately, they both confirm the semen as yours. Very rare to find the initial tests wrong. Never known it myself, but..." he shrugs, an 'it was worth a try'.

I hold Abi's waist and look deep into her moist eyes, "I definitely didn't do anything. Someone, somehow, must have..." My explanation falters. The corners of Abi's mouth turn up slightly, but it's not really a smile. I release her and sit heavily back into one of the chairs. Its legs splay slightly. How can it be my semen? It can't be. I know I didn't... A drip of sweat runs along the curve of my left armpit and starts down the underside of my arm until it meets cloth. I fold my arms: it's chilly in here today. My left leg twitches a couple of times and then begins to shake. I press my foot flat against the floor to stop it.

Abi glances towards James. He holds his hands apart, palms upwards. "Steven, I know Charles thought it was clever to have Abigail as one of your law team. It was, but now the PTI is finished and the documents have arrived there are some things I need to ask you which... might be awkward."

"PTI?"

"Pre-trial investigation – the police investigation. They sent over all the evidence documents with your court summons yesterday morning."

"Already?"

"Yes, five days early, unheard of, well, in the UK anyway."

"I guess they must be very confident," I sigh.

"Let's hope it's over-confidence," says James, positive as always. "I haven't let Abigail see the papers yet, not without your say so." His eyes shift in her direction. "She wasn't too happy about that." I bet. Strange to hear her called Abigail. I only ever do that for a joke.

"Of course she can see them. There's nothing that I wouldn't want Abi to hear and I haven't done anything, so if there's more stuff in there, it's wrong too." I receive a proper smile, if a little pained, this time.

"The judge has suggested we hold a preparation hearing in three weeks time. There's lots to discuss with you being British and all the media attention, and stuff like that. Officially it is the start of the trial, but really it's just administration. There won't be any evidence given."

"Whatever. You know best."

Lars reaches into his briefcase and pulls out a slim ring binder. "This is case..." he shakes his head slightly as James pulls out a huge lever arch file, "with all rubbish taken out. Just evidence, statements, not all forms. I start translate, but..." I notice that James's file already has a forest of sticky notes protruding from the top edge.

My eyes move from one serious face to another. "I take it that there is more bad stuff in here, then?"

"There are some points which don't exactly match your story, as well as some more forensics."

"More forensics?"

"I'm afraid so." I slowly shake my head. Abi looks steeled for the worst.

"Just go through it one point at a time, then," I whisper.

James opens his file, grabs the first sticky note, and turns to the relevant page. He stares at me, his eyes flick towards Abi, and then back on me again. His next breath out is short and disapproving.

"Let's start with the forensics then. This is the report from the post mortem. The cause of death is stated as asphyxiation, caused by a loop of some sort of thin cord. They haven't found the length used, but there were some fibres and apparently it's a manufactured at *Suomen Kaapelitehdas*."

Abi makes an audible gulp.

"Which is the same for just about every piece of rope in Finland," I snap. "Besides, I only ever worked on the steel cable side of the plant."

"Quite," says James ignoring my tone. He continues, "The rumours we heard were correct, the body was found naked." It doesn't sound right to hear her called 'the body'. An image of Arwen lying face down in the snow seeps into my mind. I shake my head to remove it.

"The only defence wound, if you can call it that, seems to be a broken finger nail. That's unusual. The coroner is of the opinion that the clothes were removed either after or on the point of death." He raises his head to catch my eye. "Also unusual, given the forensic evidence is that there are no signs of forcible intercourse either pre or post mortem."

"There you see," I say, looking towards Abi, "someone planted it."

"That's one possibility," James continues in a level tone, "however, in support of the semen evidence, investigations also revealed some material fibres which they have traced to a particular colour of Marks and Spencer's boxer shorts, which are only available in the UK. Two such pairs were found in your hotel room."

"Well that doesn't stack up for a start." A small glimmer of hope lifts me slightly in my seat and I stare imploringly at my wife. "Tell him why it couldn't possibly have been me, Abi."

"Boxer shorts?" she confirms. I can see she is as quick on the uptake as ever. James nods.

"Well, Steve never wears boxer shorts except in bed. He always says..." a smile almost surfaces, "that they let stuff dangle about too much to be comfortable."

"You see, so it's like saying I went out to Hanne's party in my pyjamas. That's not likely, is it?"

"No. Good. It's a start, but..." James hesitates.

"But what?" says Abi.

"But one could possibly argue that if you had worn them the night before, a piece of fluff might stick and then fall off later."

"Sounds a bit unlikely," I say.

James shrugs, "All forensic evidence is unlikely to one degree or another. It mostly relies on things being accidentally left behind." He turns over a couple of pages. "There is something quite strange here though. As well as your semen being found in the..." he makes a face as if tasting something unpleasant, "vaginal sample, they also found spermicide. It's been analysed as coming from a Russian brand of condoms."

"How does someone use a condom and leave semen behind?" says Abi.

"It is a good point," says James, "but as thousands of surprised mothers discover each year, accidents do happen."

"I wonder what brand of condom Kari uses?" I muse.

The barrister flicks right to the back of his file to a page marked by a green sticky note. "The police have considered this too. Unfortunately, this brand appears to be available in vending machines all over Finland."

"Did they ask Kari?"

"Surprisingly, yes, Inspector Aaltonen actually seems very thorough."

"There are many, many statement," adds Lars.

"In Mr Varis's statement he claims not to have had sex with Arwen for several weeks," continues James. He also states that they never used condoms as she was on the pill." He flicks to a different green sticky. "That she was on the pill is confirmed by both her mother and the toxicology."

"So that doesn't really help us... or hinder us, does it?" says Abi.

"No," says James, but I'm not really listening. She said 'us'. Still us. Amazing how one word can make your heart leap.

"Steven?" James raises his voice slightly.

"Sorry." I stop staring at my wife and try to refocus my attention. "Is that it for the forensics?"

"Yes."

"But there's more?" I can tell from his tone that there is.

A yellow sticky note this time. "This is a transcript from an interview with Kari Varis. They asked him about his argument with Arwen. Lars, can you translate it as you go? My Finnish is still a bit rusty." He pushes the binder across the mottled formica table top towards his colleague.

"I try," says Lars. He clears his throat and begins reading:

Aaltonen – We have witness who say you argue with Ms Saarinen outside the Hanne Bar.

Varis – Yes, it true. She was angry at me all evening, but after we leave, we start to shout.

Aaltonen – What was argument about?

Varis – It was about the future, how...

"What is word when something become no point because of what happen later?" Lars interrupts his flow.

"I think we would say 'ironic'" says James.

"Yes, that it." Lars restarts:

Varis – It was about the future, how ironic. She have some stupid idea to be a singer. I keep say to her to be real. Yes, she sing quite well, but everyone want to be singer. It is not real. It one in million chance. I say, enjoy singing, but have normal life here with me. Reach up for dream and fall over feet - "It is a Finnish proverb," explains Lars.

"I knew it," I mumble under my breath.

Aaltonen – But Ms Saarinen did not agree?

Varis – No. She say I should support what she want to do. She is more determined than I see before. She did not listen. So I say, OK, you do what you want. But she say, you always say that, but you never really mean it.

Kotka – There is no answer to that.

Aaltonen – And that was the end?

Varis – No. Then he walk past with his British friends.

Aaltonen – He?

Varis – Steven. As they walk past, Arwen looks at him. She do that all evening. I think she just find him funny, a funny old foreigner, but maybe...

Aaltonen – Maybe?

Varis – I not know, but I not like how she look. Then Steven say, 'I not do it again.'

Aaltonen – And what you think he mean by that?

Varis – I not know. I ask Arwen the same thing. She sigh and shake her head. Then she say, he mean he is not going to get us back together again. And stupid, I say that I not know we had split up. She say, well you do now.

Kotka – You like a tissue, Mr Varis?

Varis – Thank you. Sorry.

Aaltonen – Quite alright. Is that it?

Varis – No. There is more.

Aaltonen – When are ready.

Varis – I ask her why she cries, she know I love her, and then - I see this every time I shut my eyes at night - then she puts hands on side and say, I know you love me, but you not know me.

"No, 'know' is not right word," says Lars, "It mean more..."

"You don't understand me?" says Abi quietly.

"Yes, that it," says the Finnish lawyer and continues to read in his slow sing-song accent:

– She look down road and I see Steven turn next to bank, towards lake. She say, I want more, Kari, I want more than Mahikkala. I need know if I can sing. Steven understands.

Aaltonen – What she mean, Steven understands?

Varis – I not know, but it make me very mad. I say lots of things. I not remember.

Aaltonen – Try.

Varis – I say things like, Steven understands, do he? Do his wife know he understands you? How many time a night? What you been doing? Is that why we have not? All time she stay quiet. Then when I finish, she say, 'grow up' and walk away.

Aaltonen – And you see her go down street next to bank?

Varis – Yes, but not now. First, I hold her arm and ask her where she goes. She push me away and say..."

Lars pauses for a moment and glances towards Abi. I notice the hint of a grin form on James's lips. Lars backs up slightly:

– She push me away and say, go off home little boy, I go to talk to a adult.

I suspect that 'go off home' may not have been an exact translation.

Aaltonen – And then she walk down the same road as Steven Carter?

Varis – Yes.

Aaltonen – You did not follow?

Varis – No. The way she push me, I know not to follow. I ran to Harri's house.

Aaltonen – Yes, we have hear that."

Lars stops reading, raises his head and catches James's eye.

"So Kari admits having a big row with Arwen then?" I say.

"Yes," says James, "but we also know now why they released him." He tries to turn forwards in the sheaf but his fingers can't get a purchase. Unselfconsciously, he licks his left index finger which does the trick. "Very dry in here," he comments. "There's a whole wodge of statements. Apparently, Kari made so much noise banging on Harri's door that it woke up half the neighbours. Of course, the first thing anyone does when they're woken up in the night is look at the clock, so there are about three independent confirmations that he was there at exactly 02:24."

"Where's Harri's house?" I ask.

"The house of his parents, Mr and Ms Hesso, is *Ainonkatu*, 17."

"It is more than fifteen minutes' walk from the Hanne Bar," says Lars, "in opposite direction to lake. It not possible even to run to lake and back to the house in twenty minutes. Inspector Aaltonen got person from Mahi summer sport club to try it."

"Maybe he got a lift part of the way?" I clutch.

"The police think there still would be no time. It is even longer by car and there is also running in the woods before even reach the main road. Also, it take some time to strip a body and er..."

"So Kari Varis has a cast iron alibi?" says Abi.

"It seems that way," says James, turning to face her, "and from the statement, he comes across as believable, don't you think?"

"Yes," I sigh, answering for her. He never did seem like the type, but who then, who? My left knee begins to tremble again. "Could we have a minute's break? It's all pretty intense."

"Of course."

I stand and pace up and down the longest side of the room. After a minute, Abi rises and leans with her hand against the beige paint, blocking my path. "Stop it. You remind me of a tiger at the zoo."

"I know why they do it. When you feel trapped, it's comforting to keep moving." I sink my head into Abi's shoulder and inhale. "Why is this happening to us?" I whisper.

"I wish I knew."

I push myself gently away, still holding onto both of her shoulders. "You do believe me, don't you?" My voice is small and pleading.

"Yes, I believe you," says her mouth. Her eyes, well, I think they're trying to believe. Before I can stop them, my lips curl slightly in disappointment and Abi knows she hasn't lied well enough. "I'm trying, I really am trying," she sobs, but a shake of the head transmutes tears into venom. "Why did you talk to this girl? She's obviously your type. Why couldn't you just stay out of trouble... like Mark?"

Like Mark... I don't have any answer for that. Not one that won't wreck another life. I shrug, I can't help it; I know it will infuriate her more. Big red self-destruct button: press.

"And what did she mean: you understand her?" Abi shouts, accenting the 'you'.

"Well, obviously you think it means I was shagging her senseless, don't you? You might as well believe it, everyone else does." My voice cracks and I slump against the wall, gasping in between sobs.

James clears his throat and says in a level voice, "You see, this is exactly what I meant when..." He doesn't finish. Independently, but exactly simultaneously, Abi and I shout, "Oh, shut up." Startled, we turn our heads sharply, lock eyes for a moment and then dissolve into a fit of giggles: beautiful, hysterical, maniacal giggles. We cling on to each other, leaning heavily against the wall for support. For thirty glorious seconds it is all one hilarious convoluted joke.

"Sorry James," I say as my shoulders stop shaking and I catch my breath. Abi lifts my chin slightly with one finger and plants a brief kiss on my lips.

"Just tell me," she says.

I stand up straight and begin to pace again. "I wasn't trying to get into trouble. I just kept bumping into her and finding that we had stuff in common. And when I heard her sing, well, she sang Whitney Houston better than Whitney Houston for goodness sake! I told her she should have auditions and do it professionally. She told me she had a place at Kuopio to study music but she hadn't gone. She didn't dare leave her life behind, but she'd've been mad not to go." I shake my head. "All that talent, such a waste."

"You did like her though," states Abi.

"Yes, but I love you, I'm married to you." I return a stray strand of black hair to behind Abi's right ear. "Look, it probably happens to everyone who's married: occasionally you meet someone, and you can't help wondering, what if? But it's only wondering."

Abi regards me carefully and I can see a decision being made, "So if she had caught up with you along the road or in the wood for her 'talk with a grown up' what would have happened?"

She's really pushing the boundaries, but what the heck, I've already fallen over the edge. "I imagine we'd have had a long chat and then I'd have walked her back to her parents' house, wherever that was, given her a friendly hug goodnight and prevented her from being killed by some maniac. Hell, I wish that had happened."

"And if she'd suggested going back to your hotel room?"

I exhale sharply. "You really want me to tell you? You want to know the truth?"

"Yes."

"The truth is: I don't know what would have happened." Abi is silent. "I'd like to think that I'd have politely declined, but would I really? It never happened, so I don't know." Still no response. "Can you truthfully say that there's no one out there, no situation that would ever tempt you to stray? How could anyone possibly know?"

"Stop," she says and places a finger over my lips. "Just hold me." I grip her tightly, like it matters if I let her go. It does.

There is silence for some time. Eventually, a well spoken English voice laced with irony says, "I guess if I were an American, I'd be cheering and clapping right now."

"Oh James, just let everything be normal for a bit longer," sighs Abi.

"I'm sorry, but we've only got twenty minutes left before they chuck us out and I'd like to talk about the witness."

"What witness?" we say in synchronicity once more.

"Will you two stop doing that?"

We detach from each other and sit, but Abi shuffles her chair closer and places my left hand between hers.

"Sorry if it seems like I'm rushing, but the longer we have to form counter arguments the better."

"No, you do your job. I'm very grateful," I say. James smiles and continues, "The police have found a taxi driver who saw Ms Saarinen cross the main road that night. There's a statement here. Lars would you be so kind, again?"

Lars opens his own file to a page of double spaced type. Above, perhaps the first half, there is red handwriting.

"I was taking a customer home from town. It was something after two o'clock. Two fifteen maybe. I was driving along the two lane road, when I saw a girl cross the road up ahead. She did not use the crossing. She seem in a hurry. If I had not been slowing down to turn to *Pankkikatu*, I would have had to press the brake. I remember laughing: she had party shoes on and nearly slipped as she stepped back on to the pavement. She had dark red hair and, I think, a light brown coat." Lars slows down as he reaches the end of his pre-prepared notes.

"Then after I make turn, a man cross the road just in front of me and I do have to press brake. I curse this man for not looking. I see him well in the headlights. He was weared a blue army coat, black hat and gloves, scarf in front of his mouth and nose, and metal frame glasses. When I come down the road half hour later with next customer I see nobody."

"So the police think that was me?"

"They had this man compare various coats and metal frame specs. He picked out exactly the same thermal coat as you were wearing and almost the same shape glasses."

"But I wasn't there, I was ahead somewhere in the wood. And I don't wear a scarf over my nose. My glasses would steam up all the time if I did that."

"Interesting point," muses James. "That wouldn't have occurred to me… for obvious reasons. Still, the problem remains that the prosecution think they have a witness who saw you behind Arwen and that is significant."

"Of course it's significant," I say with some excitement. "This guy must be the actual killer. I mean if someone is somehow going to fake forensic evidence, wearing the same clothes as me is child's play. I mean, I virtually never went out in anything else."

"It's not exactly an amazing identification, is it?" says Abi. "I mean, I've seen blokes wearing those coats since I've been here. They're not uncommon."

"No," says James, "on its own it's nothing, but it does add to the burden of proof, and, of course, rightly or wrongly, a man following a woman is viewed very differently from a woman following a man."

"So they're going to say I spotted her following and then lay in wait, or something?"

"I suspect so."

"But surely if I was going to do that, I'd have done it in the woods, out of sight, wouldn't I?"

James shrugs. "Anyway, in one of your police interviews you said that you waited for a couple of taxis to pass before crossing the road. I suppose that's how they found this witness."

"Damned by my own mouth again." I shake my head. "Can't we try to find one of the cars I saw?"

"Of course, that's the main reason for asking. Any holes we can pick in the prosecution case, however small, are vital. Can you remember anything about those two taxis?"

I rack my brains, but it was weeks ago. I tense one corner of my mouth in resignation, "I wasn't really looking, I was drunk…"

"OK," says James, "but how did you know they were taxis? If you remember they were taxis, you must remember why you thought they were taxis. Were they like vans or saloons? With lights on the top?"

"Wait," I close my eyes; my forehead tenses with the strain of recall. "I think they were people carrier types, not as big as vans, two identical cars. There were people in them."

"Colour or badges?"

"No. I can't remember."

"Keep trying, something more may come. You've given us a bit more."

There's a sharp knock at the door. Time's up. All too short again. I lean in my chair to steal a kiss from Abi before Lars rises to open the door.

"I'll bring you some new books tomorrow," she smiles.

"Nothing too depressing, please. Bye."

The guard enters and ushers Lars and Abi out of the room. She mouths, "Love you" as she crosses the threshold. James has been rather slow to gather up his papers. He glances towards the door and then towards me and I realise it's been on purpose.

"Steven, I want you to think very carefully about this semen evidence," he whispers in passing. "Remember we're talking life sentences here. It isn't worth hiding anything" He reaches the doorway and, without turning, says in a louder voice, "Think hard."

- - -

"YOUR ABIGAIL seems to be handling it pretty well, considering." Hiltunen passes over this afternoon's compulsory coffee ration. I sip tentatively, mulling his comment.

"Yeah, I guess so. She's amazing. I mean I must have been a total knob to have ever thought... but..."

"But, what?"

"But it's so difficult. The evidence is all so bad. If it was the other way round, I don't know what I'd be thinking. Sometimes I think I can see doubt in her eyes. And all this shit James started about the semen doesn't help."

"She's bound to have doubts. Don't everybody, about most things?"

"I know, but we've never had arguments like this before. They're not about how you squeeze the toothpaste tube. They're about trust and love and stuff. It's scary."

"It's good that you're talking."

"I suppose. I mean, sometimes it's all fine and I wonder what I'm worrying about."

+ + +

CHAPTER 28

"I don't really think you should read these, Steve."

"How bad can it be? I don't want anything held back from me. I'm a big boy now." In happier times, Abi would have made some lewd sarcastic comment about that last sentence, but now it passes without note.

"Here you go then." She hands over a couple of red tops from the previous week. The headline on the first is 'Defence minister in sex romp claims'.

"He should have read up on his 1960s history before getting into that," I comment.

"It's a she," says Abi, almost grinning.

"Now there is a first. Where am I, then?"

"Page 6."

I turn over to be greeted by a half page picture of a vaguely familiar woman showing a lot of flesh above and below her dress. Inset in the bottom left corner is what looks like my passport photo. The headline reads, 'I Cooled it with Chiller Killer'. I squint at the photo.

"That's Denise, isn't it?"

"She's milking it for all she's worth," says Abi.

About ten years ago, just after I started work, I had a small thing with Denise. She was an admin assistant; I was the new engineering trainee. Everyone seemed to think it was expected and we went along with it. I'd never been out with a woman who was so, well, girly: someone who really did tell you not to touch her until her nails were dry; who took half an hour after you arrived to finish getting ready; who claimed she didn't fart. It was never going to last and it didn't, though she dumped me whilst I was still finding it all amusing enough.

But I'm reading that she had a lucky escape from an intense guy who was strangely attractive but always scared her. 'He used to sit and stare at me whilst I painted my toenails. It always gave me the creeps.'

"I could never believe how much effort she put into the bits no one was going to see," I comment, briefly glancing up from the text. It's exaggeration, supposition and innuendo. Anyone's a monster in waiting by those measures. Somehow it doesn't seem real. Not about me. "That doesn't seem too bad," I say. "At least she didn't mention my axe collection."

"Don't say things like that, they could be recording," scolds Abi lightly. She knows I always fall back on ironic humour.

"Sorry. That was a joke, OK? I am still allowed humour, aren't I?" I say, looking up towards the lens. Today Abi's here on a family visit. It's nice to be on our own, but the video may be rolling.

The other article is more of the same. This time it's an old university acquaintance making his fast buck. Apparently, the way I talked about women concerned him. 'Always talked about their sense of humour, or their smile, or their hair, like he was holding something back, never daring to mention the physical stuff.' There is a quote from a psychologist saying that it is typical for disturbed people to avoid mentioning the things that trigger their darkest thoughts. I get halfway through this rubbish and raise one disbelieving eyebrow.

"Yup," she says, "you appear to be a weirdo, because you're not, generally, a complete misogynist bastard!"

"Nice. Have your folks been getting any trouble again?" About a week after my arrest some hack joined the dots and went door knocking round Abi's family.

"They get a few calls now and again. Apparently, my Dad shouts 'innocent until proven guilty!' and then slams the phone down."

"I always did like your Dad."

"Steve..." She fretfully twirls a lock of hair around her index finger.

"What is it?"

"I had a call from the library yesterday. They need to know when... if, I'm coming back. I mean, they've been really good, I've had, what, almost three months' leave now."

"What are you saying?"

"They want me to go back to the UK for a couple of days. They've got a temp they need me to train. I owe it to them. I was thinking just after the prep hearing."

"It's OK, you go. Heck, I've been the one leaving you behind enough times over the years. Best not burn any bridges, just in case."

"Don't talk like that."

"James found any taxi drivers yet?"

"No."

"Well then," I shrug.

CHAPTER 29

I am Steven Carter and I know the charges against me. Formalities over, the judge motions me to take my seat: not a wooden bench, a cushioned plastic chair with felt pads on the base of its metal legs. Wouldn't want to scratch the lovely parquet floor, would we? Somehow I'd expected the district court to be more impressive: all carved wood, crests and Latin mottos: too much telly again. In fact, apart from the monolithic panel across the front of the room, we could be in a school assembly hall. Behind the panel on a slightly raised platform, the judge sits slightly left of centre. She wears no wig or gown, a high backed chair seemingly her only badge of office. In front of her, the built in table supports a microphone, an open file and a glasses case. To her left are three vacant chairs which will hold the lay judges.

James had a lot of fast talking to do when Abi and I found out that there is no trial by jury in Finland. It's such a given in the UK, one of those things we view as cast in stone, one of our human rights, but round the world it's actually pretty rare. We had visions of a cranky old judge dispensing summary justice with the wave of his mallet. Of course, this was as wrong as the idea that anyone other than a Brit would still be waving a mallet in the twenty-first century. 'Put it like this,' James had said, 'would you rather your fate was decided by twelve complete novices or four experienced judges?' Makes you wonder whether our system really is such a good idea. Anyway, whether I like it or not, come the start of the main trial, there will be three lay judges in addition to the one professional who will, together, review the evidence and agree a verdict.

My involvement in this closed hearing is now over. James and Lars have begun discussing practicalities with the judge and the Prosecutor. Although it is all being translated for my, and to a certain extent James's, benefit, I find my mind drifting. My eyes flick towards Abi, who James has sat at the other end of our table. In spite of the official court clerk doing the same, she is taking her own shorthand notes. Trying to seem useful, I expect.

The discussion begins with press handling – the judge is giving out strict guidelines regarding witnesses talking to journalists. We came through to the secure internal courtyard this morning, but even so, several photographers tried to flash through the one way glass of the transfer van as it entered the alleyway.

Next there are issues around translation. It seems that the usual lay judges have markedly different competencies in English. Might this cause problems? Would someone more skilled in English from a neighbouring district be better? The judge's Finnish sounds very deliberate and exaggeratedly sing-song to my ears. I wonder if this is a posh accent? She's in her fifties with blonde hair that's turning white; no, I suppose, really, it's white hair with a few remaining blondes. In one of his less helpful moments, Lars let on that she has a reputation for harsh sentencing. Still, Finland is supposed to hand out the shortest prison sentences in the world – and it won't come to that, anyway.

I miss the translation conclusion. They've started talking about who will examine the defence witnesses. There are rows of windows high on each of the side walls: too high for photographers to poke telephoto lenses through. I can see the deep blue sky of a scorching summer day. Despite the hum of ceiling fans, the temperature is rising steadily. Lars's shirt has already darkened at the armpits. Wouldn't it be lovely to sit, legs dangling into the cool of a stream, the shade of oaks above? A small white fronted bird flies low over the water and disappears downhill. Barefoot, I follow, splashing through the flow, stepping carefully over weed covered rocks. The bird has alighted, bobbing on a smoothed boulder. I stumble as pebbles move underfoot and with a whistle, the bird disappears around the next bend. Reaching the white stained rock, a lake glitters ahead through the branches. Pine branches now. A path winds downhill among the trees. Arwen is purposefully striding along it, eyes forward. I try to call out, but a sudden cold takes my breath. I try to run, but the water has frozen: my feet are held fast.

My eyes refocus on the aluminium window frames and the lilt of Finnish words re-enters my ears. An involuntary shiver passes through me and I turn my head to see a perspiring James regarding me with a quizzical expression. No one else seems to have noticed. He raises his gaze to the translator and I realise that they have moved on to setting the date for the trial. It will be winter before I am here again.

"I'VE HAD AN IDEA about the forensic evidence," I say and take a sip of real ground coffee from the lid of Lars's plastic flask. Heavenly.

James and Lars lean forward. It's not what they're thinking. I can see the words, 'I thought you might' written all over their expressions: Abi is in the UK.

"Look, I know you think maybe I was having sex with Arwen and I don't want to say in front of Abi."

"It would make the prosecution case a lot weaker," interrupts James.

"Maybe, but it isn't true and I'm not going to lie in court."

"OK, I would never advise you to do that, but then what is your idea?" James sits back. I'm still not sure he believes me, and he's certainly disappointed.

"Well, obviously the main problem with this semen evidence is that it's mine, so I've been thinking: how could anyone get my semen?"

"Go on."

Despite the fact that it's only men in the room, I blush. "Well, I'm a bloke, I was away from home for months and I haven't been playing around so... well, if someone were to rig something up in the hotel plumbing they might have been able to catch some of my semen, every so often..."

They both get the point without me having to draw a diagram. On this one occasion I am quite happy that Abi is not here. I mean, I guess she knows it happens, she just doesn't want it poked in her face, so to speak.

"Sound a bit like James Bond," says Lars doubtfully.

"I didn't say it was a good idea, it is a bit farfetched, but it's the only thing I can think of."

"No... It's good," says James. "It gives us something to work on. We can have your room and the hotel plumbing inspected for signs of tampering. And if we do find anything then that leads us straight on to investigating hotel staff and guests, I suppose. We'll have to get the relevant court orders, etc. but that should be no problem." James scribbles some notes with a more animated flourish than I have seen for a couple of weeks: something to get his teeth into. He bangs a full stop through the page and regards me with a levelled expression, "Don't get your hopes up too much though. Like Lars says, it is a long shot. Still I've heard stranger stuff. Was there more?"

"You mentioned about hotel guests, well..." I shift uncomfortably. "I'm not the only person staying there who could have M&S boxer shorts. Keith always seems to have a bit of a cave man attitude towards women. He..."

"Let me stop you right there," interrupts James. "Aaltonen is one step ahead of you. You're right, Keith does have four pairs of the relevant boxers. Unfortunately, he also has an alibi. In your statements, you mention that Keith left Hanne's party early. The woman he left with has come forward. He was with her all night."

"Can we believe her?"

"She's married..."

"Her husband work on ships," inserts Lars.

"So I think that gives it some credibility. She risks a lot by coming forward."

I sigh, "Well, I didn't really think... he's not... but everyone thinks it about me."

There's a pause whilst James's fingers dance across the screen of his phone. Lars retrieves his empty lid from the table and reaches into his bag. "We think you might want to see this."

He hands over a Finnish newspaper. Almost the whole of the front page is taken up by a photo. It's strange. Unsettling. A pale coffin with ornate handles sits in the foreground, an elaborate bouquet of lilies resting on its lid. Behind it and to the side are a group of people, family I suppose. They're all dressed in black except for one item of red: a red scarf, red gloves, a red tie. My eyes alight on a woman with hair dyed bright red. It's Til. Next to her is Harri sporting a red handkerchief tucked in his jacket pocket. Directly behind the coffin is a woman, my mouth drops open... no, the face has seen more years, but, gosh, the resemblance is strong. Arwen's mother is standing straight and stiff, her husband, I suppose, to the right. Her hand is resting on the shoulder of the young man to the left. A brother? The faces are small on the newsprint, but I realise it's Kari with slightly longer hair and a beard. A single red flower is pinned to his lapel.

"This is Arwen's funeral?" I ask. Lars nods.

"It looks like a wedding photo, but..." I whisper.

"We do that in Finland," says Lars. "We take photo of the death, as well as the baby or the wedding. Why not? It happen to everyone."

"So people might put this photo up on their sideboard to remember her by?"

"Some people, maybe."

"Wow, that's..." I'm not sure if I think that's good or bad, "different." Two tears trickle down my cheeks.

"Why do they keep using that picture?" I ask, suddenly annoyed, pointing to the inset photo. It's the same one as on the telly.

"If I was going to be cynical, I'd say that maybe the police think a picture of a fresh faced girl will get a bigger public reaction than one of a glamorous young woman," says James.

"Or perhaps her mother still think of her as little girl," Lars ponders.

"Whatever, it doesn't look anything like her. Not how she was..." More tears. I sniff loudly and pull out a tissue. "I'm sorry... I just wish I could have been there. All that red..."

CHAPTER 30

I hear Abi's laugh as the guard opens the door. Her laugh! She's smiling like I haven't seen since... well, since her party. Even James's professional poker face seems lighter than usual. Abi's kiss is long and lingering. She seats herself in the chair next to mine and waits expectantly for James.

"Well, Mr Carter, if your wife becomes any more useful, I'm going to have to start paying her," he says, very formally. "She seems to have found you your witness."

I glance between James and a now beaming Abi. My brow furrows in question.

"I was thinking about what you remembered: about the two taxis," says Abi, the pride clear in her voice. "It occurred to me the other day that maybe they weren't taxis. Maybe they were company cars or for a club or a sports team."

"So for the last fortnight, Abigail and Lars have been talking to all the hotels, clubs, restaurants in Mahikkala trying to find groups of about eight to fourteen people..."

"Had to be about that number, or why two cars?" interrupts Abi.

James continues, "A group of people who left in two people carriers at about 2am on the night in question."

"Also from the direction they were heading, they pretty much had to be from out of town." Abi turns to Lars, "Everywhere was really helpful once we told them we were working on the Saarinen case. Lars did most of the talking."

"We did not always say we work for defence..." shrugs Lars.

"Two days ago we spoke to the VPT women's volley ball team," says Abi, "and they remember you!"

James pulls a couple of papers out of his briefcase. "Great work this, Abigail... and Lars." Abi blushes. "Charles did tell me you were smart, but, well, you have to see things for yourself."

I grip Abi's nearest hand and squeeze gently.

"This is a joint statement from two of the team. I'm afraid they don't remember you for very flattering reasons. Lars, if you would:"

- We went to Mahikkala because the team night out. We have college next day so we leave early: at 2am. Our trainers were driving. When we are on to two lane road, we see this guy. He wear a dark army coat, black hat and glasses. We laugh because he look very drunk. He wobble and he look like he talk to the lamp post.

"That would have been me," I grin.

- We call out to our trainer who say, 'I hope he know his way home.' and we see someone coming down road, so we say, 'it all right a friend follows him.' Person was too far to see what they like.

"Sometimes drunk people die of cold," says Lars, explaining the trainer's comment.

"And this is from their coach," says James, replacing the paper in front of Lars.

- We drive back from Mahikkala. It must be about ten past two. Two of the girls call out, 'Look at that drunk, he talk to the post.' I said, 'I hope he know his way home.' He was wearing one of those blue army coats; a hat; I don't remember what else. I didn't see anyone else, no cars or people, but girls say that someone was coming down side road. Two lane road is straight for half a kilometre there. Definitely no one cross road just in front of man. I would see in lights. After we pass I see the man cross road in rear mirror. I see nothing else.

"So it confirms your version," says Abi, returning the squeeze. "Arwen following you, not the other way round."

"And that there was someone else following her," I say.

"I'm not sure I'd go that far," says James, his serious law voice returning, "but what it does do is establish doubt about what the prosecution witness saw and if we can do that with all their evidence..." He doesn't need to spell it out. "There is one other good thing. At least, I think it's a good thing." He smiles diffidently at Abi. No, can't have been, barristers don't do diffident.

"James has offered me a job!" says Abi, like a small child announcing the winning of a funfair goldfish to her parents: hoping for, but unsure of approval. Before my brain has got anywhere near processing this into a question, James continues in a rush, "Obviously, Abigail's library have been very kind to keep her position open for her, but she is now on unpaid leave. Your employment payments reduce next month, so her finances are, well, precarious."

"But there's no way I'm going home without you," says Abi, almost fiercely.

"Of course," says James. "I wasn't really joking earlier. Abigail has done some very useful work and she is still your chosen legal counsel. It seems quite reasonable to formalise the arrangement with remuneration."

I can't think of a reply that doesn't sound like something out of a Famous Five book. I give up trying, "James that's... that's very decent of you, but surely this must break a whole load of rules somewhere?"

"If we were in the UK, then, perhaps, but..."

There's a certain sound in the silence after James trails off. I recognise that tone: "This was Charles idea, wasn't it?"

James spreads his hands wide in capitulation. "That guy is so good at finding his way round inconvenient laws, he really ought to go into politics."

"So, it's OK with you?" says Abi.

"Yeah, why would it not be?" She looks relieved.

CHAPTER 31

"I'm afraid the searches at the hotel have turned up a blank," James announces. The three serious faces across the table have told me as much already. Abi shifts in her chair uncomfortably and glances towards James, who nods. An unsure Abi is always a cause for worry. I wrap my feet around the front legs of the chair and tense my leg muscles.

"Steve, you're being accused of murder," she says quietly.

"I know."

"That might be life in prison."

"I know." Where is this going?

"Is there anything you're not saying, because you don't want to hurt my feelings? I can take it. It's not worth throwing your life away." Her words sound rehearsed.

I struggle to hold in my anger and my words come out slow and clipped. "OK. Arwen and I were secret lovers. We had been for weeks. That night, at the party, we sneaked into the kitchen after the caterers left." I hold Abi's eyes wanting to see the hurt land home. "She loved the risk, she was so hot..." I can't continue with it. The trembling of Abi's bottom lip makes me relent. "Is that what you want me to say? Is it?" I turn my fury on James. "You've set her up to ask me this haven't you? Don't hide behind your lawyer face, you bastard. You even got her to practise, didn't you?"

"Yes, but..." says James, voice level.

"Don't 'but' me! You're my lawyer; you're supposed to believe me. I've already told you that I never had sex with Arwen. I wasn't lying. I'll say it again. I – never – had – any – kind – of – sexual – relations – with – Arwen – Saarinen! OK?" I stand and start to pace the far wall. "For crying out loud, we've just had people taking my hotel room apart searching for evidence of my own masturbation. Isn't that enough of an indignity, without you implying..."

"I just don't see how the forensic evidence stacks up otherwise, unless..."

"Unless I did kill her." I finish for him. "Thanks James, for that vote of confidence. And as for you," I stop and turn towards my wife. "Don't you know me? Don't you know that if I'd really done anything it would eat away inside me? I'd see accusation in your every glance, a double meaning in your every word. I wouldn't be able to stop myself telling you. That's what real love is, isn't it? Sharing: whatever we do together feels good; whatever we hold back hurts us." I stomp towards the door and yank it open to the surprise of the guard beyond. His hand reaches down for his baton, but only rests there as I make no further movement.

"We're finishing early today. These three are just leaving." I hear the sound of chairs scraping on the lino floor behind me.

"Stand away from door, Carter," says the guard, grimly following procedure, even though I suspect he can guess something of the situation. I step backwards and turn towards the side wall, leaving the door to swing. The guard steps forward to hold it before it shuts. I fix my eyes on a fleck of white showing through where the paint has been chipped. There are sounds of packing up, punctuated by sniffs. It takes a massive effort not to turn after each of those sniffs.

"We'll be in again tomorrow," says James. I make no response and shortly the last of the three shapes in my peripheral vision moves through the doorway.

"We go, Mr Angry Man," says the guard. He shakes his head, "lawyer here to help you, no?"

"It doesn't always feel like that," I say as I pass in front of him and through the doorway. Ahead of me, through the glazing of security doors I can still see Abi, James and Lars waiting for the second set to be opened. Abi is leaning, head against the white wall, sobbing. James reaches out a comforting hand. Her shoulder drops away from his touch and then I am given a gentle nudge in the back and have to move out of the line of sight and back to my cell.

"I'M SORRY, it's just so hard. Sometimes I don't know what to think; I can't think." Abi is holding both my hands in hers, piercing me with her grey green eyes. Who could resist?

"I'm sorry too, I was cruel. Too much time in my own company, too much time to think: it makes me too sensitive." We kiss tenderly. I hope James and Lars are having the decency to look the other way. I don't know how long we stand, resting our heads on each other's shoulders, feeling the warmth of our cheeks, the scent of our necks. A long sigh - the sound of deflation - escapes from Abi and we raise our heads. James is studiously leafing through a sheaf of papers neatly stacked on the familiar table. Lars is pouring out the first lid of filter coffee. Our movement causes them both to look up.

"Steven," says James, "I must apologise for yesterday. It's... it's easy to forget that I'm dealing with people. Sometimes, I get too caught up in the law."

"I know you're just trying to do your job, and I know it might be easier for me if I said something was going on with Arwen, but it wasn't and you and I are just going to have to live with that."

"Remember the way you just said that," says James.

"What?"

"You can be very convincing sometimes. You sound naturally honest. We can use that. Lars and I did some hard thinking last night. It seems like we're stuck with this forensic evidence, which is difficult, very difficult; I'm not going to understate that." His face has turned serious. "So what is your defence? It's got to be that this evidence is so contrary to everything else we know about you that somehow it must be untrue."

Lars takes over: "We must have witness to speak of your good character, we must show you like Arwen, not want to hurt her. We also get Abigail to speak."

"Can she do that? Be a witness as well as on the law team?"

"Why not?" says James, "If you were representing yourself you would be counsel, witness, and defendant."

"We have also the witness who see you on road and..." Lars pauses.

"And we'd like you to take a polygraph test."

"A what?"

"Lie-detector. It can be a risk and the judge may not put much weight on its evidence, but in this case it seems like there's nothing to lose."

"Ah..." I pause. My eyes flick towards Abi; this seems a surprise to her too. Then I focus on James. This is sharp; very clever in several ways. I clap out slow ironic applause. "Hell, that's genius. I'd get offended for being manipulated, but I want brains like that on my side!" Abi looks confused.

"They're asking me to put my money where my mouth is. I think old James here is taking it as a given that the test will say I didn't kill Arwen. If it doesn't, well, at the moment the forensics have got me stuffed anyway. No, he's far more interested in the answer to something like, 'Did you have sexual intercourse with Arwen?' Aren't you?"

James raises his hands in surrender.

"The test will come out saying that I didn't, and then he can use that to argue that the forensics must be wrong. But, he's also thinking that if the test says I'm lying, he can argue that I did have sex with Arwen, and I'm denying it out of misguided loyalty to my wife."

"James, you devious sod," says Abi, smiling.

"I would like to pass Lars some of the credit for this idea," says James.

"Umm," says Lars, unsure if he really wants this accolade.

"Yes, by the way," I say, "of course I'll do it. When?"

"In two weeks you have medical and mental state examination. We organise for then."

CHAPTER 32

"Haw, haw, haw... so that's why we got this bundle of fun to come. I just love the pol-y-graph." His face morphs into a broad grin. "Course I already know what answer you're gonna give to THAT question!" I snort, shaking my head with eyes raised. Hiltunen closes his notebook, leaving the pencil inside as a marker. "There ain't no more, right?"

"No, that's it... I mean, there must've been other stuff in between, but it doesn't all stick. You get enough for what you need?"

"I sure think so, but we still got the little test to come." He holds my eye. "Thank you Mr Carter, you've been very... open. Sometimes it's like extracting molars."

"So you believe me?"

"You know I can't say that right now. You'll get to read my report soon enough." He rises and holds the door wide. "Now I gotta prepare for a while." There's a short conversation in Finnish with the guard in the corridor. "Paavo will bring you down to the testing room when I call. While you're waiting you can stretch your legs or..." His eyes twinkle with amusement. "I'm sure we can spare some paper if you're dying to note down the 'Psycho-anal-ysm Blues'.

"There's not much room in my head for lyrics at the moment."

"I guess not."

MORE THAN AN HOUR LATER, I'm all wired up and ready to go: blood pressure monitor inflated and squeezing, heart rate electrode taped under my shirt, further electrodes on my forehead and fingers, lens observing my eyes.

"Remember, just yes or no and look right ahead at all times."

"OK."

Dr Hiltunen's voice is level and expressionless, his eyes fixed on the laptop screen between us. "Is your name Steven Carter?"

"Yes."

"Are you British?"

"Yes."

"Have you ever stolen something from a store?"

"Yes." In my peripheral vision, I see his eyebrows rise slightly before he can stop them.

"Did you see Arwen Saarinen in the forest by the lake on the night she died?"

"No."

"Have you ever had sexual thoughts about a man?"

"No."

"Do you like strong cheese?"

"Yes."

"Did you find Arwen Saarinen sexually attractive?"

"Yes."

"Manchester United is your soccer team?"

"No." Come on, I live in Manchester!

"Your favourite colour is red?"

"No." Light blue, obviously.

"Do you remember walking back from the lake on the night Arwen Saarinen was killed?

"Not really, but..."

"Yes or no?"

"No." Where is he going with that one? I can feel myself starting to sweat.

"Do you love your wife?"

"Yes."

"Have you ever told a lie to your employer?"

"Yes."

"Did you ever have any type of sexual relations with Arwen Saarinen?"

"No."

"Did you kill Arwen Saarinen?"

"No."

"Do you want to have children?"

"Um..." This one catches me out completely. "Yes, I suppose so, eventually."

"Just yes or no..."

"Yes."

"Do you think my beard looks dumb?"

"No." The automatic lie falls out of my mouth before I can stop it. I think I see a slight widening of the psychologist's eyes. Maybe I imagined it.

"Did you love your mother?"

"Yes."

"Were you in love with Arwen Saarinen?"

"No... well... define 'in love'?"

"To your own definition of the words."

"No, then." The corners of his mouth turn upward slightly.

"Do you like cold weather?"

"Yes."

"Have you ever slightly bumped someone else's automobile and driven off without telling them?"

"No."

"Do you think I'm clever?"

"Yes."

"Have you seen Arwen Saarinen's body?"

"No."

"Do you like it in at the remand centre?"

"No."

"Do you like your wife's cooking?"

"Yes."

"Do you know who killed Arwen Saarinen?"

"No." I wish I did.

The psychologist's eyes rise from his computer.

"Thank you Mr Carter, that was most enlightening. I'll be sending my report, along with the polygraph results in about a week or so." His smile turns into a childish grin. "Neat question, the one about the beard, don't you think?"

"Very clever," I say. He nods ever so slightly in acknowledgement, then turns and knocks twice on the door.

As the guard enters, Hiltunen leans back, resting his elbows on the chair arms, palms together. "I got a little piece of advice for you, if you wannit."

"Go on," I say, pulling off the electrode tape with sudden, pain reducing tugs.

"Before your trial, you tell your Abigail everything you told me... Everything."

I stare sceptically for a moment until the guard motions me forward. "Fun over now," he says.

As I approach the doorway, a strangely accent-less voice emanates from the bald psychologist, "Good luck, Mr Carter." I double take, but the guard grips my arm and I'm steered into the corridor before I can respond.

CHAPTER 33

"Well?"

James lifts a neatly bound report from his brief case. Stapled copies bearing the same elaborate crest are already in Lars and Abi's hands. "It's about as good as we could have hoped for. The psychological evaluation makes very interesting reading."

"He was a strange guy," I say, "I think he made up a whole persona just to put me at ease. I had a feeling something wasn't quite right, but I kept on talking all the same."

"Well, whatever, you seem to have said the right things... listen to this. He reads from the third page: the English summary.

"I find the subject, Mr Steven Carter, to be of sound mind and, considering the circumstances in which he finds himself, he remains remarkably well balanced. As you will see from the detailed comments, I find nothing to indicate a tendency towards violence or any other serious criminal behaviour. His main character defects appear to be over confidence in his own abilities and a certain naivety about matters of the heart and mind.

"Whilst particular details of his story seem to stretch credibility, I detected no signs of untruthfulness in the essential points, a diagnosis which is backed up by the polygraph results (section 2). Therefore, I reach the following conclusion: Assuming that Steven Carter is not the most accomplished liar that I have ever encountered, he certainly believes that he was not involved in the death of Arwen Saarinen. Although there is the issue of his lack of recall of the return journey from the lakeside (section 1.4), I find no evidence of memory trauma and consider his explanation of being 'lost in thought' quite plausible."

"That's good then isn't it? That was what we were hoping for?" James and Lars nod. Neither of them is smiling, though.

"Yes, but we have to remember that when this type of report says 'certainly', the judges will be thinking 'possibly', 'probably' at most."

"It's obviously not an exact science," I say scanning James's face warily. His eyes slip sideways towards Abi. My heart sinks as I follow them. I knew her greeting was too brief. I thought it must be the report, but it's more than that. "What?" Abi continues to scrutinise the page in front of her.

"Come on, I know that expression, speak to me."

"The lie-detector test: it says you lied twice." There is a note of icy accusation in her voice which scares me. I furrow my brow and snatch the report from the table in front of James. "Sorry, may I?"

"Be my guest."

I flick to section 2. There is an A3 fold out bar chart indicating the size of the physiological responses to each of the questions. The blocks of colour are much longer in two cases. I know one must be the beard question. I scan quickly down the key to 'do you love your wife?' I let out my held breath. It's not that one. "Oh..." My eyes alight on the corresponding question. Bollocks, that's barely any better.

"He says that you have one of the strongest lie responses he has ever seen, which makes the test more valid," she says, not looking up.

"Which from a legal point of view is excellent," inserts James. Just at the moment, I couldn't care less about the legal point of view.

"He says you lied first at the trick question about his beard, but then again when asked about your feelings for Ar..." She half swallows, half chokes on the name.

"Abi..."

She talks over me, eyes still fixed on the page. "He says that this lie is consistent with your naivety about love. That you think you can control who you love with your conscious mind, but your unconscious reactions show that to be a lie."

"He also states his opinion that whether or not you were in love with Arwen, it has no relevance to the case," inserts James, reaching again for the positive.

I ignore him and start again, "Abi, look at me. Please." After five interminable seconds, her moist eyes meet mine. "You know I was a bit stupid about this girl, you know we had a lot in common, that I liked her, that I..."

"...found her sexually attractive," she quotes.

"Well, yes, but I didn't do anything about it. Maybe that weird mind doctor is right and I was deluding myself, but I was trying hard not to be in love with her. The night she was killed I was so embarrassed that I vowed to start avoiding her."

"Don't say that in court," interrupts James.

"What?"

"Well, you're avoiding her permanently now, aren't you?"

"I didn't mean..."

"I know that, but it's just the sort of thing the prosecution will pick up on if you're not careful."

Abi and I stare at each other; perhaps this final comment from James has placed some context on both our thoughts.

"I'm sorry," I say quietly. "I've brought all this on you. I'm a daft stupid bugger who doesn't deserve you."

"There's nothing else?" Her expression is melting.

"No." I interlock my fingers into her outstretched hand. There's a moment of sweet silence.

"Shoplifting?" says James, eyebrows lifted.

Abi rolls her eyes and laughs, "Nicked a marble from a toy shop when he was a kid!"

IT'S A DIFFERENT SET OF WALLS, but the Formica table and plastic chairs could be the same: standard government issue. The paint is a cold arctic blue; so much more cheery than the magnolia of the remand centre; not. They might as well put a sign up: 'Abandon hope now, all who come to court'. We've turned a couple of the chairs on one side of the table towards each other and we sit, arms on knees, facing each other, husband and wife in silence. One of Abi's hands rests in mine. I suppose it's the tension before tomorrow, maybe this depressing room, but something isn't right: a difference in Abi's eyes? I'm just getting paranoid.

"It's really cold outside - minus twenty-five it said in James's car," says Abi. Oh, to travel in a car, not an armoured van, anywhere, I don't mind.

"I hope he had the seat heaters turned on?"

She nods. "They're wonderful when you first get in. Like standing with your back to an open fire." We lapse into silence. Somewhere out in the holding block a door slams.

"James is confident," she says.

"I know, I hope he's right."

"He is." She squeezes my hands. "You'll be out soon. What do you want to do first?"

I've been daydreaming about this for weeks, but I hardly dare speak it. "I want to walk somewhere open: a forest, a beach, anywhere with no fences. I want to buy something frivolous from a crowded shopping centre. I want to sit up all night, playing board games, drinking wine, eating cheesy biscuits until I look like one."

She smiles, "Midnight feasts." There are a lot of happy memories in those two words. "I'll see if I can get some in. I have to nip down to Helsinki this afternoon."

"Blowing your hard earned cash in the Nordic boutiques then?" I tease. Surprisingly, she's suddenly sheepish.

"Thought I'd better have a new suit for the trial."

"Good idea. And I'm to wear the blue one?"

"Yes, that's the one James thinks would be best."

"He does like to manage every little detail doesn't he?"

"It's his job, he prides himself in his thoroughness," says Abi, leaning back and stretching, hands above her head.

"I'm lucky Charles found him." Silence again.

The corner of my mouth twitches with remembered disappointment. "So you're really going to sit behind us tomorrow. I'd feel a lot better with you beside me."

"I do want to," she says, purposefully avoiding eye contact, "It's just that..."

"James thinks it looks better because you're a witness as well." Abi doesn't answer; we've already been through this with James. I shrug. "I expect he's right." I reach for her hands again and close my eyes. They feel the same as they always has: fingers so long and thin, quite different from my stubby digits. She should have been a piano player.

A sharp rap on the door precipitates hasty hugged goodbyes. "See you in the morning then. Love you."

"You too," she says, as the guard motions her into the corridor.

CHAPTER 34

Despite falling snow building on the window ledges, if anything the temperature is hotter in here than last time. Expectant bodies are packed tightly in the rows behind us, each one pumping out a couple of hundred watts. Despite being told to face forward at all times, I can't help but glance towards Abi. I never get that far. Heads turn towards my movement: heads with accusing stares. I flick past Harri, but Arwen's mother's eyes drill into me before I can stop them. They're the same: wide, bright, but vulnerable. I wrench my head back forward, feeling hot with shame and guilt. Why? A flicker of frustration passes in my direction from James, but he's concentrating on the Finnish, trying to get ahead of the translation.

James has also advised me not to make eye contact with the judges, even when testifying. 'The barristers ask the questions, so look at them. If you stare at the judges they'll think you're trying to be intimidating. Of course they will try to be objective, but they're still human. If you frown they may think you're remorseful and hence guilty; if you smile, they may think you're weird or not taking it seriously and therefore guilty; if you keep a neutral expression then you are detached and calculating and therefore guilty. Best not to look at all.' I can see what he's saying, but it's difficult not to be curious about these four people who hold the future of my life in the balance of their opinion. I snatch a few furtive glances. They seem like ordinary people. There are no beauties or strange hairstyles, no one especially tall or fat, just two average men and two average women. I think that's good, isn't it?

Once the main judge has called the court to order, the Prosecutor, Advocate Talus, takes his place on the right side of the room, just in front of the judges' platform. He stands at a desk whose pale, slab-like frontage mimics the longer judges' bench. Directly opposite him, on the left is an identical desk, currently vacant. Chief Judge Kivelä motions that I should rise from the defence table and take my place at the witness stand for the reading of the charges. I'm escorted by two burly guards who take up positions behind me.

I stare straight ahead, concentrating on Talus, trying to block out aloof stares from the left and hatred from the right. Just at the moment, tunnel vision would be great. Through the translator I hear him outline the basic facts of the case. "Nineteen... naked... frozen... forensic..." Certain words seem to scream in my ears despite the flat, precise tone of the English. After some time, he pauses, lifts his notes and reads the next sentence. I recognise the word *'murha'* and know it's the charge. My head moves slowly from side to side. How am I here?

In addition to the criminal charge, the prosecutor also informs me that the victim's family are claiming compensation for their distress. Like mere money can replace her... I'm still mentally fuming, when I realise that the Prosecutor has reached the question: "Do you admit or deny the charges brought by this court and the deceased's family against you?"

"I deny all the charges." I really want to say more, but James has drummed into me I must only give the formal answer. Anything else would seem argumentative.

Low whispers from my right increase as the translator finishes and I return to my seat, eyes welded to the floor.

"AS YOU CAN SEE on the map labelled figure one," says the court translator in precise accent-less English, "the woods form a ring around Lake Mahi." Advocate Talus is describing the relevant geography to the judges. He speaks a sentence and then waits for the translation. It makes for slow going, but in true Finnish fashion, is scrupulously fair on the English speakers present. The explanation continues, "This is only broken on the north side where the town itself reaches the lake. The dual carriageway runs east-west between the town and the lakeshore until it is level with the market square where it turns through ninety degrees and narrows. East of this, the woods begin again adjacent to the *LähelläMahi* Hotel."

Behind I can hear the occasional rustle of papers and wrappers. People are beginning to realise quite how long winded and boring some of the evidence will be. I daren't look, but I imagine books being opened and mints being popped into yawning mouths.

On the table in front of us are three black files. Inside each, a mass of plastic wallets contain copies of all the pertinent documents. I glance at the map of Mahikkala. With my brain used to imagining black lines as working machines, the geography is obvious. Come on, get to something interesting. Not too interesting though.

Shortly, a further sheet is projected on the large screen behind the witness stand and I turn to the next page. It is an enlargement of the area of woodland south of *Pankkikatu*. There's a red cross marked by the side of one of the footpaths. I'm pretty sure it is the one I would've walked down. How close behind me was she? Why didn't she call out?

A murmuring from behind returns my focus to what is being said. The Prosecutor appears to be talking directly to Arwen's parents. "I apologise for these distressing photos, but you must understand that due to the nature of the case, I have no choice but to show all the facts." The chief judge already said something similar earlier. A picture flicks up on the screen. As one, there is an audible intake of breath around the court. "Pure heart string tugging," mutters James under his breath. "No need to show that yet."

The photo is a wide angle snow scene: dark green pines laden with white, sparse undergrowth pushing hoar coated twigs above the blanket. Beautiful, until you look closer. A few meters to the left, orange poles marking the edges of a ski path can be seen above low mounds of snow: concealing bushes, I suppose. In the distance, a lamp post stands incongruously against the foliage. But all eyes are drawn to the middle distance where the top of something blue-grey can be seen in a small hollow beside a couple of young trees. Strewn in front, a heap of black material is half covered by a brown coat. She was wearing a black dress: my mind is only filled with that thought. The blue-grey, it must be... The volume of chatter is increasing as the assembly realise what they are seeing. Judge Kivelä raises her right hand and calls for quiet. Behind, a sob breaks the returning silence and I realise that there are tears on my own cheeks.

"That explains why the body wasn't found until the Saturday," I hear James whisper to Lars. I can't help a flash of anger as I hear him say 'the body'. How can he be so dispassionate? Those blue-grey pixels were a person: a fabulous person. I continue to stare at the photo and the heat subsides. He's right, of course, the place she's lying wouldn't be seen from the path. Just doing his job.

I'm sure there are worse photos to come, but for now, it seems that the judges have decided to break for lunch. Everyone starts to leave the room. After a few minutes of low chatter, shuffles and scraping, James glances over his shoulder, and then whispers, "Now." I turn to see the only people remaining seated are my two guards, intransigent on the front row, directly behind the defence table. In the centre of the room, a hungry queue is inching its way through the double doors, all facing away, drawn by the promising smells emanating from the in-house restaurant opposite. All except Abi, who is bringing up the rear. She raises a hand in a half wave and her lips part in a pale, nervous smile. I return the gesture and lift the corners of my mouth. I expect it looks more like a grimace than a smile. The guards stand and Abi turns away as I'm escorted through the side door. Rather than taking me back to the holding cell, they usher me into a visiting room where a flat seeded roll lies beside a bowl of meatball soup. I wonder if anyone has spat in it.

IMMEDIATELY ON OUR RETURN, the prosecution call their first witness. To my surprise, at least, it's Kari. On reaching the witness desk, he turns his head towards me and stares defiantly. I fix my eyes on the table.

There is a small swearing in ceremony which is not translated.

Talus begins, "Tell the court your relationship to Arwen Saarinen."

"She was my girlfriend for the last three years."

"I am sorry. Say if at any point you wish for a pause in the questions."

"I will answer any of your questions. Justice for Arwen is all that matters."

"On the night of Thursday 28th February this year you and Ms Saarinen attended a party at Hanne's Bar in Mahikkala. Can you describe for us what happened that evening?"

"Arwen worked in that bar. Hanne had paid off the loan on the place and all the staff and best customers were invited for a big celebration. It should have been a great time. Hanne knows how to throw a party." Once the translation has finished, I understand the chuckles from the crowd, thirty seconds earlier.

"I believe there was a free bar for the first hour?"

"Yes, there was a lot of very fast drinking and everything that goes with that."

"So you and Ms Saarinen also consumed a large amount of alcohol?"

"Not that much, actually. Arwen was in a strange mood: she kept bringing up an old argument. We should have been enjoying it, but it was tense between us and so neither of us drank that much."

"We'll come back to that argument in a moment, but for now we can see - on page six - from the toxicology report, that by the time of Ms Saarinen's death, her blood alcohol level was only twice the legal driving limit." That is next to nothing out here. "The report states that for a regular social drinker, this level of alcohol would be unlikely to cause significant loss of physical or mental faculties. Would you describe Ms Saarinen as a regular social drinker?"

"Yes, but she was pretty much sober that night."

"How would you describe your own state?"

"I did have a couple more than Arwen, but I wasn't drunk."

"But some people at the party were very drunk, including the defendant?"

"Yes, Steven and his English friends could hardly stand up some of the time."

"Isn't that just an opinion?" I whisper to James.

"Yes but it's not worth annoying the judge with an objection. Do you object?"

"No, I suppose it is fairly accurate." James shrugs the matter closed and faces forward again.

The Prosecutor glances towards our whispers, as if expecting a formal interruption. James raises his hand slightly in apology and he turns back towards his witness. "Can you describe how the defendant acted towards Ms Saarinen that evening?"

"He was drunk; he seemed to be pestering her."

"Tell us what you remember."

"I came back from the toilet one time and he was talking to

Arwen. She looked uncomfortable. I don't know what he had said. Then later, he asked her to dance. She refused, but he just kept trying to pull her out of the chair. She twisted free, but sat back heavily. The chair nearly fell over."

"So you're saying that the defendant was physically violent when Ms Saarinen refused to dance with him."

"Yes."

I glance towards James. His face is betraying nothing. I suppose he must have been expecting something like that.

Kari describes the rest of the evening and his argument with Arwen. It's all pretty much as the police statement.

"And those were her last words to you?" Unlike Lars, the court translator does not shy away from translating the expletive accurately.

"Yes," says Kari, his voice cracking. "Can I have a minute?"

"Of course." He breathes fast and deep, bottom lip quivering slightly. After a few moments, he gulps, masters himself and nods.

"So Ms Saarinen then followed the defendant past the bank and towards the lake?"

"Yes."

"I realise it must be very distressing, but I have to ask you one more thing: do you believe Mr Carter and Ms Saarinen were having a relationship?"

"I didn't think so, I thought she was just being polite to a customer, but I did see them sing together one night at karaoke and then I wondered.

"What made you wonder?"

"For a moment they were singing like... like they were in love. Then they saw me in the crowd. And now, why would she follow him if there wasn't something?"

"Indeed, why would she follow him?" Advocate Talus turns to the judge and a few seconds later the translator says, "No further questions, madam."

James replaces Talus at the Advocate's desk. When he addresses Kari, in Finnish, I realise that he has regained his previous fluency. After a few seconds, the translator echoes his tone. "I am also sorry to have to ask you distressing questions, but it is my job to try to protect an innocent man, so I must." Kari nods. "Would you say that Ms Saarinen was a physical person?"

"What do you mean?"

"Did she often touch people, hug them, things like that?"

"Yes, I suppose so."

"And she liked to joke and have fun?"

"Yes, of course."

"So when the defendant tried to pull Ms Saarinen out of her chair for a dance and met some resistance, is it possible that he thought she was messing about?"

"She wasn't playing, she was annoyed."

"Of course, I'm not asking that. You have known her much longer than my client. What I'm asking is, could Mr Carter have been mistaken and the incident you describe have been the result of a misunderstanding?"

"I don't know," says Kari grudgingly.

"OK. Did Mr Carter say or do anything immediately after he had this misunderstanding with Ms Saarinen?"

"Yes, he apologised like the English do: lots of words." There are a few chuckles from behind me.

"I see," says James, his voice a spider's web. "So when, according to your police statement, you caught hold of Ms Saarinen's arm to stop her walking off, you knew she was annoyed, but you did it anyway?"

The fly answers, "Yes, but it was different, I'm her boyfriend."

"And after she pushed you away, did you apologise?"

"No, but..."

"I see, so you claim the defendant was physically violent towards Ms Saarinen and yet you admit that you yourself did worse a few minutes later?"

Kari's eyes flick towards the prosecution table. I can't see if he gets any response, but his eyes slide towards mine. They are burning with hate. "Yes, but I didn't kill her and he did."

For the first time Judge Kivelä intervenes, "Mr Varis, do not state your opinions about the accused, unless asked for. Mr Hainsworth, continue."

"Mr Varis, you mentioned that you saw Ms Saarinen and Mr Carter singing karaoke together. Can you tell the court about your relationship with Ms Saarinen at that time." Kari seems confused. "Had Ms Saarinen ended the relationship a few days earlier?"

"Well, she said that... but she didn't really mean it."

"And did you get back together on the night of the karaoke?"

"Yes."

"Why was that?"

Kari glances towards the prosecution once more. "We talked and then Arwen sang a song to me."

"And who suggested she sing a song and chose which one?"

"Steven," he answers quietly.

"The defendant?"

"Yes."

"So you could say that he helped you and Ms Saarinen repair your relationship?"

"I suppose so."

"Does that sound like the actions of a man who wanted to have your girlfriend for himself?"

"No," says Kari, simply.

"*Kiitos,*" says James and returns to his seat. That seemed to go well. I glance towards him, but his face is expressionless. This guy would be a master at poker.

A WHITE HAIRED MAN, uncannily a Mr Saarinen - apparently a common name in Mahikkala - is the next witness called by the prosecution. He's the taxi driver who claims to have seen me crossing the road after Arwen. His testimony could have been read from his witness statement.

"Mr Saarinen," says James, beginning his cross-examination. "Just so I am clear, are you any relation to the deceased?"

"Maybe, distantly. I think perhaps all Saarinen in Mahikkala are related somehow, but I did not know the girl."

"Thank you. You are sure that the woman you saw was Ms Saarinen?"

"I saw a red haired woman wearing a light brown coat and black party shoes at the right time, in the right place. Who else could it have been?"

"But you were not close enough to see her face clearly?"

"No, but it must have been her." I think I can detect some impatience in the man's voice and he taps his thumbs against the sloped sides of the witness desk.

"Did you see anyone cross the road in front of this woman?"

"No, but I saw her almost as soon as I turned out of *Eteläkatu.*"

"I'm sorry, just so we can all understand, can you show us *Eteläkatu* and your route on the map?" The clerk flashes up the Mahikkala plan on the screen and passes Mr Saarinen a laser pointer. He turns it, searching for the button, tests it on the palm of his left hand and points at the screen.

"I picked up my customer here on *Eteläkatu*." He indicates the next road west of *Pankkikatu*. "Then I drove down the street and made a left turn on to the dual carriageway. I saw the woman cross here and as I turned into *Pankkikatu*, I nearly hit the man in the army coat."

"May I ask why you drove south along *Eteläkatu* and then turned immediately back north up *Pankkikatu*?"

"The one-way system: my customer lived in the north of Mahikkala but *Eteläkatu* is one way."

"Ah, thank you, that is quite clear now. So you were not on the dual carriageway for any length of time?"

"No."

"So it is possible that someone could have crossed the road a little ahead of the woman and you would not have seen them?"

"Yes, it is possible."

"Did you see any other traffic on the dual carriageway?"

"No, I don't think so, I don't remember any."

"Now, turning to the man who walked in front of your taxi, could you repeat what you remember about this man?"

"He was wearing a blue army coat, black hat, gloves, and scarf like the ones on the table there." He indicates the clothing exhibits which the prosecution produced during his testimony.

"And metal frame glasses?"

"Yes."

"The glasses on the table there, marked as item seven. I believe you chose those as being most similar to the ones you say the man was wearing?"

"Yes. I chose from many at the police station."

James glances towards Lars who catches the judge's eye, receives a nod and rises. He retrieves the glasses from the table. "I need also yours" whispers Lars. I slip them off and place them into his waiting hand. He holds the two pairs of specs side by side and approaches the witness.

"Are these two frames the same?" When they were closer, I could see that the other pair was slightly squarer, smaller, and gold, not silver like mine.

A shadow of disconcertment passes through Mr Saarinen's voice. "Not exactly, but quite close." Lars passes up the two pairs to let the judges make the comparison for themselves.

James continues: "Not exactly? So you can't say for sure what the glasses were like?"

"No, but they could have been his." He points in my direction.

"OK." James pauses whilst Lars returns the specs to the appropriate places. I'm glad to be able to see detail again. "Was the man you saw the defendant?" This question seems to take everyone by surprise: there is whispering on the prosecution table and murmuring from the crowd.

Slowly Mr Saarinen answers, "I don't know, it might have been."

"I'm afraid, 'might have been' is not good enough for a court of law, sir," says James. "Why don't you know?"

The slightly riled answer comes back to him: "Like I said, his face was mostly covered up."

"He was wearing the scarf over his mouth and nose?"

"Yes."

"You're absolutely sure about that?"

"Yes."

"But what about the man's eyes? Could you see his eyes?"

"Yes, I mean, not to see the colour or anything, but yes."

"Thank you, I am finished now."

The clock between the windows on the left hand wall shows that it is almost 4pm. The chief judge beckons James and his counterpart forward for a brief discussion. Before they have returned to their tables, Judge Kivelä rises, calls an end to the day, and sweeps out of the side door. I throw a quizzical expression towards Lars.

"Not enough time to do next part before five and best not to split," he explains.

"That went OK, I think didn't it?" I say.

James answers, "Yes, but tomorrow morning they're going to hit us hard with the forensics."

CHAPTER 35

Abi has taken a different seat this morning: at the extreme left hand end of the front row. No flies on her. Now if I glance left, she is the first thing I see after blank wall. I'm going to need every one of her tiny smiles this morning. The prosecution are leading up to it gently: the first witness is the skier whose dog found Arwen's body. His testimony is simply a matter of places and times. James asks him if the scene already shown in that photograph is different from how he remembers. It isn't.

Then comes the scene of crime officer and with him more photos. I feel a little queasy as the first close up is projected. Somewhere at the back of the room there is a small commotion followed by quickly retreating footsteps. Arwen is lying face down, her arms bent at the elbows, both hands close to her neck. Her right leg is bent with the heel of that foot resting back against her straight left leg, just below the knee. Apart from a light dusting of snow which has accumulated on the back of her hair and in the small of her back, she's naked, but I find nothing sexual about the scene, just tragic.

The Prosecutor is asking the officer to summarise the findings of the forensics report for the judges. I can see a pile of copies awaiting distribution in front of his assistant. Even in another language, I can hear his careful, respectful, businesslike tone.

"This photograph shows the deceased in the position in which she was found on the morning of Saturday March 1st. Although there was no recorded snowfall between Thursday 28th February and the afternoon of Saturday 1st there was quite a strong wind on the Friday night. We believe that the snow accumulation seen can be explained by blow off from the surrounding trees.

"Apart from the tracks of Mr Varjo's skis and the footprints of his dog, we found no other signs that the scene had been disturbed since the approximate time of death. There was only one set of footprints to and from the body." A photo flicks up of a line of footsteps overrun by ski tracks. Then a close up of one print: "These impressions were made by flat soled shoes of between sizes 40 and 44. Unfortunately the snow accumulation makes it impossible to determine more than that. However, the size makes the perpetrator far more likely to be male. Also it would be somewhat unusual to wear flat soled shoes along such paths, given the small amount of grip they give."

"We conclude from the single set of prints that the deceased was carried to her final position by her attacker, either after death or when unconscious. It then appears that her clothes were removed and the arms and legs arranged to the positions you see here. It is not clear why her arms were placed in the manner shown, but it appears that the right leg was bent to..." there is a slight falter in his delivery and he glances toward the part of the room where yesterday I saw Arwen's mother, "allow access to the vagina." There are gasps and angry whispers from all over the room, the hubbub gradually rising in volume until the judge raises her hand, *"Quiet."*

"Continue," says Kivelä. "We must understand every aspect of the crime, however unsavoury."

The officer nods and the awful picture defiles the screen once more, "The position of the right leg, together with the flattened area of snow here and the pathologist's evidence indicates that sexual intercourse occurred." He glances in that same direction again. "Mercifully for the victim, from the lack of any signs of struggling, it appears that this occurred when she was already unconscious or most likely after death."

"Have you been able to determine where the attack actually took place?"

"Not exactly, although we believe it to have been on the main path, adjacent to where the killer's foot prints leave it." A photograph of the corresponding area appears. It's a relief to have the other one removed. "As you can see, this is a busy track which had seen more than a day's worth of skiers passing before the body was discovered. Any signs of a struggle on the path have been erased. However, we can make suppositions as much from what we can't see as what we can see. We have very carefully checked the edges of all the paths, right back as far as the dual carriageway. We found children's footprints, dog tracks and some off path skiing, but nothing suspicious. This makes it the balance of probability that the attacker was known to Ms Saarinen."

"For the benefit of the court, can you explain how you reach that conclusion?"

"Yes," the officer seems to stand slightly taller, proud of his deductions, "The ski track itself is quite narrow, but it is bounded on each side by flat ground with only occasional low bushes. The taller trees do not grow within five to ten metres of the track. For a forest it is quite open. It would be difficult to take anyone by surprise in such a place. In any case, I have already said that we found no marks to indicate someone hiding to the side of the track. Therefore the attacker must either have been waiting in the open for Ms Saarinen or following her. If following, the path is frozen snow, it would be impossible to walk quietly. No, Ms Saarinen must have been aware of the presence of her killer for some time before the attack. A mobile phone was found amongst her belongings. Would she not have used it if she felt threatened?"

For the first time, the prosecution have put forward an argument that I haven't heard James discuss. It's a clever piece of logic. I bet Aaltonen had a hand in that. I turn my head slightly and glance towards Abi. Strained is the only word I can think of to describe her expression.

"Thank you, I think that is quite clear," says the Prosecutor, "I believe there are a couple more pieces of important evidence?"

"Yes." He indicates to the clerk and a picture of a crumpled black dress, half covered by a tan coat is projected. Beside the coat a small black-leather handbag sits propped against a party shoe. "The clothes were found as you see them here, approximately one metre from the victim's feet. Her underwear and the other shoe were found beneath the dress. Notice that the clothes are not lying as they must have been removed. In fact they are reversed, making it likely that the killer searched through them before leaving the scene. The contents of her handbag, including a purse with over 60 Euros in it, were untouched, making robbery an unlikely motive." He nods again to the clerk. This photo shows the other mirror-polished shoe, inside which can be seen the upper half of a mobile. Although the picture is quite tightly cropped, in the upper right corner the end of a bra strap can be seen, bright against the snow. Before I can stop it, that part of my brain has already thought, 'emerald green, what other colour for a red head?' How can I think something like that now? I sink slightly in my chair, thanking my lucky stars that telepathy is only found in fiction.

"Her mobile phone was most likely turned off by the killer. Despite extensive analysis, we did not find any significant forensic evidence on her clothing. Hair samples from the victim's boyfriend, Kari Varis, and friend Tilia Riikonen were found on the coat, but this is normal."

"And the other piece of forensic evidence?"

"Most significantly, we found some fibres:" he glances towards the judges, "a piece of fluff, in the snow close to the top of the victim's legs."

"And you have analysed these fibres?"

"Initially we had difficulty as they seemed to be a mix of cotton and synthetic materials not normally found in Finland. However, we requested the help of our friends in the British Metropolitan Police and they were able to identify the sample as coming from navy blue boxer shorts sold by the British shop Marks & Spencer. They are very unusual outside the UK." Mutterings from behind indicate people are drawing the obvious inference.

"And was a pair of matching boxer shorts found in the accused's hotel room?"

"Yes, in fact, two pairs were found." The mutterings rise in volume as Talus turns to James and indicates with a wave that he can start his cross-examination. There are shouts and I feel hate burning the back of my head. Judge Kivelä raises her hand and glares. Such is her authority that quiet returns without need for words.

James straightens the front of his jacket as he rises. He addresses the last point first: "Can the fibres you mention be positively identified as coming from one of my client's pairs of boxer shorts?"

"No. Only that the fibres come from that specific design and manufacturer."

"So the fibres found could have come from any pair of navy blue Marks and Spencer boxer shorts?"

"Of that specific design, yes."

"Are you aware that in the last year, M&S have sold over 100,000 pairs of this design?"

"I know it is quite common in England, but not in Finland."

"I agree, this design is not readily available in Finland, but anyone could have bought a pair over the internet. Also, there are thousands of people who travel between the two countries each year. Is it not possible that any one of these people could have purchased such underwear and brought it to Finland?"

"Yes, it is possible," says the CSI, somewhat grudgingly.

"In fact, isn't it true that several pairs of identical boxer shorts were found by investigating officers elsewhere at the Central Hotel?"

The officer shrugs, "This is true, but in the room of one of the other British guests."

"So this evidence does not in any way firmly link my client to the scene of the crime?"

"Not really, I suppose, but when you link it with the pathologist's..."

"I'm only talking about the evidence which we have heard so far," interrupts James, voice with a slightly firmer edge to it.

"No, then," says the expert.

"Thank you," says James. I hope he sounds as good in Finnish as the translator makes him sound in English. He opens a leather bound notebook, jots a couple of words, pauses, pen in hand for a moment and continues to the next point: "I must complement you on your thorough analysis of the scene of the crime, however, I do have a couple of further questions. You mentioned that your team searched the ski tracks for signs of a struggle and for footprints, but you must have had limited time to do this. There was a heavy snowfall on the Saturday evening."

"Yes, but this is normal in Finland. We knew the weather front was approaching, we called in all back-up teams to search, photograph, and where necessary cover over the crime scene on the Saturday afternoon."

"But nevertheless, it must have been a rush and something could have been missed."

The officer stands straight backed, "I believe we assessed the situation and deployed sufficient resources to ensure that nothing was missed."

"OK," says James, moving on, "you state that you believe the forensic and circumstantial evidence points towards Ms Saarinen knowing her attacker. It is a well thought out theory, but it is just a theory is it not?"

The CSI has obviously met lawyers like James before and realises what is coming. "Yes, if taken on its own it is just the greater balance of probability, but it adds to the weight of the evidence as a whole."

James ignores the comment and presses onward, "From the evidence found and in your professional opinion what is the percentage probability that Ms Saarinen knew her killer?"

"I'm not sure I can put an exact figure on it."

He glances towards the chief judge, but before she can speak James says, "I'm not asking you for an exact figure, just a rough guide. You said it was the 'greater balance of probability', surely," his eyes also turn towards Judge Kivelä, "the court should know how much greater you consider this probability? Is it a little more, say 55%, much greater, say 95%, or somewhere in between?"

The judge's nod is noted by the expert witness and pursing his lips, he says, "Very approximately, 80%"

"I see, thank you. So, 'very approximately' there is a one in five chance that Ms Saarinen did not know her attacker."

"Yes. I see you are as good at mathematics, as you are at law, Mr Hainsworth." A few titters reverberate around the hall.

James smiles ironically but does not allow himself to be sidetracked. "Rather than Ms Saarinen knowing her attacker, is it possible that she mistook her attacker for someone she knew?"

The officer considers for a moment, "Yes, it is a possibility, but not a likely one."

"So, if a person dressed in similar clothes to my client, with a scarf covering most of his face, was following Ms Saarinen, might she have turned, seen who she thought was a friend, and waited?"

"Of course this is a possibility, but it's more likely that your client himself was the one following."

"We'll see about that later," says James, no doubt trying to lay seeds of doubt, "but for the moment, you do admit that the killer impersonating a friend of the victim would fit the scene of crime evidence?"

"Yes, if he happened to buy his underwear from England." The chuckles are louder this time. I know what James is trying to do. He can't do anything else. I'm just not sure it's working, not against this smart Alec anyway.

"OK," says James, "But in summary, there is none of your evidence which definitely links the defendant with the crime scene? Am I correct?"

"None of my evidence, no," comes the careful reply.

James glances down at his notes. "My other question relates to the location in which Ms Saarinen's body was found. Don't you think it is somewhat unusual?"

"What do you mean?" For the first time, the investigator seems slightly unsure of himself. James asks the clerk to re-display the main view of the scene.

"You say yourself that the killer has taken the trouble to carry the victim away from the scene of the initial attack, where they would not be seen from the main track, and yet, after the killer has finished his gristly business, he makes no further attempt to hide the body?" James lets the blazing red dot of his pointer rest on the postcard like line of snowy boughs to the right of the picture. "Even when within a few yards, there are dense trees where a body might lie undiscovered for weeks or months? Why turn off the mobile phone, but not hide the body? How do you explain that?"

The officer shrugs, "When you have seen as many tragic scenes as I have, you come to realise that those who commit such crimes do not always think logically."

"However, in this case, I believe the killer was acting extremely logically," says the defence barrister casting his eyes towards the lay judges. "I believe he moved Ms Saarinen's body from the site of the initial attack to a specific location where the body would not be found immediately. He turned off her mobile phone to hamper any search, but I believe he left the body where it would inevitably be found in a few days. And why would the killer want that? Because he had planted evidence implicating someone else for the crime: someone who would most likely be leaving the country in a few weeks' time."

The Prosecutor raises his hand, and the judge nods, "Does the defence have any evidence to back this up? I was under the impression that he was cross-examining my witness, not making a statement."

James smiles broadly and turns towards the prosecution table, "If my fellow Advocate would wait for a moment he will see that I am forming a question for his witness. I admit it is rather a long question, but..." He turns back towards the pathologist, "Could my explanation for the location of Ms Saarinen's body be possible, given your knowledge of the crime scene evidence?"

The expert rolls his eyes, "It seems possible... but improbable."

"Thank you, you may retake your seat." A look passes from Lars to James as he sits down. I don't think that went as well as they had hoped and we all know what is coming next. I glance towards Abi: the skin is tight and pale across her forehead, devoid of its usual glow. The next deep breath is marked by a tension in the left side of my chest. My head is above the surface, but the ladder seems just out of reach and the water is cold as death.

A small man shuffles to the front of court: on the heavy side, bald on top with smoothly slicked sides and small round glasses, unremarkable, but right now my nemesis. I stare at him, hoping in some mad way that I can make him forget his evidence by sheer willpower, but I'm totally distracted by his first photo. It's a close up of the back of Arwen's head, face down in the snow. Her hair, her glorious hair: dark, matted and mostly under her face, except for the two braids. I'd forgotten about them. They snake away towards the right side of the photo, where a tiny seedling pine breaks the surface of the snow. Somehow they alone still seem fresh, unspoilt, alive. If you just look at that side of the picture, she could be lying, laughing, snowball in hand, ready to grab a leg and pull me down beside her. I resist an impulse to close one eye and block out half the vision of the other. It'll take more than a raised finger to make this go away...

The pathologist's laser is following a purple streak below her hairline. The image changes to an extreme close up of this mark. Further views show that it is virtually continuous around her neck. You don't need any medical training to see she's been strangled. I wait for the translation: "The victim has been asphyxiated by a length of narrow rope which has been held in a loop with some kind of slip knot. You can see the mark left by this knot here." He indicates a bulge in the purple line behind the left ear. "There is also some light bruising in the small of the back," a photo of the area has a dotted line superimposed over a largish area. To the untrained eye it barely looks any different from the surrounding blue-white skin. The picture changes again to a close up of two fingers. On one of them the nail is broken and an arrow indicates some blue fibres caught on the sharp corner.

"There are not any defence wounds, only this broken nail. We believe the fibres come from the rope which was used as the weapon. It may be some comfort for the deceased's family that I believe her death was very quick. The most likely scenario is that once the rope had been placed around the victim's neck, the attacker used a knee against the victim's back as leverage to pull the loop tight. The victim made an attempt to pull the rope away from her neck, breaking a nail in the process. Such was the small size of the rope that this would have been almost impossible." He reaches into his jacket pocket and pulls out a length of thin blue cord. A loop has been made in one end which he places over his left wrist. As he pulls it tight with his right hand he says, "This is the type of rope used, together with a similar knot. As you can see," he jerks on the free end and the rope digs into his wrist causing the skin to go white, "this knot allows less force to be used than with other forms of strangulation. It means the attack could be carried out with only one hand or by a person of lesser strength..." The expert witness trails off and his eyes flick towards me. I have never been more conscious of my light weight frame.

"So you have been able to identify the type of rope used?" prompts the Prosecutor.

"Yes, as well as the fibres on the nail there were several more embedded in the victim's neck and together with the patterning on the skin, we can match it to a grade of blue, six millimetre thick general purpose cord."

"And who manufacturers this grade?"

"*Suomen Kaapelitehdas.*" I don't need a translation for that.

"The work place of the defendant?" says the lawyer, just in case any of the judges hadn't realised the significance.

"I believe so." Again there are dark mutterings from behind and I shift uncomfortably, tensing my buttocks and then releasing.

I see James roll his eyes and I whisper, "along with just about every rope in Scandinavia..."

"I know, it's pure theatrics again. We'll refute it later." Maybe we will, but right now it seems to be performing its purpose just fine.

After allowing a suitably long pause for the hubbub to die down, another question is posed: "And the time of death?"

"Taking the rate of freezing and other factors into account, I would usually estimate between midnight and 4am on the morning of Friday 29th February. However, as the witness statements indicate that the deceased was still alive at 2am, we can be reasonably sure that her death occurred between two and four."

"Thank you. Can you now summarise the findings of the toxicology tests?"

"Yes," the small man shrugs, I suppose impatient to get to the more significant stuff, but the prosecution seem intent on leaving the 'best' till last. "There was nothing except a moderate amount of alcohol in the blood. This would be unlikely to have caused any noticeable effects for the average person." Perhaps prompted by an unseen expression he adds, "Oh, and the victim was using the contraceptive pill."

"You also discovered some very significant forensic evidence?"

The expert runs his fingers through what is left of his hair and pushes his glasses back up his nose as he chooses his first words carefully, "On internal examination, we found traces of two fluids. The first was a lubricant. We identified this as being used on various types of condom manufactured by the Sultan company." He pauses, and I brace myself for the hammer blow. "The second fluid was male seminal fluid containing sperm. DNA testing from this sample is a positive match to the DNA sample taken from the defendant."

There is uproar from behind me: scraping of chairs and angry shouts. James leans towards me, "Don't turn roun... ow!" A mobile phone bounces off his shoulder and clatters across the floor, scattering loosened buttons behind it. Judge Kivelä is on her feet shouting and waving people to sit down. I feel something touch my chair and turn to see that the two burley guards are standing directly behind us facing towards the crowd. Between them, I can see a man being walked down the aisle, one arm held firmly up his back. I'm fairly sure it's Kari. The judge bangs the flat of her hand down on the table several times and her voice growls above the din. The translator cannot match the tone of authority, but there is already silence before he begins. "If we have any more outbursts like this, I will remove all spectators from the court room and we will continue behind closed doors. Anyone causing trouble will be ejected immediately and may face criminal charges." The judge pauses to read her watch. "Has the prosecution finished with this witness?"

"Almost, madam."

"Continue and then we will break for lunch."

"Thank you, we will be brief." He turns towards the expert witness who has been supporting himself on the desk with one arm, wearing a bemused expression at the proceedings unfolding in front of him. I guess the pathologist's usual clientele are somewhat quieter...

"For the benefit of the court, can you state the reliability of the DNA tests."

"Given good samples as we have here, they are completely reliable. Unless the defendant has an identical twin then the chances of an incorrect match are millions to one against. In addition, the results were checked independently at the Helsinki City Laboratory and in the United Kingdom."

"So there could be no mistake that the semen found in Ms Saarinen's vagina was that of the defendant, Mr Carter?"

"None."

"Thank you, that is all."

He's timed it impeccably of course. We'll now break for an hour and the only thing on people's minds will be my semen and what that means. Before leaving the court, Judge Kivelä approaches James, who stands. She says in near perfect English, "I must apologise. I have never had an Advocate assaulted in my courtroom before. Are you alright?"

"Yes, madam, it's no problem." He shrugs, "I imagine the young man finds the whole situation very difficult."

"I don't suppose he was aiming at you," I say. Both of them turn their heads towards me in surprise.

"No, I suppose not," says the Judge and bustles towards the side door.

I spend most of the next hour pushing tasteless carrots around my plate rather than actually eating them. When it is time to return to the courtroom, James's eyes are fixed on me all the way from the door to my seat. I know what he's thinking, but he knows better now than to ask directly. Taking my seat, I lean towards him and whisper in his ear, "Someone planted that semen... somehow. That's the only explanation." He nods, his expression one of someone who had hoped but did not expect.

"Well, we'll do the best we can with that."

I wait anxiously for Abi to retake her seat. I just need a smile, even a forced one will do. Even from a few yards away I can see that she's been crying. I can understand that: it seems pretty hopeless to me right now, but when I catch her eye she doesn't seem to want to hold it. Back straight, hands in lap, eyes down, don't be ashamed of me, Abi, please. Wetness starts to form in the corner of my own eyes. Just let this afternoon go a bit better. I suck my bottom lip between my teeth and wait for the pathologist to take the stand.

"As it has been on all our minds during lunch," begins James, "let us start with the internal evidence. Sir, do you not find it strange that a condom appears to have been used, but also to find seminal fluid and sperm? Surely one would expect this to be caught and removed with the condom?" A subtly different murmur travels round the court, but is swiftly silenced with a poisonous stare from the Chief Judge's seat.

The pathologist smoothes the sides of his hair once again, "It is not unusual to find both fluids present. It is usually indicative of different sexual encounters, but there are several other possibilities..."

"Before we consider the other possibilities, let's just talk about that." James appears to study his notes for a moment, but I'm sure it's just for effect. "So there is no way of telling if the spermicidal fluid and the semen both came from the alleged actions of the killer or if one or both came from a previous sexual encounter?"

"The evidence of such fluids does not last long within a living body. Any previous sexual contact would need to have been one, at maximum, two days previously."

"So one possible explanation for the evidence as you found it is that some time on Thursday 28th or Wednesday 27th February, Ms Saarinen and Mr Carter had a consensual sexual liaison and then later the actual killer used a condom?"

The expert looks momentarily confused and glances towards the prosecution's table. "But in the defendant's statements..."

James interrupts quickly, but has to wait for the translator. As I hear the words, I'm equally confused. Didn't I just say...?

"I'm asking a theoretical question," says the defence barrister. "Is that a possible explanation for the evidence that you found?"

"Well, in theory, I suppose, yes." The pathologist seems slightly rattled and pushes his glasses back up his nose.

"What are you doing?" I whisper to the man standing beside me.

"Trust me," replies the lawyer. Short of yanking him back down into his chair I don't have much choice. The idea does cross my mind though.

"OK. Going back a step, you were saying that there are other possibilities for the presence of both condom lubricant and semen?"

"Yes," the pathologist's sparse follicle resources receive another check, but he answers with more confidence again. "Perhaps the killer did not apply the condom correctly or ripped it, or... as it would have been very cold, perhaps it came off." He shrugs, "Any of these could explain this evidence."

"I'm sure you are correct, but I would also like you to consider this possibility. Suppose the killer used a condom for his own despicable act, but then deposited a sample of someone else's semen in order to implicate an innocent party. Would this fit the evidence you found?"

This line of attack is clearly more expected and there is no sign of nervousness in the expert's answer, "Yes, of course it is an explanation, but the killer would have had to obtain a sperm sample from the defendant without his knowledge and then keep it from degrading. This seems quite fantastical."

"But possible."

"Yes, possible," the pathologist rolls his eyes slightly as if accepting an outrageous solution from a precocious student. He's not wrong, it does seem fantastical, but how else...

James changes tack, "Apart from the internal evidence, were there any other signs that suggest forced intercourse had occurred?"

"No."

"There was no bruising of the genitals as is normal in such cases?"

"No, but this is an unusual set of circumstances. I apologise for being graphic, but in rape cases the victim is usually conscious and understandably tense. The attacker must force their way in. Here the victim is likely to have been dead before the act occurred. Little force would be necessary."

"OK, perhaps not strictly necessary, but you are asking us to believe that the attacker - who has just murdered the victim in a most brutal fashion - then gently and carefully has intercourse with the body? This seems unlikely to me."

"But possible." The pathologist apes James's phrase. Something about the way my barrister's shoulders relax as the witness speaks makes me sense that something has gone right. 'Thank Thor,' chimes the part of my brain where humour used to reside.

James opens his hands. "Let me describe to you another possibility. Suppose there was no intercourse at all; suppose the killer just planted the semen evidence to implicate my client; then there would be no bruising, would there not?"

"There would not, but what about the condom lubricant?"

"You said yourself that this could be from a previous sexual encounter. So my possibility would fit the facts?"

The pathologist is slow to reply, but grudgingly nods, "Yes, as I said: if the attacker had obtained a semen sample from the defendant. But that is a big if."

"But possible."

"*Kyllä, mahdollista.*" I could hardly fail to have learnt the Finnish words by now and can hear sarcasm is his 'yes, possible' reply. The translator is good but he doesn't do intonation. Not for the first time, I wish I was better at languages.

"So it seems to me," says James, turning towards the lay judges, "that this forensic evidence leaves us with many questions and many unlikely possibilities. There are some facts and some theories, but nothing that fits together perfectly. Can you use such evidence to convict someone? Forgive me, I am thinking out loud," he says, heading off the stirrings on the prosecution table. "I have two more questions for your witness. You said that the rope used was made at *Suomen Kaapelitehdas* which is indeed the workplace of my client. Are you aware of how many rope manufacturers there are in Finland?"

"Not many, I think."

"*Suomen Kaapelitehdas* is the only significant company: they have 60% of the domestic market. Over lunch I did a quick internet search for the type of blue rope you showed us earlier. How many shops in Mahikkala sell this type?"

"I don't know."

"Three, at least, just in Mahikkala! Imagine how many places it could be bought in Helsinki. I hardly think my client's place of work can be considered relevant. I have no more questions, thank you," says James, nodding respectfully to the witness.

"Hopefully that muddied the waters a little," he whispers as he retakes his seat. I risk a glance towards Abi and I'm rewarded with a wan smile. It's a sunbeam on my solar panel: recharging.

CHAPTER 36

When I first saw Katri's name on the list of prosecution witnesses, I admit I felt a little betrayed. 'She witness you return to the hotel. They ask her to make a statement, she has no choice. It is civic duty,' Lars had said. 'Maybe she just wants to see you again,' Abi joked on one of our better days. Well, here she is, giving her full name, even paler than usual, gripping one corner of the desk tightly.

"Ms Juhana, on the night of February 28th this year, I believe you were working on the reception of the Central Hotel in Mahikkala?"

"*Yes,*" she says, without waiting for the translation of the prosecutor's question. She realises her mistake and blushes in apology, "*Anteeksi.*"

"I know this is slow and unnatural, but do wait for the translator before answering," says Kivelä smiling encouragingly.

The first question is repeated, then, "And the defendant, Steven Carter was staying at the Central Hotel at this time?"

"Yes, with the three other English men."

"Ah, yes, his work colleagues at the rope factory." Out of the corner of my eye I see James shake his head slightly. "And did you ever chat with Mr Carter?"

"We try to be friendly to all our guests. We like to make them feel part of the family, particularly if they are staying a long time. Sometimes this is difficult, sometimes easy. The four Englishmen, they liked to joke, they liked to chat. They were funny. We all liked them, and it was good to practise our English."

"So it would be normal for Mr Carter to stop and chat for a few moments when passing through reception?"

"Yes, normally." She shifts her weight from one leg to the other and her eyes flick towards me.

"Describe what happened on the early morning of Friday 29th February from two am onwards."

"It was quiet, I was the only one on the desk. Everyone else was at Hanne's party. Just after 2am a few people came back: two of the Englishmen, John and Mark, and then my two work colleagues, Dea and Raakel." I notice she pairs them separately. Good old discrete Katri. "We all chatted for a few minutes. They were quite drunk. It sounded like a good party."

"And did anyone mention Mr Carter?"

As she starts to answer, Katri's eyes flick to her right again, but past me this time, towards Abi? "I asked where Steven was, and I think John said something like 'gone for a walk, don't ask.'"

"And what do you think he meant by that?" says the barrister.

"I don't know, but you can ask him, can't you?" I suppose she must have seen him in the witness waiting area, somewhere out front.

"Yes, I will do that later." The flicker of a smile plays on the prosecuting lawyer's face. "So after a few minutes you were alone in the hotel reception area again?"

"Until about 3am when Steven came back."

"What was Mr Carter wearing?"

"He was wearing the blue army coat, black hat and gloves and a black scarf. He always wore those to go out."

"And he paused for a chat?"

"No, I asked him if he was as drunk as everyone else, but he said he couldn't stop, he had to go and do something."

"Did he say what he needed to do so urgently?"

"I didn't understand. Sometimes his accent makes it difficult."

"But it was unusual for him not to chat?"

"Yes, but..."

"Thank you, Ms Juhana, that is all of my questions."

I lean towards James, for once, my memory for conversations is going to be more than just an annoyance to my wife. "She's forgotten what she said to me first," I whisper. The voice of Judge Kivelä causes James to lift his head. "Do you wish to cross-examine this witness?"

"Yes, madam, if I could have one minute?" A nod of consent.

"She asked me why I was looking happy," I breathe into his left ear, "and what I said was that I had to go and write something down." James raises his eyebrows; somehow this has never come up before. I can see his mind racing for a way to use these facts as he saunters across to the Advocate's desk.

"Ms Juhana," James flashes his most winning smile, "are you sure you remembered all of the conversation you had with Mr Carter?"

"I think so... but it did not seem important at the time." She seems slightly flustered. Careful James.

"Do you remember how Mr Carter seemed when he arrived back at the hotel?"

"What do you mean?"

"What mood was he in? Did he seem worried or sad, or perhaps he was smiling, or..."

Katri's hand goes up to her mouth on what must have been the word smiling. "You are right, I'm sorry, I asked him why he looked so happy."

"You thought he looked happy?"

"Yes, he was grinning like someone had just told him a joke."

"I see... and there was nothing unusual physically about him or his clothes? No caked on snow, or wet patches, or rips, or anything else which might have indicated that he had been doing anything other than going for a walk?"

"Not that I remember."

"How was he wearing his scarf? Over his nose?"

"No, it must have been round his neck, I could see his smile."

"Thank you. You also said that you didn't understand some words used by my client due to his accent. Could he have said, 'I need to go and write something down?'

Katri cocks her head slightly to one side, "Maybe, but I don't really remember. I think he did say something about that the next day."

James pauses, hand partly over his mouth, as if considering whether to continue. He makes his decision and lowers the hand. "Ms Juhana, you knew Mr Carter quite well, well enough to invite him to your birthday party." There are a few murmurs from behind. "Think back to that time; ignore anything you may have read in the papers; how did he seem to you as a person?"

"Like a nice guy, funny," again her eyes flick towards me. "Someone who loved his wife." Oh, Katri, I could kiss you! "I could not believe it when he was arrested, but what they are saying about physical evidence..." Then again... I expect to see clouds cross my barrister's face after her last comment but he almost seems pleased.

"Ah yes, the rumours about forensic evidence." Of course, Katri hasn't heard the pathologist. "Let me ask you one last question. If it wasn't for these rumours would you think there was any likelihood of Mr Carter having committed this crime?"

Katri pauses for a moment, I'm holding my breath, "No, I would think he was the last person to have done it."

"So if there was any condemning forensic evidence it would go against everything that you know about the defendant?"

"Yes, it would."

"Thank you, Ms Juhana, you may leave the desk." James is wearing a smile of relief. He took a risk and it paid off.

Judge Kivelä is staring at the small gold watch laid flat on the table beside her notes. Her eyes squint slightly with calculation, "I think we have time for one more witness, could you bring Ms Tilia Riikonen?" she asks a steward. On reaching the witness desk, Til blatantly turns her head towards me and glares. I wither under her burning sapphires, but I'm not going to look down... guiltily. I shake my head ever so slightly and mouth, "No." It clearly falls upon deaf eyes. Til tosses her hair, which has returned to its usual blonde streaked black, and faces the clerk.

"Don't ask her the same question," I whisper to my attorney as the swearing in takes place. He shakes his head, dismissing the obvious. The opposing barrister stands, "Ms Riikonen, state your relationship to the deceased."

"Arwen was my best friend. I knew her as well as anyone, probably even better than Kari."

"When was the last time you saw her?"

"On the day of Hanne's party; she called round at about 6pm. She wanted..." Her voice falters, so she waits for the translator. "She wanted me to do some..." she squeezes her eyes tight shut to prevent the tears from flowing.

"Would you like to take a moment's break?" asks Judge Kivelä.

"No," she replies almost fiercely and takes a deep breath. "She wanted me to plait some braids for her. We often did each other's hair." Til looks momentarily confused at the whispering her statement has caused amongst the spectators. She hasn't seen the photo: chestnut braids, still heartbreakingly perfect against chilling snow.

Talus ignores the background noise. "How did she seem?"

"There was something on her mind, but she didn't want to talk about it. She was often like that. I thought it was about Kari. Maybe it was."

"And then she left to go to Hanne's Bar?"

"Yes. The last thing she said was, "See you," in English."

"In English?"

Til shrugs, "We picked up a few phrases from Steven and his friends, things that seemed like real English, not what you learn in school."

"Now, can you tell me about what happened later that night?"

"I was staying over at Harri's house." Til glances towards where I suppose he must be sitting. "Kari woke us up banging on the door at about half past two in the morning."

"In your statement you say it was 02:24am?"

"Yes, Harri has got one of those LED clocks... Shall I go on?"

"Do."

"Kari was in a right state, hammering and bawling his eyes out. He woke up Harri's parents and some of the neighbours. He was massively out of breath, he'd just run all the way back from Hanne's."

"And did he say why he'd done that?"

"He didn't stop, he kept on saying, 'She's left me again, she's gone off with that English bastard. She says he understands her. Haven't I always done everything for her?' Stuff like that, over and over."

"By 'that English bastard' he meant the defendant?"

"Yes," she harpoons me with a stare once again, "an accurate description, as it turns out." There are only a handful of affirming sniggers. When I hear the translation, I wonder if seeds of doubt are beginning to spread.

The barrister glances apologetically towards Kivelä and carries straight on, "What was your reaction to Mr Varis's news?"

"I wasn't that surprised. Like I said before, I knew something was up with Arwen and there was definitely some sort of connection between her and Steven, so it wasn't out of the blue. I was worried about her, though. What she was getting herself into... with a married man."

"Can you describe this 'connection' between Ms Saarinen and the defendant?"

"You could just see it sometimes when they were talking. They would kind of get lost in each other's eyes. And they kept on bumping into each other around town, accidentally on purpose. Arwen would say something like, 'Steven likes this, or Steven does that,' and I'd raise my eyebrows. Then she'd say, 'I just like him, OK? He's funny.' I think she was trying to convince herself as much as me."

"You thought these hidden feelings were returned by Mr Carter?"

"I wasn't sure, it was strange. He never hid that he was married, but he kept on talking to her. They seemed to love dancing and singing together, but then when she split up with Kari, he got them back together. It was like he couldn't make up his mind."

"Or like Ms Saarinen, he was trying to deny his true feelings?" I just know that Abi's narrowed eyes are fixed on the back of my neck. We've been through it all before, but when you hear it again... What was I doing?

"He did once say to me that he was confused. But it seemed more. I know he was having dreams about her. We teased him about that." Til's eyes stray towards me, the stone in them seeming to soften for a moment, but then they narrow once again, "It was as if he was trying to fight an obsession... I thought he was just a nice, funny, slightly mixed up bloke. I suppose they all seem like that."

"They?"

"Murderers."

James starts to stand, but Judge Kivelä waves him back down, "Ms Riikonen, I realise this is difficult for you, but refrain from these snipes at the defendant." Her stern eyes turn towards the prosecution, "Mr Talus, you will control your witness."

"Yes madam," says Talus with all the contrition he can muster, "I only have a couple more questions." I can't quite see from my angle but I think he fixes Til with a stare before continuing.

"So, Ms Riikonen, the defendant said to you that he was confused about his feelings towards Ms Saarinen?"

"Yes."

"But you felt that he was understating the problem?"

"Yes."

"From what you know of Ms Saarinen, do you think it is possible that she might have offered a relationship to Mr Carter and then withdrawn that offer?"

"In the state of mind she was in, she might well have done that."

"Something that might have tipped a man struggling with obsession over the edge... No further questions, madam."

We'd been wondering what motive the prosecution were going to come up with. Now we know. Lars is discussing something with James. I touch James on the arm and whisper, "Til looked out for Arwen like an older sister. She's not only angry because she thinks I killed Arwen, she thinks she got me all wrong and that bugs her. She's really proud of how good she is at reading people."

James nods slowly and screws up his eyes in thought, "Yes, that could be useful." He writes a couple of words at the head of his current page of notes and as always pulls down the front of his jacket as he stands. "Ms Riikonen, you are understandably angry, but from your answers I can see that you are a perceptive woman. You notice things about people, don't you?"

"Yes." Til screws up her eyes slightly.

"Would you say that reading people was one of your talents, something you are very good at?"

"Why..?"

"You've given some views about what you thought Ms Saarinen and the defendant were thinking. Are these views worth anything?"

Til draws herself up and steps straight into James's pitfall. "I'm very perceptive about people, ask anyone who knows me."

"And yet you did not consider Mr Carter to be any threat to Ms Saarinen? Your best friend, who you cared for like a younger sister?"

Til looks devastated, her bottom lip starts to tremble, "I know this. Don't you think I curse myself for this every day?"

James raises his right hand in apology, "I'm sorry Ms Riikonen, I don't mean to cause you distress, but you can't have it both ways. You can't expect us to believe that you could see my client's inner feelings, and then curse yourself for not being able to see his alleged inner feelings. Either way your intuition is not as good as you think."

Til glares at James, knowing he has tricked her. She dabs the corners of her eyes with a tissue. "Maybe I know what a man in love looks like, but I've never met a murderer before."

It's a good answer. My barrister doesn't let it linger. "Let me tell you a way in which your reading of people could be completely correct. If my client is innocent then your intuition stands correct and Mr Carter is just a 'nice, slightly confused bloke', someone who perhaps got a little too close and then backed away, someone who was unfortunate enough to be in the wrong place at the wrong time and someone who has been framed for a murder he did not commit. That fits with what you felt doesn't it, Ms Riikonen?"

"Yes, but so does my answer," she says stubbornly.

"But Ms Riikonen, you haven't any real evidence of what my client may or may not have felt about Ms Saarinen, have you?" Til is silent. "I mean, it doesn't sound very likely to me that a man who was in love with her, would reunite Ms Saarinen and Mr Varis."

"I didn't think so at the time," starts Til, slowly, as an idea forms. Then she moves into gear, "but afterwards she never stopped talking about how wonderful Steven was for getting them back together. Every time they got close and then backed away, she seemed to like him more. If he was really clever, he couldn't have found a better way of making her fall in love."

"Oh, I see, so now my client is an ultra skilled seducer? Come on, Ms Riikonen, you stretch our credulity! This is just supposition and guess work, you don't have any real evidence about my client's feelings, do you?"

Til looks at the floor and shuffles her feet.

"I have no more..." Til's head snaps up and she interrupts James, I catch the first word, *"Yes"* but the rest of the sentence is beyond me. I can see the reaction to it though. Heads rise on both tables. Immediately, James glances towards Lars who shrugs ever so slightly.

After eternity, the translator starts, "Yes, I do: you should read his song book."

"Madam, may I confer with my client for a moment?" After receiving a nod from the chief judge, James approaches the defence table and leans over it so that our heads are only inches apart. "What song book?" he whispers.

"I write songs sometimes, in a small notebook. I showed it to Arwen and Til once, but they're just lyrics, it's not a diary or anything."

James stares for a moment, then straightens up and returns to his stand. "Ms Riikonen appears to be referring to some fictional writings which my client does for recreational purposes, not hard evidence. I have no further questions for this witness, madam."

"You just read it," says Til to the prosecution table as she leaves the witness desk.

"We will now adjourn for the day," announces Judge Kivelä.

"ABI..." I start, as the solid door closes behind the retreating guard.

"Not now," interrupts James, his raised voice echoing slightly off the cold walls: more 'abandon all hope' blue. "Why didn't you mention this song book? I can't defend you if you don't give me all the facts."

"I don't see how it's relevant. Like you said, they're just art; you can't take anything from them." This is pointless, James, just let me talk to Abi. Her eyes are scaring me. "For crying out loud, James, I haven't told you about every single thing I've ever done, have I? I mean... I mean, what about work stuff? I must have sent hundreds of emails, but they're all about the project: designs, deliveries, timescales. We haven't been through all of that, have we?"

"No, but you can bet the police have."

"Well, they must have been through the song book too, so they can't think there's anything important in it."

"Maybe there is no problem," says Lars, "But this minute, Talus reads through it. Carefully."

"So is there anything we should know about?" says James, modulating his voice. Still silence from Abi. Why isn't she saying anything? I roll my eyes. I suppose I'm going to have to get this legal crap out of the way before I can find out.

"It's a small hardback notebook. Abi knows all about it, I've used them for years. I jot down ideas and lyrics for songs when they come to me. It's a complete mess: half a chorus here, a few notes there, maybe even a couple of shopping lists. There's a dictaphone as well. I hum the tunes into that."

"Why does our dear friend Ms Riikonen think it's so important, then?" asks James.

"I showed it to Arwen once and Til was there." Abi's mouth drops open. This is making it worse. I gabble on, "I know, I'm usually so private about it, but she was such a good singer, we talked about music. I told her about my song writing. She asked to read one, so I showed her the *Without You* song." I turn appealingly towards my wife, "The one about you."

"So Ms Riikonen thinks this song is about Arwen?" says James.

"Maybe, but I accidentally left the book with them and they read some of the unfinished stuff. I don't know what bit she's thinking of. I hadn't given my songs any thought until that session with Hiltunen. I wrote all sorts of things, but it's just bad poetry about everyday stuff really."

"That's it, there's nothing more than that?" Shut up, James, I need to talk to Abi.

"Look, I didn't write any songs about killing women or humping dead bodies and it hasn't got, 'I love The Stranglers' written on the front cover or anything. Can we just leave it?"

"Okay," says my lawyer, frowning slightly. He glances from me to Abi and back again. "You two obviously want to talk. Apart from the last, I think today went quite well really, considering... plenty of doubts for the judges to mull over."

"Let's go over here," I say and we move our chairs to a corner. The two lawyers busy themselves on their laptops. "I know what you're going to say."

"What am I going to say?" Abi purses her lips.

"Something about 'being lost in each other's eyes'."

"It wasn't easy to hear."

"I'm sorry. I'm scum..."

Abi twirls a strand of her raven hair round one finger. "Was she really so attractive?"

"Oh Abi!" I stretch the left corner of my mouth. "I suppose she must have been. Not more than you, though. She was just there. It all happened so gradually. I didn't realise until I was feeling it. I did fight it though. I thought I'd won."

"Won?" Her voice is suddenly strange.

"Yes. On the night she was killed, I thought I'd finally got her out of my head. Finally seen sense."

"Shame you couldn't have done that a few days earlier."

"I know."

"Oh Steve." Her hand ruffles the front of my hair like you would an exasperating child.

CHAPTER 37

Inspector Aaltonen cuts an impressive frame as the final prosecution witness: calm, confident, thoughtful, sure. Why does the man have to be so good at his job? He's been going for half an hour, running carefully and methodically through the investigation, prompted as ever by prosecution questions. Even the judges must be getting bored with the number of times he has said, 'We found no evidence...' 'We found no evidence of tampering with the DNA samples; we found no evidence to support the defence's assertion that Mr Carter has been framed by another perpetrator; we found no evidence to suggest that the plumbing system at the Central Hotel had been tampered with in any way, etc., etc.' One by one the doubts James raised yesterday are being discounted as unsubstantiated. Rather to our surprise, there has been no mention of the song book. I half expected to see it as I entered this morning, lying open, red highlighter marking the condemning words. Maybe it was nothing.

"Inspector, we come to the question of motive. Could you describe the results of your investigation into this matter?"

"Yes, although here things are less clear. There is little hard evidence, but from the things we do know, we can understand where the truth must lie." Aaltonen pauses, as if waiting for a question, but Mr Talus clearly thinks he is fine on his own. "It is not in doubt that the victim and the defendant were well known to each other. It is the depth of this relationship which is unclear. However, something made Ms Saarinen follow Mr Carter down *Pankkikatu*. He had some sort of hold over her. What was that? We also know that by the end of *Pankkikatu*, the follower has become the followed. What does that say about the defendant's motives?

"As you have heard from my scene of crime officer, the evidence indicates a strong likelihood that Ms Saarinen knew her attacker. So, perhaps this is a crime of passion: the result of some argument which has taken place on the footpath? An argument about sex or about leaving a wife? It just happened, I didn't mean to. This sounds plausible, yes? But think!" Aaltonen's eyes slide towards me, an expression of utter contempt filling his face.

"Is it likely that anyone would just happen to have a length of rope in their pocket after having been to a party? No. Even if they did, if an argument turned violent, would the victim allow the attacker time to tie a slip knot in the rope without resisting or using their mobile phone? No again." He lets this sink in. "In my professional opinion, the rope and the knot make anything other than a premeditated murder impossible." Another long pause. My left leg begins to shake again. I can see where this is going. "This leaves the sexual aspect of the case as the most likely motive. Mr Carter became obsessed with Ms Saarinen and determined to get what he wanted, even if it meant killing her first."

Even after the previous warnings, angry whispers swarm around the courtroom. It's the full works: 'Murder 1' as they call it in the States; pre-planned, cold blooded killing; certain life sentence. OK, so this is Finland, with just about the most liberal sentencing in the world. 'Life' usually only means about 12 years, but you can't count on that. It only takes a more hard line government to be elected and it's clang, tinkle, plop: there goes your key down the drain. I glance towards Abi, who is shrinking into her usual seat. Realisation of the same implications is etched on her face. 'You'd have to let her go,' says despair. 'Don't think like that... not yet,' says hope.

James is standing, the prosecution must have finished. I blink a couple of times to re-concentrate on the translation. "Inspector, you have already stated many times this morning that 'you found no evidence' for this or that. It seems to me that this case is characterised by a lack of evidence against my client?"

Aaltonen is not going to be riled and answers calmly, "On the contrary, there is firm forensic evidence against your client."

"There is some forensic evidence which if interpreted in one way could possibly implicate my client, I agree, but that appears to be all there is. Inspector, did the police find amongst my client's belongings any evidence of his having committed this crime?"

"Specifically what evidence are you referring to?" Aaltonen knows how to play the game. My Advocate has assumed as much.

"Specifically, did you find any of the victim's hairs or fibres from her clothing on the clothing of my client?"

"No, we did not."

"Did you find any traces of the rope used to kill Ms Saarinen in Mr Carter's belongings?"

"No, we did not." Aaltonen's face remains calm.

"Did you discover records of Mr Carter buying such a rope?"

"No, we did not. But he could have obtained some from his place of work."

"Inspector, as you are fully aware," James's voice is full of frustration, "Mr Carter worked on the metal rope side of the factory. *Kaapeli* safety rules would have required him to sign in and be escorted around other parts of the plant. Is there any evidence that he made such a visit?"

"No, there is not."

"Did you find any condoms of the appropriate Russian brand in Mr Carter's room or amongst his belongings?"

"No we did not, although they were for sale from a vending machine in the Central Hotel reception."

"As they are in almost every hotel, bar, and night club in Finland," adds James, presumably sarcastically. "So, other than the two items disclosed by the CSI and the pathologist, you found no evidence linking my client to the crime scene?"

Aaltonen considers for a moment, "We did find a needle matching the species of tree found around Lake Mahi on one of his shoes."

"But my client does not deny walking through the lakeside wood."

"No, he does not," says Aaltonen. I suspect he only mentioned this weak piece of evidence to remind the judges of that fact.

James returns to his question: "There is no other evidence, is there?"

"No more is necessary."

"So you expect us to believe that my client has carefully removed all traces of the crime from his belongings and yet he carelessly leaves two pieces of forensic evidence at the scene of the crime. This does not add up."

"In my experience," says Aaltonen, holding his hands wide apart to leave us in no doubt about how broad this is, "every person makes mistakes. The more stressful the situation, the more mistakes are made. Fortunately in my line of work, crimes are extremely stressful even to those who commit them. I look for the mistakes and so find the criminal. Your client made only two mistakes, at the scene of the attack when the stress was at its height, but they were enough."

I think Aaltonen wins that round, but James counters, "Did you not consider that the real killer might have planted these two pieces of evidence in order to implicate my client?"

"Of course, we inspected the hotel at the request of the defence, we interviewed a number of witnesses, but there was nothing to indicate the presence of another person."

"So you stopped investigating this possibility?"

"I judged that the evidence against Mr Carter was strong enough for all resources to be best spent investigating him. This is normal once a suspect has been charged."

"But it is a possibility; perhaps you didn't investigate hard enough? Maybe something will turn up?" says James, taunting the prosecution with the possibilities of the defence witnesses. Aaltonen remains silent. "We have also heard your theories about my allegedly sex obsessed client, scheming to kill Ms Saarinen to satisfy his desires. But this is just theory, isn't it? Little more than guess work?" The barrister continues without leaving space for Aaltonen to answer, "You said yourself the evidence indicates Ms Saarinen followed Mr Carter. How could he know she was going to do that?"

"Your client did speak to Ms Saarinen on several occasions during the evening. Perhaps more was said than was heard by the witnesses. Perhaps, your client was hoping for an opportunity and one presented itself. There are several possibilities."

"Or perhaps your guesses are wrong and it is not my client but the real killer who had such an obsession? You haven't got any real evidence about that, have you?"

"Maybe something will turn up," parrots Aaltonen. James studies him curiously for a moment before dismissing him.

And so that's it. Apart from the summing up, that's the case against me: a bit of fluff, some wrigglies, and a whole lot of hearsay, as James succinctly put it. 'Worry if anything unexpected happens', he said. Nothing has, has it?

CHAPTER 38

First up for my defence are Abi's star finds: the coach and two young women from the VPT volleyball team. It's nice to see disconcertment spread across the faces behind the prosecution table as the coach makes his statement.

"And you are sure that no one crossed the road ahead of the drunk man?" clarifies James.

"Yes, the road is straight and it was a clear night." The coach seems uncomfortable with his predicament of being a defence witness in such a notorious case. He shifts his weight from one foot to the other every so often, but he's an honest man under oath.

"And there were no other vehicles?"

"No."

"So if a taxi driver saw a woman cross the dual carriageway and then nearly hit a man in the middle of *Pankkikatu*, it must have been a different man at a different time?"

"Yes, it seems so."

"And the man you saw, waiting, crossed the road after you had passed?"

"Yes, I saw in the mirror."

The cross-examination is brief, questioning the date and time, but our witness's story holds.

The two women are called separately, but give almost identical evidence. The prosecution barrister tries a bit harder this time and the second woman bears the brunt of it.

"How can you be sure that the drunk man was the defendant?"

"He was looking so silly, talking to the lamp post, it sort of sticks in your mind."

"But you had been out partying that evening. Exactly how drunk were you?" I've seen doubt in the looks this woman has cast me, but she's not about to be insulted.

"We'd had a few, but not so many as to forget anything. Both Inna and I picked him out from that set of photos. We're not both going to be wrong are we? It was definitely him." She glowers at the barrister.

"Okay. The person you saw in the distance down *Pankkikatu*. How did you know this person was following the drunk man?"

She considers for a moment, rubbing the corner of her mouth with a finger and then says, "We didn't know for sure that the person was following the defendant." She emphasises the last word. "We just assumed. It was deserted except for two people. The one in the distance, in the pale coat, was walking towards him. We just assumed they were following, we didn't know. Not for sure."

"So this might have been some completely unconnected person on their way home?"

"I suppose so."

"Thank you. I have no more questions for this witness."

Unexpectedly, James leaps to his feet catching my elbow with his forearm as he does so, *"Anteeksi..."* he starts, but he's not talking to me, *"I'm sorry..."* I can see the excitement in the way the middle finger of his left hand is tapping against his thumb as he talks. My hair has gone grey by the time the translator starts, "I'm sorry, Madam, but may I pick up on something the witness has just said?"

Judge Kivelä raises one eyebrow, "Of course, but I must also allow a further chance for cross-examination."

"Of course," says James, "Thank you." He turns towards the witness and flashes a reassuring smile. "Don't worry, I just want to clarify something you said a few moments ago to my Prosecutor colleague."

"Okay."

"In your original witness statements, you said that the person in the distance down *Pankkikatu* was, and I quote," he lifts one of his binders and reads from it, "'too far away to see what they were like.' Have you remembered more?"

"I don't understand."

"A few moments ago, you said that the person was wearing a pale coat."

"Oh... did I not... I don't know why." She stops for a moment and gathers her thoughts. "When we made the statement they just asked if we could see what the person looked like, what colour clothes they had on. I can't tell you what colour it was. It was dark and everything in the distance looked kind of orangey in the street lights."

"But you have remembered something?"

"Yes. When he," she nods towards the prosecution table, "asked me how I could remember the drunk man so well, I saw a picture in my head of the man, him," she waves her hand in my direction, "talking to the lamp post. Behind him, way in the distance is the other person." She closes her eyes as if reliving the scene, "It's a pale dot, not a dark one."

James walks from behind our table towards the clerk, makes a request in a lowered voice, and the picture of Arwen's clothes with the light brown suede type coat sitting on top of the pile appears on the screen.

"This is the coat that the deceased was wearing. Could this have been your 'pale dot'?"

"Yes, I think so."

"So it seems even more likely that the person you saw was Arwen Saarinen... Let me repeat the question I asked you earlier: you saw the defendant waiting to cross the road, you saw someone who was most likely the deceased approaching in the distance. If a taxi driver also saw a man cross *Pankkikatu* behind the deceased then how would you explain that?

"I would think it had to be a different man."

"Thank you. Now I'm sure Mr Talus will wish to ask you a few more questions."

Talus rises to his feet and clears his throat, "Ms Klami, I wonder why you suddenly thought of this information now and it was not in your original statement?"

She shrugs and widens her eyes, "Well, you made me think about it. I didn't realise that I knew anything else, but it turns out that I did."

"Are you sure that this is not a trick of your memory? The

particulars of Ms Saarinen's clothing were well publicised in the media when the police were originally appealing for witnesses."

"I never heard about that. I didn't know anything about this until Mr Rintala spoke to us."

"You didn't hear about this case?" Apparently, the TV news has been full of it for months.

"I don't watch the news. It's so boring."

The barrister can see he is getting nowhere so instead he asks the judge to recall the other woman, Ms Tiensuu. Unfortunately, she can't verify her team mate's claim, but I see the corner of James's mouth rise slightly when she says, "But Hel has a much better memory than me, so if she says that then it must be right."

"We'll call that a nice little unexpected bonus," whispers James, as she leaves the stand. May they keep on coming!

The next few hours should be easier: character witnesses, all chosen to sing my praises. John is first and the judge has decided there is time to squeeze him in before lunch. He's wearing a modern dark grey suit. It's very formal, but slightly on the small side. He must have borrowed it. As far as I know, the only posh clothes that John owns involve kilts, sporrans and the like. 'There's nae point being a McLeod unless you flaunt it.' Reputedly, he even went to job interviews in his traditional dress. James, no doubt, had other ideas.

It's a very strange experience, listening to someone who spends most of his life taking the piss, reeling off a string of compliments. And for practicality, James swaps to asking the questions in English, so I can hear both sides. Apparently, I'm reliable, trustworthy, a joy to work with. "If there's a problem you can just pass it to him and he will find an answer." He must be talking about someone else... "Violent tendencies? I've seen more fight in a packet of jelly babies." That must have translated well into Finnish: a few titters echo round the hall. "No, Steven's one of them new men, all feelings and equality. He wouldnae get hold of a girl's hand without asking first." I roll my eyes at John's hyperbole.

Things get a little stickier during cross examination:

"Mr McLeod," says Talus through the translator, "You say that the defendant is so meek and mild that he would even ask before taking a girl's hand and yet on the night of Ms Saarinen's murder, the defendant was seen trying to drag her out of her chair."

"Aye, yes, I saw that. There was nothing in it. Arwen, God rest her soul," he says glancing quickly in the direction of the family, "had been arguing with her boyfriend for half the evening. Steven wanted to dance and he knows she likes one too, so why not ask? Then she says yes and no at the same time, he gets confused and thinks she is messing about and tries to pull her up. Hardly a big deal. If you'd have seen the expression on his face when he thought he'd accidentally hurt her, you'd know he had nothing to do with this. Not in a million years."

The prosecuting barrister ignores this comment and refers back to earlier, "You said that Ms Saarinen said 'yes and no at the same time'? What did you mean by that?" Beside me I hear James's breathing pause mid-breath.

"She was fighting it as much as he was. Their mouths said one thing, but their eyes said something else."

"So you think Mr Carter was fighting his feelings for Ms Saarinen?"

"Careful John," mutters James under his breath.

"Oh, yes, but I didnae say he was losing." John uses exactly the same tone that I know means he's got you fooled in a wind up.

"What do you mean by that?"

"I'm saying that Steven could control himself. Better than most people I know. I spent several months with him in pubs and clubs. More than one time some woman has virtually thrown themselves at him, but he's walked away. If you've ever met his wife, it's not difficult to see why that would be." In former times I'd have accused him of smooth talking Abi with that one; now I could kiss him... well, almost.

"Good answer," mouths James.

Talus narrows his eyes and, perhaps as a calculated risk, asks, "Mr McLeod, can you actually give the court an example of one of these women?"

John stares at the Prosecutor for a moment. "You want me to tell you about one of the times Steven had to get himself out of a pickle?"

"Yes."

"Okay... well..." John seems like he's stalling for time. Come on, don't let me down. He glances towards me, the corners of his mouth twitching as if to control an inappropriate urge to grin. "There was this lassie, Tytte." Just the name makes me cringe. "It was my fault really. Keith Smith and I had been pestering Steven to come to the Copacabana club on a Thursday evening." He shrugs. "It's something you have to do when you're in Finland." A few chuckles and snorts rise from the public seats – everyone knows he means 'ladies night'. "Anyhow, he finally gave in one time and..." John's voice fades away as I begin to daydream over his edited version.

+ + +

I'M NOT SURE whether to be relieved or insulted. 'Ladies night' is in full swing. As far as I can see, the main premise is that the women feel they can be more forward than usual. It's a bit like being caught up in one large hen party. Only, as you can imagine in a night club named after a Barry Manilow song, everything is a bit more sedate and (how shall I put it?) caters for the more experienced woman. I don't think I'm the youngest person in here, but I'm pretty sure I'm the youngest bloke.

Immediately after we parked ourselves round one of the many oval tables, Keith and shortly afterwards, John, were hoiked out of their seats and are now progressing round the glitter ball dance floor in various states of entanglement. I'm not sure whether I'm too young, too ugly, or if the expression of incredulity on my face is too obvious, but after twenty minutes, I'm still sitting at the table. I sip my drink slowly and try to feel superior.

"Still no bites, Stevie boy?" says John as he takes a chair, perspiration shining across his high forehead. He shares a brief peck with his partner before she heads off towards the bar.

"Fortunately, it seems I'm too much of a tiddler for all these sharks."

"Oche, you'll get snapped up soon enough." His hand waves in front of my face making biting shapes.

"Piss off." Eyebrows rise. "That doesn't count. Anyway, someone's already getting you a drink by the look of it." John's partner flicks him a long distance smile as she waits for the drinks to be poured. "She's gorgeous... for her age."

John ignores my banter, "Aye, she'll be a tricky one to leave behind, for sure."

"Did you meet her in here?"

"No, she owns the outdoor shop."

"What, where you got the thermal coats from?"

John shrugs a silent, 'It's got to happen somewhere.'

"Is that Keith's girlfriend," I ask, nodding towards the dance floor.

"Maybe tonight's. Keith goes for quantity, whereas I prefer quality."

"Don't you feel guilty?"

"Only after I come," says John, quickly, as if describing an unfortunate medical symptom to the doctor.

"Gross. That was an image I didn't need."

We sit in silence, watching Keith spin his magic on another drunken house wife until John's lager arrives.

"Tuu, this is Steven, Steven, this is Tuua," says John doing the formalities. Up close I think that Tuua looks a bit like Debbie Harry when Blondie reformed in the '90s. Obviously older but still has it, whatever 'it' is.

"Ah, Steven, John has told about you."

"All good, I hope." I refrain from saying, 'John never said you existed!'

"Are you alone?" asks Tuua.

"Yes, I always got picked last for the school football team too."

Tuua smiles. "John say you are funny."

"Did he?"

"I meant funny as in strange."

"I love you too, darling," I say and stand to pay a visit. I return to find John and Tuua are once more strutting their stuff.

"*Oletko yksin?*" A woman in one of those dresses that seems to be made from strips of silver foil is pushing her younger friend firmly towards me. She seems fairly drunk already.

"*Sorry, English?*" I say by way of explaining my blank look.

"You on own?" Not again.

"My friends are already dancing." I indicate towards Keith who is just turning his partner round with his right hand whilst letting his left hand rest on her spinning waist. Where did he learn to do that stuff?

"Oh, Keith," sniggers the older woman and says something in Finnish to her friend.

"Would you like to sit?" I ask. The younger woman looks slightly disappointed but joins me at the table. Her friend raises her hands slightly, her job seemingly done, and returns to a raucous gaggle two tables away. There is a slight pause. This is Copa, Thursday night, I know where this could go. But I don't want to be rude and it's boring watching other people have a good time. What the heck, I'll be careful...

"Steven." I say and shake her hand. I receive the 'oh, how quaint' smile I was expecting.

"Tytte."

The way she pronounces it doesn't sound Finnish and it rings bells. Holiday... fjords... breakfast... gorgeous jam. "Is that like the berries?"

"Joo, joo," she says, briefly forgetting about English. "Normally nobody know that."

"They're called something different here, aren't they?"

"Puolukka... but my father is of Norway."

"So he named you after his favourite sauce?"

"Nice and sweet," she grins.

"Goes well with ice cream."

She regards at me for a moment, realises I am teasing, and gives me a gentle nudge, "My friend tell me Keith is bad boy so I better watch for his friend." This warning does not appear to have been a discouragement. "Where you from?"

"England. Do you live in Mahikkala?" I say, trying to divert from the next question.

"No, Espoo. I stay here for work training." She points towards the group of women, now somewhat depleted by the dance floor. "All from round Finland."

"What do you do?" Heck, they always ask it.

"Dancers on pole." She laughs at my surprised face. "No. Only after many drink! We travel shop people."

"Travel agents? I hope you're staying in a good hotel."

"Central Hotel."

"Remind me not to book a holiday with your shop," I laugh.

"Why? Where you stay?" She almost looks offended.

"Central hotel also."

"You funny," she says and takes the final sip of her drink.

"Would you like another?" I raise my own empty glass slightly.

"Vodka orange juice."

As I return, mixes in hands, Keith and John are just leaving the dance floor. Their partners appear to be retreating to powder their noses.

"Who's your friend, Steven?" asks John.

"This is Tytte, this is John and you already know 'bad boy' here." Tytte laughs and takes the drink out of my proffered hand. Keith seems momentarily wrong footed. Not often I manage that. I linger over my next sip of G&T to prolong Keith's discomfort. "Tytte's friend told her to watch out for friends of 'bad boy' Keith. What have you been doing?"

"Stuff you only dream about," says Keith, but then spoils the effect with a more concerned, "Which is her friend, then?"

"The one in the foil," I say pointing towards a glittering figure, now on the dance floor.

"Oh her," smirks Keith. "That was just a misunderstanding. Very easy when you don't speak the lingo." He pauses to drink some of his now warm alcohol. "Aren't you going to spin this young lady round the floor then?" I suppose I asked for that. "Steven here thinks that this kind of dancing is silly," he continues.

"You no like to dance?" Tytte looks at me as if someone has just told her that I have halitosis.

"I love dancing. It's just I usually do... disco type dancing. I've never done arm in arm dancing."

"He's a Finnish foxtrot virgin," says John. I roll my eyes.

"No worry, I be gentle," laughs Tytte, pulling me up.

I mouth insults back at John and Keith as I'm dragged to the dance floor.

"OK, what do I do, then?"

"You hold here," she says, putting my right hand round her waist. "Other hand hold mine." Fortunately, she is only a few inches shorter than me, so we do match up reasonably well. "Now, slow, slow, quick, quick, slow, slow..."

"I love it when a woman tells me what to do," I say. Hell, I'm turning into Keith, it must be the dancing. I start reasonably well. I've seen the others do it; it's just a different dance. My eyes slip sideways towards Tytte's face, which is a mistake. There's something in her eyes which makes me stop counting. Our legs tangle as I do a 'slow' after only one 'quick'. No feet get squashed but it's a close thing.

"*Anteeksi.*"

"You doing so well," says Tytte and we start off again. She's pulled me slightly closer. We're OK for another minute or so: I concentrate hard on where I and my feet are going. I can feel Tytte's left hand moving down from my waist and on to the curve of my bum. Our legs muddle once again, I stifle an 'ow' as one of her heels presses down on the top of my shoe just above the toes.

"My fault," I say and can hardly not look towards her. 'Kiss me,' her eyes are saying, but I feel totally immune. Why don't I fancy this woman? There's nothing unattractive about her. She's pleasant enough, nicely proportioned, not skinny, but not large either; curves in all the right places, cheeky smile. Is it that she's coming on to me? Whatever it is, I need to get out of this somehow.

"Shall we sit down?" I ask.

My dance partner appears keener than I had expected. I'm worried she thinks I'm after a less public snog. Tytte keeps her arm around my waist as we walk and it stays as we sit.

"Not bad for first try," says Tuua who has rejoined John. Keith's partner is also at the table, but he makes no effort to introduce her.

"Good teacher," I say automatically. Tytte moves her hand to my knee and squeezes slightly.

"You need to learn to do some twirls," says Keith.

"I had enough trouble counting the steps without getting distr... acted." Tytte just moved her hand higher up my leg. John is trying hard not to guffaw. Just as I wonder quite where she is going to put her hand next, she presses down on my thigh and pushes herself out of the chair.

"Toilet."

"She's nay one to hang about," chortles John, glancing after her retreating back.

"Yes, Steven gets to tickle Tytte's titties tonight," Keith chimes in.

"Oh, grow up," I grumble. "Look, I don't feel too well." I stand. "Tell her... just tell her that I think she's gorgeous but that the curry I had earlier has given me the runs and I've had to split."

"We had Chinese earlier," says John.

"Whatever, just tell her," I say retreating from the table. Keith is staring at me like I'm from another planet. I am.

- - -

THE AUTHORITATIVE TONES of Judge Kivelä calling recess for lunch wrenches me back to the present. As the spectators stream out of the hall intent on hot, thick stew and tangy berry sauces, I turn my eyes to the left. They reach Abi and I have to blink. For the first time in weeks, there is a touch of warmth in her skin and teeth in her smile. It's not much, but I'm sure I've John to thank for it. I raise the corners of my mouth in half-hearted reply. He may have made me out to be a saint, but I can remember why I felt so impervious to Tytte's charms... and it was mostly to do with red hair.

CHAPTER 39

"HE's nice to talk to: he listens. It's easy to forget that you're talking to a man." Out of all of Hanne's testimony that little throw away comment was the one which almost brought a smile to my lips. I'd 've cross-examined her on that one:

'So Ms Ryti, is that meant to be a compliment or an insult?'

'Both,' she grins mischievously from behind the bar.

'And when you forget that I'm a man, does that make me more attractive or less?'

A giggle, causes me to turn my head and there is Reddy standing next to me, a stack of empties in her right hand... Stop it. STOP IT! Concentrate, it might matter.

"Ms Ryti," says the Prosecutor, "you told Mr Hainsworth that you were sure Mr Carter could not have committed this crime. Do you have any qualifications in psychology or any other relevant subject?"

Hanne's sky blue eyes glare from under a fringe of curls, her expression as defiant as her latest out-of-mode hair style. "Yes," she says. James throws me a quizzical glance to which I shrug.

"Ms Ryti," says Talus, "I must remind you that you are under oath. Exactly what qualifications do you have?"

"I have the most useful qualification anyone could want for understanding people: I have worked behind a bar for almost twenty years."

"But you don't have any academic qualifications?"

"Are you saying that practical experience counts for nothing?"

Talus is clearly unsure of how to answer this. James appears slightly smug at his opposite number's discomfort. Before he has time to answer Hanne continues, "I've seen just about every type of person there is and believe me, after a few drinks, they tell you things they wouldn't even tell their best friend."

Recovering his poise, Talus asks, "And did Mr Carter give you any of these revelations?"

"Not really, he seemed pretty together."

"Then how can you hold such a firm opinion on his innocence?"

Hanne rolls her eyes as if this is the most obvious thing in the world, "Because, I got to know him and he respects and cares for women. Whoever did this does not respect women. Let me tell you a..." Talus tries to interrupt, but Hanne says, "You asked me a question, so wait for the whole answer." There are a few sniggers. Everyone likes to see a lawyer get a taste of their own.

"One time, when Steven and the other English came into my bar, there was a very loud, very drunk woman. Everyone could see something was wrong with her. She started talking to them, saying things that didn't make sense. Steven asked her if someone was hurting her." She catches the eye of the female lay judge. "Yes, he dared to ask... Steven and Mark, they persuaded me to help her, to take her to her house. Maybe if a woman brought her home, the beating would not be so bad. But some weeks later, they saw her again with a broken leg. Steven came to ask me again to help her. I still go, but the door is always shut. It's a man like her husband who should be standing there," she points toward me, "not Steven. Do you care for a stranger and then kill a friend? I think not."

"I have no more questions for this witness." Talus gets it in finally.

"Good little anecdote," says James, reaching for a different file during the hiatus. "Let's hope Mark can do the business too."

Too much praise and people start to question it, so James keeps the character stuff to a minimum and quickly gets to specifics, "Mr Hatfield, was it normal for the defendant to go for walks?"

"Yes, he went on a wander almost every weekend." Mark's cheeks are slightly pinched with tension. Hopefully people will just think it's court nerves. Unless Raakel is out there somewhere, I guess I'm the only one who knows the real source. Don't worry. No one will ask that.

"Sometimes these walks were by Lake Mahi?"

"Yes, it's the nearest bit of countryside to the Central Hotel. I went with him a couple of times."

"And was it unusual for him to walk at night, even late at night?"

"No, that had happened before. Lots of the paths round the lake are lit all night and there wasn't exactly much daylight at that time of the year anyway. It wasn't a surprise when he said he was going for a stroll, that night."

"The night Ms Saarinen was killed?"

"Yes."

James moves to a different tack, "You were present in Hanne's Bar on Saturday 1st March when the defendant was attacked by Mr Varis?"

"Yes."

"Had the defendant been acting in any way unusually since the previous Thursday night?"

"No, not at all."

"Please describe to us what happened."

"Steven and I were sitting at the bar talking. Suddenly, Kari came in and knocked Steven off his chair and started kicking him on the floor." When the translation into Finnish has ended, I can't tell if the whispers around the room are murmur of surprise or admiration. Perhaps both? Judge Kivelä raises her hand. "The bouncer pulled him off, but he kept yelling things like, 'I know it was you.'"

"What was Mr Carter's reaction?"

"He had to pick himself up to start with, but he didn't know what Kari was on about. Then Kari told us Arwen had been killed and Steven looked gutted, we all were."

"So he reacted like anyone would on learning the death of a friend?"

"Yes."

"And what evidence did Mr Varis have for thinking that Mr Carter had killed Ms Saarinen?"

"Only that he had gone for a walk in the same woods."

"Thank you. It seems that many people in this case are willing to jump to conclusions on the basis of scant evidence."

Perhaps this story wasn't the best one to bring up. Maybe James thought that the prosecution would in any case. Whatever, the first thing that Talus asks Mark is, "I would like to ask you a few further questions about Saturday 1st March. After Mr Carter had learned of Ms Saarinen's death, did he threaten violence towards Mr Varis?"

Mark screws up his brow in confusion.

"Did Mr Carter and Mr Varis argue?"

"Oh, that." Again Mark's brow furrows as if he's trying to work out why this is important. "Kari kept saying that Arwen had followed him, so they must have met and Steven must have done it. Then Steven said that he had seen Kari and Arwen arguing, and he was obviously violent, so Kari was the more likely suspect. I suppose that was when they might have started fighting. Hanne told them both to grow up and they calmed down."

"So Mr Carter did not step towards Mr Varis in a threatening manner?"

"Maybe, but Mr Varis had just beaten him up and called him a murderer. What would anyone do?"

"You don't think that this argument was to hide Mr Carter's own lack of shock at the news and to try to move suspicion away from himself?"

Mark looks suitably gobsmacked at this suggestion, "No, he didn't know anything about it. You can't fake a reaction like that, especially when someone's just beaten you up. We were close then, I would have known something was up."

Talus almost seems to smile, as if all this has been leading towards Mark admitting that we were close. Why?

"If you were close, as you say, presumably Mr Carter discussed his thoughts and feelings with you?"

"Yes, we talked quite a bit. I suppose we kind of acted like each others' wives," He blushes as he realises the alternative implications, "I mean, not like that... I mean, just someone to have a whinge about things to."

"Like a brother?"

Mark latches on to this, "Yes, like that."

"So you must have known exactly what Mr Carter felt about Ms Saarinen."

Mark's mouth hangs slightly open; his eyes flick toward me and then back towards the Prosecutor.

"Let me remind you, Mr Hatfield that you are under oath."

"He did like her, but he liked his wife too." Mark's eyes stray past mine to the far edge of the room.

"Surely Mr Carter loved his wife, didn't he? Does that mean that when you say 'like' he actually loved Ms Saarinen as well?"

"Maybe, I don't know. Can I have some water, please?" The clerk reaches for one of the upturned tumblers stacked at the left side of his table, pours a glass and passes it to Mark. He takes a sip, loosens his tie slightly and then takes a gulp.

"Sorry," says Mark, "Dry mouth."

Talus has been waiting, motionless, mantis-like in his patience, "Quite alright. Now, come on, Mr Hatfield: you say you were close, but you do not know if he loved her? Or are you protecting your friend?"

"No... no, he doesn't need protecting, he's not done anything wrong. He just got a bit carried away, that's all." Rather than prompting once the translation is complete, Talus merely raises his eyebrows. A white faced Mark continues, "They did seem to have a lot in common..."

"And."

"They talked together quite a lot."

"Mr Hatfield, did Mr Carter ever say that he was in love with Ms Saarinen?"

Mark can't help but glance towards me.

"Mr Hatfield?"

"Yes, he did, but he said it didn't matter because he was married and she had a boyfriend and it would never go anywhere."

"But Ms Saarinen split up from her boyfriend, didn't she?"

"Yes, but..."

"This witness can be dismissed," says Talus firmly. As Mark is leaving the desk, James notices my glum face, "Don't worry, that wasn't too bad. Put it together with what John said and you were in a spot but climbing out of it." He purses his lips, "Wish I knew where Talus is going with all this love stuff, though."

CHAPTER 40

Hiltunen, the strange psychologist, is playing a different character in his repertoire today: 'the expert'. The wild beard has been smoothed down and gone are the inane grins and hearty laughs. In their place, precise sounding Finnish is being uttered from above an immaculately pressed suit. He's done well for me so far, describing his impressive qualifications, the lengths to which he goes to ensure the accuracy of the test and my particularly strong lying response. James pushed him as far as agreeing that, 'According to the evidence of my tests, I find it very unlikely that Mr Carter committed this crime.' But I'm not getting my hopes up too much. As I've been warned, knocking this type of evidence is easy:

"Dr Hiltunen, you must be aware of the independent studies carried out into the accuracy of polygraph evidence?" says Talus. "Can you state what percentage of the time the polygraph was proved to be correct?"

Hiltunen's face stretches into something between a grin and a grimace, "I believe it was about sixty percent."

"Sixty percent? We would expect fifty percent just from guessing, so are we saying that your evidence is just a little better than guessing?"

"No, what we are saying is that some people are very poor at doing the test. If an independent study were done on my results alone you would find a much higher success rate."

"But Dr Hiltunen, as there is no such study, we have only your word for that."

The psychologist raises his chin so that he is peering slightly down his nose, "Indeed, but I have been called here as an impartial expert, have I not?"

"Yes, but even experts can be over confident in their own abilities," counters Talus. "Is it not true that in many other European countries, polygraph evidence is inadmissible?"

"Of course, but not all countries are as enlightened as Finland." I notice that even Judge Kivelä's impassive expression briefly moulds into an ironic smile at that one. Talus leaves the point and moves on. Yesterday, after the prosecution had rested, I heard James and Lars discussing why they hadn't called a different psychologist to rubbish lie detector evidence. 'They must want to use something from the report, Talus can't be that stupid.' We'll see now, shall we?

"Dr Hiltunen, you qualify your report with, and I quote: 'Assuming that Steven Carter is not the most accomplished liar that I have encountered.'" Talus leaves his words hanging for a moment, "There have been several documented cases of clever people fooling the lie detector test in the past. Mr Carter is an intelligent man, is he not?"

"He appears to be, but..." The psychologist trails off. It's a proper grimace this time.

"Were you going to say, 'but he does not seem like an accomplished liar to me,' Dr Hiltunen?"

"Something like that," he replies, head shaking, "to which you will reply, 'well a good liar wouldn't appear to be a good liar would he?'"

Talus nods his head once, "Thank you, doctor, that is all my questions."

Great! So just when I'm about to give my side of the story, the word liar is fixed in everyone's heads. "Let's just get on with it," shrugs James.

There's no avoiding the stares. I fix my eyes on James's mouth as he's recommended, but to the left and right, eyes peer, accusingly, curiously, sympathetically? Well, I can hope. 'Don't look at the judges, don't look at the judges,' I chant inside my head whilst waiting for the translator. I grip the sides of the desk and begin. I am guided through that final evening with gentle prompting. Once I am uneventfully returned to the Central Hotel, James turns his attention towards the chief judge, "Madam, as I mentioned to you, the defence would like to do a small demonstration for the court using the defendant. May we proceed?"

It takes twenty minutes of waiting and shuffling before I am standing in a small internal courtyard towards the rear of the building. High above the granite walls and triple glazed windows, the brightest stars are piercing the twilight.

"Mr Carter, please pull up the scarf." I turn back towards James and blink into the floodlight. For a second after I raise the dark wool to cover my nose nothing happens; then I exhale; my glasses immediately steam up. I take them off, wipe them on a cloth handed to me by Lars, and return them to my face. They cloud over once more. I repeat this a couple of times, before James says to the assembled group of judges and officials, "As you can see, it is not terribly practical to wear a scarf over your nose if you have spectacles."

"Mr Carter," says James, once we are all reassembled in the warm, "you state that after turning on to *Pankkikatu*, you walked along the road, waited for two cars to pass, and then crossed straight over the dual carriageway. Is that correct?"

"Yes."

"But a taxi driver claims to have almost knocked over someone dressed similarly to yourself as he turned into *Pankkikatu*. How do you account for that?"

I try to keep my voice low and steady as James has taught me, "It must have been someone else. I crossed the road at the top of *Pankkikatu*, next to the bank, and no cars drove past me; only those two on the dual carriageway."

"Mr Carter, the coat, gloves, hat and scarf, did you wear these often?"

"I only had one set of cold weather gear, so I wore them every time I went out."

"Every single time?"

"I think so, yes."

"And you bought the items in Finland?"

"Yes, well, John did actually. He bought us all a set from the army surplus store in Mahikkala."

"So anyone who had seen you about town would have known what you wore and could easily have obtained duplicate clothing?"

"Yes."

"The taxi driver also stated that the man wore metal framed spectacles, but he could not fully identify this man because he had pulled his scarf over his nose. In light of this afternoon's demonstration, what do you have to say about that?"

"That's something I would never do. As we showed, my glasses would keep steaming up and I wouldn't be able to see where I was going." There is a faint whispering as those in the main seating block, who were not present for the demonstration, realise the point.

"But the witness says that he could see this man's eyes," says James.

"In which case, I can only think of two explanations: Firstly, that the man was holding his breath. That doesn't seem very likely, not if he was nearly run over. The second was that there were no lenses in the glasses."

"They were pretend spectacles?" James has used that word on purpose and wants me to echo it.

"Yes, pretend glasses, worn by someone pretending to be me."

"Why would someone pretend to be you?"

"So that he could kill Ms Saarinen and pin the blame on me." James raises the corners of his mouth very slightly in acknowledgement that I remembered to use her surname. It still doesn't sound right. I take a deep breath; I know what's coming next: James's 'trust me'.

"Mr Carter, did you have sexual intercourse with Ms Saarinen between Tuesday 26th February and Thursday 28th February this year?" Talus leans to whisper to his colleague. He doesn't seem surprised.

"No, I did not." Talus's head whips back forward even before the translator starts. Now we've got his attention.

"Did you ever have any sort of sexual relations with Ms Saarinen?"

"No, I did not."

"Mr Carter, are you aware that if you admitted to having consensual sexual relations with Ms Saarinen in the days before her death then the prosecution's primary forensic evidence would be called into question and this might substantially help your case?"

"Yes, I am aware of that."

"Then why are you denying it?"

"Because I am in a court of law and I have sworn to tell the truth. However convenient it might be, I cannot admit to something which I did not do."

"But this might save you from a long prison sentence?"

Talus stands and speaks to Judge Kivelä. "Is my Advocate colleague inciting the defendant to perjure himself?"

"Madam, the defendant has already stated his wish to tell the truth, I am merely exploring his motives," says James.

"Be careful, Mr Hainsworth, you are on thin ice here," says Kivelä over the top of her reading glasses. James turns toward me once more and repeats the question.

"It was tempting to lie if that would help my case, but I don't believe anything good comes of lies in the long run."

James pauses, affording a quick glance towards the lay judges. "So you deny any sexual relationship with Ms Saarinen even though this might make your conviction more likely?"

"Yes."

"In which case, please can you clarify for us the exact nature of your relationship with Ms Saarinen?"

"To start with we just had a laugh occasionally over the bar. Then we bumped into each other around town a few times – and it was accidentally. We found we both liked to dance and sing karaoke. Even though I love my wife, I found myself feeling something for Ms Saarinen. I told myself it didn't matter. Mark tried to warn me, but I thought I knew better. She knew I was married, she had a boyfriend, she didn't seem interested in anything except friendship: what was the problem? If she'd been more forward, I probably would have run off."

"But then Ms Saarinen split up with Mr Varis."

"Yes, but that wasn't anything to do with me. That was because he was holding her back."

"Can you explain what you mean by that?"

"Yes, Arw..." I falter, realising my mistake, oh what the heck, "Look, I never even knew what her surname was until after she was dead." I've lost my thread, but James steps in, a sure hand to guide me back on track.

"You were going to explain why Mr Varis was holding Ms Saarinen back."

"Oh yes... Ms Saarinen, she wanted to be a singer. In musicals: Broadway, the West End, that kind of thing, but Kari just wanted a little housewife in Mahikkala. The thing was, though, she had an amazing voice: really, truly special. Anyone who heard it must have known that." I can't help it, my eyes flick towards Arwen's mother. There's an odd expression on her face: rueful. I don't dare stare, but I can't help but wonder about her voice too. I return my attention to James's mouth. "And she had a place at the Music academy in Kuopio, but Kari persuaded her that there was no point going. Just getting a place there means you're one of the best in the country. Such a waste..." I trail off, wetness in the corners of my eyes.

"But you brought them back together?" says James.

"Yes, well, it probably would have happened anyway, but I gave them a nudge. Kari was desperate to get back together and it was clear that Arwen still loved him. It seemed like she wanted to give him another chance, but didn't know what to say."

"So what did you do?"

"We were at a karaoke night; Arwen had chosen a song for me to sing; she still hadn't sung my choice. So I found a great song called *We belong* and persuaded her to sing it to him. By half way through they were already arm in arm."

James lets that settle for a moment. "But you still had some feelings for her?"

"Yes. You can't just turn emotion on and off like a tap. I tried to avoid her, but we met at the singing and then at Hanne's party. Like has been said already, everyone was a bit drunk and I had a bit of a misunderstanding with her and pulled her arm. She seemed fine about it, but I was ashamed."

"You were ashamed?"

"Yes, I suddenly realised how stupid it was to have a wonderful wife, but to be acting like a teenager with a silly crush. That was partly why I went for a walk by the lake. I wanted to think things through."

"I see. So, at any point did you believe that Ms Saarinen returned your feelings?"

"No. I thought she liked me, but not in that way."

"So it was like a teenage crush?"

"Yes, I don't know what John and Til meant about the staring. Arwen was just like that: she was an intimate person. She'd keep eye contact much longer than most people would. She'd stand right next to you, or put her hand on your shoulder, but she wouldn't mean anything by it." I take a deep breath and sigh, "She was lovely, but I was married. My wife's lovely too. It's just one of those things. If you've been married a while you'll almost certainly meet someone who makes you think, 'What if...' You can't stop yourself finding someone attractive. It's what you do about it that matters."

I can tell from James's face that I'm doing OK. He throws me a tiny encouraging smile whilst the translator finishes. If he's sticking to the plan we should be close to the end. "Why then, Mr Carter, do you think that Ms Saarinen followed you towards the lake?"

"I've been thinking about that. She's supposed to have said that I 'understood' her. I think she wanted reassurance. She was going to leave her boyfriend for good and follow her dream. She wanted someone to tell her she was doing the right thing. I would have done that."

"But you never got the chance."

"No, because someone else killed her, someone who seems to want to push the blame on to me."

"Thank you, Mr Carter, I have no more questions."

In the hiatus, I risk a glance towards Abi but her eyes are already turned towards the prosecution barrister who clears his throat to attract my attention. "Well, strangely, it seems my colleague for the defence has already done half my cross-examination for me. So you admit, Mr Carter, that you had a crush, an infatuation or obsession with the deceased?"

"I think obsession is over-exaggerating the way I felt. It sounds like I was out of control. I wasn't. 'Crush' is about right."

"Oh is it?" Talus peers at me ominously. My armpits feel clammy as I wait for the hit, but he seems to recoil from the strike and asks, "But you admit that you found Ms Saarinen sexually attractive?"

"Yes."

"And you admit that you thought she did not return your feelings."

"Yes."

"And at the party in Hanne's Bar, Ms Saarinen had made her lack of feelings toward you particularly clear when she refused to dance with you?"

"Yes, I thought so."

"So I put it to you, that you had been consumed by your obsession for some time. Here you were, a man away from the comforts of home. Who wouldn't be attracted by a young woman such as Ms Saarinen? And yet sometimes she seemed to be leading you on and sometimes pushing you away. It must have been maddening."

"I wasn't like that."

Talus ignores me, "So you decided that you would take what you wanted anyway when the opportunity presented itself. You made a garrotte from a piece of rope and kept it ready."

James starts to stand, but I answer, "I don't even know how to make a garrotte. Just because I work in a rope factory doesn't mean I know how to tie knots."

"Then after the party in Hanne's Bar, you see Ms Saarinen on *Pankkikatu* and follow her into the forest. It was all too easy."

I raise my eyebrows: has this guy not been listening? "But we've just proved that I was in front. Ar... Ms Saarinen was following me. The person who the taxi driver saw was someone else, the real killer."

Talus flashes a humourless smile, "I agree with you, Mr Carter that the person the taxi driver saw was the real killer." He breaks for translation at that point and as I hear it come through I'm wondering how these words match up with the expression on his face. They don't. "But are we to believe in this fantastical other man, for whom there is no evidence, when there is a perfectly simple explanation for the witness statements?" I stay silent. I can see he's going to tell me anyway. "Mr Carter, suppose the defence witnesses are correct and you crossed over the dual carriageway for the first time ahead of Ms Saarinen. Suppose, having crossed the road you looked back up *Pankkikatu* and saw Ms Saarinen approaching? Now, as you have said yourself, you did not know that she was going to follow you; you are still not sure if she is following you, but what a chance! You enter the forest, but quickly take the first path to the right which brings you back to the dual carriageway opposite the end of *Eteläkatu*. From there you cross back over the dual carriageway and return towards *Pankkikatu*. Perhaps you conceal yourself behind a parked car or in one of the many apartment doorways. You see Ms Saarinen arrive at the dual carriageway and begin to cross. You hear a vehicle approaching and raise your scarf to hide your face for the few seconds whilst the car passes. You can hold your breath for that long. As Ms Saarinen reaches the far side, you start to follow, but unexpectedly the taxi has turned into *Pankkikatu* and you have to jump out of its way. Then you cross the dual carriageway for the second time and follow your victim into the trees..." There is a triumphant gleam in his eye as he says his last sentence, "The real killer is you." I'm still silent, thinking hard. This makes no sense, but why not?

"This fits the facts, does it not, Mr Carter?" gloats the prosecuting barrister.

"No, it's not right, it didn't happen like that. It doesn't make sense," I stall for time. Think, THink, THINK! It all comes in a rush and I can hardly get the words out fast enough. "Right, firstly you've got me running two or three hundred metres in the time it takes Ms Saarinen to walk half way along *Pankkikatu*. How am I supposed to do that when I'm wearing these flat soled shoes?"

Talus shrugs, "The pavements were gritted, it had not snowed for some time. Indeed, at the very time we are talking about, Mr Varis was running home along similar streets." This guy is just as good as James at thinking on his feet. Anyway, that wasn't my main point.

"But your little story assumes I'm some cold monster stalking an unknown victim. All this doubling back doesn't make sense, because I knew Arwen, I was friends with her. If I'd turned round and seen her following, I would've just waited for her. There wouldn't need to be any running around and hiding, would there?"

Talus runs his eyes along the three lay judges. "In my experience, criminals rarely think logically in the lead up to a crime."

"I see, so I'm clever when it suits your story and stupid when it doesn't?" I notice the corners of Lars's mouth turn up slightly. Talus is too professional to be baited and moves on.

"So what happened, Mr Carter, when you followed Ms Saarinen into the forest? Don't her parents have a right to know?"

"I didn't follow her into the forest. I didn't see anyone whilst I was walking by the lake."

"Come on, Mr Carter, we have witnesses who saw you and Ms Saarinen near the wood. You admit that you had a 'crush' on her, and we have irrefutable forensic evidence that puts you at the scene of the crime. Why waste time with this charade anymore? You caught up with Ms Saarinen, didn't you?"

"No."

"She rejected your advances, didn't she?"

"No... I never saw her."

"You couldn't stand it anymore, could you? You took the rope and..."

"Stop it!" I interrupt the translator, "I didn't kill her. Look at me." I indicate my slim frame. "How could I overpower a fit young woman, let alone carry her body for tens of metres across the snow?"

"Come now, Mr Carter, are you telling me you've never lifted your wife?"

"Yes, but a dead weight..." I trail off, deciding that's not a good scientific argument.

"Were you going to say a dead weight feels heavier, Mr Carter? How would you know?" Out of the corner of my eye, I see James's worried face, alert for my answer.

"No, I was going to say, 'a dead weight is meant to feel heavier because the person is not helping you lift them.' But I don't actually know if that's true."

"Ah, a very clever answer. Mr Carter, I have no more questions."

As I'm escorted back to the defence table I try to catch Abi's eye again, but she's staring at the floor just in front of her feet. Look at me, please. I guess she must be nervous. It's her up next.

"Apart from the bit at the end there, that wasn't bad," says James in a hushed voice. "You still sound nicely honest."

"That's because I'm being nicely honest," I mutter, but James's attention has been caught by Judge Kivelä.

"Mr Hainsworth, I'm still not happy that your next witness has been present in court during all of the proceedings so far. It is most irregular."

"Madam, I understand that it is unusual, but as one of the defence counsels, she has a right to be present and to give evidence. There are several cases, Pirinen verses the state, 2001, for instance, where a counsel has also given evidence."

"I am aware of the precedents, but your witness's evidence may still be affected by something she has seen or heard in court."

"I understand your concern, madam," says James, "but such an argument could also be applied to the defendant."

"That has always been their privilege."

"However, in this particular case," continues James, "I think that the witness's evidence will hold more weight specifically because of what she has heard in court."

"We shall see," says Judge Kivelä. She removes her reading glasses from her nose and turns towards the Prosecutor, "Do you have anything to add, Mr Talus?"

"No Madam, I agree that it is unusual, but I am not going to object."

Kivelä considers for a moment, "In any case, we shall finish here for today and continue in the morning. Court is adjourned until tomorrow at nine-thirty."

As the spectators begin to file out, I turn towards Abi once more. There's no meeting scheduled for tonight, so I have to make do with her mouthed, "See you tomorrow," and a dilute smile. I raise a pair of crossed fingers and she does the same. Dilute: watered down, faded; that seems a good description for her today. My eyes follow her with concern as she stands and shuffles towards the exit. Hey, if things go quickly, it could be midnight feast time tomorrow night!

CHAPTER 41

'Confident and professional', James must have said. 'And when you look at Steven, smile.' I've already been on the receiving end of two of those soul warming beams. I know they're kind of false, but I'll take anything I can get.

"Ms Carter," says James, "How long have you been married to the defendant?"

"Six years, six fun years," She smiles at me again. Her dark green suit contrasts beautifully with her jet hair, freshly re-dyed by the look of it. Warm make up conceals the pasty nervousness that I know must be in there somewhere. I fall in love again, for the thousandth time.

"So you must be very familiar with the way that he dresses?"

"Yes," she grins slightly, "Like most men, he has three or four favourite things that he wears again and again until they are full of holes." A few higher pitched chuckles follow the translation.

"And what, if I may be so indelicate, is his opinion of boxer shorts?"

"He doesn't like them, he says they... he always says they're uncomfortable to wear under trousers. He only ever wears them at night instead of pyjamas - and then only sometimes."

"So it would be unlikely that your husband would have worn boxer shorts when attending the party at Hanne's Bar?"

"I would say that he definitely wouldn't have worn them."

"Thank you for clarifying that. You are aware that fibres from boxer shorts similar to your husband's were found close to Ms Saarinen's body? How do you account for that?"

"They must be from someone else's or maybe they were put there on purpose."

"Planted to throw suspicion on your husband?"

"Yes."

"Ms Carter, you have heard the accusations against your husband. It must be very distressing. You have also heard him admit that he had a crush on another woman. How do you feel about that?"

This time Abi's smile for me is slightly disappointed, "Well, obviously, I'd prefer it if that hadn't happened," her eyes return to the barrister, "but I understand what he means when he says that sometimes you grow feelings for someone without realising it at first." She shrugs, "Earlier this year, before all this happened, I was in a club with some friends. A man asked me out. I didn't think I'd shown him any interest, but he still asked me. Of course, I said no. Like Steven says, it's what you do in the end that matters."

"So you don't believe that your husband had a physical relationship with Ms Saarinen?"

"No, I just think he forgot for a while that he wasn't eighteen anymore."

James's face takes on its most serious 'law' expression, "Remembering that you are under oath, has your husband ever shown any tendencies towards violence?"

Abi almost laughs, "No, that's why this all seems so crazy. He's not a macho or angry man at all. Quite the opposite really, he's quite emotional, cries fairly often. It's one of the things I like about him. He's never been violent towards me and I've never seen any sign of it with anyone else."

"So you have complete faith that your husband is in no way connected with the murder of Ms Saarinen?"

"I'm sure he isn't."

"Thank you Ms Carter." Well, that was short and sweet.

"Hardly seemed worth it," I whisper to my right as James retakes his seat.

"Don't you believe it," says James under his breath. "It's amazing what weight people place on the opinions of the wife. She did well." As he says the last, he throws an appreciative smile towards the witness desk. I'm not sure that Abi notices, she shifts her weight from one leg to the other and glances apprehensively towards Talus as he makes his way to the Advocate's stand.

"Ms Carter, I am glad to hear that you have faith in your husband. So rare these days... Ms Carter, would you say that your husband is a clever man?"

Abi's brow furrows, "Compared to whom?"

"Compared to an average person."

"I'm not sure how clever an average person is." She's making him work for it.

"Come now, Ms Carter, your husband has a good degree from one of the top universities in England, he has a professional job where he is respected by his peers, surely that counts in his favour?"

She pauses for a moment and then says, "OK, I suppose he's about as clever as you then."

James stifles a snigger. "She is quick," he mutters.

"I see," Talus's face briefly lights in an ironic smile. "Extremely intelligent then." He returns to his line of attack, "And has Mr Carter ever been known to lie to you?"

Abi considers for a moment, reaches up for her hair with her right hand, but lets it drop back down again. James must have reminded her about the twirling. Then her face cracks into an unexpected grin, "I should think he has told me that I look great when I haven't really, but not about anything important."

"I see," says the prosecuting barrister. "Ms Carter, are you aware what this is?" All eyes turn towards his right hand which contains a small, dark green hard-backed notebook.

"It looks like Steven's song book."

"Crap," I hear from my right. James is on his feet immediately. "Madam, it seems that my prosecution colleague is introducing new evidence in the middle of a cross-examination."

"Is this true?" Kivelä peers sternly to our right.

"Madam," says Talus, "This is the defendant's song book which was mentioned during Ms Riikonen's testimony. We did not manage to locate and evaluate this evidence until after we had rested."

"Bullshit..." I hear James mutter under his breath.

"There are things contained within this book that are particularly pertinent to the line of questioning that I would like to put to this witness. It therefore seemed sensible to introduce it now."

"'s more like it." More commentary from my right.

"I realise that it is irregular, but, Madam, the importance of what is written in this book will be very apparent."

"What is apparent to me," says James, "is that the prosecution are trying to ambush my witness. This evidence should have been presented as soon as the prosecution were aware of it... They could have asked for an adjournment. Instead they seem to be twisting the process for their own benefit. I move that it be excluded."

Kivelä picks up her fountain pen and jots a couple of notes, "Mr Talus, I am not happy with this game that you appear to be playing. If I am not content with how you continue I may yet follow the defence's request and exclude this evidence. However, Mr Hainsworth, the prosecution is correct when they state that the significance of this evidence was only discovered towards the end of their case and because of that I am willing to grant a little latitude. I will allow the Prosecutor to continue."

James starts to object, but Judge Kivelä raises her hand to him, "Of course, I will also allow the defence to examine this evidence, either with this witness or by recalling a previous witness." Her face twists into a wry smile, "An ambush is only successful if the weapon is sharp. If the weapon is blunt you need not worry, but if it is sharp, justice requires it."

As James sits he leans towards me, "Well, he clearly thinks there's something significant in there," he says, flicking his head towards the Prosecutor. I have no other response than a shrug.

"Thank you Madam," says Talus, and turning back towards Abi, "Ms Carter, are you aware of what your husband writes in this book?"

Abi glances questioningly towards James, but he's not allowed to help. She's on her own. "He writes ideas for songs, lyrics, notes, that sort of thing."

"Will your husband usually tell you about a song which he is writing?"

"Usually, but he doesn't like me to read them before they're finished, before I get a performance."

"And were you aware of any lyrics that he was writing whilst he was in Finland, earlier this year?"

"Yes, a couple: there was one..." Abi blushes slightly, "There was one about missing me. *Without You* I think he called it and another about..." She trails off.

"About what?" presses Talus.

"Well, it was about domestic violence, but he wasn't writing that from experience, it was because of the woman they met."

"Ah, yes," he turns a few pages of my note book, "the song, *Enemy Within*, is about the woman that Ms Ryti mentioned in her testimony?"

"Yes."

"Very interesting. So Mr Carter generally writes about things that he feels or people that he meets?"

Abi seems unsettled. We all thought Talus was going to make more of the domestic violence and now he seems to have let her off the hook. She answers in a rush, "Yes, those are usually the sort of things."

"I see... Ms Carter, are you aware of any other songs or lyrics that Mr Carter wrote in the time between his arrival in Finland and the death of Ms Saarinen?"

Abi glances towards me curiously, "Not really, he said there were various bits that were unfinished."

"Did he? What does your husband do when a song is finished?"

Abi glances towards me again, "He usually writes it all out neatly again on a new page."

"Does he?" Talus strides forward and hands Abi the book open at a particular page. "Then this one looks like it has been finished. Could you read it to the court?"

Abi's eyes flick from Talus, to James, to me, to Kivelä like a trapped animal.

"Do as asked, if you are able," says Kivelä gently.

"*Suddenly I see you in clarity*," starts Abi. Her voice catches in several places, but she pushes on to the end. "It's quite short, maybe it isn't finished?" she says quietly.

Talus reaches for the book, "You say that your husband writes about things that he feels or people that he meets. What do you think this song is about?"

Abi's eyes slip to the floor, "I don't know."

"Are you aware that one of the nightclubs in Mahikkala is called Clarity?"

Abi stays silent, but I don't think Talus was expecting an answer. He carries on anyway, "I think this is about Mr Carter seeing someone he desires in the nightclub. Someone he thinks could be special: *'the one'*. He feels like he is sinking under the weight of his desire."

James is on his feet again, "Madam, this is pure supposition. We're talking about song lyrics here. This is not a statement."

"I have to say I agree with the defence. Mr Talus, this is not evidence."

Unfortunately, Talus doesn't seem surprised, "I would agree too, Madam, but there is more, much more, and together I am sure that they shed considerable light on the defendant's feelings and frame of mind at the time of the offence."

"Alright, Mr Talus, but it had better improve, and quickly. I'm running out of patience."

The prosecuting barrister moves forward once more. He holds the notebook in front of Abi, but does not hand it over this time. His fingers push a folded sheet, stapled at the corner, to one side, so that she can see the writing beneath. "This song is again copied out neatly. Don't you agree Ms Carter?" He turns a few pages, "And this one?"

She leans forward and a frown starts to form. Abruptly, she straightens up, but as she does so she catches my eyes. I see suspicion. Come on Abi, they're just songs!

"Yes, they look like it," she says carefully.

"I will read this one, I think." Talus paces back to his desk and reads, "*I must be fast asleep and dreaming...*" I wonder how it translates? Inevitably, he accents the *'knock on the head'* and *'inebriated by your love'* lines. Without a pause he continues, "And this song has the title Harmony..."

Abi is staring at me as she listens. Her eyebrows are slightly raised, her pupils full of questions. How do you convey, 'I know what it sounds like; I did go a bit far, but I never stopped loving you; I'm sorry, I just got confused, but I didn't kill anyone.' by your eyes alone? I don't think I'm doing it well.

Talus comes to a halt at his table, "Difficult listening, isn't it Ms Carter?"

"They could be about anyone, they could be about me," but Abi's voice lacks conviction.

"Before my Advocate colleague complains again," he throws a cold smile towards our table, "I will accept that these are song lyrics and their meaning is not completely clear... but cast your minds back to the testimony of Ms Riikonen. Did she not say that Mr Carter had admitted to dreaming about Ms Saarinen? Did she not say that they liked to sing together, that there was some sort of connection?"

Abi looks slightly dazed. Again her eyes fix on James for help, but Talus marches on. "Ms Carter, as I read this next one..."

An exasperated sigh escapes to my right, "How many more...?"

"... I want you to think about what conversations you were having with your husband. What he was telling you at the time he was writing this song? And I want you to consider if he was being truthful with you."

Why did I have to write a song called *Out of my mind*? What was I thinking? I wasn't thinking it would be read out in a court of law, that's for sure. I hear a sharp intake of breath from the witness stand as Talus reaches *'flaming red hair'*. Bollocks. Tears start to pour down Abi's cheeks at the word *'obsession'*. Why did I have to use that word? It's only a song. Why can't anyone see? And it'll be *Deep* next... I steel myself for Talus's scathing comments about smuttiness and who, exactly, I was thinking might *'like it deep'*, but he steps back and shuts the book. Maybe the innuendo doesn't translate? Maybe he doesn't think he needs it...

"Pass Ms Carter a tissue," says Talus to the clerk who reaches down with an open box. "I'm sorry, but I still have a few more questions."

Abi dabs her eyes and cheeks and wipes her nose. She's not looking my way on purpose. "It's alright, I'm ready."

"Ms Carter, what was Ms Saarinen's most noticeable physical feature?"

"Her red hair." James turns his head and glares accusingly at me: this mess is my fault.

"So who do you think that this song is most likely to be about?"

"Ms Saarinen." Abi looks like she's been side-swiped.

"At the time your husband wrote this song, in the weeks before Ms Saarinen's murder, did you converse with him often."

"We phoned each other several times a week."

"And during those phone calls, did he at any time mention singing or dancing with Ms Saarinen?"

"No..." she pauses and we make eye contact, hers are narrowed. "Well, he might have mentioned her once or twice, but never as anyone important."

"Not as someone who he was writing love songs about or someone who he could not get off his obsessed mind?"

"No," says Abi in the hushed tones of defeat.

"So, it appears that the defendant misled you about his feelings for Ms Saarinen. And you are his wife: the person who knows him best. Does it sound to you like he only had a 'crush' on Ms Saarinen? He has said this under oath."

Abi doesn't answer, but her eyes fix on James.

"Ms Carter, I must remind you that you are under oath."

"I don't know," says Abi, finally.

"So if you don't know, that might make him a very clever liar, Ms Carter?"

"I don't know."

"I see. You're unsure." I glance to my right, Talus looks like a falcon, just about to... "A few minutes ago, you stated your absolute faith that your husband had not killed Arwen Saarinen. I will ask you again: could your husband have killed Arwen Saarinen?"

Say something Abi! Why is she not saying anything? Her eyes roam the room, flicking towards the Judge and then fixing on me. The view beyond the windows has more warmth than her stare.

"I d..." abruptly she stops and the ice turns to... pity is it? "No... no, I can't believe he had anything to do with that."

"You don't sound very sure Ms Carter?"

"I am, I am," she says quickly.

"Alright. Madam, I have no more questions for this witness."

"BUT THEY'RE JUST SONG LYRICS!" I protest.

"Why can't you see this?" shouts James. "What the hell is the matter with you?" His raised voice bounces around the bare walls of the interview room where we've adjourned until lunch, at least. Longer if James thinks we need it. "Your own wife won't be in the same room as you, because she thinks she's just perjured herself and you can't see what all the fuss is about?"

"I can see what the fuss is about, I just don't understand it. It's fictional writing. How can a court of law take any notice of it?"

"Steven, don't you understand? Your whole defence has never been about facts. We don't have any facts. Only the prosecution have any facts. All we have is feelings. I've been trying to build up a feeling of doubt against the evidence and a feeling of trust towards yourself. It's all we have. Talus has played us at our own game. He's given that trust a big knock. Even Abigail felt it."

"She'll come round when she's thought it through. He just surprised her in there."

"You think so?" James sounds incredulous.

"So you're saying it's hopeless: I'm up the creek without a paddle? It was your idea to have her as a witness."

"Oh I see, and who said there was nothing important in your song book? Talus would have called her as a witness or something if we hadn't. My error was in believing you. I knew I should have read that song book myself before continuing."

Lars raises his hands, "This take us nowhere, the question is what we do now. There is never no hope."

"Put me back on the stand," I say, "Let me explain what it's like to write songs, how you exaggerate things." I reach to pick up the book which has been burning a hole in the table between us. "Look, there are other lyrics that he didn't mention which I could read, I'm sure they'll shed a different light on things."

"But if we put you on the stand again, the prosecution will be able to cross-examine you again."

"What harm can it do, now?" I sigh.

"Go on then, show me..." James leans forward, a spark of interest returning to his manner.

CHAPTER 42

It's after two by the time we have reconvened. The prosecution team seem relaxed, confident. They probably had a long enjoyable lunch. A movement in my stomach reminds me of the lack of mine. Still, that's the least of my worries. I've scanned the crowd twice and I still can't spot Abi. She can't have given up on me?

"We're just awaiting my colleague," says James to Judge Kivelä, "He should only be a few moments." As he finishes speaking the rear doors open and Lars enters with Abi at his side. She slips into one of the back rows, too far to see her expression, as Lars continues down to the front. He whispers briefly to James, who stands. At least she's here.

"Mr Carter, this morning we heard extracts from this song book. It seems that the prosecution would have us believe that your song lyrics are like diary entries, revealing your exact thoughts and feelings. But that is not so, is it? Please can you explain a little about the song writing process, so that the court may understand more fully.

"May I have the book, please?" Lars comes forward with it. It's such a little thing in my right hand. Why didn't I just chuck it in the lake? It's mostly in my head anyway. I take a deep breath. "Generally, something happens to give me an idea. It might be something from real life, or on TV or anything. For instance, we met this woman who was clearly being abused by her husband. It was awful, so unfair, it was like she'd got an enemy but he was within her house. So I got the song title *Enemy Within*. I didn't know her full story, so I made one up. Mr Talus never read you the lyrics for this one." I read them slowly one line at a time being translated. The little prima donna inside whispers, 'It won't rhyme in Finnish, the effect will be spoilt.' 'What the hell does the art matter?' replies my conscious brain. "It's a mix, a little of real life and a lot of fiction."

"Just like the other songs which were read out this morning," says James.

"Yes. Just like them. I danced in a nightclub, so I made up a story about being carried away by the dance. I had a vivid dream so I made up a racier one. It's still a dream, even in the song. I get a couple back together with karaoke, so I make up a song in which the music itself is the metaphor for falling in love. It's as much about falling in love with Abi, my wife, as anything."

"And what about *Out of my mind?*"

"Well, I had a bit of a crush. I've already admitted it. I got a bit confused. It was silly. It gave me an idea, but when you're writing a song, you take an emotion you're feeling and exaggerate it. You don't hear many songs say, 'I think about you occasionally'; 'I like you a bit' or 'you're not bad'. You write, 'I can't get you out of my mind'; 'I'm obsessed'; 'You're gorgeous'. It's art, not fact. It has to sound good."

"In fact, Mr Talus did not even finish reading the whole song, did he?" For the first time, I notice the prosecution paying more attention.

"No. Like I said, these songs are not finished. They're the first draft, that's all. I hadn't worked out all the tunes and that often changes the words round a bit. And quite often new bits get added in."

James indicates to the clerk and a scan of the *Out of my mind* page is projected. "You see at the bottom here: an asterisk?" James's laser pointer dances near the bottom of the screen, "This refers to some words written two pages further on." The second page flicks up: below a hand written stave sprinkled with crotchets and entitled 'possible bass line', four lines of text are marked with a matching asterisk. James reads them:

Maybe I need a reboot up the backside?
Maybe a stirring pep talk at the track side?
All I know is: you are in my mind
I can't let this life of mine unwind

"Can you explain the meaning of these lyrics in the context of the song, Mr Carter?"

"Yes, they are meant to show that the imaginary protagonist of the song does realise he needs to snap out of the way that he's feeling. His emotions aren't out of control, there's just a conflict."

James nods slowly, "In a similar way to when a married couple argue they are still in control of their emotions. Only if violence results have they lost control?"

"That's right," I agree, "My emotions were confused, and I did argue with myself, but I never lost control and I certainly never resorted to violence of any kind."

I can hear the blood pounding in my ears in the silence as James lets that settle. "Mr Carter, I believe you have something else you would like to read?"

I swallow down the lump in my throat, "These are the lyrics of a song I wrote the night Kari hit me in Hanne's Bar, the night I found out that Arwen had been killed. It seemed so tragic that someone so young, someone with so much promise should be snatched away. That's the inspiration, but it's a song for anyone who's lost a friend or a loved one before their time. It's called *Requiem for you.*

As I start to read, there is some muttering from where Arwen's parents are sitting, but before I reach the first chorus there is total silence. I expect most people don't need the translation. I manage to hold back, until my eyes stray towards her mother: those same eyes glistening below greying hair. My voice catches and regret rolls in synchronisation down either cheek. "Please can someone tell me how I could write this, if I had killed her?" I choke as I finish.

James smiles towards me with sympathy exaggerated for the court's benefit. "Madam, I have finished with this witness."

A slapping sound startles me, and all heads turn, searching for the source. A second one and it becomes apparent that Talus is clapping slowly and deliberately as he walks to the stand. "I must complement the defendant on his acting skills. That was truly touching... But allow me to answer your question. I will tell you two reasons why you might have written these words. Firstly, as is common, perhaps you felt a sense of regret for the crime you had committed: for the young life you had taken. Secondly, perhaps you realised that you had made mistakes and in writing such words were attempting to throw suspicion away from yourself."

"Do I really seem like that to you?" I sigh.

"It is not a matter of who you pretend to be. It is a matter of what the evidence shows that you must be. We have put forward the evidence of your own hand, which reveals the turmoil you felt inside, and reveals it to an extent that even your wife is clearly shaken by the revelations. Yes, you and your team come up with some clever replies, but this is all they are: clever words."

James stands, "Is Mr Talus already giving his closing statement?"

Talus holds his palms wide in front of his chest, "I am just warming up for it, madam. One more thing, if I may?" He nods towards the clerk. The press photo of Arwen appears on the screen. "Let us not forget the weight of forensic evidence which links Mr Carter to the crime against this poor girl. Madam, I need no more time with this witness."

Talus returns his pen to his inside jacket pocket. My attention moves from him to the picture, to James, back to the picture. I'm not having this. "You're not giving me a chance to reply."

Talus comes to a halt with his folder hovering a few inches above the desk, "Sorry?"

"You've called me a liar and a murderer and you haven't given me a chance to respond. I've still got something to say." In the corner of my eye I see James shake his head ever so slightly. I'm not going to take any notice of that. I point towards the screen. "This photo, it makes Ms Saarinen, Arwen as I knew her, look like a little girl. I don't know how old it is. She wasn't like that."

Talus tries to interrupt, but Judge Kivelä intervenes, "Mr Talus, it is you who projected this photo during your cross-questioning, if I can call it that. You can hardly complain if the defendant wishes to comment on it."

Flouting all advice, my eyes pass between the four judges. "Mr Talus would like you to think that Arwen was an impressionable little girl, easily manipulated by an older man. She wasn't like that at all. She was a vibrant young woman who knew her own mind and had decided to follow her dream. I liked her cheeky humour and was in awe of her singing voice. I would never have hurt her. One day, I wanted to see her in 'Evita', to lean towards the person in the next seat and whisper, 'I used to know her before she was famous.' Now I can't. It's tragic... But on top of that," I point towards Talus, "he says I killed her. Imagine what that's like," I say, still addressing the judges, "Imagine what it's like to find that a friend has been killed; to be questioned by the police; to think that you're helping catch the killer only to find that they arrest you. Imagine what it's like when they tell you that there is evidence, impossible evidence, linking you to the crime. Imagine knowing that somebody somewhere is trying to pin this crime on you. Someone so clever that even the police don't believe he exists. Imagine sitting in this court room, hearing the Prosecutor repeat over and over that you are some kind of monster." I pause and breathe out a long sigh. "I don't know how to convince you, but I did not kill Arwen Saarinen. Please, believe me."

Judge Kivelä stares from Talus to James, both of them give a small shake of the head. "Mr Carter you may return to your seat. I believe that concludes the evidence in this case. Mr Talus, when you are ready, you may begin the summary of the prosecution's case.

CHAPTER 43

Talus rises, one loose sheet of paper in his right hand. He moves to the right of the court and grips the edges of the Advocate's desk. "Let us first remember the victim in this case. Arwen Saarinen, a talented young woman, her life brutally cut short last February in the woods close to Lake Mahi." A photo appears on the screen. It's of Arwen as I knew her, but wearing a smart navy suit and cream blouse. For an interview, maybe?

"There you see, they had another one all along," I breathe to James.

"Of course they did. One point to you for making them show it."

"We are here," says Talus to the judges, "to provide justice for Ms Saarinen and her family and to make sure that a dangerous and devious criminal is removed from public society. In such a case as this, we must show that the defendant, Mr Steven Carter, had the means, the opportunity, and the motive to commit this crime before we can convict. We have demonstrated these three facets quite clearly and it is beyond any reasonable doubt that Mr Carter committed this crime." He pauses, well aware that James cannot now interrupt. "Let me summarise the evidence for you. Firstly, let us take 'opportunity': this is simple, for Mr Carter has been unable to deny that he was present in the woods on the shores of Lake Mahi at the time of the crime. His proximity to Ms Saarinen just prior to entering the forest has also been verified by several witnesses. Is it credible that they did not meet as he suggests or that he just went for a walk 'to think things through' at two in the morning? There is no doubt that Mr Carter had the opportunity to commit this crime.

"As for the 'means', we have heard that Ms Saarinen was attacked and strangled using rope tied in a special slip knot. This rope is easily available from several shops close to where Mr Carter was staying or, indeed, from his place of work. We have also heard how the evidence suggests that Ms Saarinen must have known her attacker. Surely she would have used her mobile phone if a stranger had approached her in such an isolated area? Mr Carter was well known to Ms Saarinen." The barrister turns away from the judges and briefly refers to his notes. When Talus looks up his face is a picture of disgust and revulsion. It crosses my mind that when mocking my so called acting skills earlier, the playground taunt 'takes one to know one' would have been an appropriate response.

"Not only does the attacker kill Ms Saarinen but he also defiles her body. Perhaps this is the true intent all along, but it is where Mr Carter makes his major mistake. Although he carefully wears a condom for the despicable act, somehow it leaks and an amount of semen remains with her body. Remember, there is no doubt that the semen found is that of Mr Carter... Now the defence will tell you some fantastical tale involving a mystery man who plants evidence to pin the crime on the defendant. I ask you: where is the evidence of this mystery man? The police have not found any, the defence themselves have not found any. There is no evidence, because there is no mystery man, there is only Mr Carter. We are not in one of his country's Sherlock Holmes stories. The evidence shows what it shows. There is no conspiracy.

"Because of the weakness of their case, the defence have also raised the possibility of Mr Carter having had consensual intercourse with Ms Saarinen in the days before her death. However, they knew full well that under initial questioning, Mr Carter denied ever having sex with Ms Saarinen. To change his story in court would appear bad so they came up with another complicated, twisted argument that went something like: why would he deny something that could get him off the hook? Again this smacks of desperation. The defence have no evidence, they just play with words." I shrink further into my seat. He's right, what do we have, really?

"In contrast, to back up the semen evidence, we were able to present to you a sample of fibres found next to the victim's body which match the brand of underclothing worn by the defendant: underclothing which is very unusual in Finland. Again a hard fact!

"Finally we come to 'motive'. The defence will say, 'he has no motive, this girl was his friend, why would he kill her?', but we know the truth. We have heard it in the words of his own songs. Steven Carter had an obsession and he couldn't keep his mind off Ms Saarinen's red hair. You have heard from witnesses how he fawned over her and you have heard how Ms Saarinen may have encouraged this somewhat; how sometimes she was close to him and sometimes more distant; how this was the perfect way to grow an obsession. And then that final night at the party when Mr Carter himself admits he had too much to drink and got a bit carried away: so carried away that he pesters Ms Saarinen for a dance until she has to push him away. A normal man, perhaps, at the start, an emotional man we are told, but a man who loses control as those emotions grow, who lets them rule his actions.

"We may never know if Mr Carter somehow lured Ms Saarinen to the lakeside or if it was just the chance he was waiting for, but he was clearly prepared for such an eventuality. Initially she followed him down *Pankkikatu*, but then the pursued became the hunter, closing in on his prey a few yards into the wood. Did they argue? Did she refuse him? Only Mr Carter can tell us. Whatever the circumstances, he took the rope, strangled her, carried the body to a more private location and then abused it. Make no mistake, the evidence for this is quite clear." Talus turns slightly and gestures dismissively in our direction.

"He has no defence. If you strip away all the emotion, all the smoke and all the mirrors that my extremely competent colleague has created, you will see his case for what it is. They have pulled on our heart strings; Mr Carter has played the victim; it has all been very clever, but there has been nothing of substance which refutes any of the evidence the prosecution has presented.

"The psychologist hired by the defence was most illuminating when he qualified his analysis by saying 'unless Steven Carter is a very accomplished liar'. We have heard how accomplished Mr Carter was at hiding his feelings from his wife and you've all heard how persuasive a speech he can make. This is a devious, dangerous man who even tries to manipulate a courtroom for his own ends. We cannot allow such a man to remain in society."

"You owe it to Arwen Saarinen to deny her killer his normal life, just as he denied Arwen her future, and you must protect the public from the schemes of this violent man. In order to do this, you must find the defendant guilty on all charges."

As he says his last words, he fixes each judge in turn with a penetrating glare. He spins on his left foot and glides back to his table, the grim satisfaction of a task well executed chiselled across his face. My belief, my dignity, my self-worth are splashing wildly, flailing to stay above the surface, Talus's every sentence another lead weight in my pocket: dragging down ever harder. Wouldn't it be easier just to let myself drown?

"Hey, Steven," nudges James, "don't look so down, we haven't done our bit yet. And we get to go last! The judges will only be thinking about my words by the time they retire."

"What's the point?"

"Hey, remember what your friend Charles says, 'It's never over until the verdict and even then that's just a first opinion.'"

I manage a weak smile as he stands. Unlike his opposite number, James carries no notes to the Advocate's stand. The man must have one hell of a memory. I expect he's practised this once or twice too.

"The prosecution have talked about facts; they have talked about 'hard' evidence, but let us remember that no one piece of evidence can stand on its own. The man covered in blood is not always the killer. He may have held his dying wife lovingly in his arms after her attacker has left." James spreads his arms wide, "However strong a piece of evidence may appear, it must be seen within the context of the whole case.

"Now with this case we have a problem: despite what my learned colleague has told you, the prosecution's case hangs on just one piece of evidence. Without it, I am sure this case would never have come to court. I refer, of course, to the semen evidence, but before we deal with that, let us review the rest of the supposed evidence against my client.

"The defendant has given a perfectly acceptable reason for his presence near the scene of the attack. This has been supported by witnesses. Let us remember that there is no doubt that Mr Carter walked along *Pankkikatu* first and was later followed by Ms Saarinen, who according to her boyfriend seemed to make an impulsive decision to follow him. Remember, she was following him...

"Then there are the sightings from the drivers. The prosecution would have Mr Carter running in circles to try to fit the seemingly contradictory statements, but it is quite simple, there is no contradiction at all, because the taxi driver saw a different man. Yes, a man wearing similar clothes, but half of Mahikkala was familiar with the cold weather outfits worn by the four British engineers. Who was this other man? Why was he following Ms Saarinen? Why was he impersonating Mr Carter?

"The police claim that the scene of crime evidence points towards Ms Saarinen having known her attacker. However, this line of argument is equally valid if her attacker was impersonating someone that she knew. So we can learn nothing from that." James makes a dismissive gesture with his left hand and forges onward. "The crime was committed using a rope and the prosecution have made much about my client's employment in the rope factory. Come on! He designs complex wire cable machines; he has nothing to do with simple fabric cords that are available in almost any hardware store. Again, this is not evidence."

He starts to pace behind the desk: a couple of deliberate steps towards the raised area whilst talking, a slow turn and then retreat whilst waiting for the translator. The judge's eyes are following.

"And now we come to the prosecution's big piece of evidence: their only piece of evidence. But let's examine this carefully, what do we have? One sample of the defendant's DNA, chemicals from a condom and a small piece of fluff. All found pretty much next to each other. So during the whole time the defendant is supposed to have strangled, carried, stripped and interfered with the deceased, he only leaves three pieces of evidence: all in the same place at the same time. The prosecution would have you believe that my client is some kind of criminal mastermind and yet they also want you to believe that he made basic errors. It does not stack up. Remember how it is strange to have indications of condom usage, but semen present; remember how the fibres come from a type of boxer shorts common in the UK and worn by other people present in Mahikkala; remember how my client would not have worn such clothing except in bed; and remember that DNA from other persons was found on Ms Saarinen's clothes but this has been discounted because they were her friends. It makes you wonder, does it not?

"Now consider that not one piece of forensic evidence has been found amongst the defendant's clothes or possessions which links him to the crime. The prosecution would have you believe that Mr

Carter carried a length of rope around, waiting for a chance to use it. This rope leaves enough fibres on the victim for it to be identified, and yet mysteriously leaves no traces in the defendant's pockets. None of Ms Saarinen's DNA, no fibres from her clothes, no condoms, nothing." James smiles ironically, "It is as if he was not there, that he did not do it! The evidence is contradictory: again, it makes no sense... unless, unless you consider the other man. A man clever enough to decide to pin a despicable crime on someone else; to disguise himself as that person; to carefully commit the crime making sure to leave no evidence except that which he wanted to be found: evidence which he had somehow obtained previously from the defendant. An unusual situation, perhaps... but it fits the facts, it removes the inconsistencies and it explains why no one who is close to the defendant can understand how he could possibly have committed this crime... because he did not."

James glances back towards the prosecution's table. "My Prosecutor colleague has called it 'a twisted argument' but I strongly disagree. I've just described to you how the whole prosecution case hangs around one piece of DNA evidence, one piece of evidence which does not seem to fit. Mr Carter could have nullified this evidence by admitting to consensual sex with Ms Saarinen. He could have easily used the excuse of not wanting to upset his wife for any inconsistencies with earlier statements. But he did not; he chose to tell the truth in court. Do these seem the actions of a guilty man?"

Halting his traverse, eyes roaming the judges, James shrugs exaggeratedly, "And why? Why would Mr Carter, who admired and respected Ms Saarinen, wish her dead? There is no reason, so the prosecution have resorted to fiction, using Mr Carter's creative jottings as some kind of proof of an obsession. This is like trying to prove that Shakespeare was a homicidal maniac because he wrote Macbeth! Are we to believe this nonsense above the testimony of his work colleagues, over a business woman who has no reason to support him, over the analysis of a respected psychologist?

Yes, Mr Carter had a little crush and perhaps went a bit further than a married man ought to, but this is no basis for assuming that he had developed an all consuming physical obsession. As you heard from Mr McLeod, the defendant passed up the chance of physical gratification on previous occasions. Does this sound like someone who is losing control?

"Mr Carter is not the perpetrator of this crime, he is the second victim of a devious man who assumes the identity of another to commit his terrible crimes. Mr Carter appears to be quite normal, not because of some extreme acting ability on his part, but simply because he is not unbalanced. He is an ordinary man caught up in an awful situation. The evidence against him is contradictory and inconsistent and the stated motive is pure fantasy. Of course there must be justice for Ms Saarinen and the perpetrator of this terrible crime should be removed from society, but if you convict Mr Carter you will not be serving justice. You will be sending an innocent man to prison. Can you risk that if you are not completely sure?" James raises a pointing finger to harden his final words, "And you will be sending a message to the real killer that he has got away with it, that his method works, and he is free to kill again. Can you risk not restarting the police investigation?

"Yes, we need justice for Ms Saarinen, but we cannot find it in this court on this day. You must return a verdict of not guilty and allow the police to continue their search. Only then can true justice be served."

"How was that then?" says a satisfied James as he retakes the seat next to mine.

"Good," is the only thing that comes out of my lips. How can anyone convict me after that? I sit in a daze of imagined biscuits, wine, and late night loving touches as Judge Kivelä calls the recess. I wonder if they'll have decided before the end of the day?

CHAPTER 44

Any briefly held confidence has evaporated by the time - two and a half days later - the lay judges re-enter the court room. I focus on their faces as they take their seats. Three serious faces, all seemingly intent on their shoes. That can't be good.

"Well, now we'll see," says James. I glance behind, it can't do any harm now. Lars says that Abi is at the back somewhere, but I can't see her. Why won't she come back to her original place? I've been going out of my mind wondering what she's been thinking these last couple of days, but she won't see me. I know Lars is in contact with her. All I've got out of him is that she's OK, but she wants to wait for the verdict. What does that mean? He avoids more specific questions. He's a lawyer; he's bloody good at it.

Judge Kivelä sweeps into the room with an expression that years of practise render completely inscrutable. She calls the court to order, places her hands flat on the desk in front of her and stares straight towards me. Rather than stopping after whole sentences, her words are translated a few at a time.

"In the case... of the state... versus Steven Carter... we have considered... all the evidence... and are all in agreement... On the charge... of the murder... of Ms Arwen Saarinen... we find the defendant... *syyllinen.*"

The ice cold water rushes over my head. My limbs are locked rigid, their fight past. I sink, blood throbbing in my ears... it fades... to leave... numbness. Pastel, diluted people are shouting. A man slumped behind a table is dragged to his feet by two uniforms. A voice of frost liquefies the atmosphere. What does it mean? What is it saying? Who is Carter? The uniforms float the man to the door, along rivers and down waterfalls to a square tank: enclosed, stagnant, lifeless. The man gradually dissolves until there is no man and no tank, only a solution rippling now and then with the passage of time.

SOMEONE OPENS THE TANK and the man precipitates uncomfortably into the corridor. He's guided to another ta.. room where...

"Steven!"

"Has he said anything since the court room?"

"Abigail, you try."

"Steven." This voice feels warm and familiar, like an old settee in front of an open fire. "They say you might be in some kind of shock."

'Ah, so that's what the man has,' I think.

"Steven." That warmth again. A current catches me and starts to pull down towards the man's head. Blood throbs in my ears.

"Abi," he... I say. I try to reach forward, almost overbalancing as my movement is pulled up short by the steel circling my wrists.

"Steady there," says James.

I plant my feet wider apart and my gaze passes along the three coming to rest on Abi. "They're wrong. I didn't do it." Her eyes flick down to her lap where fingers are writhing over each other.

"Ah," says James, "We weren't sure if you even realised what had happened."

"I remember her saying *'syyllinen'*. Nothing was real after that."

"They find you guilty of all charges," says Lars quietly.

"All charges?"

"Premeditated murder and desecration of a body," says James.

I shake my head slowly. "Why did they bother with the second one?"

"Err," says James, suddenly tongue tied. "The reason we came... I've done all I can... I can point out it's your first offence; I can try to argue that you couldn't have been in your right mind, but it's Judge Kivelä and she's determined it will be a life sentence."

"You need prepare yourself for tomorrow," says Lars.

"So soon?"

"It's five days since the trial, Steven," says James.

"Five days?"

"This isn't the first time we've... well, Lars and I, have visited," he shrugs.

"Lars and you?" My eyes linger on Abi's smooth features. Her eyes flick up, catch mine, and flick straight down again. I don't need to say anything more.

James pushes his chair back and starts to stand, "I'm sorry about the way things have turned out. We'll see where we go next after tomorrow." I nod, but I don't move my eyes from Abi's face. She rises, carefully looking anywhere but at me.

"Abi..." The pain in my voice stops her movement. Inhaling deeply, her eyes meet mine. "Please..." I whisper. Shoulders slumped, she walks round the table and as her face approaches mine I gaze deep into her pupils and see... guilt. Guilt? She pecks me on the cheek: an anyone kiss, and straightens up, glancing toward the door where James and Lars are waiting. I want to shout, 'It's me, Abi. Not anyone, me! You just kissed anyone,' but what's the point? What is the point, full stop.

CHAPTER 45

James has made his arguments, weak as they are. Talus has urged for the longest sentence possible. It's all down to the lady with the half moon glasses. I don't think Talus will be disappointed.

Judge Kivelä, coughs once. The small amount of low chatter from the spectators instantly dies away. "The prisoner will stand." The translator's tones are slow and solemn.

"Steven Leslie Carter, you have been found guilty, firstly on the charge of murdering Ms Arwen Saarinen, and secondly on the charge of desecrating her body. The first offence carries a mandatory life sentence, for the second, we have determined a sentence of seven years." Kivelä removes the reading glasses which have been perching on the tip of her nose. "I have reviewed your barrister's arguments and the psychological report and I can find no reasons for leniency. This case, due to the youth of the victim and the aggravated circumstances surrounding her death, has been one of the most distressing that I have presided over. You have shown no remorse for your crime, instead, you have tried to manipulate the emotions of this court in a vain attempt to avoid punishment.

"It is my personal opinion that you should be removed from society on a permanent basis. However, as in Finland we do not *'let the lynch mob have its day'*, you will..." A sudden anger rises: how dare she quote from that song? I interrupt the translation, raising my voice, "Why would I write that if I'd done it? Tell me why?" A few angry shouts from behind answer mine and an image of all those hunting rifles silences me even before Kivelä herself intervenes.

"Even now you cannot accept you have lost," she says shaking her head. "You will serve a life sentence... I am fully aware that in this country that may mean you are released after only twelve years. I personally intend to prevent that from happening. My campaign against these 'standard' pardons will intensify. I will be writing personally to the President on the matter. She leans forward, fixing me with cold eyes, "You will have plenty of time to reflect on the lives you have ruined." The nearest lay judge leans and whispers something in her ear. "Ah, yes, and you are ordered to pay damages to the family of the deceased. We have agreed on the sum of 250,000 Euros."

Firm hands appear on my shoulders and I turn my head to see that my two guards have stepped forward. There is an explosion of noise. Kivelä doesn't even attempt to control it, but shouts over the hubbub, "This case is complete. Court dismissed." Around Arwen's family, people are standing; there are cheers. Mr Saarinen is shaking Kari by the hand. Til is hugging Harri. But in the eye of the storm, Arwen's mother sits motionless, staring unblinkingly forward. *'It won't bring her back now will it?'* I think, as I'm firmly manoeuvred towards the side door.

SITTING HERE you wouldn't know which side of the fence you were on; wouldn't know... until you looked at me. The fence in question is the razor topped boundary between Korikylä remand centre and the prison proper and my institutional blue shirt tells you all you need to know. I still find them demeaning. I guess I'm meant to. Otherwise, the lawyer room, as the guards call it, is pretty much a copy of the one a few hundred metres away: white above, dark green below, merging between with pale green walls. I feel a certain affinity to the four plastic chairs and Formica covered table, held captive as they are by screws to the lino covered floor. I smile at my little pun and continue to wait.

The metal door opens and Lars enters, he nods towards me, then turns, obviously surprised that he is not being followed. His eyes are caught by something beyond the door and he purses his lips ever so slightly. The door blocks my view, but a second later Abi walks into the room closely followed by James: so close that I've got a feeling he might have his hand in the small of her back, pushing. They part, but she doesn't take the seat next to me, instead the opposite corner: the furthest away. It's as before, she doesn't need to say a word.

"Hello Lars, James, Abi. Do you like my new shirt? I wore it especially for you."

"It match your eyes," says Lars, copying my humourless tone.

"What's it like out in the real world?"

"Still cold," he shrugs.

James glances at his colleague with slight annoyance and says stiffly, "Mr Carter, we've come here to discuss your options for an appeal hearing."

"Mr Carter," I parrot and snort out a short breath. "Can't be too familiar with convicted felons in your position, hey, James." I stress his first name.

Ignoring my comment he continues, "I'm afraid that you haven't really got many options. You can only gain state funding for an appeal if there is significant new evidence. Which, obviously, there isn't. You could appeal anyway, if you can find someone who would fund the legal costs, but I must warn you that these could be considerable."

"Can I find someone who would fund the legal costs?" I ask, my eyes fixed on Abi. Silence. She stares at her writhing hands. "What would be the point anyway, without any new evidence?" I say, not breaking my gaze.

"There is that," says James slowly, a trace of uncertainty in his voice.

I drink in the black hair, smooth cheeks, those oh so green eyes. One corner of my mouth twitches with disappointment: "Abi, why are you here?"

She raises tearful eyes, "I've come to say goodbye, Steven."

"Ah, I see..." I breathe out slowly. "So you're not going to stay and try to find some evidence of the other man then?"

"No."

"Why?" I can see she knows that it's so much more than one question.

"I stopped believing you, Steven." Her voice is barely more than a whisper and moist trails line her cheeks.

"And without belief there is no faith, and without faith there can be no love," I intone. Did I get that from some long forgotten school assembly?

"I don't know who you are any more. Maybe I never did..." her voice cracks.

I shake my head and sigh, "I'm still me, it's you who've changed."

"No," she says, almost shouting, her eyes screwed up, tears pouring freely.

"Please, Mr Carter, none of your mind games, thank you."

I turn my head sharply towards James, "It's like that is it?" He holds my glare with steady, firm eyes. "Ah well, if my wife doesn't believe me, then I must have done it, mustn't I?"

"Is that a confession?"

"Do you want it to be? Will that make it easier for you?" James ignores my question, but I see something register in Abi's expression. I take a few deep breaths and swap to the other thing which has been preying on my mind. "What happens about the damages? They're not going to make..." What do I call her now? Her, that's it. I wave one hand in the direction of my wife. "...her sell the house are they?"

"They calculate your total money and your wife's circumstance and take as much as will not leave her in hardship," says Lars.

James takes over. "But as all of your assets are jointly held in the UK it will be extremely difficult for the Finnish courts to collect. In which case, the state will have to compensate the Saarinens."

"It wouldn't even cover half of it anyway." I try to catch Abi's eyes, but they're still fixed on her lap. "You do what you like with everything... What's mine is yours..." I grimace, "I'm sure Kivelä has got plans for me to pay it all off with eternal washing up anyhow."

She doesn't reply, but her next few breaths become steadily more sniffy. Unsurprisingly, James intervenes. "I still have to have your formal answer about the appeal."

"I can't see that I have much choice. I won't be appealing. Not at the moment anyway. Maybe something will turn up, you never know."

"Maybe," says Lars.

"In that case, there is nothing to sign and we are done here." He starts to stand. Abi virtually jumps up, leaving Lars sitting beside me. He extends his right hand, "Farewell, Steven," he says and glances towards the two making for the door. Unconsciously, his head shakes slightly.

"You too, Lars." James raps on the door and the guard starts to open it.

"Abi." She turns back towards me, apprehensively. "Have a nice life... for me." James puts a firm hand on her arm and guides her out into the corridor. Tears flow down my face. As he stands, Lars squeezes my left shoulder, then he too is gone.

I'm not meant to approach the door, but I can't help myself. I stand at the end of the table, moving my head from side to side trying to find the correct angle through the small wired pane. There they are, waiting for the first security door to be opened. Abi is standing, shoulders hunched, sobbing. James reaches out a comforting hand, cupping her right shoulder. She raises her face towards his and through the tears a weak smile surfaces.

I turn away, not wanting to see more and retake my appointed seat. 'What do you do?' I think. "*What do you do?*" I shout at the top of my voice and thump my forehead into the unyielding table.

CHAPTER 46

Well who said prison was so bad? The Finnish system is an example to the world. It's all about re-orientation and betterment: I've done my 'lifer plan'; I've started my 'self improvement' classes; *I can talk base Finnish to you now, if you lick;* I've never been fitter - twenty press-ups straight off. Am I fooling you? No, thought not. They could feed me caviar and truffles, provide a five star suite, but I'd still fade. And the worst of it is you hardly feel it happening. You're turning from colour to shades of grey and you can't even see it. You've forgotten what real vivid colour is like. I thought I was coping, beating it, beating them, but I'm not, I'm dissolving, losing... myself... my mind? Losing the capacity to feel.

It takes something like this to bring it all back. The paper in front of me is black on white, but it could not feel more vivid. It's luminous purple and orange stripes with cyan dots; it's burning plastic; it's soap in a cut; it's an application for divorce.

"It's James, isn't it?"

Lars, shifts uncomfortably in his seat, "I am not allowed to say information about my client." His eyes meet mine, "I am sorry."

I shrug, "No hard feeling, Lars, I know you're just doing your job." My hands stray to the paper and turn over the first sheet. "I know it's him anyway. I could see... the last time."

Lars says nothing, but it is a confirming silence. Eventually, with clear distaste Lars speaks again, "My client request that you sign this paper. Things will proceed without it, but it make the process easier."

"For her," I insert.

"For her," nods Lars.

It's tempting to be petty... but what's the point? I don't want to bug her, I want her to understand, I want her to feel, I want...

I reach forward for the plastic biro placed between us on the table, "I'll sign, Lars, but on one condition."

"Steven, I not..."

"It's only a small thing," I interrupt, "All I want is that she reads what I'm going to write on the back of this sheet." I lift the stapled papers by the rear page, where the words, 'I, the undersigned, do...' flame in their iridescent monochrome.

"I will pass on," says Lars. He raises his palms to the ceiling, "but I cannot make her see or listen."

"She'll read it if you tell her it's there. She won't be able to stop herself. I do know Abi... Just give me a few minutes." I flip the sheet over and start writing. These words have been in my head for months:

Not for you

There was a day when I saw you smile:
that was the day that I knew.
You can see a spark fading, feel a kiss lose its meaning;
it's anyone, but it is you.

They say that all's fair in love and war;
the pieces that fitted together before
have altered their size and their shape.
Yes, all's fair in love and war,
the old rules matter no more,
you just have to follow your heart.
But why does your heart have to change?
And why does the sun turn into rain?
And what do you do?
When the smile on her face is not for you?

There was a time when I saw you glance:
you thought that I didn't see,
but I can remember a time long ago
when that look was given to me.

They say that all's fair in love and war;
the pieces that fitted together before
have altered their size and their shape.
Yes, all's fair in love and war,
the old rules matter no more,
you just have to follow your heart.

I'm holding our love in my hands.
We used to hold it together.
I can feel that it's broken:
cracks with sharp edges.
Now a meaningless token,
it's only waiting
for me to lose my grip.

They say that all's fair in love and war;
the pieces that fitted together before
have altered their size and their shape.
Yes, all's fair in love and war,
the old rules matter no more,
you just have to follow your heart.
But why does your heart have to change?
And why does the sun turn into rain?
And what do you do?
When the smile on her face is not for you?

    Self torture by song lyric. I turn back and sign on the two dotted lines. That's it then, my life has officially ended.

CHAPTER 47

"Time's up Carter."

I halt, chin halfway to the bar and hang, biceps tensed against my weight until the ache becomes a sting.

"Nothing wrong with your arms."

"It be while before I begin sit-ups." I lower myself and carefully place my feet on the tarmac. The guard smiles ruefully. "Everyone love their new bendy spoons," he says, swapping to English. He holds the cage door open.

"I bet they do."

It's been like this since I left the infirmary: solitary exercise, separate meals, a guard hanging over me at all times. At least Jarno is civil, not all of them are. We pass through two sets of CCTV monitored plexiglass doors and take a left towards the 'special' block. The scar just above my underwear line twinges slightly with each step. Maybe I overdid the exercises. It's amazing what damage someone can do with the sharpened handle of a plastic teaspoon.

"Home sweet home," says Jarno, ushering me into the narrow cell. At least I'm on my own now: the one benefit. They've said they might move me to Turku 'for my own safety.' More likely it's too expensive to keep up my personal bodyguard service. The high security section in Turku: where all the paedophiles, child killers and other status boosting targets are hidden away. I flop on to the firm mattress and wonder whether it would be better to be at the top of the pile. After all, I'm only a homicidal necrophiliac.

It doesn't get easier: the green walls are a constant sickening reminder. Almost two years and I'm still mourning. Not for Arwen, don't be daft. All said and done, I hardly knew her. No, I'm mourning for Steven and Abigail, Steve and Abi, S & A on the bottom of Christmas cards; always written with her curly flourish. Maybe you don't think 'mourning' is the right word, but it is. The mysterious joint entity that we had become died with the slashing downward blow of the word *'syyllinen'*. Perhaps it was already dead, slowly garrotted, each revealed betrayal tightening the cord? Whatever, I feel grief. In some ways I think it's worse than if she were dead. At least then there would be an end, an undeniable bottom to lie crumpled on, a place to wonder if it's worth climbing out of. Not just this endless falling; with always a small hope that maybe, just maybe, someone might throw me a rope and start pulling upward.

It must be awful for the parents of missing children. I mean, obviously it's awful, but the not knowing: it must drive them mad. I bet sometimes they end up wishing for a body so the hoping can end. I know there's no hope. Not one letter, not even an email in all this time. But you're still out there somewhere. We were one once; you know my most intimate details; we've shared the kind of thoughts you can only tell one other person. Do you tell him? Does he know you like I know you? Do you ever think about me? You must do: the places we've been, the people we know: all reminders. How many times has your Dad called him Steven? How can you stand it? Do you compare? 'He drives more aggressively than Steven'; 'He's not as sweaty as Steven was'; 'Steven never did that.' What if one day his shine rubs off? What if…

"Stop it!" I say out loud.

I've been thinking about that rope quite a bit lately. I reach for a sheaf of printed papers on the narrow shelf above me. No pens for song writing: too sharp, but I can type them into the PCs in the library. I just have to memorise any changes. My eyes skim the familiar words of the top sheet and in my mind a synthesizer intro dances above an insistent double beat:

Enough Rope

You were my continental breakfast:
My very own all action packed lunch.
You were my Sunday afternoon tease.
Where were you when it came to the crunch?

It isn't that I blame you, I'm angry with myself.
It wasn't you who put me on this cold and lonely shelf.

Someone gave me enough rope,
(and before I knew it, I'm swinging.)
Enough rope to tie my life in knots;
Enough rope to pull our love apart;
Enough rope to snare me in a net;
Enough rope to strangle your heart.

If I had enough rope to climb out of here,
to pull myself free of these bindings,
could I re-weave all our threads
or are there just too many loose endings?

You were my stylish dinner jacket
Worn at the last supper of my life,
But when it came to the midnight feast,
My darling, you just twisted the knife.

It isn't that I blame you, I'd've done the same myself.
It wasn't you who put me on this cold and lonely shelf.

Someone gave me enough rope,
(and before I knew it, I'm swinging.)
Enough rope to tie my life in knots;
Enough rope to pull our love apart;
Enough rope to snare me in a net;
Enough rope to strangle your heart.

If I had enough rope to climb out of here,
to pull myself free of these bindings,
could I re-weave all our threads
or are there just too many loose endings?

All the emotions I've poured into this music come flooding back. I feel angry, betrayed, let-down, de-loved, but most of all just sad for what's been lost. I cast the papers across the bed so that my tears don't wet them. I know the words off by heart anyway.

Is the strangle line tasteless? I don't care. I'm guilty now. Everyone thinks I did it. Sometimes I think I must have. Am I mad? Can't I remember? I know I can't remember walking back to the hotel, but I was composing… and drunk. Sometimes I dream about Arwen: snow, pine trees and red braids flowing away from pink cheeks; never blue-grey like in the photo, always pink. Is this a blocked memory trying to surface or is my subconscious torturing me for my stupidity? I'm sure Dr Hiltunen would have something pithy to say about it.

CHAPTER 48

Something's happened... Four years, 2 months, 17 days and something has changed. The guards are different. I can't explain how. I think Han puts his finger on it best as I hold his feet for sit-ups: *"It's like they don't know how to treat you today,* Limestone."

I've had that nickname since the second stabbing incident. Nothing ever really happened after the first time. They never moved him or me. I had my little time with a shadow; he got some touchy-feely therapy. Some people never change, but he wasn't too clever: trying the same thing twice. I'd been replaying that moment in the canteen over and over, every push-up, every lift, wondering what I should have done. Half way through his lunge he got the tray in his face, two hands round his right wrist and my backside in his stomach. Blue shirts scattered right and left as I shoved back hard and heaved his off-balance weight against the unyielding wall, pinning the offensive hand away from my body. Within seconds one of the guards had knocked the shard of glass from it with a baton.

As you can tell, I'm quite proud of my little scrap. Childish, really, but there is something weirdly satisfying about the primeval solution to a problem. I suppose they don't call it survival of the fittest for nothing. And it did solve the problem: he got transferred and everyone else seemed to lose interest.

We swap over and Han pushes hard on the top of my feet as I pump my solar plexus, hands behind my head. A pair of polished black shoes appear next to my left shoulder. Jarno is holding a sheet of paper. *"Ten am tomorrow, legal visit."*

"Who?"

"*The firm requesting the visit is called 'Sneck and Rintala'.*"

"*Lars,*" I say, a little bubble of hope tickling my stomach.

"*I'll fetch you from your cell at nine-fifty*, Mr Carter." He turns and heads along the wire to pass on another message.

"*Someone's getting out soon,*" says a grinning Han.

"*I told you I was innocent.*"

"*Oh, yeah, me too,*" says Han, letting go of my feet just at the point where I need his weight the most.

"*Paskiainen,*" I swear.

"*Anteeksi*, Mr Carter," he parrots, with heavy emphasis on the 'Mr'. No one's called me that in a long time.

THE BUBBLE IN MY STOMACH has grown into a writhing knot. I glance up at the clock for the hundredth time. Ten past: don't do this to me. I watch the second hand's progress with the sort of interest that can only be mustered when you don't see an analogue clock very often: it's a nice, smooth sweep. To the side of me the handle clicks and the door swings open on its solid hinges. Lars enters, grey highlights now almost fully framing his apologetic face.

"Long time through security," he shrugs. Following him in to the room is the reason why. "Steven..." he trails off, not offering his hand for obvious reasons. I expect he almost said, 'long time no see' but thought better of it.

"Lars," I say, wiggling my right shoulder which is as near as I can get to a handshake with them cuffed behind my back. The corners of his mouth turn up in a way which makes the knot clench tighter. He regards me appraisingly, "You look... healthy."

"You look greyer."

"It is looking after all these young people." The woman standing to his left smiles politely at her boss's joke. "This is my student, Ms Linna." I nod at the dark grey suited young woman. She's blonde, modestly attired and completely ordinary looking, but I bet today's security detail made sure they took their time. Not many women visit here, particularly not young ones. "First time come to closed prison," adds Lars by way of explanation.

"And you trust her with such a notorious criminal as me?" I raise my eyebrows.

"We see about that," says Lars enigmatically.

One of Ms Linna's hands moves up to her mouth unconsciously. I'm not a nervous nail biter myself, but I can see the signs.

"*Sit down, we do this in Finnish now, you know?*"

"*Ah, I see you've been keeping your brain active*, Steven." Lars takes the seat opposite me and pulls three thick binders out of the briefcase which Ms Linna has heaved on to the table. I can't help smiling faintly. Lars follows my eyes. "*Here is an example of what I was telling you about cultural differences, Kitti. Mr Carter is thinking that it was rude of me to let you carry the heavy bag.*"

"*But I'm young and... oh.*" The implication hits her.

"*Lars is correct,*" I say, "*I was smiling in a very British, sexist way. Forgive me. Finland is so better in that way.*"

"*And so much worse in others,*" says Kitti. Lars opens the first file and turns to a yellow sticky note.

"*Come on, do not keep me holding on,*" I say. "*Has someone found some new evidence in my case or what?*"

"*Yes, but it's better than that.*"

"*Someone has confessed?*"

"*Steven, Steven, just wait a moment and I'll tell you.*" Lars pulls the sheet of paper out of its plastic wallet. "*About a month ago there was an incident in an apartment in Tampere. A young woman was attacked with a hammer.*"

"*So he has moved town...*"

"*However,*" he continues, speaking over my comment, "*it seems that the woman had a strong skull and some martial arts training. When the police arrived she was bleeding from a head wound, but the man had a broken wrist, dislocated shoulder and was unconscious due to a blow from a toaster.*"

"*A toaster?*"

"*Apparently it was the nearest heavy object to hand.*"

I can't help but grin at the mental picture of someone being sideswiped by a toaster. "*But how does this link up with my case?*" I suppose it makes sense to start from the beginning, but I just want to know what it means. Am I out of here? I stretch the cuffs apart, letting the metal dig into my wrists.

"*No one did link it. In fact, to start with, the police weren't exactly sure who they should be arresting. A number of witnesses claimed to have seen the woman's boyfriend enter the flat just before the incident. He said he was home alone. Friends said that they had been arguing recently.*" Lars pauses, he can see that he's got my interest now. "*The toaster man said he was a passerby who* saw a scuffle on the doorstep and was hit when he went to help. The police were questioning the boyfriend about a double attack when someone took a closer look at the toaster man's mobile phone, or to be more precise, a deleted video file on it. An almost complete recording of the incident was recovered. The woman's account of what happened was fully verified... There is one detail of the woman's statement that I think you will find particularly interesting." He pushes the file towards Kitti who has been following closely. She places a finger on the appropriate line and quotes:

Sergeant Ylinen – You have a security chain. Why didn't you attach it before opening the door to a stranger at that time of night?

Ms Verkko – I didn't think it was a stranger. There is a frosted glass window in the door and I thought I could see my boyfriend.

Sergeant Ylinen – What made you think it was your boyfriend?

Ms Verkko – The man, he was wearing the same type of hooded coat as Pel wears. Even for a second after I opened the door I didn't realise it was someone else. Not until he stepped forward.

"Has someone show this to Aaltonen?" I'm starting to tremble with excitement: sweat cloying under my arms. *"It is just the same."*

"He knows, but let us finish!" Lars pulls the file back and flicks a page. *"A small plastic bag and a pair of latex gloves were found under a chair near to where the man was lying. Ms Verkko stated that they were not hers. The bag was found to contain a number of skin cells, hairs, and clothes fibres which matched the boyfriend."*

"Materials ready for placing down to put the murder on someone else." Lars nods. "So someone see the sameness with my case and contacted Mahikkala?"

"*Oletat poliisilta paljon...*"

That seems to translate as *'You have a lot of police...'* I query, *"What? Many police officers?"* Lars frowns in confusion. I try again: *"Sorry, I think I did not understand."*

"'*Oletat... paljon*' not '*Olette... paljon*'. It means 'you expect a lot of', not 'you have a lot of,' inserts Kitti.

"Ah, I see, thanks."

Lars raises his eyebrows slightly in an expression which I take to be simultaneous pride and amusement at the confidence of his student. *"As I was saying, you expect a lot of the Finnish police. There wasn't much 'joined-up-thinking'. No one linked anything at that time."*

"So how?"

"They may not have seen the link, but the Tampere police did do some thorough work. Amongst the arrested man's possessions were some keys. They *found that the keys were for a summer house and, I think by delivery records, they found the summer house near Oulu."*

"That's a long way from Tampere."

"Yes, but this man has moved around quite a lot."

"They find something in the summer house." It's a statement: Lars is here; they must have.

"Many things," Lars turns a few more pages to a plastic wallet of photos. *"A knife, a hunting rifle, a modified freezer, and... some rope. Does this look familiar?"* Lars turns the file so I can study the bottom photo. A small coil of narrow blue cord ends in a knotted loop.

I'm momentarily lost for words. My eyes mist over and a lump catches in my throat, "This is <u>the</u> rope?" I croak, forgetting all about Finnish.

"Yes, and with Ms Saarinen's DNA on it still." I close my eyes and let out a long sigh. Relief floods down my face. A couple of the tears fall on to the file. I can't wipe them off.

"I'm sorry," I splutter between sobs.

"No matter, that is why we have plastic cover," says Lars, pulling the file out of range. He busies himself mopping up whilst my breathing gradually steadies to alternate sniffs and blows.

"I'd nearly given up hope," my head moves from side to side, "sometimes I thought maybe I had done it – my dreams play tricks."

I notice that Kitti is studying me intently. Lars's eyes follow mine and he reaches into his pocket for another tissue.

"One of the less known jobs for barrister," he grins to his student, rises from his chair, leans across the table and offers the tissue. I push my nose forward and blow deeply. I note with detached amusement that the consummate professional returns the soiled tissue to the opposite pocket. Reaching back to the first pocket he then gently removes my glasses and wipes my face with a second tissue, starting with the tracks down each cheek. *"Kiitos paljon, Lars".*

"Under the circumstances, I think it's the smallest thing I can do." He glances towards Kitti and shakes his head with a wry smile. "Notorious criminal!" he says, slipping my glasses back on.

A thought strikes me: *"Who is it, who is this man? Do I know him?"*

Lars grimaces, *"I said he moved around the country a lot... which is easy if you work for a large hotel chain,"* he turns one more page and spins the file.

Familiar faintly mocking eyes meet mine. My brain tries to

reconcile this new fact against my memories. Lars allows me to sit until my head stops spinning and homes in on a single frustrating thought: *"Did they ever even question him about Arwen?"*

"I don't think so... No, Mr Erik Lahtinen has been very clever at avoiding suspicion. Three times, at least."

"There are others?"

"Ms Saarinen was number two, they think..." says Lars.

"From the date stamps on the other video files," adds Kitti.

"There is a video of him killing Arwen?"

Lars's face is full of distaste, *"Apparently, yes, and of two other murders – you are not the only prisoner receiving a visit this morning."*

"Really?"

"Although, unfortunately, the first case never came to court. The accused took their own life."

"I can relate to that." There is silence while I ponder how tempting that thought has been. My eyes flick back to Lars, *"What happens now? I can walk out with you today?"*

Lars smiles, judging that I'm too intelligent to be totally serious, *"If only it were that simple. No there will have to be an appeal and then a presidential pardon, but this will be big news and the courts hate justice-murder, so it will be fast tracked, you could be out in a month."*

"Justice-murder? They have not killed me yet." The corners of my mouth turn up slightly, *"Unless you two are... angels?"* I don't know the last word in Finnish.

Lars rolls his eyes at the thought and continues, *"It's what we call a 'miscarriage of justice', from the old days when we used to hang 'em."*

"So I am a victim of justice-murder? I think that is better than the English. What about when I am out?"

"You can expect compensation... your loss of earnings for the last five years, the stress, the loss of reputation, there are many arguments."

"Will you do that for me?"

"It isn't exactly my field, but certainly someone in my firm can deal with it. But, I have to tell you, it is not a quick process. It could be a year or more."

"So I will have to get a job straight away? Have I got any money left, from... from before?"

"Actually, you have." Lars shifts in his chair. *"Your ex-wife..."*

Abi. You were wrong. You probably know that by now. I hope you feel it. Abi! The heat of the name melts in my mind like a fine malt whisky, leaving a cherished aftertaste. Am I still in your heart like you're in mine? Could I re-weave... Lars has stopped speaking and is staring at me. *"Sorry, could you say that again?"*

Without comment, he repeats, *"Your ex-wife has left an account in your name. I believe it contains half the proceeds of the sale of your former house, plus your share of other assets. The Finnish government never managed to get any of it."*

"I see." That's so Abi: decision made; no half measures; nothing of mine to link her to the past, not even my money.

"That should keep you going until the compensation arrives, if you want it to." Lars holds my eyes, "It is good to bring you happy news for the first time. I apologise for not doing better job in the past."

"Don't worry Lars. You stayed professional when others didn't and I thank you for that." I stand and turn, moving my arms to the side as far as they will go, proffering my right hand. Lars reaches across the table and we shake awkwardly.

"And now we need you to write the appeal papers. Kitti?" He motions towards the door. Jarno's wide frame enters, unlocks and stands close behind me, whilst I rub my wrists.

"We keep you informed," says Lars as I sign the documents. "I expect to hear a date in the next week."

"Are you out, Limestone?" says Jarno.

I turn my head and grin, "Innocent, just like I always said."

Jarno reaches down to hold my arms whilst he reapplies the cuffs, "You not tell, in case someone get jealous."

"I think they already know. Besides, I can look after myself." I glance round at the two lawyers and growl whilst flexing the arm muscles bare beneath my short blue sleeves. The growl morphs into a laugh.

"Limestone?" grins Lars, pushing the files in Kitti's direction.

"The hard limey. Don't ask how I got it."

Kitti glances up slyly from her packing. "Limestone dissolve in water, yes?"

"As you've seen," I say, smiling with the whole of my face.

CHAPTER 49

The reflection in the full length mirror contains no blue. Somehow it doesn't seem right. I reach down to the glass coffee table and pick up a few more cheesy biscuits. The food shelf of the mini-bar is already empty. Most of the evidence is in the bin, but a couple of wrappers have fallen short. I'll tidy up later. It's quarter past midnight and I'm slouched across a double bed eating snacks – alone. Beside the open packet, a miniature Glenfiddick stands, still half full, beside a tumbler. One sip and I'm coughing like a teenager. I suppose I'll have to break myself in gently.

That wasn't the only disappointment today. I don't know why I even let myself hope. It was a stupid little fantasy. I couldn't help it. I've seen it in too many films: the man walks towards the camera, back to a barbwire topped gate, a sports bag over his left shoulder, a jacket held jauntily over the other, his incredulous expression matched by the spring in his step. Out! He's out. Just before he reaches the main road a car pulls up – just as you knew it would. The window slides down and a dark haired woman with soft grey green eyes says, "Thought I'd forgotten yer? Jump in." The woman floors the accelerator even as the man lowers himself and he's forced back into the seat.

"Hey, no one's going to put me back in there," says the man, leaning across to kiss the woman's cheek.

"Not if I can help it," she says and moves her hand from the gear stick to the man's knee. The camera switches to an overhead shot of the car as it retreats down the wide straight road into the setting sun.

There was no car and no green eyed woman. I glance round the room at the detritus of my solo midnight feast and say to my reflection, "This is not helping." I slip shoes on to my feet, the key card into my top pocket and let the door spring shut behind me. I wince at the noise, remembering too late that others may be sleeping.

At least gassy lager doesn't make me cough. To the left of my low leather settee, a counter stretches along the atrium: at this end a bar, towards the other the reception desk. Around a neighbouring table, a group of five business men, still in their suits, jockey for the attention of their single female colleague. Even with their slurring I find I can follow most of the banter. Just the sort of stuff that Keith and John were masters of. The main doors slide open and the hiss of the warm air curtain muffles the voices. When it subsides, I twist my head, surely that is... ah. The familiar voice is emanating from the ceiling mounted TV. I swivel round and zone into the sound.

"*...relieved that his ordeal is over,*" says Lars, standing close beside me, speaking to a forest of outstretched microphones. "*Remember that he has been imprisoned for five years for a crime which he had nothing to do with. All this attention is somewhat daunting. Just a couple of questions.*"

The picture cuts back to the studio where a picture of Arwen, that girlish one, is projected behind the presenter, "*Almost exactly five years ago, nineteen year old bar worker Arwen Saarinen was brutally strangled after a night out in her home town of Mahikkala. Following one of the largest investigations that town had ever seen, English engineer Steven Carter was arrested. Despite always protesting his innocence, Mr Carter was convicted on the strength of forensic evidence: evidence which it now turns out was planted by the real murderer.*" The picture switches to a slow panning shot of a lakeside cabin. Red and white tape criss-crosses the door.

"*In disturbing developments, reported first here on TV1, a number of* 'Snuff movies' *were discovered on a laptop computer in this isolated summer house. One of those videos is believed to show the attack on Ms Saarinen.*" Now we get a clip of someone with a bag over their head being escorted from a side door and helped into the back of a police car. "*Last week, Mr Erik Lahtinen, owner of the summer house and former resident of Mahikkala pleaded guilty to three counts of murder and one count of attempted murder. In each case, another man had been convicted on the strength of fabricated forensic evidence. Let's see what the exonerated Mr Carter has to say.*" And there I am. I suppose it's nice to have two minutes of fame, rather than infamy.

"Mr Carter, how do you feel to be out?" says a disembodied voice.

I can see the disappointment in my own eyes. The searching glances beyond the cameras. I force my face into a fake smile.

"It's great; it's strange." I glance towards the prison wall just yards away. "I haven't really done anything yet." Shrugging towards the camera, I retreat into bad jokes *"It is still cold out here."*

"What is first thing you are going to do, Mr Carter," shouts another voice.

"Probably run away from you lot." A laugh causes me to glance sideways. One of the bar staff is standing with my empty glass in her hand, staring up at the screen. Her eyes start to move in my direction, but I quickly look back to the screen.

"Mr Carter, are you going to seek damages?"

"At the moment I'm just happy to be out. It's good to be believed... *vihdoinkin.*"

The presenter reappears, this time beside her a bespectacled expert. *"We are joined now by our law correspondent, Mr Pern."* He flashes a TV smile. *"How was it that Lahtinen was able to manipulate..."*

"That was you, yes?" The voice from the other side of the table is strongly accented. My eyes run up the dark grey trousers, past the empty glass and white blouse to pony-tailed blonde hair. I smile and raise my shoulders in the affirmative.

"You are funny."

"It's not easy to know what to say."

She glances towards the bar and then sits in the chair opposite so that our heads are nearer the same level. "You been in prison for five years until today?"

"Yes," I say, simply, and tug at one shirt sleeve where it stretches tight over a bicep, "My old clothes don't really fit any more."

"Lots of time for exercise." She pumps an imaginary dumbbell with her right arm.

"Yes, but I would rather have joined a gym." That laugh again.

On the screen, a picture of Erik is now superimposed behind the law expert. "You must hate him... and police."

"He's not my favourite, no." I shake my head, "I don't know what I feel at the moment. I kind of feel unlucky and lucky at the same time." I thumb towards the screen. "Have they said how they caught Lahtinen?"

"I not know."

"Pure luck, that's what it was. He tried to kill another woman in

Tampere. Hit her on the head with a hammer. But she hit him back with a toaster."

"A what?"

"*Leivänpaahdin!*" Her hand goes to her mouth to cover the snigger. *"I know,"* I say, *"You expect that..."*

"Speak English," she smiles coyly. Ah, practise... I remember.

I raise one eyebrow, "If you insist..." Her smile broadens. "You kind of expect that if you get released it would be because someone had been working on your case. You know: the holidaying detective who read about me in a local paper and thought that 'something didn't seem quite right' or the investigative reporter who looked at my file with a 'fresh pair of eyes'. But it wasn't anything like that. It was the simple fortunate fact that Mr Lahtinen happened to pick on a woman who was handy with a toaster! Instead of his next sick fix he got a sore head and life imprisonment. Couldn't happen to a more deserving bloke."

I let go of the invisible toaster between my outstretched hands and gaze back into pale blue eyes: there's a mixture of amusement and confusion. I get the feeling that she has only understood half of what I've been saying. A sudden shudder runs through me as an image of the same expression in a different barmaid's eyes jolts into my brain so strongly it's almost as if I'm seeing it.

"Are you OK?" She reaches forward to put a hand on my knee.

"Have I gone white?"

Her concern turns to a smile. "A little, like you see a ..."

"Ghost?" She nods. "Maybe I did. I'm sorry, you reminded me of someone." Her hand retreats and she turns the glass in her fingers, unsure of what to say.

I purse my lips and swap to Finnish, *"The woman who was murdered, Arwen. I did know her. She work in a bar like you. Sometimes I talk to her like this. The way you look just then when you not understand everything I say, was just like her."* A hand goes to her mouth again, but this time the expression behind it is surprise, a little freaked out, perhaps.

The clock above the counter says it's approaching one a.m. *"I have a flight to England in the morning so I think I go to bed."* She nods dumbly. I glance back as I'm waiting for the lift. She's still sitting in the chair staring at the glass in her lap. Her eyes lift, meet mine, and flick straight back down again. "Are you always going to haunt me, Arwen?" I mutter as the doors slide open.

CHAPTER 50

"You're a good friend to Abi. I can see that; you always have been, but I've got to see her. I just have to."

Charles swirls the spoon around the empty cup once more and then twists his wrist to check the Omega: he's due back at the Old Bailey in fifteen minutes.

"You know I'll find out where they live in the end. Don't make me have to follow James home from his chambers or something sordid, please."

Charles runs his fingers through his grey tinged fop and shrugs. "Steven, what happened to you was terrible. I can't imagine... and I'm sorry I couldn't have done more at the time."

"I'm not sure that I was totally happy with your choice of barrister," I smile ironically. Charles raises his hands. "I don't really blame you. How could you have known?"

Charles glances around the swanky coffee bar. There are too many people close by for him to swear in public. "Stuff happens..." He leans forward with an imploring expression. "The thing is though, it has happened. We can't put the clock back. Abi is with James now. I agree it's not your fault and it's not fair, but it's a fact. Please don't wreck more lives trying to change it."

"If she wants to stay with James, I can't change her mind. I know her better than that," I say quietly.

"Steven," says Charles, pulling a napkin towards him, "I'm going to give you their address, but there's something you need to know."

His voice changes to a slow controlled tone, which I suppose was perfected describing grisly case details. "It's not just James and Abi, they've got a kid, a daughter, Eleanor."

There wasn't really much hope left, but Charles just forced the last bit out: a toothpaste tube, rolled up tight, squeezed dry, fit only for the bin. I follow his hands as he folds the napkin, presses a finger along the crease, pulls it quickly in half. The tear is ragged and uneven.

"How old?" I say slowly.

"Two."

"I'll not break up a family," I croak through the big lump in my throat.

"Good man," says Charles, his hands running from pocket to pocket of his jacket.

In spite of the circumstances, the corners of my mouth rise slightly. "Would you be looking for one of these?" I pull a pen from my coat pocket.

"I'm sure someone must steal them," says Charles reaching over the empty cups.

"From a judge?"

I CAN'T HELP BUT COMPARE with our modest two bedroom starter home as I scrunch up the gravel driveway. If it comes down to whose is bigger, James has clearly got it where it counts. As I pass between two Mercedes, I note the child seat in the back of the people carrier with a sigh. Before I even reach up for the bell, the panelled door opens. I've never seen James look so nervous. He forces his pale face into an approximation of a welcoming smile, "We thought you might be coming today."

"Charles," I say. James nods.

"I never planned it," he gushes, "it just happened. We worked together so closely. That time in Finland was so intense. We never got together until we were back in the UK."

"You were lucky no one murdered her and framed you for it then," I smile humourlessly.

"I did the best job I could for you. It wasn't a case I could win. Lahtinen covered his tracks too well."

I have an urge to rant, but he's probably right. No one could have won. The redness subsides and I reply quietly, "I know. It's only your extra-curricular activities that I have any problem with."

"She... we thought it was best to move on." James realises that I'm still on the doorstep and ushers me into the entrance hall. The central staircase splits into two balconies and it feels like there should be a large chandelier hanging in the double height space between. Not Abi's style, though.

"You know what happened then?" I ask.

"We've been following it on the net. Abigail's been pouring over every detail... You know how she is." I nod. "She does feel terribly guilty, you know." He holds my eye and I can see the caring in his. "Please don't upset her too much." He loves her as much as I do... did... do. It's unbearable.

He leads me to a door on the right, "They're in here."

"Hello, Steven." Abi is perched on the edge of an amply cushioned easy chair, holding a wooden block towards an unstable looking tower. A small hand reaches for the brick and places it down too firmly. The blocks scatter sideways.

"Hello, Abi," I say, taking the sofa, "and the demolition expert must be Eleanor." I remember the packet in my left hand. "I've got something for her, if it's OK?"

"Ellie," says Abi, "this is Mummy's old friend Steven. Say hello."

Ellie looks up from the remains of her building project suspiciously. Her eyes alight on the small parcel. "Present!"

We all grin. "I can see she's got her priorities right," I say, passing it into waiting hands.

Abi's eyes are full of small hands struggling with sticky tape and I take the opportunity to reacquaint myself with her features. Part of me had sort of hoped that she would have let herself go after the baby: loose jogging bottoms only partly covering expanding backside, that kind of thing, but it's pretty much the Abi I've always known: smooth neck, petite nose, heavy, constantly plucked brows framing those grey green eyes.

"Dolly," says the small voice. What do you buy a two year old girl these days? I don't know.

"Say, 'thank you.'"

Ellie pulls off the remaining paper and raises her head to fix me with an all too familiar smile, "'kyou."

"I think you've made a hit there," says Abi.

"Would you like tea?" says James, who has been standing in the doorway.

"Yes, please." Abi nods also: I know hers will be black with a quarter teaspoon of sugar. 'Just not quite sweet enough,' I used to joke.

We sit, both watching dolly start to rebuild the tower. At the same moment, we glance up at each other, share an awkward smile and immediately look away. Mugs clank from somewhere across the hall.

"You're looking well," I say.

"You're looking..." She struggles for the word, but I see her eyes stray towards my arms.

"Pumped up?" She nods. "Physical exercise passes the time and you can set yourself goals. Stops you going completely mad."

"It must have been terrible."

"Being locked up isn't the worst thing. It's knowing what everyone thinks you are: that no one believes you anymore." Abi gulps and her eyes drop to the floor. She's going to cry any minute. I carry on quickly in a lighter tone, "James seems to be doing well," indicating the room's plushness with the rotation of one hand.

"Deputy head of chambers, now, aren't you dear?" she says as James reappears with a pair of mugs. He nods as he pulls out the bottom table from an oak nest and places the drinks between us.

"I'll be in my study... if you need me," he says, retreating quickly. We both take our mugs and sip at the hot liquid.

Abi takes a deep breath, "Do you know about your Dad?"

"Yes, the executor wrote to me in prison."

"The home contacted me. They still had me on one of their lists. I'm sorry."

My eyes fill up and I twitch one corner of my mouth, "His mind died a long time ago. That wasn't him, not really." We lapse into silence again. The distant roar of an overhead jet is not completely muffled by the double glazing.

"I read the song," she whispers, a tear trickling out of her left eye. "I didn't speak to James for a week. He was going crazy."

"I'm sorry, it was a bitter thing to do."

"I deserved it," she says between sniffs. "And then when Charles rang to say that someone else had been arrested, after all this time. I..." Our eyes connect for the first time in the way they used to. I can see myself reflected in her pupils: my whole self, my soul. It feels like falling. "I should have believed you," she chokes and her eyes slip down towards the building project.

"There were times when even I thought I must have done it, times I couldn't bear to be myself in case I had done it."

"I'm so, so sorry," Abi sobs.

"If I had never..." My voice catches and I join her. We stare at each other across a chasm of natural wool carpet, weeping uncontrollably, sharing the grief of our loss.

Ellie stands and places a hand gently in her mother's, "Mummy, why cry?"

Abi gasps for breath and forces a smile, "A lot of things happened before you were born: things that Mummy can't change even if she wanted to." Ellie puts out her arms and they hug. I turn away, the might-have-beens are too painful. After a few moments spent in concentrated glasses cleaning, I hear a brick being picked up, take a deep breath and face back towards my ex-wife.

"I know we can't change anything... now," I glance towards Ellie who has laid Dolly on a bed of three bricks, "but before I go..." I raise my right hand to my chest. I can't think of the right words and tears start to flow again. "There'll always... be some of you... in here." I shudder uncontrollably and struggle in my trouser pockets for another tissue.

Abi stands and reaches for the mantle shelf where an open box sits incongruously between two African statues. She pulls one out and passes it toward me, sighing, "and you in me." As I wipe myself up, she takes a deep breath in and out and stretches towards the ceiling, her t-shirt parting company with the top of her jeans.

"That stomach must be the envy of the toddler group."

"Huh," she laughs, shaking her head, eyes rolling. Then as I stand, she reaches down and scoops Ellie from the floor. "Is Dolly going to come and wave good bye to Steven, then?"

The feeling's gone

I just had to see you, of course, I know that it's over,
and your green eyes still reflect my soul.
Spinning, churning, reeling, burning,
my mind bursts open: a flood of emotion,
and leaves a blank where feeling used to be.

They said our match was lit in heaven,
and I thought the fire would be eternal.
Now the feeling's gone
but I just can't move on.

In my mind's eye, he says I'm glad that that's over,
and you hold him as I walk down the path.
Swelling, sobbing, straining, throbbing,
my heart's exploding, with pain overloading,
to leave a void where once there was your love.

They said our match was lit in heaven,
and I thought the fire would be eternal.
Now the feeling's gone
but I just can't...
They laughed and said our souls had mated,
I never thought that life could part us
Now the feeling's gone
but I just can't move on.

So you are my old flame.
I can't relight it, I don't want to fight it.
So you are 'my former'.
'Ex' is the letter, how can I do better
in this world?

They said...

MY EYES FLICK between the song lyrics and the white envelope on the table beside them. Has the feeling really gone? There's definitely been a certain numbness for these last few months. Limbo: neither dead nor alive; that about sums it up. I suppose I could visit old friends, but they were all 'our' friends. Even my old work colleagues would remind me of you. I don't want to go anywhere near Manchester.

And then this letter comes and with it, a thought. I pull the unheaded paper from the envelope and read the last paragraph again:

"You understand that from a legal point of view, until the finishing of any claim, I cannot officially apologise. But, as the man in charge of the original investigation, I feel a responsibility for your imprisonment. Recently, some facts of your case have come on to my desk. Although it cannot make up for your losses, I think this information would interest you, so I feel duty to ask you to visit me in Mahikkala at your convenience. Perhaps if you come to deal with your compensation claim? Yours faithfully, Jari Aaltonen."

I stare out of the window, across the guest house's flagstone yard. Dreary London rain is still falling: it's an easy decision. I reach for my mobile and key the word 'optician' into the search engine.

CHAPTER 51

I glance back towards the steel framed doors of the Central Hotel through eyes blinking against the chill wind. From outside, the illumination of the reception area serves only to emphasize its tiredness: the once pristine granite now scuffed and chipped. *'Time for a face lift,'* I commented to Raakel earlier. *'Me or the room?'* she'd replied. She's the only one left from before.

The breeze is bitter, but it's not really cold. Not like I remember it. The Finnish hate this time of year. *'Kelirikko'*, they call it: slush everywhere for weeks, frequently refreezing to myriads of treacherous rinks. I pick my way through crusty puddles, wondering if I should invest in some wellies.

It's no surprise to see that Hanne has not been resting on her laurels. A retro, handwriting style, neon sign has replaced the former silver letters and the interior follows a similar theme. I've never been in a 1950s American diner, but I guess it must have been something like this. I pick my way past leather topped stools and pale Formica tables.

I order a beer and then ask the blue shirted bar man, *"Is Hanne here?"*

"She's out back. Shall I fetch her?"

"No, no, I wait."

The large mirror down the left hand wall is the other survivor of the makeover, although it has gained a border of black and white tiles for its trouble. The me who stares back, doesn't look quite right. I catch a movement in the corner of my eye and turn to see Hanne doing a double-take.

"Steven!" She almost sprints round the bar and kisses me on each cheek. As she pulls back, I'm surprised to see a glint of moisture in her eyes. "No glasses," she says pointing at my naked face.

"Contact lenses. A new look – like here." I indicate the decor.

"You like it?"

"I'm all in favour of new looks," I say diplomatically.

She holds my eye and then grins ruefully. "You not like it."

"I'll reserve judgement until I'm used to it... Anyway, judgements have been known to be wrong."

A expression of concern crosses her face, "You can laugh now?"

"What else can I do?" Even though the moisture has returned to her eyes, there's something about Hanne now, maybe she's just older. "What's this?" I say, pointing to the tear which has just started to traverse her left cheek.

"I not know... you remind me... of before." I can tell that her 'before' is different from mine.

"I never got chance to thank you for going to court."

"It not do much good." She catches the tear with a finger and shakes her head.

I shrug, "But thank you, anyway. I suppose it didn't make you the most popular person around here?"

She returns the shrug. "I survive, and I become strong," her voice gains a defiant tone, "and I choose." She waves her right hand in front of my face. A delicate silver ring adorns the fourth finger.

I furrow my brow in confusion but receive no help from Hanne's twinkling eyes. "There's a Mr Hanne now?" I try diffidently. "Who is the lucky fella?"

"Not a man," she says with such a mischievous grin that I can't help myself.

"So it's true what they say about Finnish women and moose?"

She rolls her eyes and bats me across the arm with the back of her right hand. "A woman... wolf balls for brain," she laughs dredging up one of Keith's long forgotten insults.

"Cool," I say. "I thought there was something different about you." Her expression clouds slightly. "No, no, I mean you look more happy in yourself: like you've found your place."

"I have," she beams. "Katri and I are together now four years."

"Not Katri who used to work at the Central Hotel?" I say, perhaps a little too quickly.

"No," she laughs, throwing me a quizzical glance. "Different Katri. You must meet her."

"I'd like to." We stand grinning at each other in silence for a moment. *"I forget, we can talk in Finnish now."*

"You learn in..."

"In prison, yes."

She regards me appraisingly. *"How long are you staying here?"*

"I not know."

"Your wife, in England?" I shake my head. The corners of her mouth rise. *"You should go and see Katri: the other one. She's the deputy manager of the LähelläMahi Hotel now."*

I nod. The guy behind the bar interrupts, *"Sorry, Hanne, the driver needs you to sign the receipt."* She glances towards the kitchen door. *"Sorry, I'll be back in a few minutes."* As she stands, she looks me up and down. *"Nice muscles, by the way."*

"You have not gone fully 'over to the dark side' *then?"* I grin, probably blushing slightly.

"Both teams have their appeal, but now I've found the best player," she grins over her retreating shoulder.

"I'M AFRAID *we don't give out the addresses of employees, sir."* Typical that Katri should be off work this afternoon. I glance at my watch. I'm due to meet Aaltonen at six."

"Telephone number?" Another shake of the head. I ponder for a moment. *"I am old friend..."*

"I know who you are..." says the grey haired receptionist.

I look up sharply from the mobile I've been holding hopefully. *"Oh, OK. You know that I never did anything then?"* She shrugs almost reluctantly. *"Katri say good things about me at the trial. I want to thank her."* The woman still seems doubtful. *"Could you ring her and then she decide if she wants to see me? It would be very kind of you."*

Muttering under her breath, the woman retreats into the back office, presumably so I can't see her dialling. A minute or two later she reappears with a slip of paper in her hand.

"She says you can go, but she's in the middle of painting her lounge." The older woman shakes her head as if the very idea of DIY is ridiculous.

CHAPTER 52

I step up to the slush free veranda, press the bell and then shuffle backwards. After a few moments, the slatted front door opens outwards. I wonder how many British people are knocked off pine verandas in Scandinavia each year due to that little difference.

"*Come in,*" says Katri, but wariness seems to hang around her pale face. Wet paint assaults my nostrils and we pass the frayed edges of old sheets protruding from a doorway, demarking the edge of the redecoration zone. "*Sorry, you caught me in the middle of...*" Her strawberry blonde pony tail bobs in front of me down the pine block hallway to the kitchen at the rear of the house.

"*You know I speak Finnish now.*"

She turns and a slight colour comes into her cheeks, "*I saw you on the TV. Would you like a coffee?*"

"*Yes. Milk, no sugar, thank you.*" I stand peering over the work surfaces through wide plate glazing to the largely still snow covered garden beyond. "*Nice house.*"

"*Soon it will be better,*" she says.

"*White?*" I ask, pointing at the drops on her old blue jumper.

"*Just the undercoat. The colour is going to be green... for the spring,*" she indicating a colour chart lying on the table. A pale but cheerful shade is ringed in biro.

"*Green for a new start, I like,*" I say, as she spoons coffee into two mugs. Clicking the kettle switch down, she turns and regards me once more.

"Are you here in Mahikkala for long?"

"I am not sure. The policeman, Aaltonen, has invite me here. He says he has interesting things to show me – from my case."

Katri shifts her weight forward and back, then pulls in her bottom lip, "I'm sorry I testified against you in court. I didn't want to, but I was on the desk that night... it was my duty."

"Is this why you look worry? You worry that I come here to be angry at you for speaking at court?" I grin broadly, "Katri, what you say about me was better than some of my witnesses. I remember think that I could kiss you for some things you said."

She blushes prettily and looks away. Did I go too far? She busies herself with the coffee. As she hands me the hot mug I notice her glance down at my bare left hand.

"Your wife is here with you?"

I lift the hand and study its fourth finger. It feels quite normal to be ringless now. "She divorced me after I was in prison. She marry my lawyer, can you believe? They have a daughter."

Katri's hand goes to her mouth. Was that sympathy or to hide a smile? "You poor man."

"It has not been the best five years ever." I take a sip of the coffee; it's surprisingly tasty for an instant. Katri motions that I should sit down at the small pine breakfast table. She joins facing me, hardly any distance away. Her only make-up is a few spatters of paint on her right cheek, but there's not a line around her eyes. I can't see any difference in five years. "You have not change at all."

"Not much on the outside."

"I have an idea about Finnish women – why you all look young."

She grins, "We don't all jump in ice lakes, if that's what you think!"

"Only stupid men do that... No, it is because of the dark."

"The dark?"

"No sun for half the year, no sun tan, no lines," I indicate round her eyes with a finger.

She leans back in her chair, brings the mug up to her lips once more and then smiles: one of those wide, comfortable smiles that I used to enjoy so much. She's about to tease me.

"Someone has changed a bit on the outside, though."

"Contact lenses," I say, although from the direction of her gaze I don't think that's what she means.

"Yes, and..." she twinkles.

"*Oh, you mean these,*" I say, patting a bicep. "*I had a lot of time for exercise... I worry that perhaps it make me look like a thug.*"

She shakes her head, "*No, I like it. No tatuointeja though?*"

"*Tatuointeja?*" I ask.

"*Drawings on your body,*" she laughs.

"Oh, tattoos?" I say, realising with embarrassment that the root word is almost the same in Finnish. "*Sorry, I still have trouble sometime with the huge long endings you Finns put on words.*"

"*I find the same with all the little words in English.*" Katri grins, remembering this old piece of banter, previous held in the English language. Both of us are so lost in memories it's a moment before we realise we're still holding eye contact.

I raise my eyebrows and draw imaginary letters across my chest. "K-A-T-R-I F-O-R-E-V-E-R," I spell out loud.

"*Yes, like that, yuck!*" she says, thwacking my arm with the colour chart.

"*No, I never want any of them.*" As she takes another swig of coffee, I scan round the room properly for the first time. It really is a swish kitchen: solid wood fronts, stainless steel built in appliances, halogen, maybe even induction hob.

"*A deputy manager has to spend her money on something,*" she says.

"*No one else to spend it on?*" I ask, fearing that I've misread everything, as I always used to.

"*No,*" she says with a twinge of sadness. A little bit of hopeful madness takes hold of me before I can hold it in check.

"*What ever happen to that man you tell me you like, the one 'who was taken'?*"

Her eyes widen slightly, but she plays along. "*He went away for a while...*" There's silence. Bollocks, why did I say that? She glances to the left, towards the digital clock on the microwave. Double bollocks.

"*I am sorry, you need finish your painting?*" Her expression, which appears to mirror mine, gives me a little comfort.

"*Yes... but...*" She holds my eye, expectantly; at least that's what I hope that look means.

"*I have to go to Aaltonen at six, but maybe after, would you like to have a meal? Eight o'clock?*"

That broad smile again, "*I'd like that... and after,*" the smile changes to a grin, "*as you're older now, maybe I can teach you arm in arm dancing?*"

"*I'd like that.*" I say, copying her contraction.

As I pull away from the front of her house, the whole of me has prickles. You know, when you've sat with one leg under your backside and your foot goes numb. Then you stand up, the blood starts to flow again, and it prickles. I feel prickles all over. My heart is pumping them round my body. I take one hand off the wheel. It's trembling.

The clock below the speedometer tells me it's way too early for Aaltonen yet, so I pull over next to a small park. On the verge, just beyond the front of the car, some ornamental flowers, daffodils, maybe, have pushed up a few green shoots where the snow lies less deep in the shade of a small birch. An idea forms like the water droplets on the overhanging twigs, warming in the afternoon sunshine.

Green shoots

Winter turns into spring,
the sunlight touches everything,
cold melts away.
Your breath unfreezes my heart
(yeah, the thaw is coming.)
Numbness begins to depart
from the warmth of your smile.

Green shoots push up through the snow
reaching for the daylight:
reborn again.
The promise of your arms,
the sparkle in your bright eyes;
can I recall the strength to be alive?

Buds explode into leaf,
shaking off the season's grief,
time must move on.
You pump new blood through my veins
(and the prickling's started)
Purge me till nothing remains:
Cleaned by the touch of your love

Green shoots...

I have been in hibernation,
now you're making me wide awake.
There used to be no consolation,
now you've given my mind a shake.
I thought my path was a dead end:
Somehow you've got me on the mend.

Green shoots push up through the snow
reaching for the daylight:
reborn again.
The promise of your arms,
the sparkle in your bright eyes;,
you've made me feel like I could be alive.

I don't care if it's hopelessly optimistic: way over the top. I'm just happy to feel something. Happy to sit, consumed by possibilities rather than memories. Maybe I'll even sing it to her someday.

CHAPTER 53

"*Quiet here tonight,*" I comment as Aaltonen leads me past rows of empty cubicles, screen savers winking from every desk.

"*Big hockey game. I thought this would be a good time... to avoid any embarrassment.*"

He's probably right; I expect there are still a lot of people here who worked at putting me away. We reach what appears to be the largest office at the end of the floor. I note the small brass plaque on the substantial door.

"*Police Chief Aaltonen now then?*"

He gives me a slightly uncomfortable glance and indicates that I should take a seat. "*I was promoted soon after the Saarinen case. I'm afraid I may have profited from your conviction.*"

"*Glad to be a help.*"

Wincing, he unlocks a drawer in the imposing desk and pulls out a slim blue document wallet. I smile inwardly at the other trappings of Aaltonen's status: the high backed 'power chair', the glass fronted shelves weighed down by learned tomes, the framed certificates. Keith would call it TBS solidified, but with Aaltonen I suspect that, rather than affectation, it has all been carefully chosen for maximum effect.

"*Nice office, intimidating,*" I comment.

"*Isn't it,*" he says deadpan, but with a slight twinkle in the eye that suggests humour lurking somewhere under the stiff exterior. Joining me at the conference table which occupies most of the rest of the room, he flips open the lid of an ultra thin laptop, pulls a memory stick from the wallet, and connects it.

"I have spoken to Lahtinen. He has been surprisingly forthcoming about the case: boastful, even."

"I saw in the news that he spend a lot of time saying that the police were stupid."

Aaltonen takes my implied insult on the chin, *"Perhaps we should be ridiculed. We... I failed you and the other ones."* It sounds as much a matter of professional pride as personal regret.

"It is shame the first one did not have a toaster."

His lips purse into what might pass as a smile, *"Yes, we can all be very grateful to Ms Verkko."*

Strangely, I just can't feel any anger against this old school policeman. *"He was clever. I almost believed that I done it."*

"Yes, but only one man. At one time I had almost fifty officers working on the case."

"But they all investigate me!" I wink at the Chief to show him that there are no hard feelings. He pulls a sheaf of printed papers from the document wallet, though I judge from the dog eared corners that he must pretty much know it all off my heart.

"You were very close to the truth at the trial. He did copy your clothes and it was him following Ms Saarinen at the end of Pankkikatu. We were just missing one piece of the puzzle."

"The semen evidence?"

"Yes. Even there you were so close. When we were asked to search the hotel, I admit, I thought maybe we would find something, but it wasn't the plumbing."

"Erik was on hotel front desk, he had keys to my room?"

"Yes, but apparently he didn't need them. You were one of several people that he was watching, hoping to find something he could use. Apparently, one day you handed in a bag of washing which contained..." Aaltonen pauses struggling for a euphemism, *"freshly stained boxer shorts."*

My mouth hangs open and I clap my hands against the sides of my face. Why did I never think of that? The washing! Then another thought occurs and I groan, "Oh no... oh, that is too... oh..." My face screws up in one of those expressions that you make when someone has told you a sick joke: one that you shouldn't find funny, but you just do.

"What?" says a bemused Aaltonen.

I snort, shaking my head, "It would be funny if it wasn't so tragic." I remember my intent to speak Finnish wherever possible. *"I remember that time: it was just once. I had a dream, a... I do not know how to say in Finnish, a 'wet dream'"*.

"It's the same 'märkä uni'."

"Oh, OK. I had a wet dream and so the boxer shorts." I pause, and glance at Aaltonen whose expression is unreadable. *"Guess who was the star?"*

"Ms Saarinen, I suppose," says the Chief, sharp as ever. The corners of his mouth turn up slightly, *"Ironic... He used a condom over his hand to place the evidence without leaving traces of his own DNA."*

"Clever." I muse, *"So there was no really any sexual part to the crime."*

"No. It seems that was all to make you seem more guilty."

"It worked..."

The whirr of the laptop's cooling fan steps up a gear and we both glance towards it. *"What is this for?"* I ask. I think I know and I'm not sure that I want to.

"You may have heard that Lahtinen videoed his crimes..."

"I do not think I want..."

"No, no, I would not show you the actual attack, it is... distressing. But there is something before that, something that might answer some questions... about Ms Saarinen... I thought I should give you the choice to see it..."

I'm only going to wonder forever if I don't watch it. Part of me wishes Aaltonen had less of a conscience. *"Why not?"* He double clicks and a video window appears. Play...

It's a good quality but rather unsteady shot. Above the hiss of the cheap microphone crotchets of heavy breathing keep time with the quavers of rapid footsteps. Hiss, crunch, crunch, blow, crunch, crunch, hiss, crunch, crunch... Ahead, approaching a lamp post is a pale dot. The dot becomes clearer as it moves into the light and then fades as it passes beyond it. I feel slightly seasick trying to follow its progress on the bouncing image. The pace and breathing increase. After a minute or so, the dot has elongated into a person: a person with a pale coat and long hair of a darker shade. Even in between the lamps the picture is now quite clear, the lying snow on path, verge and tree a reflector for any available light. But it's an unnatural light: all is tinged with the tangerine glow of hot mercury vapour. The hair looks almost carrot orange. Her gait, which has been purposeful until now, falters and she glances back towards the camera, her face still small, but lit by the previous lamp.

"Don't stop, run..." I say out loud, but she doesn't hear. She stands, hand on one hip, waiting... As the camera shifts, there's a glimpse of chest and head: dark coat, scarf, hat. It takes up a new angle, lower than before, about the height of an arm hanging down. Less obvious, I suppose.

"He must have practised that," says Aaltonen, the picture staying centred on Arwen as she grows in the frame. The camera's approach reduces to a saunter, but the breathing doesn't slow.

"How you are behind?" she calls. The breathing catches, but there is no response. Still closer, and despite the chinny camera angle, I can see a quizzical furrow of that milky brow. One eyebrow lowers leaving the other raised and she smiles an irresistible mixture of amusement and apprehension. Her lips part and she quotes, voice full of meaning: *"I must be out of my mind, can't get you out of my mind. I must be out of my mind, can't get..."* The smile wipes and her eyes go wide, *"Who... What are you do..."* The picture lunges forward into blackness.

I stare into the blank screen, the after-image of her face slowly fading. Aaltonen stands and I sense that our meeting is at a close. He proffers a hand and as I shake it, his eyes are soft and his voice is low: "Is it better to know?"

EXTRAS!

Visit: http://peterwindridgesmith.wix.com/p-w-s for deleted scenes, suggested reading group discussion questions and more. If you enjoyed *Enough Rope*, please recommend it to your friends, write an on-line review, tweet about it, or like it on my Facebook page.

Printed in Great Britain
by Amazon.co.uk, Ltd.,
Marston Gate.